YUCATAN DEEP

TOM MORRISEY

ZONDERVAN™

GRAND RAPIDS, MICHIGAN 49530 USA

ZONDERVAN™

Yucatan Deep
Copyright © 2002 by Thomas Morrisey

Requests for information should be addressed to:
Zondervan
Grand Rapids, Michigan 49530

Library of Congress Cataloging-in-Publication Data

Morrisey, Tom, 1952-
   Yucatan deep / Tom Morrisey.
     p. cm.
   ISBN 0-310-23959-1
    1. Cave divers—Fiction. 2. Treasure-trove—Fiction. 3. Indians of Mexico—Fiction.
4. Americans—Mexico—Fiction. 5. Yucaan (Mexico : State)—Fiction. I. Title.
PS3613.O685 Y83 2002
813'.6—dc21

2002007546

Interior design by Susan Ambs

Printed in the United States of America

02 03 04 05 06 / ❖ DC/ 10 9 8 7 6 5 4 3 2 1

To Linda—
the braver of the two of us

THE PURPOSES OF A MAN'S HEART
ARE DEEP WATERS,
BUT A MAN OF UNDERSTANDING
DRAWS THEM OUT.

PROVERBS 20:5

PROLOGUE
ITZA MAYA TERRITORY,
NEW SPAIN—JUNE, 1524

Crouching motionless in the upper limbs of a sprawling banyan tree, the red howler monkey gazed out at the pit, a chasm nearly three acres in size, tan limestone walls dropping sixty feet to water that was the deep blue of approaching night.

Around the pit was a clearing nearly fifty yards deep, creeping vines and underbrush gradually reclaiming a broad, sun-whitened necklace of rock. At its periphery, the clearing gave way to jungle, a dense canopy of ropy trees and sawgrass that stretched seamlessly to the horizon in all directions.

The monkey, a well-grown male—twenty pounds of muscle wrapped in short, thick, reddish-brown fur—watched as a breeze picked up and then died, sending a silver crescent of wavelets shimmering across the surface of the water. The animal blinked its round eyes once, swiveling its fur-ruffed head to take in the whole of the pit and its clearing.

Something close to awe seemed to register in the howler's eyes. It gazed noiselessly at the open space, at the rare, cloudless purple vault of twilight sky. Then the monkey began making its way down to the ground, its long, thin limbs working slowly and easily, the prehensile tail working like a fifth paw.

Five feet above the ground, the animal stopped again. Once more, it looked and listened, a moment of caution before leaving the relative safety of the tree.

The howler had just feasted at ease in the upper reaches of the canopy, resting on slender branches that would easily bow and register the weight of an approaching predator. Now it was time to drink.

Overhanging the very edge of the pit was a rectangular limestone block, visible from any point in the clearing. Elaborate carvings graced either end of the block, but if the howler recognized these as stylized representations of its own species, it gave no indication. Nor could the monkey know how the shallow, dished spot near the center of the altar had been chipped away over the years, even though the scars from a thousand obsidian knife-points still dimpled it.

But the dished spot held water for hours after the afternoon rain, and this the red howler apparently did know. And just as the limestone altar was visible from all parts of the clearing, so it afforded a clear view of all the surrounding jungle forest. Nothing could approach the monkey there unseen.

By bending its forepaws at the wrists, the red howler could just touch its thumbs to its middle and index fingers, a trick that gave it sufficient dexterity to grasp a leaf. It plucked one from a lower branch now, and then dropped to the ground with cautious silence. Holding the leaf over its head like some fabulous treasure, the lanky primate ambled comically across the clearing, glancing right, then left, before hopping up onto the altar.

Turning to face the jungle, the red howler settled to its haunches on the warm stone surface, dipped its leaf into the shallow basin, and raised the improvised cup to its lips. It began to sip delicately, like a dowager taking afternoon tea. Then, just as the big male dipped the leaf for a second sip, it froze, glaring at the near edge of the clearing, red fur rising slowly on its back.

A young bachelor from the red howler's troop, a monkey only half the big male's size, had alighted from the lower branches of a papaya tree. Cautiously, it began to approach the altar. Dropping the leaf, the big male leaned forward and began a loud, prolonged, clicking croak, its mouth open in a wide O, exposing formidable incisors—an unmistakable warning that this drinking spot was his, and his alone.

The smaller monkey lowered its head submissively but did not retreat. Turning, it began to slowly crab sideways toward the altar.

The big male rose to its hind legs, the ruff around its face standing on end. It stamped its front feet loudly, its croak changing to an eerie howl, rising in timbre.

The little bachelor hung its head even lower but did not change course. Moving by degrees now, it shuffled all the way up to the altar and hesitantly draped one shaggy forepaw at the other male's feet.

Shrieking, incensed at the young bachelor's persistence, the big male leapt high into the air, landing with a frightening, resonant *thump,* bare inches from the offender's paw.

The smaller animal did not retreat, and the big howler leapt even higher, a dramatic display that was half tantrum, half threat. When even this did not evict the intruder, the big male leapt once more, landing loudly, stained teeth bared, ready to strike.

Suddenly, both animals froze.

The altar had moved.

With a splintering crack, the block tilted, and the monkeys sprang away, shrieking and fleeing for the safety of the trees. Behind them the entire limestone overhang sagged, weakened by centuries of rainfall, finally succumbing to gravity's inexorable tug. As the rivals watched, wide-eyed, from the tree-limbs high above, the stone gave one last mighty crack, and then plunged into the flooded pit below.

White water shot almost to the treetops, collapsing back upon itself in diminishing liquid commotion. Then the jungle was still, the rolling surface of the pool the only evidence that anything had happened at all.

Beneath the surface, the altar continued its journey; dust and pebbles streaming behind it like an ancient comet's tail. The huge limestone block weighed nearly twelve tons, yet it dropped through dark water for better than a minute without touching a ledge or an outcropping. Finally it struck bottom, raising silt that billowed all the way to the surface, a quarter of a mile above.

For days, the silt hung in the water, minuscule particles of clay and calcite drifting slowly back to the substrate from which they'd come. When the waters finally cleared, fully three-quarters of the altar lay buried in the debris at the bottom of the underwater pit. At one end, the carved head and shoulders of a single monkey-idol were all that remained above the rubble.

The stern features glared up grimly through the darkness, hollow stone eyes glaring, as if chastising a world with the impudence to treat its deities so basely.

1

CENOTE "X,"
THE YUCATAN PENINSULA—
DECEMBER, 1998

No one had ever done it before, which was why they were trying to do it.

To Mike Bryant, floating at the surface of more than fifty billion gallons of geothermally warmed water, a deep aquamarine pool in the middle of trackless green jungle, such reasoning—thinking that had seemed logical, even inspired, back home in Florida—was making less and less sense by the minute.

Mike was preparing to make a scuba dive, an experience he usually found tranquil, meditative, introspective—serene.

Today, it had all the serenity of a Roman circus.

The reporters—from *Sports Illustrated*, *Outside*, *Men's Journal*, Associated Press, *The New York Times*, and a couple of Spanish-language publications out of Mexico City—had begun arriving at dawn, shattering what little sleep he'd gotten and raising the camp's stress level by several notches.

The media had come in by helicopter, an irony that was far from lost on the dive team. The Yucatan Deep Project was so badly underfunded that Mike, his partner, Pete Wiley, and the rest of the staff—a motley collection of friends and relatives—had been compelled to stage their equipment to the dive site in a series of four overland trips from Cancún. While the media flew in on air-conditioned, professionally chartered Bell Jet Rangers, the Project's gear—everything needed for three months of camping, plus a portable compressor, industrial-size cylinders of oxygen and helium, radios, and virtually an entire dive-shop's worth of equipment and spare parts—had been ferried into the jungle months before in a Nissan Pathfinder, a Ford F-350 pickup, and a Chevy van, all personal vehicles borrowed from friends in Tulum and Meridien and Cozumel, and all much closer to the scrapyard than the dealer's showroom. Each trip had involved two river fords and continuous tonsorial assaults on the underbrush with winches, chain saws, and machetes, the road deteriorating from asphalt to gravel, to dirt and sand, to two-track, to barely discernable game trail before it finally disappeared entirely. The last six miles had been painstakingly covered on foot, blindly following headings from a handheld GPS satellite-navigation unit over jungle terrain so convoluted that Pete swore, "God must have balled this place up as a prelude to throwing it away."

The morning's biggest helicopter of all had been the converted Russian Mi-8 troop transport carrying the TV crew: an incredibly noisy twin-engine craft that had flattened one tent and nearly blown another to Guatemala with its rotorwash. After this behemoth had landed, the ashen, goateed director for the Expedition Network shoot had climbed out, walked shakily to the edge of the *cenote*, looked down, and said, "Oh. It's in a pit." That was the last Mike had seen of him. Now, up on the rim, sixty feet above the surface of the water, six people in stylishly uncoordinated khaki outfits were setting up tripods and stringing cable.

"Hey. Is this a private pond, or can anybody come in?"

Mike turned in the water and saw the familiar face—silver hair and beard framing an impish grin—not two feet from his own.

"Pete," Mike smiled. "I didn't even hear you get in."

"You were lost in the ozone, buddy," Pete Wiley told him. "Then again, I don't blame you. This is a big day."

"That it is," Mike agreed. He was silent for a moment, and his expression softened. "Pete," he said. "I want to thank you—"

"Oh, man." Pete rolled his eyes. "You aren't gonna start gushing on me now, are you?"

"I'm serious," Mike told him. "I haven't got any more business being here than the man in the moon. You're the expert. I just came along for the ride. I couldn't have organized something like this by myself. I wouldn't even have known where to begin. I still think you ought to do this one on your own. You deserve it."

Pete laughed. "Man," he said, "why would I need that? As it is, I've got enough war stories to see me the rest of the way into my dotage."

That, Mike knew, was true. If you punched up "cave diving" on the Internet, Pete Wiley's name showed up several hundred times. He'd set records worldwide, and the places where he'd explored new passages read like a world atlas—Africa, Australia, Japan, the Bahamas, South America, the Middle East. He'd already been famous when Mike had first taken a cave-diving class with him. And then—Mike had never known why— this world-class explorer had taken Mike under his wing. It had been like living in a *National Geographic* special. When it came to finding a mentor in the exotic world of cave diving, Mike couldn't have done better than Pete Wiley.

"In fact," Pete continued, "If anybody deserves it, it's you. You've done all the training dives with me. Those dive tables we developed? They're as much yours as they are mine. You deserve the spotlight. I've got half a mind to get back on the platform, take all this hot junk off, grab a cold *cervesa,* and sit this out, let you do it yourself."

"I wouldn't," Mike said flatly.

"I know," Pete agreed softly. "That's why I'm in here." Then he looked up and nodded toward a suntanned figure up on the rim. "That, and to make sure our pal up there eats a double portion of crow."

The "pal," Mike well knew, was nothing of the sort. He was an unpleasant surprise who had arrived along with the TV crew: Viktor Bellum— compact, cocky, and muscle-bound, by his own claim a former Navy SEAL. Now a minor cave-diving celebrity, he had been openly critical of many—most—of Pete Wiley's record dives. Bellum ran a dive shop in the tourist town of Tulum, conveniently near both the best-kept collection of Mayan ruins and Akamal, the center of Mexican cave diving. He did a brisk business in a sport that attracted only the tiniest fraction of Mexico's visitors, and he generally acted as if he had invented it and that his way of diving—his equipment configurations, his decompression tables, his methods, and his philosophies—were the only ones that weren't blatantly suicidal.

More than once in the previous year, Bellum—who had never met either Pete or Mike before this morning—had posted notes on Internet bulletin boards, notes always unsigned but obviously his, predicting that one of the two explorers, and possibly both of them, would be dead by year's end due to their ignorance of his allegedly superior diving technique. Somehow, those notes never mentioned the fact that, between the two of them, Pete and Mike had twenty-seven dives deeper than 500 feet to their credit—and Viktor Bellum had absolutely none.

"The Expedition Channel's 'expert commentator,'" Pete snorted. "Can you believe it? Of all people. Why him?"

"He's local," Mike observed. "He was cheap."

"I suppose," Pete reluctantly agreed. "But what makes it worse is that he flames us for months on the 'Net, and now he shows up here all kissy-face, trying to bury the hatchet. He even volunteered to carry my tanks down here for me. And can you believe it? He asked if it was okay if he chipped in as a safety diver."

Mike's eyebrows went up.

"You didn't," he said.

"I didn't," Pete assured him. "I told him that we'd been all booked up for months." He looked around, taking in the walls of the *cenote*, the water rippling in the breeze. "Well," he said. "What is it they say? That living well is the best revenge? I'd say that making history is even better. Let's do that, Mikey."

"Let's," Mike agreed.

Without another word, Pete began to kick smoothly away, swimming on his back, going over to join his support crew.

Mike looked up on the rim of the *cenote,* where Viktor Bellum was making hand motions, talking to the lighting director. He pictured the man volunteering to sherpa dive gear down to the platform. A wolf in sheep's clothing.

But at least Bellum had some idea of what they were doing. That meant that he knew how to help—and when to stay out of the way. The newspaper and magazine reporters, on the other hand, were everywhere. On the staging platform, just a few feet away from where Mike now floated by himself in the water, Pete's nineteen-year-old daughter, Becky, was speaking to three of them and definitely proving that she'd been paying attention during all those communications classes at Berkeley.

"It's pronounced *seh-NO-tay,*" the pretty, deeply tanned young woman was saying, her short, streaked-blond hair bobbing as she nodded. "That's right, *c-e-n-o-t-e*. No. No accent *grave*, although it sounds like it needs one, doesn't it? It's Spanish, but Latin American in origin; you don't find any such word in the older Castillean dictionaries. The early Spanish explorers adapted a Mayan or Indian word, *duc'not*. In cave-talk, these openings are called *sinkholes,* places where the limestone surface rock has collapsed, creating access to the water-filled cave system below."

A writer asked a question that Mike couldn't hear, and Becky replied, "We call it 'Cenote X' because it's the twenty-fourth unmapped sink that my dad and Mike located on LANDSAT satellite imagery of the area, and the sites were lettered in alphabetical order. This site actually showed up on satellite imagery only about twenty-eight months ago; as you can see, the tree cover grows quite close to the edge of the pit, and earlier satellite passes had all been made at oblique angles that missed the pit and the water below. Then NASA put up a new satellite that happened to track directly overhead on one of its passes, and this showed up on the pictures.

"We did the initial surveys on six of the sites we'd discovered two years ago, and when we got to this one, we dropped in 350 meters of plumb-line—that's about 1,155 feet—without so much as touching the bottom. Since then, we've sounded from several points on the surface, and it looks as if the tip of the debris cone—the pile of rock and rubble that accumulated as the top of this sink collapsed—lies 368 meters, or 1,214 feet, beneath our current surface level. To either side of the cone, the bottom drops off at least another 50 meters—165 feet. So the bottom of this sink-hole is believed to be roughly 1,380 feet down. You can compare that to the Empire State Building, which is 1,420 feet high. If you were to dunk it in here, you'd barely have enough sticking out of the water for King Kong to get a decent grip."

All three writers bent to make a note simultaneously, and Mike smiled, despite the enormity of what he and Pete were about to attempt.

". . . easily the deepest known water-filled cave in the world," Becky continued, "more than 350 feet deeper than Zacaton, which is also here in Mexico, and at least 450 feet deeper than Bushmansgat, a cave at the bottom of a lake in South Africa—"

There was a tap on Mike's shoulder, and he turned away from the dock. There aren't many people who can look attractive in dive gear and a hood, but the woman floating next to him did. He smiled and she smiled back.

Bridget Marceau tapped on her dive watch. Mike nodded and the two of them began to swim toward one of three large orange inflatable buoys anchored in the middle of the three-acre body of water. They swam slowly; Mike was encumbered by a pair of high-capacity titanium tanks on his back and, despite the 87-degree water temperature, he was wearing a crushed-neoprene dry suit with a brushed polypropylene undergarment, clothing designed to keep his body heat from being leached away over the next several hours. Bridget, dressed in a more conventional wetsuit, didn't have to worry as much about overheating, but she wore her own set of double tanks, and was towing four big 104-cubic-foot single tanks.

The pair swam on their backs, the easiest way to surface-swim in heavy dive equipment, and, as Mike glanced over at Bridget, their eyes met. The auburn-haired, green-eyed love of Mike's life smiled.

"You ready to do it?" she asked him aloud. Like most people deaf since childhood, Bridget's speaking voice was a little too loud, a little too nasal, a little too dully inflected.

Looking skyward, Mike made a big show of reflecting on this question. "No," he finally said, and they both had a laugh.

The two of them had met in a beginning scuba class Mike had taught six years earlier. He'd had a reputation as an instructor who did well with challenged students, even certifying several who'd come to class in wheelchairs. Bridget had been Mike's first deaf student, though, and it had taken her only five minutes underwater to show him that, in his chosen environment, what she had was not a liability but a gift.

Like all scuba instructors, Mike had a set of hand signals that he used for communication underwater, but Bridget's talent for speaking with her hands had far outshone the twenty-odd signals in Mike's limited repertoire. Bridget was a natural in the water and, over the years, under Mike's tutelage, she had progressively honed her skills, eventually becoming an outstanding cave diver, conservative in her air use, intuitive when it came to route-finding, and naturally cool under pressure.

The pair had become fast friends and dive partners; love inevitably followed. What Bridget lacked in hearing, she more than made up for in her silently conveyed, lightning wit. Yet, although dependent on lip-reading, she was at the same time the most careful and attentive listener Mike had ever met in all his years of teaching and lecturing.

She even saw humor in the fact that she shared her last name with the world's most famous mime, although that by no means made her a fan. Bridget couldn't stand the cloying, white-faced, street-corner prima donna. On their second date, she'd confessed to Mike that she'd never seen a mime that she didn't secretly long to punch out. In his book, this only further qualified her as an honest and likeable human being.

Now they were together at a crystallizing moment, at the threshold of a dive that could not help but change his life forever. He was glad that she was here for it. He watched her bubbles roil the surface and waited for her to return.

At the far buoy, three hundred feet away, Pete Wiley paused as his own tanks were being secured. He looked at his old friend and smiled.

"Any butterflies yet, Mike?" His voice carried across the water as if the two of them were floating side by side.

Mike smiled back. "The size of fruit bats."

Pete grinned broadly and nodded, the whiteness of his teeth a startling contrast to his deeply tanned face.

"That's good," he said. "For something like this, fruit bats are appropriate."

"No ki—."

Mike's reply was cut short by an unmuffled engine roaring to life on the rim above. Portable klieg lights blazed to life and lit the surface of the *cenote* with the relentless glare of a half-dozen miniature suns. On the water-level platform, Jake Stiles, a seasoned cave diver and the only member of the camera crew that Mike actually knew, stopped suiting up and waved his arms, catching the lighting director's attention. Stiles, a burly bear of a man with thick, dark curly hair and a veritable thicket of a moustache, drew his finger across his throat, an unmistakable signal to cut the generator.

The lights faded. Silence flooded the *cenote*. The generator noise wasn't the only sound that had stopped. Birdsong, the shrieks of monkeys, trilling insects—everything but the faintest whisper of the breeze was suddenly gone.

"What's wrong, Jake?" The director, his Ray-Bans dangling from a neck lanyard, was shouting, as if his underwater cameraman were half a mile away.

"We don't need the lights," Jake replied in a normal voice. "And we sure don't need the generator. Not right now."

"But the east side is still in shadow," Mr. Hollywood yelled back.

"Then it's in shadow," Jake said quietly. "Use a reflector to fill, if you want, but nothing that makes noise. And keep your voice down, man. This is real, not a commercial."

Everyone—media, project team members, film crew—had stopped to watch the exchange. Now they slowly returned to their tasks.

Two support divers swam out with inflated bicycle inner tubes, floating hoops supporting heavy plastic garbage bags, which in turn were filled with ice cubes and cold water.

Bridget got back to the surface just as one of these cobbled-up floating basins was positioned in front of Mike. The support diver gave Mike a snorkel and took his facemask. Bridget raised her wrist, looked at her divewatch, and said, "Go when you're ready."

Mike put the snorkel in his mouth, nodded to Pete one last time, and leaned forward, immersing his face in the ice-cold water.

His gasp was clearly audible through the plastic snorkel tube. For a minute or two, he shivered uncontrollably. Then he calmed down and began to breathe normally, his respirations gradually slowing as the minutes ticked past.

For good reason, Pete Wiley had dubbed the floating cold-water basin the "Face-T-Freeze." Its purpose was to trigger something called the "mammalian diving reflex," a reaction—common to whales, porpoises, seals, and just about every other mammal found in the sea—that shunted blood into the body's central core, slowed the heartbeat, and dramatically reduced respiration. Research had shown that humans had the reflex, as well as sea mammals, but only when exposed to exceptionally cold water. It was the reason that people—particularly small children—were often revived without serious organ damage, even twenty minutes or more after falling through the ice on frozen lakes. Pete had hypothesized that prolonged exposure of the face and nasal passages to extremely cold water could awaken the reflex, and help reduce the volume of breathing gases needed by a diver during a rapid descent to extreme depths.

Mike opened and closed his eyes, bathing them in the water. Every once in a while, he would draw some up his nose, hold it, and blow it back out. For a minute, this gave him the worst ice-cream headache imaginable, then things settled down. After five minutes, the sensation was oddly pleasurable.

The fruit bats in his stomach were calming as well. Months of hard work had gone into planning this dive, and, Viktor Bellum's Internet ravings aside, Mike knew that he and Pete had planned it right. Every practical precaution had been taken.

Their titanium tanks had been wrapped with resin-impregnated fiberglass so they could be filled to twice their usual working pressure. The regulators—the breathing mechanisms that delivered the breathing gases from the tank valves—were redundant; if one failed, there were backups, every bit as good as the primary. The same went for all of the critical gear: the lights, the decompression computers, the buoyancy compensators, or BCs, that allowed the diver to hover neutrally or even float while wearing nearly 200 pounds of equipment. All of these had backups and, in many cases, the backups had backups.

Still, Mike reflected, no one had ever gone from the surface to 1,000 feet using a self-sufficient system. And on this fine December morning, he and Pete were attempting to not only do that but to touch down on a bottom that was fully a third again deeper.

They were going into unknown territory, and that was one of the reasons that Pete had ruled out a tandem dive. They would be descending at better than 100 feet a minute. If two divers collided at that speed, the momentum could be sufficient to dislodge or even damage equipment.

Then there was the matter of task-loading. It would be everything Mike and Pete could do to monitor their own systems on a dive of this complexity. Neither diver could afford the luxury of keeping an eye out for a partner. And the truth of the matter was that, on an extreme dive such as this, if things went wrong beyond one trained diver's ability to handle them, having a second diver nearby would do little good; heroics were simply out of the question. As Pete put it, "At these depths, getting excited enough to get short of breath can be fatal. Narcosis, loss of consciousness, embolism, drowning—there's a whole menu of ways to die. We don't need any extras."

The only workable solution had been to make the dive as a "tandem solo"—two men descending simultaneously on separate lines, just out of sight of one another. Still, Mike inwardly wished that he and Pete could make the dive together. Pete had honed Mike's skills until the two of them stood at the apex of the small cave-diving world. But Pete was also fifty-six years old. He was carrying about thirty pounds more than he had when he was in his younger days, he still smoked a pack of Camels every day, and he had always been a tad stocky. Mike, more than twenty years Pete's junior, was by no means a health nut, but he didn't smoke, drank rarely and moderately, and the home gym was a regular part of his life.

Pete had packed in his share of supplies to the camp; that was true. When it came to the work and heavy lifting, he could do his share, and then some. Still, the older diver had become something of a father figure to Mike, and Mike couldn't help but want to watch over him.

Mike smiled around the snorkel in his mouth. In the course of his cave-diving education, Pete had twice saved Mike's life, once when a section of the ceiling collapsed on his leg over at Akamal, and once when he'd experienced a total air loss on the upstream side of Cow Spring, back in Florida. Pete, on the other hand, had never required so much as a moment's assistance from Mike.

So who, Mike wondered, was he trying to kid? Pete could take care of Pete. That much was certain.

Another tap on the shoulder. Mike lifted his face and Bridget gently removed the snorkel from his mouth. He allowed her to put the dive mask on for him; the aim now was to minimize movement, preserving his greatly depressed respiration and heart rates. Even though the water had numbed his face, he could sense the care as Bridget's fingers smoothed the silicone flange of the mask, set the top of his hood over the upper edge, and settled it gently against him. Next she put the mouthpiece of a Spare Air, a tiny tank containing a few minutes' worth of medical-grade oxygen, between his lips. He took a breath and tasted the cold gas.

OK? She asked it in sign, thumb to forefinger.

Mike nodded.

Let's dive. Sign again; thumb down, like a Roman emperor giving a gladiator the verdict.

Mike found the inflator hose for his buoyancy compensator, raised it, and pressed the purge valve. Air hissed noisily out, and he slipped down under the water, feet first. The topside sounds disappeared, and blue-green water surrounded him, punctuated by tiny bubbles drifting up from the foot-pockets of his fins and the folds in his dry suit.

Bridget took him by the arm and gently led him to where his travel tanks were clipped onto the descent line. Mike was still groggy from the cold-water immersion, but the oxygen and near-bathwater warmth of the *cenote* water were reviving him. He found the carabiners securing his tanks and clipped them onto D-rings sewn onto his harness, two tanks to each side, so they hung under his arms like ungainly metal wings. Bridget watched closely, making sure that each tank wound up in its proper place, that the big yellow numbers—1, 2, 3, and 4—were all clearly visible to Mike. She wanted to assist him but did not—all equipment adjustments, all gas switches from this point on, would be made by the divers. The extra people in the water would only come into play if something went very, very wrong.

Mike clicked his last tank into place. He checked his lights one after the other, a primary, a secondary, and two backups, switching each one on and off to make sure it worked properly. He looked at each of his three decompression computers to verify that they were running and showing his current depth of twelve feet. Finally, he set the bezel of his dive watch to zero.

Time to go.

He handed the Spare Air off to a support diver, settled the regulator labeled "1" in his mouth, and gave everyone the "okay" sign.

Bridget pointed to herself, crossed her closed hands over her heart, and pointed back to him: *I love you.*

Mike raised two fingers, his own slang sign for "too," as in "me too," something he'd invented after Bridget had gone through one of her diatribes about men being afraid of commitment. The humor did not escape her, and she waved a dismissive hand: *Get outta here.*

Mike signaled, one thumb down: *Diving.*

He raised the inflator hose and purged the rest of the air from his main buoyancy compensator. The effect was like hitting the down button in an elevator; he began to descend, his support team slipping up and out of his field of vision. Squeezing the wing-like sides of the BC, making certain that he'd gotten all the air out, he reoriented his body in the lukewarm water, going from feet-down to spread-eagle, his head lower than his knees, like a skydiver. The fingers of his left hand closed into an O around the descent line, picking up the bumps and texture of the nylon rope as it slipped through, barely kissing his skin. As the surrounding pressure mounted, his dry suit squeezed against him, and he pushed his inflator valve, adding just enough argon to relieve the squeeze. His ears, his sinus cavities, his mask, all the air spaces in and around his body were subject to the same increasing pressure, and he exhaled, gulped, and worked his jaw constantly to equalize them.

Darkness swallowed him. Mike reached down to his waistbelt-mounted battery pack and flipped a rubberized switch. The 100-watt lamp head on the back of Mike's right hand, connected to its battery pack by a waterproof cable, shot a brilliant spear of white down through the gloom. He swept it around as he descended: off to his right, broken cave wall swept distantly by, shadows changing and lengthening in the dim backwash from the light; below him, the bright yellow rope stretched ramrod-straight down into the blackness. Other than that, it was all empty water in ever-deepening shades of olive.

A plastic tag slipped through his fingers. That would be the marker for 150 feet: time for a gas switch. Mike took the number "1" regulator out of his mouth and, without slowing his descent, exchanged it with the one marked "2." This one tasted markedly colder than the other, and that was good. It told Mike that he was now breathing gas that contained helium—meant for greater depths.

Mike added more argon to his suit. Argon was the opposite of helium, four times denser than air, with tremendous insulating qualities. It couldn't be breathed; even a little argon could cause acute gas narcosis—what Jacques Cousteau had called the "rapture of the deep"—at depths as shallow as 20 feet. But injected into the empty spaces in his suit, argon would help retard heat loss from his body. As deep dives were, of necessity, lengthy dives, staying warm was a priority.

Lights coming up. That would be his safety diver, stationed at 300 feet.

Mike's and Pete's weighted lines plunged roughly parallel, two hundred feet apart, from the surface to two different points on the debris cone, about 1,250 feet down. Each diver would run his own line top-to-bottom. Then, on the ascent, each would catch a "travel line" from 300 feet, up and over to a single ascent line that ran from 250 feet to the surface. That way, Mike and Pete would have one another's company during the twelve-and-a-half hours of in-water decompression required by a dive of this magnitude, and Bridget would be able to monitor them both without swimming back and forth.

A "deco bottle" of tri-mix gas, cached for use during the decompression stops, on the way back up, was hung at 300 feet. With it was a safety diver, whose primary job at this point in the dive was to make sure that Mike didn't get hung up on either the bottle or the travel-line as he passed the junction.

Mike sank swiftly toward the safety man, who looked up, the fat, twin hoses of a Draeger rebreather unit flaring under his facemask like the world's largest Pancho-Villa moustache. The diver flashed Mike an "okay" sign. Mike answered with the same, plummeting safely past the diver, the tank, and the lines without retarding his descent. As he closed on 350 feet, he glanced to his left and saw another light aimed distantly in his direction, a dim, blue-green spark wheeling in a luminous O.

Pete. Mike returned the light signal—*okay*—and the spark went away as Pete again aimed his lamp down into the abyss. Mike did the same and retreated into a small, concentrated world, a world that consisted of himself, the water, and as much of the descent line as his dive-light could pick out.

Another soft plastic tag slipped through Mike's hand. Four hundred feet. One hundred feet below, he could just make out the green glow of a twelve-hour Cymalume chemical light stick, marking where a bottle of gas had been cached for his ascent. Mike released the line until he'd passed the tank, then he regained it as he switched regulators again, going from his number-two tri-mix tank to his number-three deep-travel tank.

The water around him was now pitch black. Mike didn't bother looking around with the light; he knew that the sink was shaped like a huge, elongated funnel, its walls flaring out below 350 feet. In any direction he might care to look now, all he would see would be more water. He raised his head, but the double-tank manifolds kept him from glimpsing the surface. Even if he could have, he knew that it would be no more than a vague, gray-green smudge in the darkness. The sinkhole had several sulfur layers where the compound was concentrated in the water, reflecting back the ambient light and closing it off from the depths below.

Seven-hundred-fifty feet, and Mike was under twenty-three times the pressure he would have felt at the surface, although, as long as he kept equalizing the pressure in his ears and adding gas to his suit, he didn't feel it. Closing in on another chemical light stick marking his deepest cache of ascent gas, he released the line, more reluctantly now, and switched to his last travel cylinder. The green glow of the stick swept by like a passing train. He concentrated on keeping his breathing deep, full, and slow.

A spasmodic, involuntary trembling started in the muscles of his upper back, migrating around to his chest and abdomen. The big front muscles of his upper leg joined in, and he clamped down on the regulator mouthpiece, digging in with his teeth so he wouldn't lose the reg' if his jaw began convulsing as well.

The tremors were caused by a condition known as "HPNS"—high-pressure nervous syndrome—in which a combination of depth and breathing-mixture changes caused the nervous system to virtually short out. It was a transient condition; not all deep divers got HPNS, and those that did didn't get it all the time. Mike had experienced it only twice before.

The first time, the tremors had scared the dickens out of Mike, even though Pete had warned him that they were possible, even statistically probable. The second time, Mike had been more ready for them. Now, he knew that the condition would go away in half a minute or so, as his body adjusted to the new mix. He continued descending, and everything calmed back down, the tremors subsiding as quickly as they'd arisen.

At 872 feet, Mike eclipsed his personal depth record. Every foot deeper was a new accomplishment for him now, and he was still breathing on the supplemental travel tanks. Another plastic tag came up the rope and passed through his hand: 900 feet—time to go to the "Big Kahunas," the main set of bottom-mix tanks on his back.

Mike switched regulators and began breathing an exotic gas mixture that was 96 percent helium, 3 percent oxygen, and 1 percent nitrogen.

Had he attempted to inhale such a mix at the surface, he would have passed out in a matter of minutes; at sea level the body requires at least 10 percent oxygen, just to retain consciousness. But at 900 feet, every breath Mike took was more than twenty-seven times as dense as it would have been at the surface. A 3-percent oxygen mixture here kept him as alert and hyper-awake as an 81-percent oxygen mixture would have, up top.

The narrow beam of his divelight picked out something drawing nearer on the rope, a small yellow disk. Mike frowned: all he'd put on his line were the depth markers. Then he got closer and saw that it was a plastic smiley-face button clipped onto the 1,000-foot marker tag. Some wag had put it on the rope before lowering it, a gift left to give him a chuckle at depth, but Mike wasn't smiling.

The good news was that he had now broken the 1,000-foot barrier—something no other diver had done before.

The bad news was that it had taken twelve minutes to descend to the "grand." If the unthinkable were to happen now—if Mike were to lose all of his breathing supplies, or if the regulators were to stop working under the extreme pressure—even if he could jettison all six tanks and become positively buoyant, it would take him a minimum of eight minutes to float back up to the surface—just enough time to become brain-dead. And that wasn't even to mention the blood vessels all over his body that would explosively embolize—rupture as bubbles boiled out of his blood from the sudden decompression.

It was the kind of thought that could sober a St. Patrick's Day parade. Still, Mike collected the smiley-button from the tag as he sank past, stuck it in the Velcroed pocket where he kept his decompression schedules, and tried to push back the dread creeping in on him from all sides, grasping at him as he dropped through the oppressive, jet-black water. They had a name for what he was feeling: "long-way-home syndrome." Astronauts got it, ice-pack submariners got it, and, right now, Mike Bryant had it.

The rope was now tagged in 25-foot increments. Mike passed 1,025 feet, then 1,050, then 1,075.

The 1,100-foot marker was just coming up when there was an incredibly loud bang, like a large-caliber handgun being discharged right next to his ear.

His dive-light went dark, and everything around him vanished under a blanket of absolute, utter darkness.

2

Sudden, irresistible panic hit Mike Bryant like a sledgehammer. His ears were still ringing; the noise had been incredibly loud.

Questions raced through his mind. Had a tank exploded? A manifold ruptured? Was he hurt? Had the pressure struck him in some unknown way? Was he blind? Was he dying?

Mike immediately tightened his grip on the down-line, but the rope kept sliding through his hand, tearing the water-softened flesh as his weight—the weight of the six tanks and all the supplemental gear, the redundant equipment added for safety's sake—dragged him relentlessly downward toward the bottom of the cave.

Involuntarily he cried out, the helium-modulated sound emerging from his regulator like a cartoon chipmunk's frantic shriek. Fins churning the water furiously beneath him, he loosened his hold on the rope and groped with his free hand, frantically patting his chest and left shoulder until he located the inflator hose for his buoyancy compensator. Finding the inlet valve, he pressed it, holding it in for five seconds, releasing for five so the rushing air would not freeze the mechanism open, and then pressing it again.

Even with the long, five-second bursts, it took a glacially long time for the BCD to inflate; more than 33 atmospheres of water were pushing back, trying to keep it collapsed. Mike felt the 1,125-foot marker slip past his hand, then the 1,150, then the 1,175. A few moments later, the down-line slowed its passage through his hand and finally stopped.

He had now put the loud bang and the loss of light together in his head; his dive light's battery pack had imploded, the tough, thick, reinforced polymer case collapsing under the quarter-ton-per-square-inch pressure of the surrounding water. Mike patted the other side of his waistbelt, found the power pack for his back-up dive light, switched it on, and was rewarded with two seconds of blessed light before, with a second loud bang, it too imploded from the pressure.

The blackness raced back in.

Now the rope began to slip in the opposite direction. He was sliding *up*. The heavy gel batteries had dropped out of the second pack as it disintegrated, lightening him and rendering him buoyant. Like a bathysphere shedding its drop-weights, Mike was bound for the surface. He fought a second tug-of-war with the ascent line, scraping his wounded hand in the opposite direction, up-ending and rising feet-first as he strained to keep a grip on the taut, unyielding rope.

Upside-down, the inflator-hose exhaust valve was of no use; it only worked when the valve was the highest point on the buoyancy compensator. Fortunately, Lamar Hires, the cave-equipment genius who'd designed much of the team's gear, had thought of just such a contingency when he made the big horseshoe-shaped air bladders. He'd put dump valves in the bottoms, as well, and Mike gave one of these a vigorous tug, releasing an invisible geyser of bubbles into the obsidian waters.

He stopped rising, sank slightly, added another five seconds' worth of air to the bladder, and stabilized. Well out of breath now, he was over-breathing the regulator; each breath it gave him felt like only half of what he needed, and the temptation was great to just rip the thing out of his mouth, and take a deep, full breath.

Of water.

Crazy. Mike fought back the urge. Back home in Florida, a cave-diving buddy of his often spoke about "the little man in your head," the guy who starts out by muttering, then utters somber warnings, and finally yells at you non-stop when you're exceeding your comfort zone.

Right now, the little man in Mike's head was screaming like there was no tomorrow.

Training kicked in. When a diver is out of breath, trying to inhale more deeply will only exacerbate the situation. The viable solution is to do the opposite of what instinct demands, to exhale as deeply and fully as possible, rid the lungs of all but their residual volume, and then inhale normally. Mike did this as red stars exploded in his vision and he teetered on the sharp edge of consciousness.

Slowly, gradually, bit by inexorable bit, the stars died out, the blackness returned, and his breathing became as easy as breathing can be when one is 117 stories underwater.

His backup lights were another Lamar-Hires invention, three-C-cell flashlights milled from solid blocks of Delrin plastic, protected by thick, triple O-rings and pressure-resistant, in theory, to 3,300 feet. Mike found one of these in its place on his shoulder strap, unhooked it, and turned the lamp-head to activate it. He got light.

It wasn't nearly as much illumination as his primary systems had provided. Those had thrown out a brilliant white shaft, the kind of light you might use to land an aircraft. By comparison, the backup lights produced the kind of light you might use to change a fuse. But they were equal to the tasks at hand: following the line, checking his depth computers, reading his gauges.

His gauges. It didn't really matter what they said; after the loss of both primary light systems, he was "turning the dive"—aborting and going up—anyhow. But just to see how much of a stew he had gotten himself into, Mike checked the pressure gauge for his main tanks.

He almost wished he hadn't. The gauge showed a little over 2,000 pounds of pressure, enough to do a one-hour cave dive under normal conditions, but only about a three-minute supply at this depth. The dive plan had called for each diver to turn around when he hit 3,300 psi on his main tanks, regardless of whether he'd reached the bottom of the sink. That would leave ample gas for the return to the 750-foot stage tank, with a tiny bit of gas in reserve, in the event of problems. But Mike had huffed and puffed nearly 1,600 psi of heliox away during the minute or so in which he'd dealt with his emergencies. He now had no reserve whatsoever.

In fact, it was worse than that.

He had to lose just over 400 feet of depth to get to his first stage tank. The standard maximum ascent rate in scuba diving is sixty feet per minute—400 feet would take a little over six-and-a-half minutes at that rate. But during the first half of the ascent, the chances of a decompression-related injury was relatively low; so, below 500 feet, the dive plan he and Pete had worked out called for a 75-feet-per-minute rate, a rate that would cover the distance in a little over five-and-a-half minutes.

Mike didn't have five-and-a-half minutes of heliox. He had about three. Two voices began arguing in his head, the one saying that it wasn't fair, that it should have been enough for him to deal with the light failures, the buoyancy problem, the breathing problem; the other saying, no, this is to be expected—when emergencies happen, they tend to cascade, one problem leading relentlessly into another.

He forced himself to listen to the rational voice, to smother the panic and frame a tactic that would deal with the situation at hand. He needed to move up quickly, but not so quickly that he would elevate his respiration and breathe the gas down even more rapidly. He held the dive-light against the face of his wristwatch to recharge the radium second-hand, then he began a rhythmic pull-and-glide up the ascent line, pacing his breathing by his watch—breathing in for ten seconds, holding it for ten, breathing out for ten and then starting the cycle over. Keeping the watch in front of his mask, Mike reached as high on the rope as he could with his right hand, pulled until that hand was at hip-height, slid the right hand up, and repeated the action.

The 1,100-foot marker came and went. Pull. Glide. Pull. Glide. Mike was neutral in the water; pulling himself up the ascent line involved no more effort than lifting a can of soda. But even lifting a twelve-ounce can of soda can cause exertion if you do it often enough, so he forced himself to listen to a mental mantra: Pace yourself; pace yourself; pace yourself.

The second-hand flicked past the top of his watch. One minute. One thousand feet.

Too slow. He'd only covered sixty feet, not even fast enough for the original dive plan. More argument raged in his mind: "Not fair!" from one voice; "Cascade, to be expected," from the other.

The little man in his head whispered insistently: *You're gonna die.*

He began pulling and gliding with both hands, counting the seconds in his head to pace his breathing. In. Hold. Out. A little short of breath, now, but here was 900 feet coming up, passing by, dropping below him as he climbed. A victory of sorts to be securely back in the triple digits, even though he'd never been that deep until this very morning. The eight-hundred-foot marker showed distantly in the output of the little three-cell light. It was getting closer, but the regulator was breathing harder now; he had to draw more vigorously on the mouthpiece to get anything at all, bottom of the barrel.

Not yet, Mike thought. *So close.*

Just below eight hundred feet, the regulator gave him its last partial breath and then it clamped down. Draw as he might, he got nothing. His big double tanks were empty.

Far up the rope, like a distant galaxy on a dark summer night, Mike could see the glow from the chemical light stick on his deepest stage bottle. There was more heliox up there, better than 135 cubic feet of it. That was an additional five-and-a-half minutes of breathing time at the tank's depth. All he had to do was get there. Get there, grab that tank, and use it to get to the next tank after that, his middle heliox mix, at the now-absurdly shallow depth of 500 feet.

But first he had to get to 750, and his lungs were already burning, demanding something to breathe. The four travel tanks were still with him, and one was a 7-percent heliox mix, marginally breathable at this depth. But Mike recognized that he was severely stress-loaded. His breathing-gas consumption had been excessive, he was tipsy from the intoxicating qualities of the high-pressure gas. If, with his judgement so muddled, he grabbed the wrong regulator, a hyperoxic gas mix would send him into convulsions in a matter of seconds. A diver could not keep a regulator in his mouth through the spasms caused by oxygen poisoning. He would drown.

He *would* drown, and he *was* suffocating. His head throbbed with the oxygen deprivation. Hot pokers pierced his lungs.

Only one option remained. Mike held his breath and—steadily, not working so strenuously that he would pass out—pulled his way up the ascent line. The light-stick's glow got closer.

Closer.

The shape of the tank was discernable now in his backup-light's feeble beam. Pressure built at the back of his throat; his lungs were speaking up, screaming for something to breathe.

All around the periphery of his vision, red stars blossomed and danced.

Hold on. Almost there.

Whoa. The tank was closing in too quickly now. He was positively buoyant again, the air in his BC having expanded during the trip up from 1,100 feet. Mike vented some air out, watched it race in shimmering bubbles up, away, and into the darkness. It seemed ludicrous: here he was, literally dying for a breath, and he was throwing air away into the water. But he couldn't breathe air, not at these depths; it would kill him.

He needed the special gas mixture in the stage tank. He needed it now.

Mike dragged his hand on the rope, slowing himself so he would not pass the tank, and his hand came to a stop at an empty D-ring bound onto the line, just below the ring to which the tank was clipped.

There was a carefully established method to the tank exchange. Mike was supposed to remove his number "1" travel tank, clip it into the lower D-ring, pick up the stage tank, clip that onto his harness, exchange the main-tank regulator in his mouth for the stage tank regulator, purge it of water and breathe from it as he advanced up the line.

Mike ignored all of that. Lungs burning, chest feeling like it was being death-hugged by a boa constrictor, he snatched up the stage-tank's regulator and crammed the silicone mouthpiece between his teeth. Relieved, thankful, joyous at having gotten to the precious reserve tank, he exhaled his stale lungful of air, and then, ready for the ecstasy of that first precious breath, he inhaled.

Nothing happened.

The regulator wasn't working.

Forget yelling. Forget screaming. The little man in Mike's head threw a full-fledged, out-and-out hissy-fit, wailing and beating his hands and feet against the floor. Mike tried, unsuccessfully, to ignore him.

Think. What to do. Think. Try to find the last of his travel heliox? Trust his judgement to grab the right regulator in a state hovering perilously close to panic? No. Think. There had to be something else. The red stars blossomed across his field of vision.

Think.

Think.

Of course. The valve was closed! He and Pete had shut down the valves on all of the stage tanks before lowering them into the water; that way, a regulator couldn't accidentally free-flow and empty its tank.

Mike's vision was pulsing now, lighter and darker. He was losing consciousness. When that happened, the autonomic nervous system would take over, overriding the will to resist breathing, taking in whatever was out there, even water. Working by feel, Mike found the valve knob, turned it, sensed the low-pressure line jumping as it filled with gas, and then, with nothing left in his lungs to exhale, pushed in on the regulator's flexible diaphragm shield.

Relief.

Sweet, cool, life-giving gas rushed down his raw throat and into his embering lungs. The panic fell away, and Mike was instantly aware of everything around him: the texture of the guide-rope in his fingers, the encircling press of the mask against his forehead, the brilliant yellow color of the ascent rope, and, off in the periphery of the dive light's beam, tiny particles of silt drifting down from the *cenote* wall above, where they'd been dislodged by his exhaust bubbles. He was 110 percent alive, extra aware after his trip to death's door.

Top-caliber biathletes can cross-country ski at a pace that sends their pulses into triple digits, drop prone into the snow, load a rifle, concentrate, and then—by the time they are ready to take their first shot at the target—force their pulse down to a meditative forty or forty-five beats per minute. An accomplished breath-hold diver, Mike could do the same thing, and he did it now, reining his respiration back to a controlled pace in the space of five or six breaths.

Working methodically now, he located his number 1 travel tank and unclipped it from his dive-harness. The lower D-ring on the ascent line was obscured by the stage tank; he groped for it for all of five seconds and then, with the giddy sensation of a man throwing money out a window, simply gave up and dropped it. A thousand dollars' worth of cylinder, regulator and submersible pressure gauge slid swiftly out of his dive-light's beam and down into the blackness, headed for the bottom of Cenote X, where it would spend eternity in the company of broken rock, mastodon bones, and whatever else had fallen in over the millennia. Mike unclipped the stage tank from the rope, secured it onto his harness, and continued up.

Sixty seconds earlier he had been on the ragged edge of drowning. Now the main dangers he faced were from the pressure changes in the upper section of his ascent. Mike pressed a button to arm the ascent alarm on his decompression computer. It was preset for 75 feet per minute; if he undershot or exceeded that rate by more than 10 percent, the computer would beep and tell him to get with the program.

He fished his decompression table out of his harness pocket and scowled at it. The dive plan, put together using expensive proprietary software, and agonizingly tweaked and refined by Pete Wiley, the most knowledgeable man in the world when it came to these things, called for a first decompression stop at 500 feet. But that was assuming the dive had gone as planned. While it was true that Mike had not dived the full 1,250 feet to the bottom, his respiration had, for at least a couple of minutes, been well off the charts. That, and the tension of the problems, would have sent adrenaline coursing into his bloodstream, tensing his tissues so they would not off-gas as easily and forcing him to retain extra levels of helium and nitrogen. It was safe to say that he was now at least a pressure compartment or two past the worst gas states anticipated by the dive plan. Penance would be required. To play it safe, he decided to put in a couple of extremely deep decompression stops.

He made the first at 650 feet, coming to a halt on the ascent line and pressing a button to silence the depth computer. He was back now, all of his skills clicking in at peak efficiency, and he controlled his buoyancy so precisely that he was able to hover in place next to the line without so much as touching it.

Mike noted the position of the second-hand on his watch and started timing one minute. Holding his dive-light against his suit to cast himself back into darkness, he looked up and could just barely trace the rise of the rope against a background of the deepest green-gray. It wasn't much, but there was light. There was still a world up there where the sun was shining, birds were singing, people were breathing air that did not come in a bottle, and Bridget was awaiting his return. Mike wasn't back to that world, not yet, but knowing it was up there was enough.

Showing the light on the watch-face again, he followed the second hand around, aware that, with each tick of the clock, even though he could not feel it, overpressured nitrogen and helium were leaching out of his blood, bone marrow, and muscles, like carbon dioxide effervescing from an opened soft drink.

As the second-hand passed twelve, Mike moved up again. For the second stop, he arbitrarily split the distance between 650 and 500 feet, coming to a one-minute halt at 575 before continuing up.

Even with the two extra stops, he still had pressure showing on the gauge when he got to the second stage bottle, at 500 feet. The water had a definite green hue to it now, and he could make out a hint of color in the rope, even without the dive light. Coming home. The switch this time went by the book: number 2 travel tank off his rig and onto the ascent-line D-ring; stage tank valve full open; stage tank clipped and secured onto harness; and old regulator swapped for the new. The whole thing took fewer than twenty seconds, but he lingered for an additional minute-and-a-half, going back to his original decompression schedule.

As he waited, he looked at the travel tank he'd just removed, and absently wondered if tank number 1 had hit the bottom of the sinkhole yet.

The bottom . . .

Mike turned his wrist to look at his main decompression computer and pressed a button to change the display from "Current Depth" to "Maximum Depth." Against a phosphorescent green background, the numerals "498" dissolved and were swiftly replaced by another figure: "1197."

Eleven hundred and ninety-seven feet. Nearly twelve hundred. In fact, his fin tips would have broken twelve hundred, easily. Only fifty feet farther, and he could have touched down on the debris cone, all the way to the floor of the sink.

Fifty feet. Less than the distance from home plate to the pitcher's mound. Less than the ten-second walk from his dive shop, back home, to his kitchen door.

He'd been close. Had he cared to direct a light downward, even the dim little low-wattage backup light, he would undoubtedly have been able to see the bottom of Cenote X. But he hadn't aimed his light down. It hadn't even occurred to him to do so at the time.

Spilt milk, Mike decided. He'd gotten close, but as the old saw went, "close" only counted in horseshoes and hand grenades.

Reaching into his zippered pocket to re-check his decompression schedule, Mike found the smiley-face button, and this time it succeeded in bringing him a grin. It wasn't as if he'd been skunked, as if he'd accomplished nothing on this fine December morning. He'd busted the grand—1,000 feet—and that, in itself, was an extraordinary accomplishment.

An even broader grin creased Mike's face behind the regulator. Since he hadn't touched down, Pete—assuming *Pete's* lights had held up—would have the conquest of Cenote X all to himself. Certainly, in his heart of hearts, Mike had wanted to reach bottom; he'd wanted it, he'd tried, and if it hadn't been for the equipment failures, he would have. But as it played out, if Pete bagged the sinkhole all by himself, it just seemed right. Appropriate. There was no better, more experienced cave diver in the world than Pete Wiley. He had paid his dues, and then some.

Mike rejoiced for his friend and couldn't wait to congratulate him. The second-hand passed 12, and he moved again, swimming up toward the steadily brightening surface.

By the 400-foot stop, Mike could make out his safety diver waiting 100 feet above. The man asked a question with his light, swiveling it around in a big, slow circle: *Are you okay?*

Mike replied with two big circles of his own light.

The schedule called for a three-and-a-half minute stop on the heliox at 400 feet; three-and-a-half minutes only, but it seemed to take forever. There were people up top—friends; people who cared about him; Bridget, who existed in a class all by herself—and the first of these was just a scant 100 feet above. Just knowing that gave Mike the exhilarated, greatly relieved feeling of a prisoner on the verge of parole.

Three minutes, twenty-eight seconds. Three-twenty-nine. Three-thirty. Go. Flushed with excitement, augmented by more than a touch of relief, Mike used his thumb and two fingers to lightly pull himself up the ascent line. He could see the question in the safety diver's eyes, so, as he closed in, Mike touched his index and middle fingers to the palm of the opposite hand and then waved both hands, palm down, over one the other: *I didn't touch down.*

The safety man nodded and shrugged, then pointed to Mike and made the "okay" sign, nodding again: *But you're still in one piece. That's what matters.*

Mike drifted to a stop, level with the diver, reached into his harness pocket and pulled out the smiley-face button. Eyes wide, the other man reached for Mike's depth computer, checked the maximum depth, and immediately began pumping Mike's hand up and down like a well handle.

"Ahh righ . . . ," he said aloud through his rebreather mouthpiece. "Way hu gho!"

Way to go, indeed, Mike thought. He had the grand. And Pete was using a different model dive light, so Pete had no doubt bagged the bottom. It was a good day's work, all around.

When he'd gotten up that morning, Mike had resented the arrival of the media, been irritated that they would be there, adding pressure to make the dive, even if Pete's or his intuition suggested otherwise. It was a long-standing agreement between them: if either one preferred not to dive on any particular day, he could stand down, no questions asked. The media didn't understand that, though. The reporters were on schedules, had deadlines, and expected to see something newsworthy in return for their trip into the jungle.

Now he was glad the reporters had come, glad that they, and their cameras, even the suddenly repentant Viktor Bellum would be there to record the dual victory when he and Pete came out of the water.

The safety diver had triggered a countdown timer when Mike got to the decompression stop. It beeped, and the man looked at Mike and extended a fist, thumbs up: *Time to move up.*

Mike nodded his assent, switched tanks, and they moved out, not directly up the main line that he'd followed from the surface, but on an angle away from it, following a quarter-inch "jump" line that would lead to the first shared decompression station, at 250 feet.

Mike looked at his watch and checked his dive time: thirty-five minutes and change. He would be better than five minutes late getting to the 250-foot deco stop, time that he had accrued handling the problems down deep and making the additional stops. Pete would be having kittens. Mike picked up the pace a bit, eager to see his old friend.

Although only 50 feet shallower than the 300-foot stop, the beginning of the decompression line was better than 100 feet away, so one stop couldn't be clearly seen from the other. But Mike was getting close enough now that he could make out details: the hundred-pound mushroom anchor ballasting the bitter end of the line, two 125-cubic-foot cylinders fitted with independent regulators, the mesh bag that would hold the squeeze pouches of rehydrating fluids.

But no Pete.

Hmm, Mike thought. *Looks as if we'll both have war stories to tell tonight.*

Mike turned around, got the safetyman's attention, and pointed to the empty deco stop. Then he pointed to himself and touched the fingertips of one hand to the heel of the other, aiming his hands off into the empty water.

Pete's not here yet. Follow me.

The safety diver looked concerned. A sawtooth profile—descending after having begun an ascent—carried with it an increased risk of decompression illness. But it was Mike's dive, and the safety man, who was on a rebreather, would be at a substantially lower risk. He nodded, and Mike turned his wrist so he could see his compass, took a bearing, and set off in the direction of Pete's descent line.

It felt strange to actually be swimming in open water, using the fins for locomotion, rather than sinking or pulling oneself along a line. For a moment, there was nothing but green water all around them, like being inside of a giant, olive-drab ping-pong ball. Then Mike began to see light ahead at Pete's 300-foot stop.

The safety diver on Pete's line must have seen them coming, because he immediately signaled: three bobs of his light up and down, followed by three sweeps side-to-side.

Hurry.

Trouble.

Heart sinking, Mike dug in with his fins, kicking with his legs from the hips down, picking up speed and ignoring the fact that his body was a mass of fizzing, decompressing gases. His safety diver, unencumbered by the bulky travel tanks, was even quicker, passing him as they raced toward the deco stop. When they got there, Mike's worst fears were realized.

Pete was not there.

The combined beams of three dive lights reached far down the yellow descent line. They could clearly see the tag for the 400-foot marker, and several yards of line beyond that. The water was absolutely empty, not even bubbles coming up from the depths below.

Mike got Pete's safety-man's attention, wagged his fingers and lifted his hand, and then pointed to the safety diver, his eyes and his dive watch: *How long since you last saw his bubbles?*

The man drew a circle around his own watch-face and held up a single finger: *One minute.*

A minute.

Only a minute earlier, Pete had been inhaling, exhaling, breathing, functioning . . . alive.

Mike was a trained cave rescue-and-recovery diver. He understood the physiology of drowning as well as anyone so trained, knew that drowning was not the sudden death depicted in the movies, but a staged process that took time. A diver running out of air would first hold his breath. That would take two minutes, maybe longer for an experienced breath-hold diver such as Pete. Then reflex would kick in, the body would try to breathe, and water hitting the larynx would trigger a second, deeper round of breath-holding, this one involuntary and lasting as much as three minutes. From then on, it varied. Most individuals would finally inhale water, but some—about ten percent of all drowning cases—would simply suffocate.

Either way, it took about four to six minutes for a person to actually drown, and as much as eight for the brain to expire from the lack of oxygenated blood.

Meaning that, somewhere down below, perhaps on this line, perhaps not, Pete was very probably still alive.

Mike's mind raced. Was there anything else that could account for the lack of bubbles? There were no outcrops in the wall on this side of the sink, nothing to deflect exhaust bubbles. There was always the possibility that Pete had gotten off-line somehow, that maybe he was doing a free ascent, simply coming up through empty water, or perhaps following the sink's wall up toward the surface. But if he was doing either of those things, he would not have sufficient gas to make it all the way up. His deep mixes would deplete quickly, and three of his four travel bottles would be toxic down deep.

Any way you looked at it, Pete wasn't going to make it up on his own.

Mike checked his pressure gauges. The tank he was on was still good, better than 3,500 pounds of pressure, but it was tri-mix with 18 percent oxygen. He was pushing it, just breathing it at this depth; it had been mixed to be used on an ascent, rather than a return to a lower level. Any deeper, and he could convulse from the excess oxygen; the nitrogen in the mix was already dimming his reasoning. And that went for the stage bottle sitting at Pete's stop as well.

He had one breathable heliox tank that held less than a minute's worth of gas. In all likelihood, he didn't have enough gas to get down to wherever Pete was, and if he did, he certainly didn't have enough gas to get himself, let alone the two of them, back up.

Plus, even if he could get down there and find Pete, even if he'd had a limitless supply of gas, Mike knew his chances of helping his friend were hopelessly slim. Underwater resuscitation is next to impossible; he'd never heard of an attempt actually succeeding.

Pete's safety diver grabbed his wrist, pointed to Mike's heliox tank, then to himself, and aimed a thumb down.

Brave man. He was volunteering to carry Mike's last bit of heliox down and try to save Pete. But the Draeger rebreathers used by the safety divers—devices designed to let the diver breathe the same small amount of gas over and over again—were electromechanical apparatus, replete with pressure seals and potential leak points. It had taken extensive re-engineering just to get them reliable enough to be used at 300 feet. Taking one below 400 was like asking for a one-way trip.

Mike actually considered the offer for a moment, then shook his head. There was no sense in throwing away two lives in a vain attempt to save one. Pete Wiley had taught him that himself, drilled it into him over their many years of cave diving together. And he'd been right.

They waited another five minutes, a forlorn trio suspended in the half-light of deep water, dive lights aimed down an empty rope, searching futilely for a hope that would not come. Then Mike signaled, thumbs-up. They left a light burning at the stop—it would never be needed, but that was the procedure—and all three of them started back up the jump-line, leaving Pete's deco bottle hanging, untouched and unused, in the middle of the dark, green pit.

All sense of accomplishment, all joy, was gone. The depth record didn't matter. Nothing mattered. The three men arrived at 250 feet and Mike vented his BC, clipping all four of his single tanks off to empty D-rings, and switching over to the 20-percent-oxygen trimix cylinder. He was very conscious of the extra regulator—Pete's regulator—hanging from the tank's valve. Throat tight with grief, Mike inhaled, pushing oxygen down to his broken heart.

Lights, a pair of them, were coming down the line above him, the twin orbs moving in perfect synchronization.

That, Mike knew, would be Jake Stiles, filming as he descended, the video lights mounted on stand-offs to either side of his camera housing. Jake, who knew the kinds of difficulties that might crop up in a record dive such as this, had agreed that he would give Mike, Pete, and their back-ups ample time to get to the deco stop and handle any problems before he came down to film. He would want shots of them swimming up the line, but they would get those later.

Jake got closer, realized Pete was not present, and stopped filming, lowering the camera. He knew what this dive was about, didn't have to ask the question, and did not need an answer. It was obvious that Pete was gone. Drifting in close to the line, Jake reached out and squeezed Mike's shoulder.

Mike put his hand on top of Jake's and squeezed back. They had both known Pete for years. They shared his loss.

More lights were coming down from above—two dive lights, moving independently. Two divers. It hadn't been planned to have anyone else come down. For the best part of a minute, Mike wondered who it was. Then he was able to make them out, and his heart sank further. The diver following up was Bridget.

And the one leading was Becky.

Wearing wetsuits and doubles sets, the two women had obviously decided to come down and share this signal moment with the two most important men in their lives.

Bridget, anxious, had fought to keep her concern from the ebullient Becky. Becky was a woman now, but she was also her father's child, convinced that her dad was invincible, certain of his ability to conquer any challenge that awaited him in the dark waters below.

As they swam closer, Bridget saw the divers grouped below and, at first, her heart leapt up, glad for the coming reunion. Then she saw that one was missing—there were only three divers, plus the cameraman. Something had obviously happened, but to whom?

And who would she want it to be? Mike, so Becky could have her father back, or Pete, so she and Mike could be reunited? Either way, the end was tragedy, and Bridget found herself motionless in the water, cramped with grief, unable to proceed as Becky swam on.

———

Bridget and Becky had shared a quirk, Mike had noticed. Neither woman cared that much for sunglasses. They owned them and sometimes wore them, but most of the time, when they were topside, Bridget and Becky were squinting in the daylight glare. It was hard to see their eyes, impossible to tell what color they actually were.

But here, underwater, in the dimmed light of this environment, they would open their eyes wide, and they were beautiful—Bridget's emerald eyes, and Becky's deep brown, alive with the spark of life and bordered by the frames of the dive masks.

Becky was close enough to Mike that he could see her eyes now, gleeful at the coming reunion, alive with the excitement of the moment.

Then she got closer and her enthusiasm collapsed. She turned from man to man, looking for her father. At last, she turned to Mike, and for one long, agonizing moment, he wished it had gone the other way around. He wished with all his heart that he'd been the one who had died.

Slightly, the movement barely perceptible, Mike shook his head.

Becky shook hers back, defiant, unbelieving. She half-turned, began to jackknife in the water, and Mike realized that the plucky nineteen-year-old intended to go down into the blackness to search for her father, a suicidal urge with only the pair of 95-cubic-foot tanks on her back. He grabbed the edge of her BC, got a grip on her harness strap, and pulled her in to him, closing his arms around her.

For a moment, she fought him, beating her hands against his chest, struggling to get away. Then she went limp and surrendered, sagging in the strong, supportive circle of Mike's arms.

She raised her head to look at him, their regulators almost touching, their mask plates no more than an inch or two apart. Behind the mask, her eyes, those deep brown eyes that he had learned to love so well, the eyes of a young woman as close to him as a daughter, were brimful of tears, pouring out their grief.

She shivered with the pain of it, and he held her.

3
DANA POINT, CALIFORNIA— AUGUST, 1999

The wave collapsed a hundred yards shy of the beach, and Elvis Hastings kicked out neatly, letting the short competition surfboard drop him gently into the cold Pacific without so much as a tug on his ankle leash.

The stretch of nearshore water known as "Trestles" was pumping today, solid blue corduroy that looked as if it ran all the way out to Catalina. And as usual, the shore break at Dana was working its magic with the storm surge, piling the big ocean swells into walls of water as big as an Orange County ranch house, the morning offshore wind holding the curl just long enough for the biggest waves of each set to go tubular—glistening, blue-green, tanker-truck-size cylinders of rolling water that are a Southern California surfer's dream.

There had probably been a time in Elvis's life when he hadn't known how to surf, but if there was, he couldn't remember it. The tops of his feet were knobby with calluses from contact with the board; under the purple and yellow Body Glove wetsuit, his knees wore the same badges of honor. He had far more than surf knowledge; he had surf sense. Elvis didn't need to count sets and look for the seventh or eighth wave—at Dana, it was almost always the eighth that would go monster. He just knew. Without even glancing over his shoulder, he knew when to hold a "bobber"—to stay where he was—and when to dig and go for it, propelling his board at precisely the right speed to synchronize with a moving mountain of water.

Right now, his surf sense told him that he could paddle right back out and get on top of the break zone just in time to catch another pipe, but

Elvis ignored it. Instead, he sat astride his yellow board, like a man riding horseback-style atop a giant banana peel, and looked out at the incoming break, an expectant smile on his face.

There were, after all, any number of things that gave Elvis Hastings joy on this earth, but right up there near the top was watching his father work a wave.

In an instant, he saw him, arms digging smoothly and strongly as he powered over the crest of a swell and then, with an agility and grace that could only come from years of riding water, Joseph "Molokai" Hastings pressed smoothly into a standing position and began traversing down the face of the breaking wave, his streaked blonde hair whipping wetly behind him, the tensed, rail-thin body as lean and hard as it had been thirty-six years earlier, when he'd caught his first ride.

A neophyte might have thought that he was going the wrong way, surfing away from the center of the break, rather than toward it, but Elvis knew better—he immediately grasped what his father was up to. He watched as the tiny figure on the distant board stepped back and kicked the nose suddenly around, going back across and then up the wave just as the froth began to whiten at the crest. Closer and closer, he rode the wave up near its white peak, arms out for balance, sinking further and further until he was practically in a catcher's crouch on the speeding board.

Above him, the wave built, water dropping off the crest just behind him now, chasing him across the face of the wave. Then it "tubed," falling over into a giant rolling cylinder of saltwater that glistened and shimmered in the early morning sun. The tail of the board disappeared behind the moving, curving curtain of water, then the rider was covered, and for four long seconds there was no sign of either man or board, just this monstrous pipe of water rolling shoreward, the white foam churning at its base.

Elvis grinned and then whooped as Mad-Dog Molokai, the king of Dana Point surfdom, shot from the open end of the pipe like a projectile leaving a cannon, man and board skipping briskly across the water, leaving a series of white dashes for a wake.

But he wasn't done yet. Shifting and leaning suddenly to his left, the surfer catapulted the board back up the face of the wave, riding it up high into the air, reaching down with both hands and holding the board to his feet as he turned it earthward, and then crashing down through the same pipe he'd just ridden, bursting through the moving wall of water like some Beach Boys version of Poseidon. Only then did he veer his board away in a sweeping curve, dropping down astride it just as he came to a halt next to his son's bright yellow surfboard.

"Righteous ride," Elvis said, nodding mellowly, a warm grin on his wet, tanned face.

"Righteous board," his father replied.

"Nothing but driftwood without the right rider," Elvis observed.

"Nothing but swimming without the right board," his dad returned, and they both laughed at the timeworn exchange.

The two men dropped prone on their surfboards and began paddling out, side by side.

"Really, Elv," the elder Hastings said as they coasted down the back of a big roller, "this is one serious blade you've carved, here. Better than any balsa board I've ever ridden."

"No way," Elvis retorted.

"Way," his father replied, nodding sagely.

Elvis kept paddling and allowed himself to bask, just for a moment, in the glory. From Sydney to San Francisco, his father was a living legend in surfing circles. A champion wave-rider who still regularly brought home the cup in the masters' category, Molokai Hastings had surfed breaks all around the Pacific basin, and had settled at Dana Point because it regularly pumped out the largest surfable waves in all of southern California. His shop, the Boardroom, was the nerve center of the Point's dedicated surfing community, a kingdom he shared with Kumani Hastings, the native Hawaiian beauty whom he'd wed only two months after meeting her in a surfing competition in New Zealand. They'd been together for twenty-eight years, a durable union based on their love for the ocean, their only-child son, and the fact that, wherever they were and whatever they were doing, they always took time at the end of the day to hold hands and watch the sunset.

Surfing skill alone would have been enough to earn Molokai Hastings his place in the International Surfing Hall of Fame. But he was equally well known—maybe even better known in some quarters—for the top-quality surfboards that he turned out at M.D. Molokai, Ltd., a small warehouse just down the block from his shop.

The elder Hastings had been the first board-maker ever to embrace numerical controls and computer-programmed milling in his craft. While other boardmakers were still shaping by look, feel, and guess, he was carving designs that were absolutely perfect in their symmetry, a process that he'd patented and then licensed out to a select few shops in Australia, South Africa, and on the East Coast. Like everybody else, he'd done most of his work in polystyrene foam, carving the board from block foam to give it lightness and resilience, and then wrapping the shaped foam with resin-impregnated fiberglass cloth to give it strength. But his real claim to fame was his work in balsa wood.

Balsa surfboards had emerged in the nineties as a purist's ride, slightly heavier than foam, but with a look and feel all their own. M.D. Molokai wood boards were things of great beauty, laminated for aesthetics as well as function, generally finished with a clear polyurethane shell that allowed the beauty of the wood to come though. Sometimes he inlaid his work, using rare, dark balsas to create abstract designs or realistic scenes on the board: chains of open-petalled flowers, a Diamond Head sunset, gulls flying wingtip to wingtip. Because of the craftsmanship, M.D. Molokai wood boards cost anywhere from six to ten times what a similar foam board would run, and because of their beauty—and the fact that most surfers lived their whole lives on the shy side of broke—the vast majority of Molokai Hastings' masterpieces never touched the water. Instead, they got used as wall ornamentation in restaurants, bars, and offices on both coasts.

This pleased their creator, but it also irked him. There were even some people who said that his balsa boards were nothing but artwork. He surfed an M.D. Molokai "Kon-Tiki" balsa every morning that he could, rain or shine, just to prove them wrong.

So for him to tell his son that he'd never surfed a better wooden board was like having Michelangelo tell a young painter, "Wow—I wish that I could paint like that."

They paddled up the face of another wave, then coasted down the back of it.

"So?" Molokai asked.

"Hmm?" Elvis replied, paddling up the face of the next big, green roller.

"Are you gonna tell me how you did it?" his father asked, grunting with the effort as he pulled over the top of the wave. "Or are you gonna make me kneel on this twig and beg?"

"Well, I used your reverse-skeg design . . . ," Elvis began. For better than a decade, a feature of M.D. Molokai boards had been their front-swept fins, or skegs, a small one near the tail and two large ones outboard of, and just ahead of the small one. They allowed the rider to swivel the board beneath himself rather than simply turning it from the tail.

"Yeah," his dad interrupted. "I know that. But how do you make this puppy jump?"

"It's not all balsa," Elvis said. "I laminated it around a core."

"Foam?" his father scowled. "No way, Elv. I tried that, years ago. It deads 'em out. This one's like—the opposite direction."

"I know," Elvis said. "But I've got this bro? Friend from college? He works at Rhutan, the aircraft designers up at Mojave. And they've been working with this expanded polymer, a titanium-reinforced honeycomb, as a lightweight fuselage component. I had him float me a piece shaped to some CAD dimensions that I e-mailed him, shot it full of foam when it got here, and used that as my core. It's like a foam-dampened series of springs running down the middle of the board. They make the board belly a little when it's loaded—the same characteristic that balsa has, anyhow, only amplified."

"Springs," his father mused, nodding, as they nosed their boards around and pointed them shoreward. "Did you—"

"—save the metrics?" Elvis laughed. "I totally did, Pop. They're all on the hard-drive, over at the shop. And I got us quantity prices on the polymer core, as long as we buy at least twelve at a time."

"Awesome!" his father said approvingly as they began paddling in parallel, their boards nosing down with the wave building steeply behind them. They rose to their feet and shot in tandem across the steepening face.

Surfers rarely work a wave together. "Dropping in"—jumping onto a wave already occupied by another surfer—is taboo in most surf circles. The split-second changes of direction inherent in the sport make close-quarters far too dangerous for most participants. But Elvis Hastings had grown up surfing with his parents, especially his father. The two men knew one another's surf-sense as they did their own; they could tell, intuitively, where and when the other would turn, and exactly how he'd work the wave. It enabled them to do what, for most surfers, would be impossible—to surf together with barely a board's-length between the two of them. They traversed, turned, kicked up, and caught air, and jetted back down the wave with a precision that would have done the Blue Angels proud. Not a word passed between them, and they rode this last wave all the way in to the beach. The rare morning offshore wind was dying down; anything that came after it would be anticlimactic.

"So what're you gonna call it?" Molokai asked as they walked up onto the wet sand.

"Call it?"

"The board. You designed it."

"Oh—I don't know," Elvis shrugged. "You and Mom are always better at that."

Molokai scowled in thought at the gleaming, honey-gold board.

"The 'Big EZ,'" he finally said. "'E' for Elvis."

"And 'Z?'" Elvis asked.

"Because it sounds cool."

"Okay. Good by me."

They carried their boards up to the truck and rinsed from Igloo jugs of freshwater, boards first, then themselves. Elvis tugged on the long zipper pull down the back of his wetsuit, peeled it off, and rinsed again, standing next to the sport-ute in his knee-length kicks.

"Polymer honeycomb, huh?" Molokai asked as he accepted the Igloo jug for a second rinse. The water had been poured in hot before they left home, and it felt great after an hour in the cold Pacific.

"You bet," Elvis replied.

"That's it," his father said with staged angst. "I'm hanging up my belt-sander. I've been styled by a grommet."

"Dad," Elvis reminded him, eyebrows arched, "I graduated with honors in mechanical engineering from Cal Tech."

"Okay. I've been styled by an *overeducated* grommet."

The two men laughed and began to towel themselves dry.

"Righteous board," Molokai said again.

"Etcetera," his son replied, saving them the longer exchange.

"But it proves my point."

"C'mon, Dad. Please—"

"I'm serious, Elv. The shop and the board business are both up twenty percent on the year. You could live—and I mean live well—on the net from the T-shirt sales alone. And you know your mom's been dropping hints for like the last two decades about moving back to the islands."

"So move," Elvis urged him. "Sell the businesses and buy yourself a piece of Kauai beachfront like you deserve. Or relocate; move everything to Hawaii and run it from there."

"I didn't start this to sell it," his father told him, shaking his head. "Or to move it. I started it because I love it. It's where my heart's at. And come on, Elv . . . it's where your heart's at too.

"You don't make something like this," he said, nodding at the Big E-Z, "on just technique and theory. It's a talent, a labor of love, and you know it."

"No doubt," Elvis agreed. "And I do love it, Dad."

"Then what could be more important than doing what you love?"

Elvis stopped drying himself.

"You really want me to answer that?"

"No," his father said. "It's just ... man, you could be set for life, Elv. Clear future; good, steady money—*great* steady money—no hassles, no worries. I just hate to see you throwing everything away."

"Gee," Elvis said, sitting down on the Expedition's big rear bumper. "It seems I remember this story. There was this guy? Joe Hastings? And the beach was his groove, but his father wanted him to follow in the family business, you know? And that's what his old man told him when he said he was gonna start a surf shop. He said, 'I hate to see you throwing your life away.'"

Molokai stopped toweling his hair.

"My father," he said, "was a car dealer. His bread-and-butter product was a car called a Rambler. In 1969, the same year I started the shop, Ramblers went dinosaur—totally out of existence."

"And even if they hadn't, it wouldn't have made a difference, would it?" Elvis asked him. "The beach was—well, a higher calling. And that's what this is for me, Dad. A higher calling."

He nodded at the crashing surf.

"Even higher," he added, "than that."

His father pulled on a Boardroom Surf Shop T-shirt, pale blue with a frangipani-blossom design running in a horizontal stripe across the front. Elvis reached into the Expedition and got out a 1950s-vintage Rayon panel-design aloha shirt, an antique replete with ukuleles, palm trees, hula girls in grass skirts, and genuine coconut-shell buttons.

"Classic threads," his father said, killing the silence.

"It's a Kameahameaha original. Traded my old longboard for it."

The men dressed quietly for the next couple of minutes.

"Uhm—your mom and I were going to drive over to the marina and catch the early brunch," Molokai finally said. "Want to come along?"

"Thanks," Elvis said sincerely. "I'd really like to, but I've got somewhere to be."

"On Sunday morning?" his father asked. "Where could you possibly have to go on a Sunday morning?"

Elvis arched his eyebrows.

"Oh," his dad said. "That."

"You guys are more than welcome to come," Elvis offered. "The music, alone, is gonna be awesome. We could hit the brunch later."

Molokai gave it a long moment's thought.

"Nah," he finally said. "Kumani hates it when the eggs Benedict sit on the steam tables too long."

He looked out at the surf line.

"Listen, Elv," he said. "I'm not all that old. I can run the shop a few more years. Three, five, six . . . whatever. Give you time to think about this. Change your mind if you want to, you know?"

"Pop," Elvis shook his head. "This isn't anything I'm going to work out of my system. Not in three years. Not in six years. Not ever. It's like staying under the curl when the wave pipes. I'm committed, you know?"

His dad looked out at the surf, saying nothing.

"But I'll tell you what," the young man smiled. "You ever get desperate for ideas, I'll be happy to come back in for a few days and lay out a kickin' new board design, save your sorry, soggy hide from bankruptcy, okay?"

It worked. The towel came flying at his head, followed swiftly by a damp wetsuit and an empty Styrofoam cooler. Whooping and grinning, Elvis took off sprinting down the wet, packed sand, his surf-legend father in gleefully hot pursuit.

4

HIGH SPRINGS, FLORIDA— FEBRUARY, 2003

The windows in the back of Mike Bryant's van were tinted so no one could see in, but changing in the van always made Bridget Marceau nervous, particularly here at Ginnie Springs.

A cow pasture when cave divers first started visiting in the 1960s, Ginnie Springs had been developed into a genuine curiosity; a carefully tended and landscaped diving resort—three hours' drive from the nearest ocean. Cave divers came to Ginnie from around the world to train in and explore cave systems such as Devil's Eye and Devil's Ear—second-magnitude freshwater springs that discharged upwards of forty million gallons of crystal-clear water a day into the tannin-stained Suwannee River. Groups of two or three divers would walk past the van every minute or so, scant feet from the windows. And even though Bridget knew that there was no way they could see her, it still felt unnerving to be standing there unclothed.

Having let herself in with her spare key, Bridget found herself balanced on one bare foot in the van's cargo space, scrunched between spare sets of scuba tanks, trying to keep from toppling or stepping painfully onto one of the brass yoke adapters, wrenches, line-reel spools, line arrows imprinted with "Underwater Underground"—the name of Mike's guiding business— or other pieces of cave-diving bric-a-brac that littered the floor. Perspiring from the heat of the enclosed vehicle, she wriggled into her one-piece swimsuit. Finally, she pulled the nylon straps up over her tanned shoulders, pulled, stretched, and breathed a sigh of relief.

Bridget opened the van's side doors and inhaled deeply. In addition to being at least twenty degrees cooler than the air inside the van, the air outside was also considerably sweeter.

Not that Bridget minded that much. She had gotten used to it, just as she had gotten used to so much about Mike over the years. His van; the clutter of his house; his refrigerator, stocked almost entirely with rising-crust pizzas and pre-cooked barbecued chickens; the twice-a-year absences, when he left to guide groups on dive trips—Bridget had gotten accustomed to all of that, just as she had gotten accustomed to his perennial uniform of jeans and a faded polo shirt; his hair, which was usually about two weeks overdue for a trim; his oftentimes taciturn manner.

Bridget sat on the threshold, just inside the van's open doors, and fluffed out a light dry-suit undergarment, a neck-to-ankle polyester-fiber body-suit. It was the type of clothing a skier might wear beneath her bibs; worn under the crushed neoprene dry suit, it would keep her warm throughout even a lengthy dive in the seventy-two-degree spring water.

She unzipped the suit and slid one long, tanned leg into it. Some of the men walking by slowed to give her a sidelong glance—and some of them were barely more than half her age. She blushed just a little, partly from embarrassment, and partly from the realization that, to a certain extent, this pleased her.

For thirty-four, Bridget was in remarkably good shape, although that was as much the result of hard work as it was of nature. Like most docs, Bridget didn't get an annual physical—she'd heard of any number of cases of patients keeling over a month or two after getting a "clean bill of health." But she did get an annual mammogram, even though she hated the discomfort. How was it one of her patients had described it to her? "Like putting your breast on a cold garage floor and asking your husband to back the SUV over it." She did a monthly self-exam as well, feeling for abnormalities while she was soaped up in the shower, just as she advised her own patients. And she checked her own blood pressure once a week, monitored her fingertips and nails for the club shapes and striations that could be the signs of heart disease, and ate a balanced diet, supplemented by a modest assortment of vitamins.

Bridget swam every day—two miles in the pool at the health club before going to work at the hospital, in addition to all the water time she saw on these long weekends in cave country. And over the last two years, she'd selectively added some weight-machine work—reverse triceps curls to tone the undersides of her arms, latissimus pull-downs for her back, abdominal twists and gluteus work to combat even the most nascent hint of middle-age spread. While the results would never get her on the cover of *Sports*

Illustrated, they did earn her quite a few sidelong glances from the opposite sex. She noticed, even when people thought she would not. Hearing-impaired people have, out of necessity, better peripheral vision than most.

Bridget slipped on a pair of insulated nylon booties, took off her watch, and looked at the time. It was two-fifty in the afternoon; the note under Mike's windshield wiper had said that his class would be coming up out of the Devil's Eye at three. Bridget knew that all of Mike's class dives ran as punctually as a boot camp. She pulled on the legs of her dry suit, slipped its internal suspender straps up over her shoulders, left the neoprene arms tied around her waist so she wouldn't overheat in the Florida sun, and closed and locked the van doors.

A couple of divers she knew were coming up the steps out of the spring basin when she got to the broad, open entry deck. They waved hello, and one signed haltingly, *How are you?* Bridget smiled and gave him a thumbs-up.

The Devil's Eye spring basin was, despite its name, a placid scene, straight out of Stephen Foster—an inviting little riverside cove of clear, blue water, overhung by ancient cypress trees, their limbs shaggy and heavy with Spanish moss. But if one looked more closely, one saw the "boil," a permanently disturbed area on the spring's surface, caused by the constant upwelling. The spring added the equivalent of a five-hundred-gallon aquarium's-worth of freshwater to the cove every second.

All across the basin, tiny bubbles broke the water's surface as well. These were, Bridget knew, cave-diver's exhaust bubbles, percolating up through anywhere from twenty to fifty feet of porous limestone. Anytime divers entered the Devil's Ear basin after mid-morning on a busy day, they could depend on seeing these bubbles, which continued to rise for hours after the last diver was out of the water and gave one the impression of swimming in an enormous glass of crystal-clear champagne.

Near the spring boil, larger bubbles were breaking the surface, causing a nearly continual disturbance. Bridget watched these; they would be the exhaust bubbles of Mike and his three students as they waited out a decompression stop twenty feet down, on the bottom of the cylinder-like Devil's Eye, next to the dark hollows that formed the apertures into the actual cave system.

As Bridget watched, the bubbles broke in more concentrated clusters—divers coming up. The bubble-path began walking across the water toward her.

Three hooded heads, strangers, broke the water's surface just a few feet from where Bridget stood. A fourth head followed, unhooded, wearing the yellow-framed dive mask that Mike habitually used so his students could pick him out more easily underwater.

"Hey, sailor," Bridget said aloud, and Mike removed the regulator from his mouth and grinned.

The three students smiled as well. None registered any surprise at the unusual sound of her voice. They were Germans, and it was a sad fact of life that, like most leading-edge American cave explorers, Bridget and Mike enjoyed considerably more celebrity in Europe than they did in their own country. The Germans weren't surprised by Bridget's deafness because they already knew about it, having read numerous accounts of the Yucatan Deep Project dives in popular magazines back home.

Good afternoon, one of the young men even signed self-consciously, bringing a grin to Bridget's face.

"Did you have a good dive?" she asked aloud, and all three nodded, their lips moving silently from Bridget's perspective as they enthused, "*Ja, sure! Ja!*"

Bridget stepped down to the water's edge, relieving the team of their two squat, green, oxygen decompression cylinders and triggering a small flood of bilingual thanks.

Back at the van, the divers quickly shed and stowed their equipment. Bridget saw Mike tell his students, "Okay, we meet at the shop at eight tomorrow morning, and I'll have your fills ready to go. We're doing Little River tomorrow, so get some rest tonight."

All three students nodded their assent, but they were young, male, and German, and if they were like most of the other young European men whom Bridget had seen in these classes over the years, they would doubtlessly hoist a few in the High Springs bars this evening. Bridget smiled to herself; the Devil's Ear system had fairly high output at the entrance, but its apertures were so large that you could move against the flow easily. At Little River, the typical cave-course dive would be fairly short—down to the Florida Room or, at most, the Dome Room—but the divers would fight a constant torrent virtually every foot of the way. If these boys took that on with a hangover, they'd pay for it. But they would live, Bridget decided, and they would learn.

Mounting a set of regulators on her twin-tank rig, Bridget watched Mike as he tended to some of the housekeeping items that came with teaching a class, helping one diver relocate a battery pack where he could get to it more easily the next dive, lending another a wrench so he could move his tanks up a little and make the manifold easier to reach. He was smiling, nodding, joking as he worked, and Bridget was certain the students would go home impressed, as hundreds before them had been, with their instructor's enthusiasm.

But Mike was tired. Dog-tired, and trying to hide it, although he couldn't camouflage it from someone as attuned to his nuances as Bridget. She could see the extra crow's-feet from too little sleep, the gauntness that had crept into his face of late, the slight bow in the shoulders of a man who had always stood ramrod-straight. And he'd been that way for weeks.

The German students left, and Mike stretched as he got ready to change out his tanks. For a moment, Bridget toyed with the idea of asking Mike to cancel their dive. She decided against it. Mike would see it as what it was—her recognition of his fatigue—and he could be vain about such things.

Pursing her lips, Bridget decided on another approach. As he bent to shut down his regulators, she touched him on the shoulder.

How much gas do you have left? she signed.

He showed her his gauge: he had nearly twenty-seven-hundred pounds of gas pressure left, well above the minimums for starting a cave dive.

I did a full shift at the ER today, she signed to him. Technically, that was true. She had put in eight hours, the same as she did almost every Thursday before driving up from Ocala. But she didn't add that her caseload had been light—some minor cuts, a few vagrants with viruses, two skateboarders who'd collided on a rail-grind, and a couple of retiree snowbirds with angina. Late in the morning, Bridget had even managed to sneak in a half-hour nap.

Why don't we just dive out what you've got there, she continued, *and call it a day?*

Mike looked up at her. The Devil's Ear was one of Bridget's favorite dives, and when she did it, she liked to work her way back through the cave system, all the way over to the small spring on the far side of the Santa Fe River, where there was an aperture just large enough that divers could poke their heads through and see canoeists passing to and fro on the river's surface, seventeen feet above. But that trip took a minimum of an hour, one way, and required each diver to start with at least 3,000 pounds' worth of pressure in the double 104-cubic-foot steel tanks they carried. In fact, for safety's sake they usually each staged in an extra tank of gas, leaving them clipped off to the line halfway in.

"Sure," Mike finally said aloud, looking up at her. "If that's what you'd like, we can make it a light one."

Bridget nodded and set about readying her own equipment, holding a tube-like oxygen analyzer up against one of the tank valves and cracking the valve so a whisper of gas would pass through. The gas analyzed as 36.19 percent oxygen—NOAA Nitrox II—and she set her wrist-mount Ni-Tek II decompression computer accordingly. Then she threaded her two regulators into the screw-mount DIN valves, snugged them against their O-rings, opened the valves, and then—as she would be unable to hear a gas leak from a blown O-ring or a damaged valve—she misted both first stages and their valves with soapy water from a small spray bottle that Mike carried for that purpose. When no bubbles formed she was satisfied that the connections were secure, despite the 3,200 pounds of pressure showing on her submersible gauge. Bridget went on to check the next items in her mental checklist, the dive tables that she would fall back on, should her decompression computer fail.

As Bridget readied her gear, Mike drank a bottle of Gatorade, replacing some of the fluids inevitably lost after breathing dry, compressed gas from a scuba tank. As he drained the bottle, he eased himself wearily onto the back bumper of the van—then lunged.

Bridget caught the movement from the corner of her eye and instantly knew what had happened. When he took them off, Mike had set his tanks and harness against an equipment rank, just inside the rear doors of the van. The tanks had been sitting nearly upright and, when he sat on the back bumper, settling the van slightly on its springs, the tanks had tipped and fallen out.

Cave divers generally link their two tanks together by means of an isolation manifold, a metal tube running from one tank valve to the other. The device gets its name from the isolation valve, located in the center of the crossover tube. Used in conjunction with the two tank valves, it allows the diver to breathe from both tanks through either regulator during normal conditions or to isolate one tank from the other, in the event of a partial air loss.

The knob of the isolator valve projects up higher than either of the two tank valves; it was this that had struck the ground first when Mike's tanks fell. Bridget found him examining the knob—bits of gravel were embedded in the rubber where it had hit, and the nickel-plated brass of the valve body was scratched. From the relatively calm way Mike was inspecting the valve for damage, Bridget assumed it was not hissing and leaking gas.

How's it look? She kept her signs small. There was no need to draw attention to the incident and inform other divers nearby, many of them Mike's former students, that he'd just dropped $3,700 worth of dive equipment on its head.

It looks okay, Mike signed back. *Good thing it was gravel it fell on, and not concrete.*

Switch out your tanks? Bridget signed back.

Mike rubbed his thumb over the brass valve.

No, he signed. *It's okay. I'll dive these.*

Bridget considered asking him to switch the tanks anyhow. It was what Mike would have told anyone else to do—switch off to some spare tanks and keep the manifold out of the water until it could be bench-tested.

She decided not to push it. Mike had been diving caves at least fifteen years longer than she. He knew more about the sport than just about anyone alive. Manufacturers consulted him on equipment designs. He inspected and repaired dive gear daily . . .

. . . And Bridget didn't want to add to Mike's stress by second-guessing him. She had to respect his judgement.

Bridget pulled the sleeves of the dry suit on, then slipped the collar up and over her head, smoothing the latex seal so it pressed wrinkle-free and flat against her skin.

She zipped the dry suit shut and squatted down, squeezing the suit and venting the excess air out of the open exhaust valve, pulled the neck seal away slightly to free the air that had moved up there, and then stood, feeling the snug squeeze of a properly vented dry suit.

Her hair came next. For most dives, she'd just braid it, but here at Ginnie the currents tended to rip, and high flow would worry at the braid every time she stopped, so Bridget gathered her hair into an impromptu bun and held it there with one hand while she slipped on a neoprene hood with the other. For most divers, this moment was a little disorienting, as the quarter-inch neoprene tended to muffle sound, but for Bridget, that point was moot.

All that remained was a familiar multi-step ritual. Bridget sat down on the van's side threshold, wriggled into her harness, and snugged up the straps—first the waist belt, low on the hips, then the crotch strap that would keep the gear from slipping if she inverted. She reached back, found her dry suit inflator hose, and connected it to the inlet valve on the chest of her suit. Then she did the last three straps: left-shoulder, right-shoulder, and the chest cinch that kept the others from slipping down off her shoulders. Running her left hand from her armpit down, she verified that her line reels were free and accessible, then she slipped her two backup lights under rubber keepers on the shoulder straps. She clipped the pressure gauge's brass link onto a stainless steel D-ring just below her back-up second stage, rocked forward onto her feet, and stood—she had rock-hard thighs from years of "caver-squats"—and that was it. She picked up her mask and fins; she was good to go.

Sitting on the back bumper of the van, Mike was just finishing with his gear. He reached back to find his dry suit inflator hose, and Bridget saw him wince.

Your shoulder? She asked him in sign.

Mike nodded.

But it's not that bad, he added in sign. He cradled his left arm in his right, pulled it, and then shook the left arm loose.

Bridget knew the story about the shoulder. It had happened years before they met, as Mike was leading a dive tour to Puerto Rico. On the tiny island of Culebrita, he'd climbed a small cliff to get pictures of some of the group swimming in a tidal pool. Climbing back down, his wet shoes had slipped on the rock and he'd fallen, catching himself with his left hand but partially dislocating his left shoulder. An EMT on nearby Culebra had relocated it for him later that afternoon, but the ligaments had stretched, leaving it with a tendency to go out on occasion. It was one of those things that could be corrected by surgery but happened so rarely that Mike didn't think it worth the time away from diving to have it done.

We can sit this one out, she signed to him. *Call it a day; go get a pizza and rent a video.*

She shrugged.

Mike smiled.

"It's fine," he said aloud, knowing she'd read his lips. "Let's just get in the water."

He'd left the fuller of the two oxygen decompression bottles sitting outside the van, and Bridget picked it up so he wouldn't have to with his game shoulder. The two of them walked in silence to the staging deck and went down the steps into the spring basin, where the water was chest-deep on

Mike, shoulder-deep on Bridget. They put on their fins, then swished, rinsed, and donned their masks, Bridget taking an extra second or two to make sure her hood seal lay atop the mask flange so it wouldn't leak.

Separately, they turned all of their lights—the two high-intensity primaries and the four flashlight-like backups—on and off underwater to verify that they were working. Bridget turned around and leaned back, submerging her tank manifold so Mike could check it for leaks; he patted her on the shoulder, and then she checked him. All of this happened without a word passing, either spoken or in sign. It was a drill they'd repeated so often that it needed no words.

They put a little air in the back-mounted buoyancy compensators and swam face-up, on their backs, toward the tea-brown waters of the Suwannee, a hundred yards down the basin. Bridget clipped the oxygen bottle off on her harness and swam with her hands clasped loosely at her waist, looking at the cypress trees that overhung the basin, at the plywood diver's-flag signboard that permanently marked the promontory near the river, at divers leaving the water from the stairs on the far side. Turning her head back, she could just make out the slightest ripple of the second spring boil and a canoe passing it on the far side.

They stopped short of the second boil, right at the edge of the river proper. The water was a little shallower here; they could stand easily in their fins. Both divers checked their pressure gauges and made sure their dive computers had automatically activated in the water.

"One minute," Mike said, and Bridget nodded. When she'd first trained with him, she had asked him what the one-minute notice was for, and he'd smiled and told her, "So you can think good thoughts." She tried to do that now, but doubt kept sneaking back in.

Mike nodded at his watch and then pointed a thumb down: *dive.*

Bridget returned the signal, and the two divers vented their buoyancy compensators as they settled into the moving water.

A confusion of eddies met them as they submerged. At their backs, water from the Devil's Eye basin pushed by as it surged out to join the Santa Fe. From their right, the main current of the Suwannee pushed by. And just in front of them, water welled up from a long, oblong depression, perhaps ten feet wide by twenty-five long—the Devil's Ear spring basin, bare limestone except for a thick limb of waterlogged cypress collapsed across it ten feet down. All around them, tendrils of brown Suwannee River water wafted through the clear spring flow like ghosts in search of a home.

They swam down into the Ear. It was late in the day; most of the cave-diving classes had concluded, and only two divers were in the big depression, waiting out their deco stops. One looked up, saw Mike, and waved. Bridget didn't recognize him; probably some former student.

A loop of polypropylene rope encircled the cypress limb, and Bridget clipped the oxygen bottle off to it, where the currents couldn't roll it away. She nodded at Mike and the two of them turned on their lights. Mike headed down to the far corner of the depression and seemed to disappear.

The Devil's Ear system is huge, with some passages as large as railway tunnels, but its headspring emerges from an aperture no wider than a phone-booth door, and a little over half as high. It's not what one thinks of when one pictures a spring—not a hole in the basin's bottom, but more of a hole on the wall. It sits nearly dead vertical, almost impossible to see from above.

That was where Mike had gone, and Bridget kicked down to follow him.

Flow, like a giant's large, insistent hand, pushed her back as she neared the aperture. Bridget remembered clearly the first time she'd dived here; she had struggled for several minutes to swim and claw her way in against the constant torrent, burning down more than 1,000 pounds of air pressure in the process.

But that had been years earlier. Now she had the procedure down pat. She simply let herself settle through the billowing outflow, grabbed the lip of rock at the bottom of the entrance aperture, and pulled herself through with one fluid motion, jackknifing and turning left as soon as she was through.

Immediately, the current lessened. The Devil's Ear cavern was huge: twenty feet from top to bottom and nearly twice that in diameter. There was a lot of water moving through, but there was also a lot of space in which to contain it; Bridget's bubbles still ran toward the entrance, but they did so at a much more oblique angle. One could easily swim against the outflow.

Mike looked her way and they exchanged "okays" with their dive lights, painting circles on a sidewall with the blue-white beams. Mike headed on across the cavern and Bridget began to follow him.

Then she stopped.

There was no guideline running across the cavern floor.

In and of itself, that was not so remarkable. Even though the first rule of cave diving is the establishment of a continuous guideline back to open water—water with surface open to the air—divers often bent that rule in the Devil's Ear cavern. During the winter season, classes entered the system with such regularity that there would soon be a tangled spider's-web of guidelines if every group placed one when they entered. So a custom had arisen; the first group into the system in the morning would set a guideline across the cavern floor, placing a plastic line-arrow next to the reel where it was tied off to the permanent line that ran through the cave system itself. Then, every group that followed would place its own line-arrow on the guideline. When a departing team removed the last arrow, they would know that they were the last group out of the system and they could remove the reel and return it to its owner.

Many long-time Devil's Ear divers had become used to crossing the cavern without running a guideline—so used to it that, regardless of whether a guideline was already in place, they would simply cross the entry cavern without one. The logic there was that the system was so often dived that it silted out only under extreme circumstances. And even if it did silt out, the Devil's Ear cavern was so simple, and the flow so potent, that a dive team lost in the cavern area could simply hover a few feet off the floor, stay in contact with a wall, and depend on being blown out the entrance aperture by the flow in the space of three or four minutes.

Except that this wasn't Mike Bryant's way of diving. He *never* bent the rule. Bridget remembered talking with him about it, remembered the serious look on his face and the way he'd deliberately articulated his words so she could be certain of reading his lips.

"You never dive casual," he'd told her. "Not ever. The cave you take for granted is the cave that's going to kill you. We run lines: all the time, every time."

So Mike hadn't skipped running a guideline.

He'd forgotten.

Bridget debated turning the dive right then and there. It was her prerogative. If she did, though, Mike would immediately see why she'd done it, and it would embarrass him. The two of them didn't need that.

But Mike had already shown so many red flags. Not running a guideline was simply one of them. The shoulder was another; it just wasn't smart to dive when you weren't one-hundred-percent, physically.

Then there was his equipment. Setting it down carelessly, where it could fall out of the van—that had been clumsy. But then going ahead and diving it, even though it might have been damaged by the fall? That was an error of judgement.

Bridget decided. She'd turn the dive. But she wouldn't turn it just yet. About ten minutes down the main passage of the system was "the Lips," a spot where two bedding planes met to form a wide "room" that was only about three or four feet from floor to ceiling. She'd wait until they passed the Lips—that would make it a decent-length dive—and then she'd turn it there, get them out before they got too deep within the system's convolutions.

Bridget hovered, letting the outflow carry her slowly back toward the entrance, while she worked by touch, unclipping a line reel from its place well back on her harness. She unscrewed the reel's thumb-lock, cinched the thin braided-nylon cord over the steel spike driven into the threshold area, and kicked back into the darkness, running the line as she went.

Mike was waiting next to the "Grim Reaper," a metal sign, decorated with a skeleton-fingered black specter, that the National Speleological Society's Cave Diving Section had placed in several of north Florida's most popular cave systems. Beginning with the block-lettered words, "PREVENT YOUR DEATH," the sign warned untrained divers that the passage from this point on was suitable for properly equipped, properly trained cave divers only: that it presented a lethal threat to those who entered unprepared.

Up to the sign, Mike and Bridget were in the cavern zone—that area reachable by ambient light during the daytime, and an area in which, even without artificial lights, divers could normally depend on being able to find their way by sight.

Beyond the sign, the Devil's Ear system was plunged into perpetual midnight. This was the cave proper. Diving here required artificial lights and the ability to navigate effectively by touch alone, should the lights fail.

Bridget rounded the sign, tightened down the drag on her line reel, and clipped it off to the end of the permanent guideline, which was anchored by a heavy concrete block. She didn't shine her dive light directly at Mike—that would temporarily blind him—but even in the backwash surrounding the lamp's beam, she could see the surprise registering in his eyes as he realized he'd forgotten to run a reel. Sign language gave them both the ability to comment on the lapse, but neither one did. Bridget simply extended her hand, all four fingers together, in the direction of the passage: *Proceed.*

Mike nodded and headed deeper into the cave.

The main passage here was huge, fifteen feet from wall to wall, and a dozen feet easily from the exhaust bubbles racing along the vaulted ceiling to the layer of clay silt sleeping on the floor. In the glass-clear water, the dive lights reached two hundred feet or more, a faint blue coloring the only hint that the outflow had substance at all.

It was here, in this passage, that Bridget had fallen in love with cave diving. Initially, she had taken up her cave training simply because it was what Mike Bryant did, and she had already identified Mike as someone who would be special in her life. Then, late in her beginning-cave classes, Mike had taken her and two companions into the Devil's Ear system, and Bridget had been, as she was on this day, the last one into the cave.

When one of the other students had breathed his air down to two-thirds of his starting pressure, he'd called the dive, and everyone had turned around where they were, making Bridget the first one in the column on the way out.

She had, at that point in her training, only recently mastered the trick of hovering neutrally in the water with the heavy steel cylinders and battery packs used in cave diving. She had taken advantage of that in the big passage, rising up to within a yard of the ceiling and relaxing, letting the flow carry her back out.

Hanging motionless in the moving water, she had enjoyed the illusion that it was the walls that were parading seamlessly past her; that she was not moving at all. Bending forward so she could gaze back down the passage, she had seen the three following divers, their forms gauzily illuminated by the backwash of their lights, and in the center of each form, their lights had been the blue of purest topaz, breathtakingly beautiful and moving in some deep and primal way.

"I looked back," she would later write to a med-school friend, "and for the briefest of instants, I had this warm and wonderful peace, the feeling that I was being followed by angels."

The walls of the big passage had been scalloped by centuries of outflow, a seemingly endless pattern of shallow, blackened, palm-size depressions, like a field of dirty snow that had lain too long in the sun. And a quirk of fluid dynamics—Bernoulli's Principle, Bridget remembered from her training—reduced the flow slightly near the walls, floor, and ceiling.

Knowing this, the two divers hugged the right-hand wall, swimming in the slower water and pulling themselves along with their fingertips to speed the swimming. They did this very deliberately—setting their fingers just ahead of the ridge of a scallop, pulling, and then lifting cleanly away. Cave divers learn early on that limestone is exceptionally abrasive, especially to water-softened fingertips. Bridget swiftly fell into the pull-and-glide pattern, her fins undulating steadily in the slightly bent-kneed pattern of a cave kick, keeping her moving fins well away from the easily disturbed silt. A glance at her pressure gauge showed that she'd used less than 300 pounds of gas pressure, not even 10 percent of what she'd begun with. She pulled. She glided. She kicked. She thought.

Dehydration. That might be one explanation for the way Mike had been acting. He'd been breathing dry, compressed gases all afternoon, wearing a hot dry suit in the sun between dives. Even slight dehydration could upset a person's reasoning abilities significantly . . .

. . . Except it wasn't as simple as that, and Bridget knew it.

The broad passage ahead abruptly ended. Mike was shining his dive light at two great slabs of eggshell-colored limestone, the great rock tablets held marginally apart from one another, as if earth herself were giving the two divers a perpetual sneer.

The Lips. They'd arrived. The bedding-plane junction, Bridget knew, would open back up into passage only another twenty feet further on. She would stick with her plan; she would follow Mike that far, and then call the dive.

Mike and she were up close to the ceiling of the passage; they would have to descend to make it through the restriction of The Lips. Bridget watched as Mike angled down, not pulling now, propelling himself on fin-power alone.

Something white fluttered down toward the cave floor. It was Mike's plastic decompression table, dislodged somehow from the pocket where he carried it. Bridget saw Mike look down, following the table, and as he did, she realized that his momentum was carrying him forward—toward the Lips, but too high.

She bobbed her light up and down three times rapidly, in warning, but it was too late. With the momentum of nearly 300 pounds of diver and dive gear behind it, Mike's crossover manifold banged into the upper limestone slab.

Pandemonium followed.

Like mercury brought rapidly to a boil, a silver funnel of nitrox gas billowed up to the cave ceiling, where it raced away in glistening, dancing sheets. While Bridget heard nothing, she knew that a gas loss of that magnitude would be like a freight train, roaring only inches behind Mike's head. Popping her back-up regulator out of its holder, she kicked strongly to close the fifteen feet between her and Mike.

Mike reached back with both hands and began turning his tank valves, shutting down both tanks individually in an attempt to isolate the leak. When that failed to alleviate the situation, he moved to the isolator, turning it, trying to confine the loss to a single tank.

That, Bridget could see as she got closer, was not going to work. The weakened manifold had broken and was rapidly jetting the precious breathing gases from both sides of the valve. He could turn both tanks off, but that left him nothing to breathe. And if either tank was on, it would lose gas continually. No matter what Mike did, he was facing one of the worst predicaments in cave diving—a total loss of his breathing supply.

Like a magician drawing scarves from a coat pocket, Bridget pulled on her back-up regulator hose, releasing all nine feet of it from the shock cords that had held it tucked in behind her buoyancy compensator. She held it outstretched toward Mike, the bright yellow color of the regulator easily visible even in the backwash of the dive lights.

Mike was reopening his tank valves, diverting some of the escaping gas back to his regulator, allowing him to breathe, although not for long. Bridget could actually see the needle creeping across the numbers on his pressure gauge, steadily making its way down to zero.

She swam around in front of him, holding the extra hose coiled in her left hand, the regulator still offered in her right. She'd dropped her lamp head to free both hands, and now it swayed back and forth on its cord below her, casting giddy, gyrating shadows around the flooded passageway.

Bridget held the regulator up in front of Mike's dive mask, only inches from his face. He continued working with the manifold, back to the isolator valve now, trying vainly to shut down the escaping gas. His eyes didn't seem to register the regulator at all. It was as if he was peering intently at something thousands of feet away.

Object fixation—Bridget recognized the symptoms immediately. Mike was so intent on trying to solve his problem that he was oblivious to any external remedy. In this state, he would keep turning valve knobs until his gas ran out and he drowned.

Bridget waved her hand before Mike's eyes. No reaction. There was only one solution. Twisting as she pulled, Bridget wrenched Mike's regulator out of his mouth and then, depressing the purge button to get the gas flowing, shoved the mouthpiece of her back-up regulator between his still-gaping lips.

Mike coughed, took a breath, and blinked. He reached back once more and shut down both of his tank valves simultaneously, trapping the last hundred pounds of gas pressure and keeping the cave water from flooding his steel tanks. The irony of that gesture did not escape Bridget; the man was together enough to keep his tanks from rusting but not together enough to save his own life. The two of them floated neutrally in the cave passage for perhaps ten seconds, neither one moving. Then Mike looked at Bridget, recognition written in his eyes, and held his right hand up, thumb to forefinger, other fingers outstretched: *I'm okay.*

He was back.

Bridget signaled thumbs-up, a purely academic gesture, calling the dive. Mike nodded, and they began their exit.

Bridget and Mike kicked steadily along in the outflow, heading back toward the entrance at the speed they would normally use, making good time but keeping their breathing moderate and preserving the remaining breathing supplies. They used the flow to help them, staying away from the floors and ceiling, hovering almost exactly in the middle of the passage. The Poseidon regulators they used were ambidextrous, capable of being used with the hose on either the left side or the right, so they swam side by side, Mike minding the hose and making sure he stayed within easy reach of his breathing supply, Bridget keeping close watch on her pressure gauge. The high-performance regulators were not prone to free-flow, but they took turns breathing, anyway, the better to avoid overtaxing the system.

All these little chores kept them from signing to one another very much, which was good, as Bridget wasn't sure what she'd say.

She certainly couldn't say what she was thinking: *This is the guy who survived Cenote X and lived to tell the tale?*

They got to the beginning of the permanent guideline and left Bridget's line reel in place—she could come back to get it later. As they crossed the cavern, Bridget motioned, one hand behind the other, and Mike moved ahead, using nearly every inch of the nine-foot regulator hose. The Devil's Ear cavern entrance was too small for two divers to go through at one time, and it was better to have Mike go through first, where, if he were to somehow lose the regulator during the exit, he could easily get to their oxygen decompression bottle.

Mike streamlined himself and aimed for the rectangle of daylight. Bridget wrapped her fingers around his right ankle to keep the two of them together, and they slid smoothly out of the limestone opening, both of them venting their dry suits and buoyancy compensators to keep from floating out of the small basin.

Bridget reached up and unclipped the oxygen bottle, handing it to Mike, who turned it on and immediately began breathing oxygen, surrendering Bridget's back-up regulator. She turned and restowed the hose, taking her time, delaying eye contact while she got herself back together.

When she finally did look back Mike's way, it was to check his dive computer. Hers was already clear, but Mike's showed five minutes of decompression required before he could go to the surface. And the trauma of the gas failure would have added to the danger of decompression sickness.

Twenty minutes of stop. She signed. *Okay?*

Okay, Mike signed back. Then he added, *Thank you. I owe you.*

Don't worry about it, Bridget replied. Then she busied herself, looking at her gauge, and kept herself busy for the next third of an hour.

Staying silent while they got out of the spring and packed the van was easy for Bridget. All she had to do was avoid eye contact. She was glad that she'd driven her own car and met Mike at the springs, because that would postpone any conversation for a while, as well. As soon as the back doors of the van were shut, she signed, *See you at your place.* Then she got into the familiar confines of her little red BMW convertible—her one luxury—and followed him on the forty-five-minute drive up through pulp pine and cattle country to Suwannee County.

Three-quarters of an hour was not enough thinking time for Bridget. Mindful of Mike's game shoulder, she headed straight back to the open airfill station behind his small shop, got a hand-truck, and came back to get the tanks—hers and Mike's—and wheel them back to the station, carefully tagging the manifold that had failed. Then she went back to her car and got the overnight bag out of the trunk.

Mike was hanging gear up to dry. Bridget signed to him, *I'm going to grab a shower.* He nodded, and she let herself in to his single-story ranch house with her key.

Her hair was still wet when she came back out onto the patio, where Mike was cooking chicken breasts on the gas grill. He handed her a cold iced tea, and she smiled her thanks, settling down at the glass-topped patio table set with plastic plates and plastic-handled flatware.

She should have grinned at the fact that Mike was finally heeding her cholesterol warning and grilling poultry instead of steak or ribs. She should have felt relaxed and comfortable, dressed in faded jeans and a scooped-neck pink top, barefoot in the low afternoon sun, looking forward to an evening of nothing in particular. But the change in Mike, the way he'd dived, and the fact that he was going along with her silence—not trying to be his usual upbeat self and make positive small-talk—had her off-center, ill at ease.

Potato salad and baked beans—Mike's attempt to round in the major food groups—were already on the table in opened deli containers, a serving spoon stuck in each. There was a plastic pitcher of tea that, even though she'd yet to try her drink, Bridget knew would be sweet, because Mike was a Southerner, born and bred, and he didn't make iced tea any other way.

Mike brought the chicken to the table, set it down, seated himself, and they began to eat.

Not for the first time, Bridget missed the prayers her mother had once led at the table, back when she was a little girl. Those had gone on until the car wreck, the one that had killed her mother and cost Bridget her hearing. Then there had just been the three of them—Bridget, her sister, and her father—at the table in the evenings, and nobody prayed before supper anymore.

Bridget waited until the chicken breast was gone from Mike's plate and all that was left was a smudge of the barbecue sauce that she hadn't been able to talk him out of using. Looking up, she signed, *Want to talk?*

"About what?" Like most signers who could hear, Mike found it more comfortable to speak as he signed.

Today. The dive.

"I'm sorry, Bridge. That was stupid. I wasn't myself."

You haven't been for a while. Is it Becky? You know I could do more.

This was dangerous ground. Ever since Pete's death, Bridget and Mike had each contributed to Becky's support while she waited for the insurance settlement to drag through court. For Bridget, this had meant a little less money into her mutual fund. But for Mike, it had meant the sale of a boat and a standard of living that most people step up from after college.

"No. In fact, I got an e-mail from her yesterday. She's got an internship for the summer, and it pays enough to cover her apartment and food. So that's actually going to get easier."

Then what is it?

Mike paused, pursing his lips, but signing and saying nothing. Then, holding up a closed fist—cave-divers' sign language for "stay right there"—he got up and went into the house.

He was back in a few minutes with an envelope, fashioned from the thin, flimsy paper that once was popular for international air mail. Mike handed it to Bridget, and she looked at the return address: "J. C. Rosaria, Ejido Mono, Playa del Carmen, Q.R., Estados Unidos de Mexico."

J. C. Rosaria. Juan Carlos Rosaria, the Mayan-descended president of the *ejido*, or land-owning group, that held title to the land surrounding Cenote X. It was Juan Carlos who had given Pete and Mike permission to dive on the property. He'd been pleased, Bridget remembered, that someone had found something to do with the hilly jungle land that formed the inland half of his *ejido*.

"Go ahead," Mike said and signed. "Read it."

Bridget opened the letter, typed, it appeared, on an old-fashioned manual typewriter.

> Dear Señor Mike,
>
> I make writing to you today because another American, the man Viktor Bellum, has asked my ejido for the permit to make the scuba in the deep *cenote* of the jungle. I say to him no, that I give this permit already to you and Señor Pete, but now he has a jurista write to me and ask the same, and I ask you what to do. This jurista can maybe make the trouble for the ejido of mine, like they did in Punta Banda, when they take the land of that ejido away, so I worry. I am not giving to him the permit unless you say OK, but if you don't say OK, please come and make your scuba quickly, so there will be no trouble for Ejido Mono. Please let me know what your wishes are, so I can make to him the reply.
>
> Your faithful friend,
> Juan Carlos Rosaria

Bridget read the letter twice, then looked up.

Let him do it, she signed.

"Let who do what?"

B-E-L-L-U-M, she spelled. *Let him dive.*

"What?"

You had your try. If he wants to take his, then let him take it.

"Bridge . . . Bridget. Come on. Pete gave his life trying to get us to the bottom of that *cenote*."

"And that's what?" Bridget replied aloud. "A reason for you to give your life as well?"

"I'm not going to die."

"You are," Bridget said. She was speaking loudly enough now that Mike was glad he did not have neighbors. "You almost died today, in a passage where you take beginners with single tanks and Y valves. And you did it because you cut corners. You're not . . . you."

She looked at the letter, noted the date on the postmark.

A month old, she signed. She almost added, *When were you going to tell me?* She didn't.

Ever since you got this letter, you've been out of it, she signed. *Think about that.*

Mike sat back, sighed.

"I'm wrapped a little tight," he said. "Juan Carlos needs me down there yesterday, if I'm going to take the heat off of him. I've got to set things up, get sponsors, cover all the bases."

You're thinking when—October? October was the beginning of the dry season, the earliest that a team could go if they wanted to move things overland. The earliest Bellum would be able to go, as well.

Mike nodded.

You're crazy.

He said nothing.

It's all crazy. Every bit of it. It was crazy from the start. We shouldn't have gone. Nothing good came of it, Bridget signed.

"Nothing good?" Mike asked. He was thinking of the record.

Maybe one thing. Maybe Forest.

Mike paused. "Forest" was the name that they'd given to a stranger, a girl no more than thirteen years old and obviously Mayan in ancestry, who'd simply shown up at their *cenote* camp one Sunday morning as Mike and Pete were going through the long weeks of preparatory dives.

Forest had not come alone. Two men had been with her, one old and one young, emerging from the jungle as Bridget was getting up to start the camp's coffee. All three had been dressed in odd clothing, poncho-like tops and calf-length pants made from a rough, hand-woven fabric: the two men carrying a blanket on which the girl was lying motionless, her right side covered with an ulcerous, festering wound. Bridget later told Mike that she knew her voice could be startling, so she had waited for them to speak first, but she had not been able to read their lips—whatever they said was neither English nor Spanish. So she had communicated with them in simple sign, indicating that she would like to inspect the injury.

It had been a terrible burn, third-degree in some places, gone horribly septic in the jungle heat. Bridget had seen burns often in her job back home as an emergency-room M.D., but never one so terribly neglected. She had led the three back to the camp, started an IV on the girl, and begun dressing her wound; Mike had just been coming out of his tent as Bridget bent to her work. Then, when Bridget had looked up to tell the men that their young companion would recover, they were gone.

The girl was conscious in forty-eight hours and up and about three days after that. She had been interested in everything but had never spoken a word. She seemed clever but would startle at the oddest things—the Coleman stove seemed a veritable source of wonder to her, and lanterns actually frightened her. "Forest," they'd called her, both because she had come out of the forest, and because somebody on the crew had just watched "Forrest Gump" on video before coming in to join the expedition in the jungle.

For two weeks, Bridget had treated Forest with intravenous antibiotics, cleaning the wound and keeping it covered with saline-soaked gauze when she was not exposing it to epidermal oxygen in the project's portable hyperbaric chamber. After several days it had become obvious that a portion of the wound would never heal, so Bridget had excised and closed it, relying on the resiliency of the teenage skin to cover the open sore. The stitches had come out two weeks later. The next morning, when Bridget went to check on her silent patient, she was gone.

The project staff had made only a cursory search for her. It had been obvious that her people, whoever they were, were completely at home in the jungle. It had also been obvious that Forest, her healing well under way, had left to rejoin them.

"Forest disappeared," Mike said.

I don't want you . . . Bridget began. She switched to speech. "I love you, Mike. I don't want *you* to disappear."

And then the tears came, and Mike was on her side of the table, awkward and on his knees and holding her while she sobbed. He stroked her hair and said, "It's all right . . ." and then remembered that she couldn't hear him, so he turned her face up to his and kissed her brow.

Her breathing settled down, and it was awkward, kneeling there next to her on the poured-concrete patio, so Mike stood up and smoothed her hair.

"I think it's time I grabbed a shower, myself," he said and signed. "Are you okay?"

She nodded.

But it didn't surprise Mike all that much when he came out of the bathroom twenty minutes later, dressed in clean khaki shorts and a T-shirt, to find her gone. The sun had just set, and the cover was on the gas grill, the dishes cleared from the patio table. Mike found them washed and standing in the rinse tray next to the sink; a tiny chameleon standing guard over them on the outside of the kitchen window screen, its motionless body silhouetted in the Florida evening twilight. And next to the dishes was a note.

> I love you. I really do. And I'll still see you, and still love you, and still care for you, but don't you dare expect me to be a part of this dive.
>
> It's crazy, Mike, and you're not doing it for any of the right reasons. Not because you want to, not because you are ready to, and not because you feel you can. You're doing it because it was Pete's dive, and in an odd way you're right. It always has been Pete's dive, and I think you know that you were there to support him all along, but it never was something that you would have done on your own. But now you want to.
>
> Why? To preserve some record? You've got a record now, and it doesn't seem to have done much for you. And maybe you think you're doing it for Pete . . . I don't want to sound callous here, but Pete's dead. You can't do anything for him anymore. Doing this dive won't bring him back to life, but it can kill you, and it will, if you try in this state of mind.
>
> I'm going home. Please don't try to follow me, and don't try to reach me this weekend. Maybe we can talk in a week or so.
>
> B.

Mike didn't bother looking in the driveway. He knew the little red BMW convertible would be long gone. He found the letter from Juan Carlos on the kitchen counter, and picked it up so he could return it to its file.

5

TULUM,
QUINTANA ROO, MEXICO—
MARCH, 2003

Slowly, tenuously, its green skin folding and unfolding in the golden morning sunlight with wary hesitance, the iguana crept toward the ripe mango on the garden wall. The lizard's paws, splayed like a child's green-leather gloves, twitched ever so slightly in wariness. For the twelfth time in as many minutes, it sampled the air with its tongue, testing its surroundings with all of its senses: searching, probing, trying to taste the possibility of a trap.

At last, the animal closed the final ten inches to its prize, nibbling at it with a delicacy one would not have thought possible for such a creature of such prehistoric appearance. It took two such tentative bites, then chewed with a gulping bob of its wattled head, pausing after a moment to lap the sweet nectar from the very center of the fruit.

Left hand cupped under his right in the classic combat-shooter's grip, Viktor Bellum placed the white dot of the Ruger P-89T's front sight on the very tip of the iguana's tail, and then crept the pistol laterally, his movement as slow and as regulated as the minute-hand on a watch. He traced the length of the four-foot animal, the gunsights intersecting the nerve-path of its spinal column, rising and falling over the hunch of its back, dropping down to hesitate in the area just beneath the shoulders, where the slowly pulsing heart would be, and then rising back to center on the head. Bellum picked a point just above and behind the eye, adjusting his sightline until he was certain he was centered on the creature's almond-size brain. Holding his aimpoint, he drew in a moderate breath and held it, index finger building pressure steadily on the trigger.

Without relaxing that tension, Bellum spun the swivel stool on which he was seated, the Ruger's hammer falling home with a sharp metallic click, the silver mouth of the pistol aimed solidly at the third button of Hector Gabrillo's coffee-stained uniform shirt.

"*Ai! Mia madre!*" the *federale* exclaimed. "It's okay, *Picuda*! It's me!"

Bellum smiled ever so slightly at his Mexican nickname—*Picuda* is coastal slang for "barracuda." The name suited him well. It should have; he'd chosen it. Still pointing his gun at the Mexican police officer, he slipped off his gold-framed Oakley sunglasses, revealing eyes so lightly brown they were almost yellow. Yellow eyes, bleached-blond crew-cut, a deeply bronzed face terminating in a squared, cleft chin—everything about him seemed square-cut and burnished in various shades of gold.

"I know it's you, *Capitan* Gabrillo," Bellum said cynically. "I knew it was you when you stepped out of the back door of my shop, half a minute ago. That's dangerous, not to announce yourself."

The Mexican policeman straightened up. "But how could you . . ."

"The same way I know that the iguana left the wall when he heard the sound of the trigger," Bellum said. "The same way I know that he left the mango on the wall."

Gabrillo nodded, obviously impressed.

"Good thing for me it wasn't loaded," he said, still nodding, looking nervously at the dark mouth of the gun.

"Not loaded?" Bellum mused. He spun back in one quick motion, and the mango vanished in a yellow mist from the adobe wall, the hollow, cracking report of the nine-millimeter pistol reverberating heavily from the walls of the courtyard.

Bellum smiled thinly at the startled police officer.

"This weapon has a decocker, *capitan*," Bellum said, bowing his head toward the still-smoking pistol. "It's a hinged plate that can be raised and lowered between the hammer and the firing pin. It was on for the iguana . . . and for you. It was thumbed off for the mango."

Bellum glanced down at the .44 caliber Smith Wesson on the policeman's hip and smiled. "You might want to get some training and learn about such things," he said. "Might save your life some day."

Gabrillo shook his head, took off his officer's cap, and mopped his balding brow. "You shouldn't be messing with that thing," he told the American. "It's not even legal for you to have it. Four years ago, up at Nogales? A gringo came across the border, then remembered that he had some *pistola* ammunition—not the gun, mind you, just a box of bullets, hidden in the spare-tire carrier of his Jeep. He even told the border guards about it, himself. No matter. They arrested him, confiscated his Jeep. He was locked up in Monterrey, three, maybe four months before the lawyers got him out. And they never did give him back his Jeep. That's the kind of trouble they give you in Mexico . . ." *May-hee-ko* was the way he said it. " . . . for fooling with that sort of thing."

"And who would they send to arrest me?" Bellum scoffed. "You? You nearly keeled over when I turned with the gun. I don't even want to *think* about what you did when I fired it.

"And besides," he added. "I do not 'fool' with this sort of thing. I take business seriously, and this"—he hefted the gun—"is business. Now, why are you here?"

"T-Tuesday," Gabrillo stammered, holding his hat in both hands like an enlisted man reporting to a superior. "Two days from now. Alvarez is going to have shipments leaving from two points on the peninsula at midnight. The American DEA and their Coast Guard have learned this, and they will intercept. Our office has been asked to cooperate."

Bellum nodded, held up his hand to show the Mexican police officer that he should wait, and—taking the handgun with him—walked into the back door of the shop. Inside, he moved a couple of twin-manifold scuba-tank sets and knelt to open the squat safe concealed behind them. From a thick stack of currency, he counted out $1,000 in American $100 bills. Closing the safe, he returned to the courtyard.

"The interception—is it on the ground or out over the Gulf?" he asked Gabrillo.

"At the airstrips," the Mexican replied, eyeing the money. "It's simpler. The Coast Guard will do air surveillance, but they'll be concentrating on the strips, up by Progreso."

"So the Americans will be fully engaged at, say, oh-fifteen?" Bellum asked.

"Yes—twelve-fifteen—exactly," Gabrillo agreed.

"Good work," Bellum told him, handing the man the money. "Let me know if anything changes."

Gabrillo grinned, as giddy at having pleased Bellum as he was over the cash in his hands.

"Anything else?" Bellum asked him.

"Else?" Gabrillo repeated. "N-No, no. Nothing."

Bellum nodded, dismissal obvious in his gesture. The Mexican police officer bobbed his head and shoulders in a silly little bow and left the way he'd come, through the dive shop.

Waiting until he was certain the policeman was out of earshot, Bellum walked back to the table where he'd been sitting, set down the pistol, and picked up a Motorola Iridium II phone. The device looked like a cellular phone, albeit with a much more stout antenna. It worked directly off communication satellites, circumventing the sometimes-intermittent Mexican landline and cellular networks.

That was Bellum's ostensible reason for owning the expensive phone. A valuable fringe benefit, though, was that the digital signal was encrypted and virtually impossible to monitor through conventional surveillance techniques. Running a dive shop and guide service was only an incidental business for Viktor Bellum. In his other lines of work, it was worth it to pay a premium for privacy.

Bellum mused for a second over what it would be worth to give Geraldo Alvarez a call and share with him the information he'd just received. Bellum had occasionally done business with the Colombian-born drug smuggler. He knew that Alvarez would gladly pay him $10,000, maybe $20,000, in return for keeping two planeloads of baled marijuana and hashish—not to mention the aircraft that would be carrying them—out of the hands of the Mexican government and the American Drug Enforcement Agency.

But then again, if he did that, the Americans would know that they had an information leak, and he would never be able to use this particular gambit again.

Bellum knew that Alvarez had figured out a way to work the American authorities' budget-consciousness in his favor. For years, the DEA had watched the Yucatan coastline for illegal departing traffic, but they had eventually pared down their resources to the bare minimum needed to intercept a single smuggler—usually, all that was needed. So Alvarez had taken to sending two shipments out simultaneously, on the grounds that, even if one got caught, the other would still get through.

Now the Americans had upped the ante and, for the first time in two years, added the resources necessary to do two interdictions at once. But that would, Bellum knew, stretch all of their available resources during the half-hour that it would take to make the arrests.

Meaning that, during that half-hour, he could fly a jumbo jet full of cocaine off the Yucatan coast, and no one would be the wiser.

What he had planned was considerably more modest. Not a jumbo jet, just a small, twin-engine Piper Seneca, piloted by a retired RAF man who'd flown stealth missions into Iraq. And the cargo would not be cocaine.

Bellum dialed a Mexico City phone number and waited as his signal bounced off a com-sat and down to a relay station, 900 miles away.

"*¿Hola?*"

He was in luck; the professor had not yet left for the university.

"It's me," Bellum said in English. "We have a window. We're going. Have your materials at the same place as last time, no later than twenty-two-hundred hours—that's ten o'clock—Tuesday night."

His contact asked the usual question, and Bellum replied, without hesitation, "Fifty thousand American, in cash. Large is fine, but have it loose. I'll be checking it."

There was the expected protest, which Bellum cut short by saying, "Fine. You want it done cheaply, you do it yourself. . . ."

As expected, the voice on the other end of the phone capitulated.

"And another thing," Bellum added. "I had to pay for this window, so I'll need to be reimbursed—five thousand dollars."

There was another squawk of protest, and Bellum grunted.

"All right," he said. "You win. I'll eat half. Twenty-five hundred. Plus the fifty large. Have it all with you when you get here. Twenty-two-hundred, sharp, this Tuesday."

He pushed "End" on the satellite phone, silently congratulating himself for the extra $1,500 that he had managed to work into the deal. Not that he didn't deserve it, he reflected. There were always incidentals to cover.

Bellum touched the cleft in his chin. That was one incidental—$3,000 from a plastic surgeon up in Santa Monica, and worth every penny; people saw that, and they just assumed you were a tough guy.

The surgeon had offered to do his nose, as well, for an additional $1,200, but Bellum had told him to just stick with the chin and the cheek bones; just enough to keep his face from jogging people's memories. Besides, he'd already done his nose, passing out face-first into a urinal at a central-Georgia Denny's, years before, in high school. Of course, that was not the story he told about it.

Hardly anybody knew the real story about the nose, just as hardly anybody knew that his eyes were really hazel, not yellow-brown. Colored contact lenses may have become an everyday item up north of the border, but they were still a rarity down here in the skinny latitudes. And lately, the contacts had served a second purpose, saving him the ego-reducing blow of having to wear glasses for the myopia that had come creeping on with middle age. The Florida optometrist had prescribed reading glasses too, but there was no way Bellum would do that. His arms were still long enough—just barely.

As for hair color, even Bellum wasn't sure about it anymore. It had been mousy brown when he'd first started to bleach it, more than a decade before. Now, he hesitated to think how much salt had crept in among the pepper.

Fake chin, fake eyes, fake hair. It went on. He'd given himself his name, as well as the nickname. At least he hadn't been reduced to wearing a girdle . . . not yet. He struggled through his hundred sit-ups every morning—there had once been a time when he could crank them out like a well-oiled machine—and that gave him barely enough strength to hold his gut in enough to impress the *peóns* . . . provided he didn't have to speak more than a sentence or two at a time.

Still, sometimes it seemed like an awful lot to go through, he thought, just to bluff and fluster some semi-literate yokel like Gabrillo.

Mexico. Bellum hated it. Hated the country, hated the heat, hated the cockroaches the size of cigarette lighters that seemed to populate the place, hated the whole dismal, backwater pall that constantly hung over it. He hated the people too, with their casual *mañana* attitudes, their defeated eyes, and their language, lazy and gratingly sibilant to his ears, even though he had been fluent in it for longer than he could remember. He even hated the women, though he regularly paid one for her company.

But most of all, he hated his father for bringing him to this country in the first place and for dooming him to return to it.

His father—the king of futility. Another tropical dreamer who preferred wasting his life in this cesspool to living in America. And then, the year he'd turned seventeen, they'd dared to look offended when they had told him to shape up or be shipped off to go live with relatives in Atlanta for his senior year of high school, and he had greeted that option not as the ultimatum they'd intended but as an opportunity to escape.

Bellum picked up the little dental mirror that he'd hidden among the dive gear on the courtyard table, carefully positioned so he would see the *federale* when he came through the door from the dive shop. A window in the back of the shop had reflected the image of the carefully positioned mango.

Add a little smoke, he thought bitterly, and he could have a full-fledged magic act.

That was okay. Already, he had made enough in his second business—the secret one—to live modestly for a while, stashed away in untraceable accounts in the Caymans, the British Virgin Islands, Dominica.

But Viktor Bellum didn't want to live modestly. He had paid his dues. He wanted his reward. And he was going to get it.

Only one thing stood between him and his goal, and that was Mike Bryant.

And from what he was hearing through cave-diving's grapevine, Mike Bryant was already his own worst enemy.

6
LAKE CITY, FLORIDA

Lamar Hires didn't do business suits; not for anything short of a wedding or a funeral, and this was certainly neither of those. But Lamar, of moderate height and muscled with the kind of build that comes naturally from a lifetime of hefting ninety-pound scuba sets, was wearing a brand-new white Dive-Rite polo shirt, just removed from its plastic wrapper that very morning, and a newer pair of Levis with fewer than a dozen washings on them. His paprika-red hair and beard were freshly trimmed, though he still wore no socks under his ancient brown Docksiders, but that was to be expected. Lamar wasn't sure if he owned a pair of socks.

Mike Bryant was dressed in similar fashion, except his polo shirt was light blue, rather than white, and the embroidery on his said "Underwater Underground." The other four men in Dive-Rite's spartan conference room were dressed in dark suits, white shirts, and ties, which marked them, in this region of Florida, as visitors.

"Coffee's in the urn behind you, and help yourselves to the donuts on the table, gentlemen," Lamar said after the introductions had been made. He was providing more than the facility and refreshments for this meeting; thanks to his connections with DEMA—the Diving Equipment Marketing Association—Lamar had a good relationship with many of the top names in dive and marine equipment. His counterparts, chief executives at four major companies, had agreed to either come in themselves or send senior people to talk with Mike, mostly on the strength of Lamar's reputation.

Mike arranged the business cards he'd been given on the table in front of him. The diving industry, once run by a few dedicated individuals who had started out making gear in their basements, had gone both corporate and global. The entrepreneurs of days gone by had sold out, for the most part, to large sporting-goods conglomerates with the deep pockets to invest in emerging technologies and the law firms to cope with the liability. In that sense, Lamar Hires was close to unique. He had bought out his old partner more than a decade before and made the investments necessary to keep up with technology, earning the distinction of being one of the few CEOs of a diving-equipment company who actually used, on a daily basis, the same gear that he produced and sold.

This also made Lamar the only person in the room that Mike actually knew—something that would have been unheard-of just a decade earlier. In fact, two of the people in the room—a Japanese sporting-goods executive and a Swiss man from a prestigious company that sold a very upscale line of sunglasses—had made it obvious in the introductions that they had never heard of Mike before. It made the room seem warm to him.

"Okay, for those of you who are certified divers, Mike and I will be taking you down to Ginnie Springs for a cavern orientation just as soon as we conclude this briefing," Lamar said. "But first, Mike would like to take you through a brief overview of what I'd have to say is a unique and promising opportunity for everyone here. . . . Mike?"

"Thanks, Lamar," Mike said, standing. "And thank you all for coming to see us today."

Seven years earlier, when Pete had been doing most of the presentations and Mike had merely been along to offer support, they'd used overhead projectors and a noisy and ancient Kodak Carousel slide projector. Now, Mike cued his "slides" from a laptop computer and did the presentation with Microsoft PowerPoint.

It was a glitzier format, but the content was essentially the same. Mike painted a picture of cave diving as one of the last frontiers left on earth— one that had essentially lain untouched up until the early 1960s, and had not truly opened up to extended exploration until thirty years later. He paid tribute to the pioneers—Tom Mount, Bill Main, Parker Turner, John Zumrick—people who had developed the techniques that made modern exploration possible. And then he talked about the modern-day explorers, people such as Jim Bowden, who was the first person in the world to dive deeper than 900 feet—a record that had stood until Cenote X—and Ann Kristovich, holder of the women's cave-diving and deep-diving depth records.

Then Mike moved on to the *cenote* itself: the rain-forest location, the evidence of a possible Mayan settlement in the surrounding area, the local geology, and finally a cross-section of Cenote X's main water-filled pit, depicted with the Empire State Building drawn alongside of it for scale. Using a bar-graph animation, he showed how close his previous dive had gotten him to the actual bottom of the *cenote,* demonstrating the feasibility of what he was proposing. Then he outlined a projected timetable and listed the various publications and broadcast media that had covered the previous dive, and additional media that might be willing to cover the next one.

It was a short talk, no longer than twenty minutes from beginning to end, but Mike felt as if he'd run a marathon by the time he'd finished. He remembered how Pete Wiley used to emerge from these things energized, pumped up by the contact and the experience. Personally, Mike couldn't wait to get out of the boardroom, away from the people with the suits and the Palm Pilots, the ubiquitous Mont Blanc pens and the yellow legal pads.

"Well, that's pretty much what we are proposing," Mike concluded, realizing that it sounded awkward even as he said it. "What questions can I answer for you?"

The four people in suits looked at one another, and then the Japanese executive bobbed his head in an abbreviated bow and spoke up. "Your previous attempt, the reason it was . . . ," and he fumbled here, because the obvious word would be "unsuccessful," and that, to a Japanese national, would sound unspeakably rude.

"Cut short?" Lamar asked helpfully. Lamar had made several trips to Japan.

"*Hai*—yes," the Japanese executive smiled gratefully. "And why, please, was that?"

"I had an equipment failure," Mike explained. "My lights—not Dive-Rite lights, by the way—different manufacturer."

He smiled as he said it. Nobody smiled back.

"So," the Japanese executive pursed his lips. "It was a former sponsor's fault that the team did not reach its goal?"

"It was an extreme situation," Mike replied, not liking the way that this was going. "Dives such as this take equipment to conditions far beyond what the average user would encounter or even imagine. It's reasonable to expect some issues. That's why we have redundancy in cave diving. I had back-up lights with me, and they worked."

At the back of the room, Lamar was nodding, encouraging Mike as he worked his way around the tricky question.

"I think I see where Katsumi is going with this, though," said another of the men in suits, an American from a marine-supply conglomerate that made, among other things, dry suits. "I mean, your partner died on the last attempt at this dive, didn't he?"

"That's right," Mike admitted. "He did."

"And people have died on Everest, on K–2, on the Eiger," Lamar added from the back of the room. "Hundreds of people have died attempting to climb mountains, maybe thousands. That's why people admire those who do—they are willing to incur substantial risk in order to achieve their goals."

"But weather is usually what turns a mountain climber around—or kills one," the American replied. "You don't have weather in a water-filled cave. We know that Mike, here, didn't make it the last time because of a gear failure. What about his partner? What did he die of? Was that a gear failure, too?"

"We don't know," Mike told the group truthfully. "We never recovered his body."

All four of the suits bent forward simultaneously and made notes on their legal pads.

"Listen," Lamar said, moving to the front of the room to stand next to Mike. "You see this gold dive watch on Mike's wrist? Rolex gave him that in recognition of the last dive."

Mike nodded and tried not to be too self-conscious about the $25,000 watch as Lamar raised his arm like a prizefighter. Mike rarely wore the Rolex, preferring to keep it in the safe at his shop, but he'd taken it out especially for the meeting.

"They don't do that for anyone except world-class explorers," Lamar continued, letting Mike lower his arm. "That's a pretty impressive credential."

"This is true," said the Swiss sunglass executive. "Then again, if the wristwatch fails, no one dies from it, *ja?*"

"That's right, Franz," Lamar agreed. "And nobody's ever died from sun-glass failure, either, so how big a check are you writing today?"

The room went still for a moment, and then all four of the visitors broke up laughing, the tension suddenly gone.

"I think that this is going to be a very big deal," Lamar said, nodding at the group. "I know that Mike is talking to Ford Motor Company about supplying vehicles for the project . . ."

Silently, Mike gulped. What Lamar had just said was true. Mike had written letters and sent prospectus sheets about the project to Ford—and to General Motors and to Dodge and Nissan and Toyota and even Mercedes. Then again, Pete and he had talked to the same companies the first time around. All had listened but none had offered support. Nor did he have any reason to suspect that the results would be different this time. But Lamar's comment had worked its magic with the visitors. They were listening intently to what he had to say.

"And Dive-Rite is, of course, going to be supplying the technical cave-diving equipment for this effort," Lamar continued.

This too was true. But Dive-Rite was not actually sponsoring the project, not providing funds to pay for consumables and out-of-pocket costs. Reputation aside, Dive-Rite was a very specialized company, and thus a very small one. It didn't have the funds to invest in expeditions other than those conducted by its own staff.

" . . . And yes, our reputation is riding on how our gear will perform in the *cenote*, but then again, our reputation is riding on how well any piece of gear performs, any time a diver takes it into a cave," Lamar continued. "Is there risk? Certainly. But it's manageable, and the potential rewards far overshadow any downside. We're planning to feature Mike and his project in our catalog the year after next, and we really think it will connect, particularly with upscale recreational divers with a mounting interest in tech-style equipment."

Mike, impressed, said nothing, and was silently thankful that Lamar was there to do damage control. Had it just been him, he was pretty sure the group would have gone back to their rental cars by this time.

"We can handle more questions later, at lunch," Lamar finally concluded. "Right now, let's go diving."

Three of the four executives were scuba divers—Franz the sunglass man was not—and Mike and Lamar took them down to the main basin at Ginnie Springs, where only the marine-supply man showed any aptitude beyond what you'd expect from a casual resort diver. Still, the adjoining cavern had long since been "safed"—its cave system permanently closed off with stout steel bars—and was clear of silt, and straightforward in its layout, simply a large, downsloping room that ended at the grill where the cave system itself began. Regular, open-water divers went into the Ginnie cavern all the time during daylight hours, and even the basin beyond was an enjoyable experience, a white-sand-bottomed bowl filled with air-clear water and populated by inquisitive sunfish.

Mike and Lamar showed their charges how to use line reels, and then they took them into the cavern itself, working behind some huge fallen blocks off to the left side, where they ran a stretch of guideline to make it look like real cave passage, and posed the visitors for photography, Lamar shooting several images with a housed digital camera so they would have some nice, staged pictures to e-mail the executives as a follow-up.

It was late afternoon by the time the last visitor had left and Bridget pulled into the parking lot with Mike's van. Lamar had left to meet a cave class in nearby High Springs.

Mike loaded his gear and climbed in on the passenger's side, leaning over to give Bridget a weary peck on the cheek. Then he folded down the armrests on his seat and leaned back.

"Tough day?" Bridget asked, putting the van into gear.

"I guess," Mike said, leaning forward out of old habit so Bridget could watch him sign. "I don't know, Bridge. It's not like it once was, you know? They're all suits, all business, all . . . distant, I guess. There are no connections any more. They want a nicely wrapped package, with no downside, and I imagine that they're big enough that they can find it. But not here. It looks as if I'm too much of a question-mark for them."

He shrugged, gazing out the van window as they passed cattle farms and pulp-pine groves, the typical North Florida landscape, and then he turned back so she could see his face again.

"Maybe this isn't meant to be," he said. "Maybe somebody else is supposed to dive X, you know? Maybe I should just stick with my cave classes and work on adding some more sport charters into the mix, make a little money for a change. I know it will be better for us."

Bridget said nothing. She reached over, took his hand, gave it a squeeze as she drove. But inside, something hidden was rejoicing, nodding its suddenly lightened head and saying, "*Yes!*"

They had dinner in Madison, fried chicken with biscuits and gravy, a typical pine-country dinner and the best that they were going to find in a town that size. To the suddenly relieved Bridget, it seemed like a celebration banquet. Then they headed out to Madison Blue Springs, once a cypress-ringed pool at the edge of a garbage dump and now a commercially operated spring with paved parking areas and a modicum of landscaping. The cypress trees were gone, cut down to keep tourists' kids from leaping from them into the spring, and the area still attracted clouds of flies, even though the dump had long since vanished. But tonight there was a soft spring breeze, the flies were on sabbatical, and the snorkelers and open-water divers had all long since left the spring basin to watch HBO at their hotels.

They were nearly geared up, just about ready to make their way down the wooden walkways and stair steps into the headspring, when Bridget noticed it—the small green display screen on Mike's cell phone was blinking.

"Message," she said aloud. Mike walked around to the front of the van, picked the phone up, and registered a moment of surprise.

"It's a text-page," he said. Mike's cell phone also worked as a text-pager—working through an operator or the Internet, it was possible to send a short written message to its tiny digital screen. But not every user subscribed to the service, and not many people knew Mike had it—he did as a courtesy to Bridget, so she could get messages when she visited. Mike rarely got text pages, himself.

"From Lamar," he said as he pushed buttons to bring up the message. Then he read for a moment and his face lit up like a kid's at Christmas.

"What?" Bridget asked aloud, still smiling.

He handed her the phone.

"BONSOLIERE SUNGLASSES ASKS WILL $50K SECURE SPONSORSHIP?" the tiny LCD characters read. "AND YOBATU SCUBA TALKING REGULATOR DEVELOPMENT AND $100,000 ADDITIONAL FUNDING . . ."

She pressed the "Next" key to read the rest of the message.

". . . FOR PROJECT," the screen continued. "NO NEWS FROM OTHER TWO, BUT IT'S A START. SO WHEN DO YOU LEAVE FOR MEXICO?"

Stunned, Bridget read the message twice. Then she handed the phone back to Mike, unable to see what he was saying, because she could not hold back the tears.

7

THE YUCATAN PENINSULA

Walking slowly and carefully, Elvis Hastings re-shot his heading with a small Silva orienteering compass, resettled the backpack onto his shoulders, and slipped the compass back into the breast pocket of his sweat-dampened khaki shirt.

Surrounded by rain forest, swallowed up by jungle that rose nearly sixty feet to a canopy offering only the faintest suggestion of blue sky, Elvis carried a stainless-steel machete that he used every thirty seconds or so to hack back the clinging vegetation, carving a tunnel through the dense, green foliage. In his pack, he carried an expensive pair of Oakley sunglasses that he hadn't worn once in the two weeks since the bus from Cancún had dropped him off at the trailhead. The jungle lightened to deep shades of green during the day and went pitch-black at night, the only natural light coming from firefly-like insects and the occasional rare phosphorescent mushroom. Twice, as he walked, he had wandered across places dappled by actual sunlight; tiny gaps in the vegetation where the limestone pushed so close to the surface that little could take root and grow, but these were not clearings—not by the longest of shots.

Once, near sundown, he had found himself at the base of an overgrown Mayan pyramid that he climbed in the deepening twilight, coming to its top well after the horizons had darkened, emerging under a canopy of stars so thick that they seemed clouds, the Southern Cross hanging bright and low over the sea of slumbering treetops.

Consulting his watch there to obtain Greenwich Mean Time, Elvis had taken out the light polymer sextant that he carried and shot sightings on three stars. He'd then turned on the Garmin eTrex pocket GPS he also packed along—an instrument he operated sparingly, because the battery life of the unit was limited—and was pleased to find that his star-sighting had been as accurate as could be expected with nineteenth-century technology. Elvis had marked the uncharted pyramid on his Mexican topographic map and then lain back to watch the sky, a luminescent bowl of salted black. The distant lights of an airliner and the steady pinpoint passage of a satellite had been the only visible reminders that people still existed in this world.

Elvis had intended to spend the night on the pyramid's summit, just so he could see the sun rise the next morning. But sometime before midnight, a jaguar had begun calling less than half a kilometer away, and while he was certain that he was considerably larger than the jungle cat's usual prey, the former surfer had decided not to take a chance. Working by the waxing and waning light of a hand-powered flashlight, he had returned down the pyramid's crumbling, creeper-thick steps to the jungle floor, found a usable tree, and spent the night as he had spent all his nights since he'd started this hike, twenty feet off the ground in a string hammock, his backpack hung beside him on a short hank of mountaineering rope.

He had read himself to sleep that night as he did every night, poring over the only book he carried with him: a thin, compact traveler's Bible with a worn, snap-flap leather cover. Each night, he started in the eighth chapter of Romans, because it was his favorite, and then returned to the schedule that would take him, like clockwork, through the entirety of both the Old and the New Testaments every six months, and had taken him cover to cover through the Bible eleven times since he'd made the decision to devote his life to what he was doing today. His wrists were getting thicker, his hands and forearms adding muscle from squeezing the grip-like generator lever on the flashlight, the only electrical device he carried that required neither fuel nor batteries, so he did not have to ration its use.

He did not see the sun the next morning. Nor had he truly seen the sun for days. The canopy swallowed it up, and he traveled in daylong green twilight, in daylight filtered through the leaves of centuries-old tropical hardwood trees.

The young hiker reached the base of the tree to which he'd shot his last heading, re-shot the same heading on the most distant tree that intersected his lubber line, and returned the compass to his pocket once again.

Elvis was being watched. He was certain of that, and he had been certain of it ever since the morning he'd left the pyramid, three days before.

Away from the primary tourist areas, Mexico was famous for its bandits. Elvis knew that. But any bandit lying in wait here, more than thirty kilometers deep into the Yucatan jungle, would have to be either out of his mind or hopelessly optimistic. So Elvis was not afraid. He had every reason to believe that the people watching him—he was fairly certain there was more than one—were peaceful, if curious, and would do him no harm.

Then again, the jungle inhabitants of New Guinea had initially been thought by their European discoverers to be a benign and friendly people—and they'd turned out to be headhunters. But Elvis thought that wasn't likely to be the case here. The people of this place had been studied, albeit rarely and sporadically. They were known to carry bows and arrows, but those were for howler monkeys, parrots, and iguana, the staples of their meat supply. Murder was virtually unknown among them.

Besides, Elvis felt he was protected. He traveled with no human companion, no soldiers or hired guards, but he felt safer than he would have had he been surrounded by a full division of battle-hardened troops. It was a feeling he had only known recently, but he was growing accustomed to it, and it was a great comfort.

He got to the tree he'd sighted on and stopped to take out his compass. As he did, he glanced down and saw it—a human footprint, broad and splay-toed, a full inch shorter than his own, pressed into the moss at the base of the tree. Even as he looked, the moss began to spring back up, the impression becoming dim and vague. Someone had been here—someone who had moved away less than half a minute before.

Feeling like Robinson Crusoe discovering his first evidence of Friday, Elvis made another sighting with his compass, certain now that his every move was under scrutiny: certain also that the footprint had been left deliberately, a test to determine how he would react. Trying hard to appear casual, he matched the compass needle to the selected bearing, sighted down the lubber line to a distant, vine-covered tree, and walked on.

Sliding the machete back into its scabbard on the side of his pack, Elvis snapped the nylon-web keeper over the hilt and secured it in place. The implement was useful—he could not have covered half the territory he had traveled thus far, had it not been for the use of it—but it could also be viewed as a weapon, and he had no desire to appear dangerous.

A deep breath, a stretch, and Elvis further slowed his pace a notch or two. He did not really have a destination—no place that he was actually walking *to*. He shot compass headings simply to ensure that he did not travel in circles, and to keep him from accidentally wandering across the border into Guatemala, which he knew to be fewer than 5 kilometers to his south. His destination was—he hoped—an event rather than a particular place. The reason he'd come all this distance was to meet, face-to-face, the inhabitants of this lush and primitive region. And if he didn't, he soon *would* have an actual, physical destination. He was running low on food and was already down to half rations, trying to stretch his freeze-dried supplies. In two day's time, he'd have to switch on the GPS, find the heading back to his pick-up point, and walk out.

Elvis's journey had started, he now understood, nearly ten years earlier, in early November, on the north shore of Oahu.

The event had been the Hawaiian Tropic International, a surfing competition that drew participants from throughout the Pacific basin, as well as South Africa, Maldives, Brazil, Florida, Puerto Rico, and even France. Though he had never been the competition surfer that his father was, Elvis had hit several of the larger events every year. He'd had sponsorship—a suntan lotion company, a swimwear manufacturer, a sunglass maker, and, of course, M.D. Molokai Surfboards. And he'd had other business in conjunction with the contest as well. The day before the competition was "demo" day—local surf shops would be sending people out to surf the M.D. Molokai line with him, just as all the other competitors would also be wooing the locals on behalf of their sponsors.

But while most professional surfers looked at their demo work as little more than a necessary evil, Elvis took it seriously. His family's income depended upon it, so, while the others would be content to just show up the day before the first demo was scheduled, Elvis always made it a point to come in a week early, study and surf the local breaks, and get familiar with the patterns and rhythms of the waves. Besides, he had family on Oahu—his mother's parents and sisters still lived outside Honolulu, and he had an uncle who lived right on the beach at Haleiwa. It was all the more reason to fly himself and his boards in early and visit.

After stopping by the Strong Current Shop the evening before and reading Hurricane Bob's morning surf forecast, Elvis had decided to surf Waimea Bay, second in local reputation only to Pipeline for monster waves. It was a weekday, a school morning, and he pretty much had the ocean to himself. A couple of retirement-age longboarders out for a sun-riser had headed for the beach and stayed in as soon as the dawn wind began building the breakers higher than twelve feet.

About an hour later, the breeze shifted and the waves began breaking to the left, so Elvis switched his leash over to his left ankle and surfed for a while "goofy foot"—right foot forward. It was fun, and he enjoyed the fact that he could do it at all. Just as many speed skaters can only turn with any degree of agility to the left—the direction in which most races are run—so many surfers, even professionals, can only surf well with the left foot forward, the natural stance for right-handed people.

But although Elvis was talented that way, it still tired him rather quickly; his goofy-foot muscles simply weren't as well conditioned as the ones he used in a conventional stance. After four rides with his right side forward, he was tired, thirsty, and ready for a break.

He rode the next wave until it collapsed, then slid back down onto the board and paddled all the way in to the beach, flipping the board over and carrying it, ankle leash still attached, over his head when the water got shallow enough to wade.

He ran up above the high-water mark, stuck the surfboard skeg-first into the sand, where nobody could walk over it and damage it, and then looked up and down the sparsely populated white crescent of beach. The boards were still up on the concession-stand windows.

"Too early in the season," said a baritone voice behind him.

Elvis turned. A lean, white-haired man in his seventies, maybe older, was standing there barefooted, wearing tan cotton trousers and a blue-and-red-striped rugby shirt. He was holding an unopened bottle of Evian water in each hand, and his voice carried a hint of Australia or New Zealand in it, as if he had grown up there, but lived elsewhere most of his life.

"Not the surf," the man added. "Season's just about peak for the surf. Then again, I'd say it looks as if you'd know that. But it's too early for the concessionaires. They won't open shop until noon, perhaps later. Come Thanksgiving week, they'll be here by sunrise, setting up chaises, staking out umbrellas, hawking cold drinks and nose zincs."

He smiled at the accidental rhyme and continued, "Be that way through Christmas, then they'll slough off a little while longer, and get back to business around Easter week. Which is the long way around of saying that, if you're looking for anything from the vendors, you'll have quite the wait ahead of you. May I offer you a cold water, instead?"

"Hey," Elvis smiled. "Thanks. I'd appreciate that."

The elderly man nodded up the beach to where a pair of Adirondack-style chairs sat in front of a small, neat, palm-shaded home.

"My place," he said with a small smile. "Why don't we go sit? You can keep an eye on your surfboard from there."

They did, Elvis settling gratefully into the rustic but comfortable chair while the older man excused himself and went into the house, coming out five minutes later with an island breakfast of sliced pineapple, coconut, cheese, and sweet Hawaiian bread. Elvis offered a small protest at the unexpected hospitality, but the older man just shushed him with a smile and began asking his young guest about his life—how long he'd been surfing and where, and how Waimea compared to the other places Elvis had surfed in his travels.

They were all things that the young Southern Californian was comfortable talking about, and he chatted amiably for five minutes, telling the older man about Surfer's Paradise, in Australia, where he had competed several months earlier, and talking, of course, about Dana Point and Maverick's and the other big-wave sites up around San Francisco and Monterey, where diehard big-water surfers headed when the forecast called for massive storm surge. Then, aware that he'd been rattling on nonstop and had yet to so much as discover his host's name, Elvis asked the genial elder to tell him something about himself.

His name, the older man told Elvis, was Alec Pemberton, and he was a Kiwi—a New Zealander—who had first visited Hawaii in late autumn of 1941 as a young pharmacist's mate with the Royal Navy, attached to the Australian Royal Marines.

"Nineteen forty-one," Elvis mused. "Hmm. Were you here then for . . ."

"Pearl Harbor?" Alec asked. "Oh, yes. I was there, in fact—at Pearl when it happened. Our unit had been dispatched to help load supplies onto a destroyer due in that afternoon. We'd gotten to the base early so we could attend chapel services—it was a Sunday, you know, and the Royal Navy required that of all enlisted men back then—but we never made it. The first strafing runs began when we were still a quarter-mile from the chapel. A mate of mine and I dove under a dock winch and it protected us. The rest of our blokes weren't as lucky. They hid under a fuel truck. It was hit and went up in flames."

Alec stared out at the water as he continued his story. "I've seen the movies they make about that day. They make it seem glorious, very exciting, don't you know? It wasn't. It was confusing and loud and utterly terrifying. I can still hear the sounds of my mates screaming as they burned, and there was absolutely nothing we could do to help them. Heaven knows we tried. We ran over there even as the second strafing runs came in and the bombs began to fall. One round ricocheted off a bollard and hit me in the shoulder. It didn't wound me—it was already spent—but it knocked me over. It was hot where it had struck me, and I carried the bruise for weeks. And by the time we got to the fuel truck, the flames were so fierce that we couldn't get near. It was too late, anyhow. The screaming had stopped, and I imagine that they were all quite dead. At least, I hope they were. We couldn't help them. But we tried."

"You were heroes," Elvis said quietly, fascinated by the account.

"No," Alec replied evenly. "We were not. We were just very frightened boys in the midst of absolute pandemonium. Either that or, if we were heroes, we were only two of thousands that day. All I know is that, having seen my mates die in those first few seconds of the attack made it very real to me, very apparent that every bomb, every burst of machine-gun fire, was more lives, no older than my own, gone in an instant: being snuffed out in pain and agony and stark, confusing horror."

That must have been awful, Elvis had thought to say, but he hadn't. Alec was obviously not done yet, and Elvis remained silent, waiting to hear what the old man would say next.

"If anything, the week after was even worse," Alec continued. "There were men in those big battleships that had rolled at their anchorages, and we could hear them, imprisoned inside the hulls, rapping with hammers, wrenches, whatever they could find, trapped there in the darkness, trying to signal us to come rescue them. But the hulls were too thick in some places for the machinery they had at Pearl, and in other places, they couldn't cut, for fear of releasing the trapped air and flooding other parts of the ship. So the Navy had to send for heavier cutting equipment and they had to work section by section, and that took weeks, which was far longer than those men had, with the air going stale by the minute.

"We heard them constantly for three days while we worked on the salvage effort. Some of our blokes sang and whistled and told jokes, talking loudly to drown out the sound of that infernal tapping. Finally, on the fifth day, the noises stopped. But I dreamed of it for weeks afterward, woke up with the terror-sweats every night, dreaming that I was trapped, alone and suffocating, wet and cold and hungry, down deep in the darkness."

Alec took a sip of water and nodded out at the blue Pacific.

"That's where most of the war was for the next six months, you know," he said. "Out there, on the ocean. Midway, the Coral Sea—people just don't understand these days how very close we came that year to losing the whole war. Oh, there was the Doolittle raid on Tokyo, and that was a tremendous morale booster for the troops in the Pacific theater, but it was a needle being jabbed at a giant, and Halsey barely got his carriers back into position in time to help defend Port Moresby.

"My unit was rebuilt, and they sent us up to try to stop the invasion of Borneo, but we never got there in time. It became Japanese territory while we were still under steam, more than a week away. So I didn't see action again until we invaded Guadalcanal, and I didn't get *there* until a month after our first troops had hit the beach, well into the summer of 1942. I'd been reassigned to a Royal Marine air squadron back then, and we shared a strip with some Yanks, Marines as well—it was the same thing for both navies; the Marines didn't have their own medics, so they would have naval medical personnel assigned to them. And as you might imagine, as we were the blokes assigned to patch them up if anything went wrong, the Marines did a first-class job of protecting us, but that also took us out of the action of defending anything if we were attacked, and three weeks after I got there, the Japanese made their first major effort to retake the field.

"I jumped headfirst into a slit-trench with another medic, a Yank from St. Louis named Slocum, and the Marines came, Johnny-on-the-spot and set up .50-caliber machine gun positions and sandbags at either end of the trench. It was late, ten at night, and the Japanese were firing with tracers so they could aim, and our lads were firing back, tracers as well, so the air was just crisscrossed with these bright streaks of yellow and white, and then mortar rounds began dropping in as the enemy tried to blow holes in our perimeter.

"They say that, in battle, a fellow gets too busy to get scared, and that may have been the case with the lads on the guns, but it wasn't the case with me. I was cowering there on the floor of that trench, with the machine-guns rattling and roaring away just ten feet to either side of me, and I didn't have anything to do but be terrified." Alec paused here and smiled. "So I did that the best I knew how. And then Slocum leaned over and shouted in my ear, 'Chin up, Alec, our fellows will take care of this.'

And I looked up, and, Elvis, there the man was with heavy machine-gun fire tracing back and forth, not two feet over his head, and he was absolutely calm, not a bit of fear showing in him. I mean, he still had his senses. Certainly, he wasn't about to go strolling around in the shot and shell, but he looked . . . serene. Confident. And I wasn't. I remember looking up as explosions lit the sky, and shouting back, 'This is hell!' And Slocum chuckled at that. He laughed like we were back in the barracks, playing cards, and I'd just told a good one. And then he yelled in my ear, 'This isn't hell, Alec. It's not even close—though I imagine some folks will be there tonight.' Then he nudged me and asked, 'What about you? I think we'll make it—but if we don't, where does Alec Pemberton end up?' And I thought about it for a moment, and I began to weep, because I didn't know."

Alec smiled and nodded as he resurrected that terrifying memory. Elvis thought it odd, but he said nothing, still mesmerized by the story. The older man offered his guest more pineapple, took a small slice for himself, and then leaned back and continued:

"The assault lasted until well after midnight, and for the next hour, Slocum talked to me, shouting in my ear. He had a pocket New Testament— one of those 'bullet-proof Bibles' with the steel covers that the Yanks carried in the war, and he had a torch—a flashlight—with a red filter, so he turned it on, and in the glow from that vermilion light, he read me Bible verse after Bible verse and told me about Christ. He told me that all men were sinners, which I had no trouble believing about myself. I was young then and single and a sailor, and I had been living, after all, as sailors tend to live. And then he showed me how I had no means of personally disposing of that sin, that nothing I could do or offer would ever be sufficient to repay it. Then he told me that Jesus . . ."

Alec paused. The hint of a tear beaded at the wrinkles in the corner of his eye.

"He told me that Jesus was God's Son, that he was God himself, and that he offered his body and his life's blood on the cross to pay for the sins of mankind in general, and mine in particular. Slocum told me that Christ paid my sin-debt for me, that he offered that payment as a gift—a free gift—and that, if I wanted to accept it, then all I had to do was turn away from a life led by sin, turn toward a life full of him, and believe.

"And I did, and suddenly the battle that raged all around us held no terrors for me, and Slocum and I were huddled there, praying together in the mud on the bottom of the slit trench. Then our lads called in the Japanese positions to our battleships lying off shore, and the big guns opened up, and for five minutes, the shells landing were so loud that we couldn't even shout to be heard. After that, it was all over and Slocum and I ran out to tend our wounded. We saved several lives that night, but one boy I went to had been torn right in two by a mortar round. It was awful; he looked more like meat than a man. He was still alive, and hurt so badly that he was past the point of feeling any pain. But he was still quite lucid, and he knew that he had only minutes left on earth, so I told him what Slocum had told me, and I saw him embrace his Savior with the last breath he had within him. And you know what? That felt better to me than all the ones that I patched up."

Elvis had felt mildly discomfited with the way the conversation was going just then, but he reminded himself that it was he, after all, who had brought up the war in the first place. And he found himself asking, "What happened next?"

"I saw the war," Alec told him. "At least, I saw much of it. And I saw the victims of the war. Not our injured and dead boys, although they were certainly victims in their own way. But the people who lived on these islands around the Pacific, people so peaceful that they were easy conquests for every invader that happened to sweep in from across the sea. I remember places like Pelilieu, up in Micronesia, the Western Carolines. The civilian population was evacuated by the Japanese before Chesty Puller and his Marines began their invasion, and we repatriated them to it once the war was winding down, but it had been destroyed, absolutely annihilated, in the meantime. I mean, if you look at the islands of Micronesia today, they are so heavily foliated that they look like clumps of broccoli poking up out of the sea. And so did Pelilieu. But after our naval bombardment, the island had been so completely battered that it was down to bare, whitened, shell-blasted rock. There was nothing left growing out of the soil. There was no soil. You can imagine what was left of the houses. The Japanese had been on the island since 1912, and I don't mean to make them sound like heroes, but they had put in a power station and a hospital and a school for the local children and modern water and sewer works, and all of it, every single bit of it, was gone, blown to oblivion. You go there today, and the trees have grown back, but they still only have electricity for three hours each evening and running water for four hours a day.

"And I saw this time after time, throughout my time in the service. I saw people coming back to places without hope, and I saw people dying of malnutrition and fever and lack of sanitation—and dying without ever knowing about Christ. So I arranged to be mustered out on Oahu, right here in the middle of the Pacific, and I got a job as a carpenter, helping out in the boom following the war. I bought property along the bay here, thinking I could sell it later on, which I did, but I kept one piece and built this house so I would have a base to come back to. I got married to my Annie, an ex-Army nurse, and she helped support us while I studied at a missionary Bible college over in Honolulu. Then, for the next thirty years, we traveled around the Pacific, building medical clinics and sharing the gospel. We came back just five years ago when Annie's heart got bad. She passed on last year."

"I'm sorry," Elvis said softly.

"Don't be. I may miss her, but she's happy. And knowing that makes *me* happy."

Then Alec squinted at the surf and looked at his watch.

"Well, Elvis," he mused. "The wind won't keep this break up much longer. Come back tomorrow—I'll have breakfast, and you're welcome to use the conveniences as you'd like. But right now, I imagine you'll be wanting to get back to your water."

Two minutes after putting his compass away, Elvis came to a place where two mahogany trees had fallen roughly parallel to one another, their trunks about five feet apart. He kicked the dead leaves away from the base of one trunk and then did the same with the other until he was satisfied that no cover remained in which a scorpion or a snake or any of the myriad spiders of the Yucatan—all of which were poisonous—could be hiding. Then he took off his pack, made a show of stretching, as if he was just stopping to rest, got out his Bible, a water bottle, and the nylon food sack containing the last of his protein bars, and sat on one of the trunks.

Fascinated by Alec Pemberton, who had lived through so much that he had only read about, and puzzled by the prospect of a missionary who did not preach at him, Elvis had returned to Alec's Hawaiian cottage the next day and the day after that and the day after that. They had talked about the islands, about change, about the blue Pacific. One night, Alec had accepted an invitation to visit Elvis's uncle's house, and he had arrived with a beautiful wood carving, a "story board" from Koror, in Palau, that he had insisted the household keep as a gift.

It was just a few days before the competition was to begin that Elvis, relaxed and comfortable now with the morning interludes to his surfing, had asked Alec, "So how long have you been retired from missions work?"

"Retired?" Alec had answered. "Oh, I'm not retired."

"But you're here."

"Yes," the old man had nodded. "But not in my retirement. You see, I used to minister to people who lived on islands all around the Pacific Rim. But lately, I only minister to one person, someone on this very island."

"Who's that?"

"A surfer," Alec smiled. "Nice young fellow—bright, friendly, very polite. Comes from a place called Dana Point, in California."

Coming from a person who had become, in the space of a week, a friend, that statement—which Elvis would have seen as threatening just a few days before—had seemed both surprising and comforting.

"I see," he'd said.

"May I ask you a question, lad?"

"Of course."

"People call this paradise," Alec mused, lifting his hand to take in the sun, the sand, the ocean, and the palm trees. "But it isn't. It isn't paradise, and it isn't heaven, not any more than that airstrip on Guadalcanal was hell when I called it that during the war. But there is a heaven, Elvis. And just as certainly, there is a hell. And the question I have for you, Elvis, is this—have you any idea which of them it is that you're headed to, and have you any idea why?"

And when Elvis had confessed that he had no answer to that, Alec had taken out a brand-new, slim, traveler's Bible, with a brown Moroccan leather cover. And he'd unsnapped the cover, opened it, and shown Elvis the places in the Bible that a man named Slocum, from St. Louis, had shown him more than half a century before. Then, when Elvis had listened and made from his heart the same decision that Alec Pemberton had once made in a slit-trench in the middle of a firefight, Alec had embraced him, and handed him the Bible. Embossed on the cover in gold were the initials, "EH."

"Thank you," Elvis had told him. "You were pretty certain of this, weren't you?"

"I wasn't," Alec had shrugged. "But He was."

After that, Elvis's perspective had changed. He'd still enjoyed surfing, still toured for his father's company, and still spent long hours working on the business when he was home. But shore breaks and surf were no longer the center of his life. At Alec's suggestion, Elvis had found a church on his return to Dana Point, a small nondenominational Christian assembly. He started attending regularly and encouraged his friends and family to join him. Some did, some did not, and some found excuses to distance themselves from him. His mother and father were in the second category—uncertain of why it was that their son suddenly wanted to spend every Sunday morning—and just as often, a couple of evenings a week—with people who, for the most part, did not surf and were not part of the community in which he'd been raised. But strange as the new interest seemed to them, they did not object. They could see that Elvis had a new peace about him, that he seemed content, confident . . . complete.

And for a year or so that was how Elvis had felt. God was in his heaven, and Elvis was surely bound to spend eternity there with him. Life was good.

Then, one Sunday evening, Elvis's pastor—a young man not five years older than the surfer himself—had talked about evangelism. He'd read from Matthew and Mark in the Bible, and showed how Jesus' last instructions to his disciples concentrated on the importance of sharing of the gospel with others.

Elvis tried this on his trips to the beach, carrying the Bible that Alec Pemberton had given him. And he found, to his great surprise, that the surfers didn't seem to mind it. Those receptive to the gospel message found much of the same joy and peace that Elvis had discovered.

And those who weren't receptive? They appreciated the fact that there weren't quite as many people out on Trestles vying for the same waves on Sunday mornings.

Then Elvis's pastor delivered a message on the parable of the five talents in the book of Matthew, and he'd explained how God has blessed every Christian with at least one gift. Some, he said, were good with children, and these might be called to serve in children's ministries. Some had the gift of patience and understanding, and they might be called to serve as counselors to troubled individuals and families. And some, he said, had been blessed several times over with the ability to share God's Word, and they might be called to be pastors, or evangelists . . . or missionaries.

To Elvis's great surprise, it was the latter to which he felt most strongly drawn.

He remembered Alec Pemberton's words, how the New Zealander had witnessed to a dying Marine and had seen him accept Christ, and how that had felt even better than saving the wounded soldiers' lives.

Having seen several of his friends come to Christ, Elvis could relate.

And then he thought of the other things Alec had said, how he and his wife had traveled around the Pacific for three decades, carrying medical hope and the gospel of Jesus Christ.

Elvis wasn't married. But the rest of the equation—being a missionary in the Pacific—seemed logical to him. He knew many of the islands, and he loved them. Ministering to them was a powerfully attractive prospect. He could see it: preach a little, surf a little, talk to people on the beach. He thought about it for weeks, although he didn't mention it to anyone, not even his pastor. There was a piece that had yet to fall into the puzzle—he just *knew* that, even though he couldn't say why—and he needed to wait and see what that was.

Then a missionary from Faith's Frontier had come to speak at Elvis's church, and suddenly everything had become absolutely clear.

Young, bearded, and very energetic, the missionary had told the church how all around the world there were tribal people who spoke languages so esoteric, so little-known, that God's Word had never been translated into them. Cut off from community with the rest of the world by the lack of a common tongue, these people, the missionary explained, lived and died without word of basic medical, sociological, and technological advances that could ease their suffering and their strife. And they also lived and died without ever hearing about the keys to eternal life. Faith's Frontier had been founded by a group of concerned Christians—most of them former military people, after World War II—with the expressed purpose of seeking out these groups and learning their languages so the Bible and other essential information could be translated into them and they could have access to the knowledge that the rest of the world took blithely for granted.

For Elvis, a connection was made as certainly as if God himself had placed the message in his hand. He knew he was supposed to give his life over to Faith's Frontier.

But that feeling, that certainty, had confused him. He was, after all, familiar with the islands of the Pacific. He'd surfed everywhere from the New Hebrides and Papeeté, to Fiji, Bali, and Okinawa. Competition coverage had made him a minor celebrity in some of those places. He knew that it was common, even Biblical, for missionaries to seek funding for their work through churches and other organizations, and he thought that, if he kept his hand in on his surfing, he might be able to get some of that funding from his sponsors—it was even possible that his mother and father might want to subscribe to the cause, and maybe that involvement would be enough to get them interested in God and church and eternal life.

And hadn't he been led to the Lord by a man who had devoted his entire career to reaching the people of the islands? It seemed logical, natural. Why, then, did he feel so strongly called to work that was so completely different from what he'd pictured? Certainly, he spoke Spanish as well as a smattering of French. But he was no linguist. Not enough to think he'd be talented at translating the Bible into new tongues. Not by a long shot. Why, he wondered, was God calling him into an area in which he had no background—and, insofar as he could see, no talent?

Confused, bothered by the seeming contradiction, Elvis had said nothing to anyone about the direction in which he felt God was leading him.

Mature enough as a Christian to know that personal troubles were best resolved through prayer and time with the Scriptures, Elvis had driven by himself up to Monterey, leaving his surfboards at home—feeling odd doing that—and had spent long hours on the coast, high above the thundering surf, poring over the Bible that Alec had given him. As the waves washed in and collapsed into snow-white foam around the Big Sur boulders, Elvis had read with fresh eyes about Moses, about David, about the apostle Paul. And in each of these cases, and many others, he was struck by the fact that God either chose to use a person who did not initially seem capable, or he used people in ways that would have seemed least likely to them.

Elvis was puzzled by this until it dawned on him: God didn't want Elvis Hastings to go do something for God—God wanted to do his *own* work, *through* Elvis Hastings. It was like most things in this new life that Elvis was discovering. It required faith. His Bible was open to the sixth chapter of Isaiah, and he'd found there the response that God was waiting for. Raising his face from his reading, he'd looked up, out over the swirling surf and the rugged Monterey coastline, past the blue Pacific, out to the distant white clouds, the nearest thing that he could picture to heaven, and he'd repeated what he'd just read: "Here am I, Lord. Send me."

God had sent him. It hadn't happened immediately. There'd been two very intensive years of seminary study, followed by a year in Faith's Frontier special language academy. While studying there, he'd read about the work of Alfred Bellamy, one of the first Faith's Frontier missionaries, and a man who'd done extensive work with people in isolated villages on the Yucatan Peninsula, descendants of the original Mayans who had first populated the region. Intrigued, Elvis had flown down to visit some of the villages reached by Bellamy and had learned that there was still at least one group, deep in the jungle, who had still not been reached with the gospel and who still resisted regular contact even with other Mayans.

He'd known then who it was that he was called to work with.

It didn't take long for the sounds of the jungle to flow back in, once Elvis was settled. He read in his Bible for several minutes when, just like that, he became aware of it. There'd been no sound, not even a rustle of leaves. But he was no longer alone.

Looking up, Elvis saw a young, brown-skinned man, about nineteen by the looks of him, even though his face already showed traces of wrinkles. His jet-black hair was cut in a manner that reminded Elvis of the Beatles albums he'd seen at his uncle's house, and he was wearing a rough, poncho-like outer garment over hand-woven knee breeches, his knobby feet shod with some sort of leather sandal.

The natural thing to do was to smile, but Elvis resisted this urge; while most Western cultures viewed a smile as friendly, he knew that there were places in the world where showing the teeth was interpreted as a display of aggression. So he nodded his head, a simple bow.

Behind the young man, Elvis could see one other, hanging back and just barely visible through the foliage, carrying two bows. His visitor was, apparently, also concerned about appearing aggressive—he had left his weapon with his companion.

What now? There weren't any hard and fast rules for this sort of thing. Elvis bowed again, this time in a moment of prayer, and asked the Holy Spirit to show him what to do.

Suddenly, he knew. Elvis opened a food bar, broke it in two, and using the flattened food-sack as an impromptu serving platter, he offered the bar to his visitor.

The young man sat, took a piece cautiously, bit into it as Elvis took a bite of his own, and grinned broadly at the sweet, crunchy blend of carob, nuts, and peanut butter.

A smile. *So*, Elvis thought, *smiling must be cool.* Grinning back, he offered the young man a drink from his water bottle and then, looking up at the other hanging back in the distance, he gestured to the space still open on the opposite log. The young man turned and said something in a language that seemed to be mostly labial sounds and hard consonants. In a moment, there were two of them facing Elvis, their bows stacked next to his machete and backpack.

So, Elvis thought. *What now?*

Introductions, he supposed.

"Elvis," he said, placing his hand on his chest.

The first young man nodded. He understood.

"Kukulcán," he replied. It was, Elvis knew, the Mayan name for Quezecoatl, the feathered-serpent god of Toltec mythology. It was the cultural equivalent, he supposed, of naming your kid after a well-known Bible character.

"Ictlatl," the young man said next, gesturing with an open palm to his companion.

"Koo-kuhl-CAHN," Elvis repeated. "Ick-til-AH-til."

The two men laughed. Apparently he had just massacred the pronunciation of their names.

"AY-uhl-vis," the first young man said in reply. Turnabout was fair play.

Elvis leaned forward, his hand falling on a splinted piece of mahogany. He broke a piece off, held it out, and said, "Wood."

Looking at one another, the two young men said a single word, together, *"Che'."*

"Cool, bros," Elvis grinned, recording the word phonetically in a water-resistant notebook. "School's in session."

8
SIXTEEN KILOMETERS WEST OF TULUM, THE YUCATAN

Incredibly noisy but showing no light, the olive-drab Huey helicopter skimmed only fifty feet above the starlit jungle canopy, too low for radar, too swift to be identified from the ground. Standing in the open doorway, leaning out on his safety line, Viktor Bellum holstered his pistol and looked down at the darkened treetops flowing steadily past, like waves from the deck of a ship. Only sixty minutes now stood between him and more than a million dollars, and Bellum was virtually giddy with the knowledge.

He glanced back into the cargo area for the hundredth time, just to assure himself that everything was there. It was. Years of planning, months of preparation, one long night of jungle stealth, a month's long wait, and then two days of packaging, and it all came down to this—a one-hour flight to a jungle airstrip and a simple exchange for a suitcase stuffed with unmarked cash. Badda-bip, badda-bang, badda-boom. Amazing.

Then it happened. The fuselage lurched and the chopper began turning. Warning buzzers erupted from the cockpit, and the pilot's voice over the intercom, calm in the way that only an American-trained pilot's can be, called out, "Bird strike . . . hang on."

But Bellum did nothing of the sort. He'd ridden enough choppers to know that, this close to the ground, with no room to autogyro, the chances of riding out a crash were slim to none. So he took the only option that he had. He unclipped the tether and stepped out into the ink-black jungle air. . . .

Bellum jerked awake, slapping the mosquito boring into his neck. Jungle, night—that's where he was, all right, but he wasn't falling. He was slouched on the worn, tube-framed seat of his beat-up old International Scout, waiting for his contact. He felt in the dark to make sure that his AK-47 assault rifle—a mainland Chinese knock-off of the legendary Kalashnikov—was still secured in its rubber clamp against the dash and that the Ruger was still resting in the holster under the mesh-and-canvas vest that he wore instead of a shirt.

A fully automatic assault rifle and a pistol. That was a lot of firepower. Especially in a country where a gun of any kind was enough to land Bellum in a jail system so rough that Amnesty International gave it six pages on their website. But the guns were necessary evils. A lot of money was going to be changing hands in the jungle this evening.

Of course, guns were of no use if you were snoring when trouble came calling. Bellum couldn't believe he'd fallen asleep.

Actually, he could. One of the hazards inherent in leading a double life was that it made you double tired. And he was that, having taught a cave class earlier in the day. He killed another mosquito, silently raking it off his skin and crushing it between his fingers. And he listened—listened for any sign that someone, or something, had crept close to him while he dozed off. But all he heard were insects, tree frogs, and the far-off calls of howler monkeys—sounds that had long been as familiar to him as his own mother's voice.

The dream came as no surprise to him. It was the same dream he always had, the only dream he ever had anymore. Nor was it simply a dream. It was memory. It had happened.

Bellum's uncle had proven even poorer than his father at keeping the rebellious teenager in line. The night of his eighteenth birthday, Bellum had been caught boosting tires from a Vadalia Wal-Mart. He'd been one day too old to be tried as a juvenile in Georgia, so the judge had made him an offer—serve time or serve his country. Bellum had chosen the Navy.

His first hitch had gone without incident, and he had almost resigned himself to straightening up, maybe moving back in with his uncle after discharge and getting a job at the local Ford plant.

Then his parents had died, and he'd found his great secret—a discovery that amounted to nothing less than a treasure map.

That had changed everything. Bellum had re-upped with the Navy on the condition that they'd send him to Pensacola and give him EOD training—explosives ordinance demolitions. Being an EOD meant he also became a diver, which was cool and was critical to his long-range plans, but the best part about the job was daily contact with HE—high explosives. These were a marketable commodity, so Bellum got good at doing more with less—pocketing a little bit of the material from each job and then selling off this nest egg, a piece at a time, to people with deep pockets and bad accents.

A friend in Special Ops showed him how to build an identity off a stolen birth certificate, and he did this twice, getting a Social Security number and a fresh driver's license under the new name, and then he used the first set to go to court and get one of the bogus names changed again to the one he used now. He lived off-base by that time and kept the pieces of his emerging new identity there, in his apartment—a PADI diver's certification (easy to get, as he already knew how) and then, over the next two years, a National Association of Cave Divers certification and, finally, instructor certs in both scuba and cave diving.

The cave diving gave him two things—a visible means of support for when he finally went back to Mexico and then, as now, a good excuse for driving out into the boonies where clandestine deals could be conducted in clandestine surroundings. The only thing the new Viktor Bellum didn't bother with was a bank account. He did all of his deals in cash, and that went into a safety deposit box.

Bellum shifted, crushed another mosquito, and leaned back, listening to the jungle around him. He rubbed his chin and felt the cleft that the surgeon had placed there.

That had been the next-to-last thing he'd done, just as soon as he'd finished his hitch. It had seemed a little extreme at the time, but the way he looked on it now, his instincts had been protecting him. Some of his customers for explosives had been Egyptian. He didn't know for sure that they were Al-Quaida, but he didn't know for sure that they weren't, either, and if they were, it was a life sentence, maybe worse, for anyone convicted as an accomplice. No, without a doubt, incognito was a very good thing.

Bellum had stayed in California just long enough to heal up and walk a passport application through the L.A. office. Then he'd hopped on AeroMexico and come back to a place he'd thought he'd turned his back on forever.

Bellum shifted his weight again, swatted his hundredth mosquito, and sprayed a fresh coat of Deep Woods Off onto his exposed neck, arms, and chest. A small tree frog climbed up the Scout's windshield, its tiny form barely outlined in the darkness of the jungle night. Bellum set the can of insect repellant on the seat next to him and tried to remember just how long he'd been back in the Yucatan.

Ten years.

Unbelievable.

Two years—that's what he'd allowed himself to find what he was looking for down here, grab it, and get out. And he'd actually found it in one: found it, grabbed it, and then lost it.

To a bird flying into a tail rotor.

He'd seen the chopper go down—seen it, gone to the place where it went in, and realized that he could come back and salvage the cargo. But jumping out of a moving helicopter was not something one emerged from unscathed. Bellum had broken his ribs, broken his arm, and sustained a concussion. When he went to hike out, he'd wandered for days in delirium, keeping just enough wits about him to claim he'd fallen on a trip to a back-country *cenote* when a *campesino* driving a flatbed Chevy had finally picked him up on two parallel ruts that passed for a road in this part of the world.

And by that time he had lost track of the crash site.

Bellum shook his head, just thinking about it. It was maddening—the Lost Dutchman with monkeys and lizards. He'd searched for the site for two more years, telling people that he was scouting for dive sites as he'd hacked his way through the bush, trying to figure out where he could have wandered from in seventy-two hours.

Finally he'd given up, resigned himself to making what he could teaching cave-diving and doing a little smuggling, dope and artifacts, on the side. Then the Expedition Channel had signed him up to be their local expert, and when Bellum walked out of the Russian chopper to look at Pete Wiley's and Mike Bryant's dive site, he had almost keeled over.

Because it had been different. There were tents and support aircraft and a cleared landing area. But there had been no doubt in Bellum's mind.

It was the place.

Bellum looked for the hundredth time at the bright green Tritium numerals of his dive watch. It was seven minutes shy of twenty-two hundred; he had been sitting here in the bush for better than twenty minutes. Not that he expected the university professor to be early; the man would not spend a single second longer in the jungle than he had to, and Bellum didn't blame him. In addition to drug runners and banditos, this was a place populated by poisonous snakes, reptiles, and spiders. Several of the tree frogs were venomous. A single Yucatan tree could contain more different species of ants than the entire continent of Europe, and some of *those* were poisonous. Just being here was chancy.

But two vehicles traveling down a jungle two-track within minutes of one another were bound to draw some attention, so Bellum had deliberately come in a half an hour early and offered himself as a sacrificial feast to the insects. He reached out in the darkness and felt the worn wooden stock of the AK, assuring himself once again that he could find it in an instant if he needed to. Then he stretched and found a new spot on the worn vinyl seat.

He checked his watch again. Five minutes to go. *El catedrático*—the professor—would not be late; of that much, Bellum was absolutely certain. The objects the man had in his possession were national treasures, and Bellum, the professor's only option for getting them out of the country, would fire up the Scout and be on his way down the trail at precisely one minute past ten if the meeting failed to materialize.

Bellum listened to the jungle noises for what seemed an eternity. Then he sat up. He'd heard something, a sound so faint that you thought you were imagining it. No. There it was—he heard it again: the noise of a worn truck engine making its way toward him through the jungle. The clatter of worn tappets and slapping lifters reassured him: no police or military vehicle would ever be in such poor condition. And it was a sign that *el catedrático* was still following instructions; he'd left his expensive Land Rover—a vehicle that could not help but attract attention in this poor country—at home and had brought a vehicle that could pass for something owned by a poor farmer.

In a matter of moments, headlights became visible through the foliage, and Bellum jerked the AK out of its dashboard mount, slapping the safety off as the truck moved closer. He was fairly certain that it was his contact closing in, but he wanted to be ready just in case it was not, and besides, it never hurt to have the client see him at quarter-arms as he arrived. Fifty percent of this business was intimidation.

He pulled on his own headlights, illuminating a rusting Dodge pickup truck, its listing bed covered by a patched canvas tarp, one man in the cab—goateed and wearing the sort of anglicized tweed cap that only a university professor would ever think of adopting. Bellum stood in the open-top Scout and motioned the man over.

"You weren't followed." It was a statement, rather than a question. Bellum had no patience for contacts who didn't exercise the proper precautions.

"Of course not," the professor said curtly in heavily accented English. He stood there, trying and failing to look righteous in baggy khaki trousers and a double-pocketed shirt that stretched obscenely over his ample belly. Then he added, "I don't know why you have me come out here, anyhow. It would be much—ah, easier—if I just hired a driver."

Easier, Bellum thought with more than a hint of disgust. *You mean less risky.*

"Maybe so," he said instead. "But the fewer people who know about this, the better. And besides, this way there's less chance that anything turns up missing along the way."

And no chance that you hold some of this back and then accuse me of lifting part of the cargo, Bellum thought to himself.

"Then why not just let me take the shipment directly to your airstrip, myself?"

"And let the pilot get a good look at you, be able to pick you out of a line-up?" Bellum chided. "Don't you know that he's the one most likely to be apprehended in this whole thing? Do you want him to take you down with him? This way, I'm the one taking all the risk. It's for your own protection."

And this way, Bellum thought, *you don't get any fancy ideas about trying to go freelance, contacting the pilot yourself and cutting me out of the deal.*

He waited, gave the professor plenty of time to imagine going to jail, losing his prestigious position and his university tenure, and then he said, "We don't have much time. Let's see what you've brought."

"But of course," the professor nodded, pulling the tarp off the truck.

In the truck bed, strapped down atop a wooden pallet, were two Rubbermaid storage bins, the kinds of containers you might buy to carry camping equipment in or store your kid's toys. Bellum approved but said nothing. The first time they'd done this, the professor had shown up with the materials crated in wooden boxes and packed in bubble-wrap and excelsior, the same as he would have done for a legitimate shipment. It had seemingly taken forever for them to pry open and inventory each crate.

The professor loosened the stout nylon straps and set them aside, and Bellum unsnapped the lid of the nearest container, removing the two-inch sheet of foam rubber that lay underneath. He clicked on a heavy police-style Mag-Lite flashlight and, holding its knurled aluminum barrel shoulder high, played the tight white beam over the contents of the bin.

Evenly spaced in a thick block of foam specifically cut to fit them were a dozen small clay figurines, some squat and round, others square-edged and embossed with intricate vine-like designs. All were dull and dusty in appearance.

Bellum thought, not for the first time, that Olmec pottery had to be an acquired taste; nothing in this tub looked as if it would fetch more than twenty-five cents at a garage sale. But the truth was that each figurine would command an easy five figures, and that was on the black market, to buyers who knew that the pieces were stolen. Were it possible to export such objects legitimately, the price per piece would easily nudge a hundred grand. Most surviving Olmec art was sculpture: figures carved in jade, obsidian, or basalt. Pottery was a far more perishable medium, and the price reflected this fact.

Bellum pulled a piece out and inspected its base, noting the *Museo Nacional de Arqueologia* stamp and the catalogue number, written there, as per tradition, with a steel-nibbed pen and indelible India ink. He checked the next piece, and then the one after that, working his way through the entire layer, checking to make sure that the professor hadn't put in any ringers or anything broken—something to try and later pawn off as Bellum's fault. He replaced the last piece, nodded, and the professor gripped the upper tray by its two knotted rope handles and lifted it away, revealing a second tray underneath.

They worked in this fashion for twenty minutes, going through three trays in each storage bin, seventy-two figurines in all, with a street value, once they reached Miami, of just under three-quarters of a million dollars.

"This is more than I'd counted on you bringing," Bellum said as he snapped the second storage bin's lid back in place.

"I never said what I was bringing," the professor replied, not looking him in the eye. As Bellum watched, the squat little man sealed the bins with a roll of security tape bearing the emblem of the University of California at Berkeley—a bit of subterfuge intended to point the finger away from Mexico if the shipment was spotted in transit.

"It's twenty-four pieces more than the last time," Bellum insisted.

"But we agreed on a price," the professor said, smoothing an imaginary bubble in the tape.

"That was for forty-eight."

"What, the *aeroplano* cannot hold seventy-two?"

"It's not that. Each additional piece is additional risk."

"For me, yes. Not for you. Your people deliver to my contacts. It is they who do the selling. You provide only the transportation, and two containers is two containers. It is the same thing."

This was true, but Bellum was not about to admit it. And it stuck in his craw that the man would try to get him to move a quarter-million-dollars' worth of antiquities for nothing.

"Another ten thousand," he said flatly.

"What?" The professor exclaimed it so loudly that the surrounding jungle went silent. "Ten thousand? You rob me!"

"When the price was fifty for forty-eight pieces? I don't think so, *amigo*. I should be asking for an additional twenty-five."

"It is not fair," the professor grumbled. "We had the price."

The fat little man made a show of thinking about it for a few moments. Then he looked up at Bellum and smiled. "Okay. I am a reasonable man. I give you . . . five thousand more."

"Tell you what," Bellum said flatly, clicking the Mag-Lite off. "Why don't you drive this junk up to a flea market in Tijuana and see what you can get for it up there? The deal's off."

"No! No!" The professor quickly shuffled around in front of him and pulled off his tweed hat, holding it crumpled before him in a gesture of sincerity, his oily pate just visible in the backwash from the trucks' headlamps. "I'm sorry, señor. It was very silly of me to argue with you in such a manner. You win. Another ten thousand for . . . for your time and trouble. Okay?"

Bellum stared at him until the man looked down at his feet and then said, "Okay. Deal. But next time, you tell me what you're bringing. I need to know what I'm transporting. You got that?"

"But of course, señor. It will be as you wish."

In truth, Bellum hoped with all his heart that there would never be a "next time," but he was not about to let this fat little blowhard know that. The prospect of continued service was the only leverage one had in arrangements such as this.

The professor scuttled to the driver's side of his pickup, where he pulled an old-fashioned Samsonite hard-shell briefcase out from the back of the cab. Setting it in the middle of the dusty vinyl bench seat, he began to count out rubber-banded bundles of American fifty-dollar bills, each bundle swollen and bow-tied by the wrinkles of circulated money. Bellum moved in for a closer look, and the Mexican shuffled sideways just a little, trying to stay between the American and the contents of the briefcase. But Bellum just shouldered him aside.

Sighing, sweat beading up on his forehead, the professor finished counting out the money. When he was done, Bellum saw that there was still an inch-thick stack of bills left in the case.

He sandbagged me, Bellum thought half-admiringly. *An inch of hundreds is fifteen thousand dollars. The little rat came ready to go the whole extra twenty-five grand.*

"There you are, señor," the professor said with a smile, nodding at the pile of money on the truck seat and sliding the briefcase into the back of the cab again as casually as possible. "It is all there. I will, of course, take no offense if you wish to count it again yourself."

"Oh, far be it from me to offend you, professor," Bellum said, knowing that the sarcasm would never translate. He took a small brown paper bag out of his cargo vest pocket and slid the two thick stacks of cash into it. "Let's get the stuff transferred, all right?"

"But of course."

But of course, Bellum groaned to himself, easily setting one bin in the back of the Scout and watching with satisfaction as the professor struggled with the other.

"It is good?" The professor asked as soon as that was done. "We are set?"

"Yeah," Bellum said. "I've got it from here. You're good to go."

"But of course . . . I mean, thank you, señor."

Bellum secured the bins with oversize tarping straps that he normally used to keep his tanks from rolling around in the back of the Scout, and watched in quiet amusement as the professor jogged the ancient pickup back and forth laboriously, twisting and fighting the wheel, muttering to himself in the pickup cab, finally getting it turned around on the narrow jungle two-track. With an ominous drum-roll of lifters and tappets, the old Chevy lumbered back up the way it had come in, the glow of its taillights tinged purple by the pall of blue exhaust.

Clicking the Mag-Lite back on, Bellum counted twenty-five hundred dollars out of the money that the professor had just given him and put it into a Zip-Loc bag. Then he tucked the bag into a pocket of his mesh cargo vest. The rest of the money went under a tray of wrenches in a toolbox that he kept bolted to the floor of the Scout behind the front seat. It wasn't a great hiding place; after the glove compartment, it was the next place anybody would look. But it sure beat driving around the boonies with a paper sack full of cash on the passenger's seat.

He started the Scout and slipped it into gear. While beat-up, it functioned perfectly; the engine, transmission, and differentials had all been recently overhauled, the shocks and tires new within the last 10,000 miles. That made the truck dependable for his cave diving, and it made it perfect for this sort of extracurricular activity—an extremely reliable vehicle that wouldn't attract a second glance from anyone back in the bush.

Bellum drove slowly, mindful of the small fortune in antiquities sitting in the cargo area behind him. Three-quarters of a million dollars, and all he had to show for it was a lunch-sack full of cash, less the ten grand for the pilot, less the thousand he'd already given Gabrillo and an additional fifteen hundred to pay his courier cut-out in Miami. That left fifty thousand, net. Good money by most standards, and a handsome return for a single evening's work, but nowhere near three-quarters of a million. Then again, he was nothing more than a glorified UPS man in this deal.

He knew that he could quite easily just hijack the entire shipment and try to sell it for himself. But the problem with Olmec pottery was that there were so many forgeries. It was possible to determine authenticity through radiocarbon dating, but few buyers would seek expensive laboratory analysis on a piece that they knew to be stolen. So the only way to get a good price on black-market pre-Columbian pottery was to be able to document provenience—where the piece had been found, and by whom.

That's what the professor brought to the table. The export of Indian antiquities from Mexico had been illegal since 1970, yet modern means of finding sites—satellite imagery, infrared photography, and magnetic contouring—had resulted in an unprecedented number of pieces being discovered in recent years—more than could be displayed at any one time in a museum. So most pieces were documented and then warehoused, never to be seen again. That made it easy for people central to the process—people such as the professor—to skim a few out and sell them on the black market. Each piece was still photographed and cataloged, just as if it were being kept, and the catalogs were public documents, accessible on the Internet, making it easy to verify the authenticity of any particular piece. That way, the artifacts, although stolen, were still provenienced, and the values remained accordingly high, especially in Asia, where the collection of black-market artwork was widely accepted.

But the one variable in this was the professor. If Bellum were to try to sell the shipment for himself, the professor couldn't run to the authorities—that would implicate him—but he could withdraw the provenience; erase the pieces from the catalog, and render them worthless.

So the best Bellum could be in this arrangement was a lowly accomplice. That irritated him. He hadn't set this pipeline up for other people to use it.

But it was okay. Soon, he told himself, he would be using it for himself, one last time, and that would make it all—the waiting, the years of rotting down here in the Yucatan, the payoffs, and the fraternization with every lowlife under the tropical sun—all worthwhile.

Ten minute's driving got him to a wide, broad swath through the jungle, a turf airstrip that had originally been put in by a logging company back before jungle preservation had become trendy. Now "eco-touring" sightseeing flights set down here for their back-of-the-bush stops, a fifteen-minute interlude in the jungle to make the tourists think they'd really been somewhere. They kept it mowed, and at night it got secondary use by people like Bellum. The DEA watched it. He knew that. But tonight, they would have their attentions directed elsewhere.

His wait here would be more on the order of forty-five minutes, but he wouldn't be drifting off this time, not with fifty-grand-plus and a king's ransom in Olmec pottery riding with him in the Scout. At least the mosquitoes had mostly retreated; it was getting late for them, and the breeze coming down the airstrip helped keep the stragglers at bay. Bellum drove the Scout to the far end of the strip, parked in the center, and waited, the assault rifle resting in his lap with a round in the chamber and the safety off.

At five minutes to midnight, he lit two highway safety flares and pitched them to either side of the runway, their two-inch, hot red jets of flame sizzling noisily in the short wet grass. He drove slowly down the strip, repeating this every fifty meters or so, until a string of bright red pinpoints outlined the full length of the runway.

Promptly at midnight, he heard the twin-engine Seneca III but did not see it until it flew right over him, a darker mass passing quickly between him and the stars. Bellum pulled on the Scout's headlamps and popped smoke, tossing a military surplus smoke grenade out in front of the vehicle, where the red plume from its nozzle wafted down the runway in the twin cones of the Scout's lights, giving the pilot an idea of wind direction and strength.

He could hear the airplane bank out over the jungle and turn back toward him. Half a kilometer out, the landing lights came on, and now he could barely hear it at all; the pilot had it throttled way back and was into full flaps, riding the ground effect off the jungle canopy, a bit of bush-piloting skill that even a cynic such as Bellum had to admire. When it cleared the trees at the end of the runway, the Seneca dropped as if it had driven off a curb, then it found its effect again and glided just a foot off the ground, finally settling to earth as the pilot pulled the nose up slightly. The engine note came back up as the pilot ran the Seneca down most of the rest of the runway on its back wheels, keeping his props angled skyward, well away from the soft turf. Then, two hundred meters from Bellum, he throttled back completely and let the nose wheel come down, wheeled expertly in place so he was pointed back down the airstrip, and stopped, his engines still running, ready to depart at a moment's notice. As the plane turned, Bellum noted with satisfaction that its five-character fuselage number began with "N"—an American number that wouldn't attract the least bit of attention on the far side of the Gulf.

Setting his rifle aside, Bellum unholstered the Ruger and jogged to the airplane, playing the Mag-Lite over the interior as the pilot took off his seat belt and headset. Bellum put the gun away; except for the pilot, the plane was empty, all seats but the front two removed. Bellum jogged back to the Scout, started it up, and backed the old utility vehicle into the open part of the "J" between the airplane's wing and its tail. Even idling, the turning props kept a torrent of wind rushing back at him as he opened the Seneca's port-side door from the outside.

The sharp smell of pepper greeted him and Bellum grimaced slightly. Drug runners often ground pepper and paprika into the packing material around their shipments, in hopes that it would disguise the contents from the dope-sniffing dogs used at airports. But the cargo area was empty except for a two-liter jug of aviation lubricant bungeed against the aft bulkhead, so the smell must have been from the plane's last run.

"Ready to load," the pilot yelled as he duckwalked back into the doorway.

Bellum looked at him—gaunt of frame, pencil-thin RAF moustache, red nose, moist eyes. He wore a fresh white shirt with shoulder boards, the kind corporate pilots favored. But Bellum smelled something strong over the pepper. Spearmint. Mouthwash.

"When was your last drink?" Bellum yelled back over the engine noise.

"Sixteen hours ago—I'm legal." The pilot smiled, adding, "At least in that respect I am."

Bellum didn't believe him, but there wasn't time to quibble, so he simply nodded and opened the tailgate to the Scout, sliding in first one storage bin and then the other.

"That's it?" the pilot asked. You could almost see the wheels turning in his head.

"That's it," Bellum confirmed. "And no, you don't have time to hop back to Akamal and pick up something else. The American radar is going to light back up in fifteen minutes. No dope. Not on this run."

"Pity." The pilot shrugged and looked at the security tape with a twinge of disappointment—no skimming, this trip, either. The thin man strapped his cargo down with broad nylon webbing that ratcheted taut. Then he returned to the doorway, hand out. Bellum unzipped his vest and handed him the Zip-Loc bag full of cash.

Unapologetic, holding a red-lensed penlight between nicotine-stained teeth, the pilot opened the bag, counted the money twice, closed the bag, smiled, and slipped the cash into a beat-up leather chart case. He looked up. Off to the side of the runway, the last fumes of the smoke grenade drifted lazily away.

"Not enough tailwind to worry about," he mused aloud. "Pickup's fifteen hundred at MIA tomorrow, yes?"

"Fifteen hundred," Bellum confirmed, giving him the name of the courier service that would be meeting the plane.

"Right, then," the pilot smiled. "Mind giving the hatch a shove?"

Bellum pushed the door closed and held it while the pilot dogged it down from the inside, then Bellum jumped into the driver's seat of the Scout and drove it to the side of the runway. The Seneca's landing lights flared back on, both engines roared, and in less time than it takes to say it, the twin-engine plane was roaring down the turf strip, rotating on its back wheels, and stepping up into the ground effect. The pilot kept it there while he built speed, brought the gear up, and doused the landing lights, then he climbed steeply away, navigation lights dark, the aircraft no more visible in the moonless sky than a shadow.

Along the airstrip, the highway flares began to sputter. Bellum checked his watch; it was a quarter past midnight. Exactly on schedule. Right now, Geraldo Alvarez was being lightened to the tune of two aircraft, plus their flight crews and cargoes, and all the big eyes in the sky were focused on that great, big, headline-worthy event, and not this puny little one.

This little one . . . fifty grand, net—out of a nearly three-quarters-of-a-million-dollar front end. *Chicken feed*, Bellum thought to himself. Still, it was better than a sharp stick in the eye. And his big one was coming.

As the last of the road flares fizzled out, Bellum started up the Scout and pointed it back east, toward the sea, toward Tulum. He had a cave class to teach in the morning, and it was a forty-minute drive back through thick jungle—jungle much like what he'd been raised in, much like what both of his parents had died in.

Mexico. Man, but he hated this country.

9

WEST PALM BEACH, FLORIDA— JUNE, 2003

The Intercoastal Waterway, that river-like strip of sea that runs between Florida's Gold Coast cities and their barrier islands to the east, was alive in the sunshine, the brilliant midday light reflected by a thousand shimmering wavelets as a warm breeze swept the water's length. Crossing the bridge with the top down on the BMW, headed into Palm Beach with the sun warm on her bare shoulders and the fresh salt breeze in her hair, Bridget should have felt like the queen of the world. But she didn't. Every mile only deepened her dread.

It was a mood very much at odds with the immaculately polished little red sports car.

Although her income was easily triple that of her middle-management neighbors back in Ocala, there was little to distinguish Bridget's home from any of theirs. She belonged to a health club rather than a country club, still watched videotapes rather than DVDs, and bought most of her clothes at J.C. Penney. There was no wine cellar in her basement, and the only original artwork in her home came from occasional visits to the marina craft fair here in West Palm. True, she had services that did the heavy housekeeping and the lawn care, but that was hardly unusual for a working woman who lived alone.

In fact, Bridget possessed only one symbol of her professional status, and that was the car. Five years earlier, she had decided that, if she was going to spend four hours a week on the interstate, asphalts, and two-lanes that connected her home in Ocala and Mike's place in Luraville, she was, by George, going to do so comfortably. So she had gone out and paid cash for a brand-new BMW 320i convertible, racing red with tan leather interior.

The Bimmer was designed to be a joy to drive, but this morning it had only served to further deepen Bridget's melancholy. Utterly impractical for a cave-diver, the tiny car had worked out for her only because Bridget had long since taken to leaving all of her bulky cave gear—the double-tank sets, the bulky dry suit, the multiple regulators with their overlength hoses, the lights, and line reels and whatnot—up at Mike's place, along with a hair-dryer, rain gear, toiletries, and several changes of weekend-casual clothes. The car had been purchased as her link to Mike, and now she wasn't so sure that the link would be needed much longer.

Bridget drove along the waterway up to Riviera Beach, where she pulled into the marina and parked in a space next to Mike's empty van. Putting the top up on the BMW and setting the folding Mylar shade in the windshield, she got out of the car and went around to the trunk, pulling out a large net duffel that she carried easily by its broad shoulder strap.

For a cave diver, that was one of the most liberating things about ocean diving—the relative paucity of equipment that was necessary to do it. A small U.S. Divers travel BC, a simple regulator with a small attached instrument console, her mask, fins, and snorkel, and a thin, leotard-like, Polartec-lined Lycra wetsuit—that, plus a towel, a folding hairbrush, and her C-card and logbook—was about all Bridget had in the gearbag. Mike would have the tanks waiting for her on the boat, along with a weight belt and four pounds of lead.

Bridget had never heard the crying of gulls, the clank of tanks being loaded, or the nervous chatter that accompanies a class of divers setting out for a new experience, but she knew intuitively that the noise would probably drown out any greeting she might call out. Which was just as well—she preferred not to call any attention to her arrival. That would be less disruptive to Mike's class—being unable to hear, she had no way of knowing if he was in the middle of giving them his customary dive-boat orientation. And given the friction of recent months, Bridget just wasn't all that crazy about shouting out a greeting to Mike anyhow.

". . . Lastly, the bathroom on a boat is called a 'head,'" Bridget could see Mike saying as she came down the gangplank to the boat, riding below dock level on the incoming tide. "And a marine head doesn't flush like your toilet at home, so you want to ask a crew member how to flush it if you need to. Otherwise, it will plug up, and plugging the head is not the best way to win friends and influence people on a dive trip."

The eight assembled divers shook slightly, which Bridget correctly took to mean that they were laughing.

"That's it," Mike continued. "If you closed the valves down on your tanks for the ride out, be sure to purge the regulators so you aren't showing a false reading on the gauge."

He looked and saw Bridget.

Hey there, he signed.

Hey, yourself, she returned.

Mike crossed the deck to take the gearbag off her shoulder, and she let him do it but pretended to be turning, looking at the boat, as he tried to kiss her hello.

So what are we diving today? Bridget asked in sign.

"The *Mitzpah*, and then Breakers," Mike replied aloud, as he had her gearbag in one hand and his dive roster in the other. Looking over his shoulder so she could still read his lips, he carried her bag over to an open spot on the far bench and continued, "These guys all have their Adventure Diver—we're working on Advanced today—first a wreck dive, then a drift."

Bridget nodded and looked around. Five of the "guys" were just that. Two were women who appeared to be married to two of the other divers. They wore wedding rings and were chatting with one another and joking with two of the men; probably two couples who went diving and hung out together. The last diver was a woman—Bridget caught herself thinking "girl"—with long blonde hair, fashion-model good looks, and a French-cut red bikini that she wore far too well. As Bridget watched, the blonde feigned helplessness with the tank strap on her BC and, like a bass sucking in a lure, Mike trotted over and pushed the cam closed for her.

Still smiling on the outside, Bridget fumed. Couldn't this little hussy put two and two together regarding Bridget and Mike? Hadn't she seen Mike try to greet Bridget with a kiss? Then Bridget realized that she had shunted the kiss away, so no—the blonde probably hadn't.

A tiny crack appeared in the brick wall that Bridget had been so carefully building all the way down from Ocala. Here she was, ready to tell Mike to act responsibly or find a new dive buddy—and she was getting all in a huff over some little slip of nothing who was half silicone and half Coppertone. Just what *did* she want, after all?

Still asking herself that question, Bridget went over and introduced herself to the single woman, speaking slowly and making certain the stranger could see that she was lip-reading. Then she pitched in and helped get the young woman's dive gear squared away as Mike walked off to attend to his other students and the single woman—"Angie," she saw from the ID Magic-Markered onto her pink swim fins—looked initially confused, and then smiled warmly, thankful for the help.

"You're married?" Bridget saw Angie asking, nodding toward Mike.

Bridget shook her head, just a bit.

"Not yet," she said.

Bridget continued to secure the young woman's spare regulator in its yellow plastic holder, but inwardly, she was bewildered.

"Not yet . . ." Where the heck had *that* come from? Here she was, ready to have it out with Mike Bryant, tell him to forget about the *cenote* dive or forget about her, and she was gushing and blushing like some infatuated schoolgirl. She pursed her lips and gave the regulator a tug.

"There," she told the single woman. "You're all set."

The blond smiled her thanks, and Bridget stood and turned—almost bumping into Mike.

I'm glad you're here, he signed. Not "where were you; you almost missed the boat."

Your tanks are set up behind your stuff, he continued. *I've got you and me on Nitrox II. And we stopped at Mickey D's on the way in, so I got you a Quarter-Pounder with cheese and some fries. They're in the insulated sack on top of my bag, and there's Coke in the cooler.*

Bridget looked coolly at Mike. He was trying so hard, trying to please her, to show her that he was a good guy, worthy of her attentions.

He'd been working outside again, she saw. His tan was approaching movie-star dark, his hair sun-bleached at the edges. His biceps moved up and down ever so slightly as he signed to her, and the barest ruff of chest hair showed over the top of the plain turquoise T-shirt that he wore above his faded red trunks. He was giving her his best even-toothed smile, and even behind the Ray-Bans, she could see his eyes sparkling with anticipation, those crows-footed eyes and that square-chinned smile that she had grown so fond of over the years. He was happy to be here, happy that they were about to set out, the ocean dive a treat and a break from the cave work that he did almost daily.

And Bridget loved Quarter-Pounders with cheese. Mike knew that, and he knew that she would have left the house late and probably wouldn't have stopped for lunch on the way, so he'd thought of her and gotten her one.

Bridget sighed. Why spoil his bliss? There'd be plenty of time to talk after the dives, she told herself. Plenty of time to shake out whatever needed to be shaken out and be done with it, if that was the case.

She smiled.

Thank you, she signed, and she hugged him. Not a kiss, but a hug. She wasn't ready for a kiss, but the hug came involuntarily, like breathing.

The deck shuddered slightly as the captain fired up the big diesel engine. Bridget quickly took her BC out of her duffel and quickly set up her gear. She grabbed the little insulated lunch sack from the top of Mike's gear bag, fished a cold Coke out of the cooler, and holding the lunch sack between her teeth, she climbed the narrow ladder up to the flying bridge, where the captain waved a quick hello as he shouted something down to the mate.

McCarthy used his charter for sport-fishing too, so the flying bridge was nicely equipped with a blue canvas Bimini top, three comfortable white vinyl captain's chairs, full instrumentation, and a broad dash liberally punctuated with drink holders. Bridget slipped her Coke into one of these, slipped her shoes off, and put her bare feet up on the open dash as she sank back in the sun-warmed chair. A dockhand was taking the stern line off. Up front, she could see the mate doing the same with the bowline, leaping aboard from the dock, the weight of his landing nudging the boat ever so slightly out toward the harbor as the vibrations from the big diesel crescendoed. The world rocked slightly with the movement of the boat, then settled out again as their forward momentum put it back on its keel.

Bridget opened the insulated bag and breathed in the aroma of the hot burger and fries. She pushed her Oakleys up on her nose and sighed. Mike looked as if he'd needed this, and now she realized that she did too. They were still due for a talk, but for right now . . . life was good.

McCarthy pointed them east, toward the Palm Beach Inlet, medium throttle now, the boat bobbing slightly in the light chop of sheltered waters. Bridget enjoyed the still-warm sandwich and looked around, amazed as she always was by the spectacle of West Palm Beach.

Just a century earlier, everything she was looking at would have been mangrove swamps and beach grass, wave-driven sand, and sun-whitened driftwood. Panthers had walked the western shore not all that long before, and saltwater crocodiles had once hunted the very waters they were crossing; alligators and manatees could still be found here.

But these beaches, where Seminole Indians had once hunted fish and shorebirds, had become some of the most opulent resort real estate in the world. Far to the right, above their low-rise neighbors, she could see the twin towers of the Breakers, one of Palm Beach's oldest hotels, and still among its finest. Sailboats and sailboards danced on the quiet Intercoastal waters, their white sails standing out in brilliant contrast to the coral-tone resorts along the shore. Through the mouth of the inlet Bridget could see the startling blue waters of the true Atlantic.

She ate the burger and finished most of the fries as well. By the time the dive boat was closing on the inlet, she was settled back in the swivel seat. The tension of the long drive down from Ocala melted away, and before they'd so much as crossed the inlet into the Atlantic, she was fast asleep.

She was awakened like a princess in a fairy tale, with a light kiss on her forehead. Blinking behind her Oakleys, smiling despite herself, she looked up; Mike tapped his watch and held up five fingers—five minutes. She nodded, handed Mike the empty lunch bag with a mouthed "thank you," and followed him down the narrow aluminum ladder.

Fully 180 degrees of the horizon was blue, open ocean now. Somewhere off to their east, barely within range of a boat this size, would be Bimini, and then Grand Bahama. But it was easy to imagine that one could start sailing into the sunrise and not hit land until Africa.

Bridget stooped to her gear bag and took out her diveskin, purple with yellow accents, opening the back zipper and shaking the suit loose, then slipping one bare leg and then the other into it before pulling on the arms and shrugging the snugly fitting diveskin into place on her shoulders. She closed the contour-conforming zippers at the ankles and the wrists of the suit, then she zipped up the back, using the extra-long lanyard perma- nently attached to the zipper for that purpose.

Bridget's dive boots were black, not purple—she believed that there was such a thing as too much color-coordination. She pulled them on and zipped the ankles shut, then she got out her mask, fins, and snorkel (all yellow, because *some* color coordination was all right), set them behind the rest of her equipment, and re-opened the valve on her scuba tank. Last, she put on her weight belt, noting that Mike had brought her a pouch-style belt that used soft, shot-filled weights—the kind she liked, because the weights didn't dig into her hip bones.

With her things ready, Bridget walked around the open deck, checking on the students. These divers were all working on their Advanced certifications, meaning that they were already certified and had accumulated a bit of experience, and it showed. No tanks were set up with the valves pointing backward, no weight-belts were being worn with the buckles facing right. Bridget noted with some satisfaction that Angie had redirected her attentions and was now buddying up with one of the single men in the group, a crewcut, on-leave serviceman who was just about falling over himself as he helped her get her gear ready.

The boat came down off plane and the vibrations coming up through the deck dropped noticeably as the captain reduced throttle and began a slow circle. Up forward, the mate stood by with a long-handled gaff— like most frequently dived wrecks, the *Mitzpah* was permanently buoyed, which made mooring at the dive-site as simple as tying up at a dock.

Bridget sat and put on her buoyancy compensator; then she stood, marveling as she did every time she went ocean diving. The equipment she wore for most of her cave dives weighed twenty pounds more than she did; standing up with it on was like performing a deep squat in a weight room. In comparison, the thirty-odd pounds of her saltwater gear felt like almost nothing at all. She picked up her mask, fins, and snorkel and headed to the back of the boat.

While everyone on the boat was a certified diver, Bridget and Mike had a routine that they'd worked out anytime they dived from a boat with students. Bridget would enter the water first, so she could be there to help anyone that needed it, while Mike would remain on the boat, assisting people topside, until all of his students were in the water.

The mate came back and tossed a current line—a long nylon rope with an orange float at the end—off the stern. There was a slight sea running, and the line would give the divers something to hold onto and keep themselves in place until everyone had entered the water. Steadying herself with one hand on the gunnel, Bridget pulled on her fins and tugged the straps snug, then stepped down to the swim deck and looked back at the mate, who flashed her an "okay." Nodding, she put her regulator in her mouth, secured the mask against her forehead with her fingertips, and took a giant step forward.

The sunlit water exploded into a million champagne bubbles as the water closed over her head. Like a curtain rising, the bubbles disappeared, and then it was all blue; blue water in every direction, the dark blue bottle-like shape of the shipwreck far below them, white sand tinged blue by distance, clumped here and there by sea-bottom growth that looked, from ninety feet away, dark blue as well. Bridget kicked back to the surface, touched the top of her head in an "okay" signal to the boat, and switched from her regulator to her snorkel, because the cardinal rule of diving with students was that you always had to make sure that you used less air than they did. Face-down in the water, Bridget kicked until her hand came in contact with the drift line, then she let her hand slide along it until she had drifted back nearly to the float.

This was one of Bridget's favorite times in a dive. She was the only one in the water, and, while she'd gone in with her regulator in her mouth, she hadn't taken a breath from it yet, so that audible telltale of a diver's presence, the gurgle of exhaust bubbles, had not yet been heard.

It was that gurgle that alerted most of the larger animals and convinced them to move off. By coming in first, Bridget got a chance to see the site as it looked normally, when humans weren't around, and she was rewarded with a view of a pair of spotted eagle rays winging their way tranquilly through the water beneath her. They disappeared under the boat and then came back. Beneath them, a big nurse shark was swimming steadily along the bottom, returning to some secret cubbyhole in the wreck.

Bridget resisted the urge to tell the boat about the rays and the shark. It could create a rush, and someone could get hurt. And besides, not all divers knew that nurse sharks, unless provoked, were essentially harmless. There was no use creating a case of cold feet.

Bridget felt the vibration of a splash up the line. The students were coming into the water. Sure enough, the eagle rays banked and headed for the open ocean, away from the dive site. She raised her head, watching to make sure that the students signaled their "okays."

They were a good group. Nobody popped a fin or lost a mask on entry, there was no thrashing at the surface—they all seemed comfortable in the water. Everyone found the drift line without mishap, and they all moved back to make room for one another. That was good too. Courtesy was a sign of comfort; a diver ill at ease in the water rarely gave a thought to anybody else. Finally, Mike giant-strided in, gave the thumb-down signal, and the students slipped slowly from sight. Mike met Bridget on the line, and they too vented their air, jackknifed smoothly in the water, and headed down, kicking steadily in the eighty-degree seawater, following the students, who swam together like a school of otherworldly fish.

The *Mitzpah* was an old Greek luxury liner, 195 feet long—small by modern cruise-ship standards, but impressively large underwater nonetheless. There was a current running stern-to-bow, and Bridget could see that Mike had briefed the students on this. Rather than descending immediately to the ship, they drifted over it, passing the pilothouse, where the mooring line was tied off around a railing, and continued to the bow, where a huge Navy-style fluked anchor and chain showed where the old ship had ridden before she went down.

The *Mitzpah* was not a true shipwreck, which is to say that she had not sunk to the seabed as the result of storm or collision or act of war or fire at sea. Rather, she had been scuttled: sunk on purpose, to create an artificial reef that would shelter and attract game fish. As sunken ships are a magnet to scuba divers, the *Mitzpah* had been "safed" before she was sent down— doors and hatches welded open or removed, her bunkers and engine cleaned of fuels and oils, her batteries, with their corrosive acids, removed.

But both Bridget and Mike knew that there was no such thing as a truly "safe" sunken ship. Years before, in the Keys, a husband-and-wife buddy team had turned up missing after a long dive on an artificial-reef "shipwreck." The divemaster had returned and spotted the husband waving frantically from a porthole, lost within the bowels of the ship. The divemaster had gone in and led him out, and then returned to look for the wife. She had drowned and was pronounced dead at the surface. But to make matters worse, the divemaster had not had enough air to decompress properly, and the man had fallen victim to decompression illness— "the bends." Not even treatment in a hyperbaric chamber had been sufficient to return him to health—the hero was living out the rest of his life as a cripple.

PADI standards would not allow students to enter a shipwreck on an Advanced-certification dive; to do that required training beyond the scope of this course. And the memory of that crippled divemaster was more than enough to reinforce that regulation in Mike and Bridget's minds. While entering a sunken ship would be a walk in the park for certified cave divers, they stayed well away from the hatches and entrances, and were pleased to see that the students did the same. There didn't seem to be any "cowboys" in this group.

Excited at the prospect of a whole sunken ship, the students swam a little too quickly, burned air a little too fast, and kicked a little too hard in their efforts to see it all at once. Bridget smiled as she contrasted this with Mike, who casually pulled himself along the ship's railing with his fingertips, stopping at the big anchor capstan to explore its nooks and crannies. A couple of the students drifted in, and he showed them what he had found—a long-antennaed Florida lobster backed into a hole under the machinery, a blue-and-black sergeant major defending his purple egg mass, and a tiny clown shrimp, striped black, white, and orange, and willing to step tenuously onto the palm of an outstretched hand.

Encouraged by this example, the students went beyond the big picture—the ship—and began to see the *Mitzpah* for what it had become: a vibrant community of every sort of creature. They found black-spined sea urchins and white-fingered anemone clustered around hatchways, sea fans taking hold on the roughened surface of rusting deck plates, a green moray eel keeping a lookout from a windowless porthole, and a school of spadefish patrolling under the awning framework outside the long-abandoned deck cabins.

Sinking to the sand near the stern, the group discovered a southern stingray hidden in the sand, the big animal shaking the sand from its disk and flapping gracefully away, like a living Frisbee, as they approached. Then they looked at the ship's propeller, bronze and still free of growth, before allowing the prevailing current to slowly drift them back toward the pilothouse. When they got there, Mike took a quick head-count and then, as a group, they started up the mooring line in pairs, Mike and Bridget going up last.

The entire dive, from the time they'd left the surface until the time they started back up, had taken only twenty minutes, well within the no-decompression limits, but the boat's crew had put a long, weighted, trapeze-like bar into the water at fifteen feet for their safety stop, and the entire group obediently arranged themselves along it. Standards called for just a three-minute stop here, although Mike had recommended five, and in actuality it turned out to be longer than even that. A huge school of baitfish had congregated in the shadow of the boat, and amberjack and Atlantic barracuda were attempting to feed on the thousands of tiny silver fish. But every time a predator came in, the fish reacted as a group, bunching into a tight ball or splitting into two sections or twisting into a Mobius-like pattern designed to distract the hungry attackers' attentions away from any individual fish. For the most part, the little fish were successful, although more than one jack or barracuda returned from the fray with a small silver fin flipping plaintively in its mouth. Finally, when ten minutes had passed, Mike knocked on his scuba tank with the pommel of his dive knife—an action that, Bridget knew, would create a distinctive ringing sound underwater, even though she had never heard it. Then Mike signaled, thumb-up, and the group rose slowly to the surface, where they arranged themselves along the driftline and took turns getting back aboard.

Bridget climbed the ladder with her weight belt on—at four pounds, it made little difference to her—then she turned and took Mike's eight-pound belt as he came up to join her. She didn't say anything to him, didn't sign. She knew that all the students would be talking at once now, the did-you-see-that exuberance, and the what-was-that-thing-with-the-antenna questions. She had long since resigned herself to the fact that she couldn't have Mike, or even the smallest part of him, after these class dives. His attention would be focused on his students.

McCarthy's boat had a shower on the stern. Bridget shrugged her gear off and secured it; then she stepped back under the shower and ran it, looking up and letting it wash back over her head. It ran her long, auburn hair straight, better than any comb, and she squeegeed the length of her hair with her hands and returned to her gear to get things ready for the next dive. The lightest possible breeze was blowing, just enough that she didn't feel the need to take the wetsuit off, although she did open the wrists and tug the zipper open at the back.

She looked up, and Mike signaled for her to go topside, so she did, getting to the flying bridge just as the mate slipped the mooring line off the davit and the captain cranked the engine back awake. Moments later, Mike joined her with his cooler, taking out a Tupperware container containing a precooked barbecued chicken breast—one of Mike's staple foods—and a store-bought container of potato salad. Bridget raised her eyebrows and he handed her a Baggy full of carrot and celery slices—Mike's concession to health food. She smiled and launched in, noting that the chicken did taste great, even though most of its nutritional value was doubtlessly long since processed away.

Mike had also brought egg bagels—with the potato salad, a double starch in a single meal, although Bridget again said nothing because it was so obvious the man was trying to please her.

He got three Cokes out of the cooler, one for Bridget, one for him, and one for the captain, who had already started his own lunch, a ham sandwich wrapped in waxed paper, taken from a small cooler that looked as if it held bait as often as it held lunch. Down below, the students were also grabbing a bite, all except for the two married women, who had pulled off their wetsuits and headed to the bow to sun themselves. This could have been vanity, but it could just as well have been a sign that one or both of them had gotten seasick before. But they were smiling and joking with one another, so either the seasickness was a distant memory or they had social events coming up and they wanted to work on their tans.

Angie and her attentive military man—a sailor, Bridget noted from the small anchor tattooed on his upper arm—came up and joined them on the flying bridge, which made for tight quarters, but the afternoon breeze had not picked up yet, and as the boat was not rocking all that much, it was all right. There were too many people facing too many directions for Bridget to follow a conversation by reading lips, so she turned and looked out to sea instead.

For several long minutes she studied a vista that was a thousand hues of blue. The only relief to the cerulean landscape was a distant cruise ship, white on the horizon. The world of emergency rooms, of operating theaters, was a million miles away. So was the world in which she and Mike had friction, even though Mike was sitting next to her, literally close enough to touch.

A fist-sized dark shape, brown like weathered and polished wood, bobbed and moved on the surface about a hundred feet out from the boat. Bridget squinted, trying to make it out, but it disappeared. Then, three or four minutes later, it was back again. In the midst of the shape, she could just discern the pupil of an ancient, inquisitive eye.

"Look," she said aloud, pointing. "A sea turtle."

Bodies pressed in around her, looking, and then Angie and her sailor went down the ladder, telling the others. Soon, every student on the boat was crowding the port rail, pointing. The turtle submerged again but only stayed down a minute this time and came up not twenty feet from the boat. It was a loggerhead turtle, and an old one, with better than a yard of shell exposed intermittently in the light chop. Mike was standing next to Bridget, watching the turtle as well, and he put a hand on her shoulder. Even through the light wetsuit, she felt its warmth, the familiar pressure of his light I'm-here-with-you squeeze. After a moment's hesitation, she put her own hand atop his and squeezed back. Then the turtle submerged again, the mate went forward to release the mooring line, and the whole boat shuddered as the diesel was restarted.

Mike settled back down next to Bridget as the captain headed the dive boat south, toward the water off the strip of Singer Island resorts. Bridget and Mike looked one another's way at the same time, and they both smiled as the wind played at their hair. But they were two people in sunglasses, he in his Ray-Bans and she in her Oakleys, and the dark lenses hid whatever messages were there in their eyes.

They were running about two miles offshore, close enough to enjoy the Palm Beach skyline. Slowly, the twin spires of the Breakers resort came back into view, and when they did, Bridget and Mike headed back down to the dive deck, put their dive boots back on, and opened the valves on their scuba tanks. Seeing this, the students began readying their own equipment, and by the time the boat slowed to a stop directly off the famous resort's beach, the whole class was dressed and ready to go.

There was no mooring buoy this time, so the mate went forward and threw a Danforth anchor, easily sighting the reef below through the clear water, and aiming for the white sand alongside. Bridget saw the mate pull on the anchor line, setting it, and she went back to the stern and waited while the drift line was set out. Then it was back to the familiar routine—rinsing and donning the mask, a giant-stride off the swim deck, the exhilarating explosion of bubbles, and she was bobbing on the floating white line, signaling an "okay" back to the boat and watching a big Nassau grouper nosing its way around a clump of coral forty feet below.

The group got in the water more quickly this time, and at a signal from Mike they all submerged and swam forward to the anchor line, which they followed to the bottom. Mike pointed to the reef, and the students all swam that direction. Then he freed the anchor from the bottom and, taking his regulator out of his mouth, purged it for five seconds, sending a white plume of huge, roiling bubbles to the surface. A moment later, Bridget saw that the mate had spotted the signal—the anchor lifted off the sand and began to ascend through the blue in jerking sporadic steps, as the mate hauled it in hand over hand.

This was the type of diving that Palm Beach was famous for. The Gulf Stream, that river of warm tropical water that runs up the East Coast of the United States, gets closer to shore in Palm Beach than it does at any other point in the country. This makes the water there warmer, and clearer, than it is at any other point along Florida's Gold Coast, and it brings tropical fish and corals similar to those one might find in the southern Bahamas. The Stream also moves northward at a steady pace, creating a prevailing current. By lifting the anchor, Mike had set the boat adrift on that current; all the dive party had to do now was drift north along the reef—the most effortless form of diving imaginable—and, when they surfaced at the end of the dive, McCarthy's dive boat, drifting as well, would be right above them.

Side-by-side, Bridget and Mike swam to the reef and made themselves neutral—neither sinking nor rising—about three feet above it. The coral heads and sponges began to pass by underneath them, like an unreeling picture, the swaying of sea fans and the undulations of schooling fish the only clues to the current that was pushing them along. The students, unaccustomed to drift diving, swam back and forth, bubbles almost constantly in motion above them. But Mike's regulator released a modest stream of exhaust bubbles only every twenty seconds or so, and Bridget's did the same as she relaxed, drifting with the ease of a helium balloon along the current, her breathing slowed to the barest of minimums.

The reef was alive with color—reds and yellows and oranges, all tinted blue by the depth. Parrotfish, porkfish, and striped sergeant majors were everywhere. Yellowtail snappers swam in fork-tailed schools around the divers, and black groupers nosed among the corals below.

The students all congregated in one spot. Someone had spotted a moray, a big green one, its mouth open in what seemed to be an aggressive display, but was actually the large eel's way of breathing. One of the students had a small underwater camera, which he raised, the flash making the smallest blue spark in the underwater twilight.

The group resumed its drift along the twisting, turning stretch of reef. They floated effortlessly past elkhorn coral, brain coral, barrel sponges, and sea fans, stopping now and then to look at a blennie peering from a dead spot in a coral head, or a flight of golden-scaled shiners hiding under an overhang, waiting for nightfall. Forty minutes into the dive, the students began to surface, two by two, each buddy pair courteously checking in with Mike before heading up. Bridget and Mike kicked ahead of the group so any stragglers would drift up on them, rather than past them. Finally, there were just two buddy teams left in the water—Bridget and Mike, and the sailor and Angie, who had turned out to be a relaxed and competent diver.

Allowing Mike to drift ahead, Bridget turned to look at a large grouper that had poked its head out from under an overhang. She had just turned to catch back up when someone began tugging insistently at her fin.

It was Angie, obviously overwrought, her eyes wide behind her pink mask. She pointed up urgently, and Bridget looked toward the surface and saw, not twenty feet above them, a shark—better than twice as large as any shark she had ever seen. For a moment, her eyes went wide. Then she realized what it was and kicked up to join it.

10

The shark was beyond big. It was huge—the length of a small city bus, swimming steadily, almost lazily, in the same direction as the divers, its great oval mouth slightly agape, a small flotilla of attendant remoras and scavengers finning steadily north in the protection of its gigantic shadow.

Bridget gasped as she neared it. A single word, something from *Moby Dick*, the Bible, she wasn't sure where, crept into her head: *leviathan*.

She looked back at Angie, motioned up and down with her free hand—"calm down"—and made the "okay" sign. Then she rapped on her tank with her dive knife—a signal that she could not hear, but one that she knew would get Mike's attention. When he turned, eyebrows raised behind his dive mask, Bridget made a fist with her left hand and opened her right hand above it—*whale*—and then held her rigid right hand vertically to her forehead, the universal divers' sign for "shark." She pointed up. An explosion of bubbles erupted from Mike's regulator as he echoed her gasp.

Mike joined Bridget in her ascending course, parallel to that of the big shark. Angie and the sailor hung back, obviously unwilling to get any closer.

Bridget and Mike got even with the animal and drifted over slightly before it, off to the side of a gaping, oval mouth that looked easily capable of swallowing any scuba diver whole. Then they drifted back. Bridget kept her hands in, close to her body, and slowly, cautiously, kicked even nearer. She made an effort to breathe slowly and evenly, keeping all of her movements deliberate and slow. She was close now; she could see the distinctive white-spotted pattern that covered the big shark's upper body, and she was aware of its black, silver-dollar-size eye taking her in, scrutinizing her. She drifted closer, touching the shark's sandpaper-rough skin, and let herself slide back along its huge, wide body—like the elastic hull of some living, alien submarine—until she was next to the sail-like dorsal fin. Cupping her hand over the thick leading edge of the fin, Bridget held on and let her legs trail neutrally behind her. In a moment, her hair was streaming back as if caught in some underwater wind. She turned and saw the seven-foot-tall caudal fin swaying back and forth, propelling them steadily, and she marveled at physical contact with a living thing so powerful and huge.

In a moment, Mike had joined her, his hand over hers, riding on the other side of the dorsal fin. He peeked around it and nodded at her, giddy with excitement. The two students stayed off to the side, visibly astonished at what they were witnessing—a pair of divers riding a shark that made the predator in *Jaws* look like a puppy.

But it wasn't foolhardiness. The whale shark—the largest species of fish in the world——was also one of the most docile. While unmistakably a shark—its broad shovel-shaped head and triangular dorsal fins made it clear that it could be nothing else—it fed exclusively on plankton, scooping them into its cavernous mouth as it swam.

Atop the shark, being steadily towed through the blue water, Bridget was beside herself with wonder. She had never even seen a whale shark before, except in the occasional TV documentary. To glimpse one in the open ocean was a once-in-a-lifetime rarity. But to touch one, to stroke one, to hitch a ride on one—that was the sort of thing that divers dreamed of. The animal was so large that it blocked out everything below; all she could see was a plain of white-spotted charcoal skin. Yet it felt so essentially *alive*. The shark seemed barely to move its huge caudal fin, but even that effort was sufficient to propel them powerfully through the water; Bridget had never before felt so *immediate*, so very much at one with the sea.

Angie still kept her distance, swimming off to the side with exaggerated full-legged scissors kicks, trying to keep pace with the whale shark. But her sailor had gotten his courage up. He swam in but began losing ground on the huge fish and missed his attempt to join Bridget and Mike on its dorsal fin. Bridget turned her head and watched as he caught the shark by the caudal fin instead. His ride lasted only a second or two. After that, the whale shark swished its tail side-to-side through one full cycle and sent the hapless sailor tumbling mask over fins through the water.

A creature as small as a scuba diver held no peril for a whale shark, but, just as a mosquito might trouble a human being, a diver could irritate the big fish, and the sailor trying to hitch a ride on the tail seemed to have done just that. The shark turned east, toward the open ocean, and began to slowly sound, gliding slightly downward through the water, heading for the depths of the Continental Shelf.

Bridget glanced at her dive computer and saw the black numerals mounting—forty feet, counting toward fifty. She tapped Mike's hand with her free hand, showed him her computer and he nodded and signaled back, thumb up. Reluctantly, the two divers released their holds and kicked upwards to miss the big, undulating caudal fin as the shark swam through, headed for blue water. Bridget and Mike hovered and watched the giant fish go, swimming steadily and tirelessly, like a living machine, until its huge, spotted form was simply swallowed up by the distant underwater mist.

The sailor and Angie caught up within a minute. Both were now down to less than 500 pounds of air, and even Bridget and Mike's pressure gauges had dipped below 1000. Mike led the group to a depth of 15 feet, where they hovered neutrally, taking their safety stop while drifting steadily on the big, broad current of the Gulf Stream.

Bridget and Mike's eyes met.

My first whale shark, she signed to him.

Mine too, he returned.

She nodded, and he added, *Glad that I saw it with you.*

And there it was; the tiny crack that sent reality flooding back in. A year or two earlier, Bridget would have signed back *me too* without even having to think about it. But now? Now she found herself breaking eye contact, looking down and pretending to re-secure her backup regulator in its elastic holder. She stayed that way until the group had completed its safety stop and begun to kick slowly up to the surface.

The excitement of the whale-shark experience, that instant sense of camaraderie that comes so naturally to people who have shared a rare or unusual experience, lasted all the way back to the dock, and then some. All of the students had dived with Mike previously, so they'd acquired his good habits—tipping the first mate just as soon as the boat was tied up, carrying all of their gear over to the freshwater dunk tanks that McCarthy had set up on his dock, and rinsing the saltwater off everything, even their masks and fins. But through it all, the magic of the whale-shark sighting kept them pumped, excited, energized. Bridget noticed the sailor looking tongue-tied and awkward as he approached Angie, obviously asking her out for an early dinner. Jaded ER surgeon or not, Bridget beamed as she saw the blonde smile and nod.

She felt Mike's callused hand on her shoulder and turned, the smile still there on her face.

"Amazing day, huh?"

She nodded.

"I was thinking of the Crab House for dinner. Do you want to leave my van here and just go over there in the Bimmer?"

Bridget almost said yes, almost automatically agreed that they would head off as they'd always headed off: A couple. An item. Then she caught herself.

Some of the doctors at the ER are away on a conference, so they're short and I'm on call in the morning, she signed. It was the second time she'd lied to Mike this week, and while she regretted it instantly, she continued, *We'd better drive both cars so I can take off for home straight from the restaurant.*

"You aren't staying on and diving tomorrow?" Mike asked, surprised.

"No," Bridget said, looking away. "I'm sorry."

And the funny thing was that, in some strange way, she was.

The van was emptier than usual as Mike headed up the road to Ocean Avenue. McCarthy's provided open-slated equipment lockers for divers on multi-day trips, so most of his gear, and his students' gear, was out of the van and back there on the dock, where it would drip and air at least partially dry by morning. And the tanks were all stacked next to the air station in McCarthy's small dive shop; the first mate would fill them at dawn when she arrived.

What troubled him was that Bridget hadn't left her gear with him. She was fastidious about that little red BMW of hers; leaving wet dive gear in its trunk was just something she didn't usually do. True, she'd rinsed the equipment and dried it as well as she could, rolling the wetsuit tightly between one of the big beach towels that Mike carried in his van and letting everything sit and hang for as long as possible before stowing it away. But normally she would have put her gear in a locker with his or at the very least put it in the back of his van, so he could drop it off with her in

Ocala on his way home on Sunday. She'd refused his offers to do that this time, acting as if she hadn't wanted to cause him any bother. But she'd never worried about putting him to any trouble before. It was almost as if—Mike banished the thought, and then retrieved it. It was almost as if she wasn't planning on seeing him again.

Her request to take two cars to the restaurant had been one warning sign. Her insistence on keeping her wet dive gear in her own car was another. And now, as Mike put these two things together with the friction of the past few months, the arguments over the *cenote* dive—well, in his mind, that raised a tidy forest of red flags.

The sun was creeping down toward the horizon when he got to the Crab House, a place he and Bridget had been visiting forever, for as long as they'd been bringing scuba classes to West Palm. The restaurant was nestled next to the western approach to the Intercoastal bridge, and part of it was built on trestles that hung out over the water. Mike drove past the entrance and parked his old van under the bridge. Bridget would leave her BMW with the parking valets, and they'd park it right next to the entrance, but a beat-up old Chevy Van didn't project the kind of image the restaurant would want, and if Mike valet-parked it, they'd put it somewhere out in the boonies. So it made more sense to save the four bucks and park it himself within easy walking distance of the entrance.

Sure enough, by the time he walked back up the hill to the restaurant, there was Bridget, changed back into a white linen blouse and red culottes and sandals, her hair tied back with a plain black ribbon, Oakleys perched atop her head, looking like a million dollars and change. She stood pointedly and watched the valet drive her four-wheeled baby the few feet to its parking place, making it clear that she wasn't going to stand for any quick tour of the avenue before it was parked. Then, satisfied, she turned. She was just putting her sunglasses away in her bag when Mike joined her.

"Hey," he smiled.

They don't look crowded yet, Bridget signed back. *Should we try to get a table right away?*

"Sure," he smiled. But again, this wasn't the Bridget he knew. Or rather, it *was* the Bridget he knew, but in a mode that he knew to be dangerous—all business, no room for sentiment. And sentiment was the only card that Mike held.

They passed the bar and went into the restaurant, stopping at the host's station.

"Do you have something on the outside of the veranda?" Mike asked the young woman standing at the station. He almost slipped her a five-dollar-bill but decided against it—that sort of thing flew in Miami, but it would be considered *gauche* here in trendy West Palm.

"Sure." The hostess smiled at the attractive couple and asked Mike, "Special night?"

"I hope so," he smiled back.

Pulling two menus out of the holder on her station, the hostess led the two of them back, down a slatted wooden ramp and through a dining room crowded with tables and nautical bric-a-brac, through the French doors folded tightly against themselves at the far side of the room, and out onto a broad wooden porch-like veranda, where the cool breeze of dusk refreshed the largely empty booths and tables. Across the Intercoastal, lights were winking on in homes and on houseboats. Over the broad wooden railing, Mike could just see the red and white running lights and the ivory outline of a big, sleek Bertram yacht, making its way south in the gathering darkness.

Bridget brightened a bit as they took seats together in a semicircular booth with their backs to the water. The veranda of the Crab House wasn't much—paper tablecloth on rough wooden tables—but the soft salt breeze and the atmosphere of the waterway more than made up for the lack of linen and polish. A candle in a hurricane chimney played flickering light and provided what Mike hoped would be a romantic mood. The waitress came for the drink order and registered just the slightest bit of surprise when she got it—a coffee and a Diet Coke. But Mike never touched alcohol the evening before a dive—which was, for him, almost every evening. And after years of working on highway-accident victims in the ER, Bridget wouldn't dream of drinking before driving.

"And could we have some bread right away?" Mike asked the waitress.

She nodded and walked back toward the kitchen, leaving the two of them alone.

"Well," Mike said, breaking the silence. "Good day, huh?"

When Bridget said nothing in reply, he repeated himself, leaning her way. He knew that she didn't care to sign in restaurants. She didn't like the stares it drew from neighboring tables.

Bridget moved the candle over, next to his plate.

"I'm sorry," she said, her voice very low, compensating, because she knew that the deaf often speak more loudly than circumstances require. "I didn't see that."

"Oh." Mike leaned closer to the candle so its light would fall on his face, wondering as he did if it was going to produce the same horror-movie effect that kids like to create with flashlights. "I was just saying that I enjoyed the day."

"Oh. Me too."

Mike nodded. Bridget nodded back. They waited. The bread came.

Bridget looked at the bread basket. Mike smiled; they'd been coming to the Crab House after their West Palm dives for years now, and this was an old ritual with them. He knew what was going through her head. It was the reason he'd asked for the bread.

"Go ahead," he said, leaning forward again so she would be able to read his lips.

Beaming, Bridget took a roll from the basket and turned around so she was kneeling on the seat cushion, her elbows up on the railing. Mike grinned. For all her womanly shapes and curves, the picture he got of her, kneeling on the seat like that, was that of a six-year-old, getting a boost to raid the cookie jar.

And she showed a childlike enthusiasm as she tore the roll into four pieces and dropped them, one by one, to the water, thirty feet below.

Instantly, the dark surface of the Intercoastal erupted as dozens of channel catfish swarmed for the bread, their barbeled snouts coming completely out of the water in their eagerness to be fed. The sun was all the way down now, but just enough light showed from a nearby jetty for them to pick the fish out. They were big, fully grown, and Mike imagined that most of the fish had lived their entire lives here in the shadow of the Crab House's veranda. Bridget wasn't the only patron who fed them. It was something of a Palm Beach tradition.

Mike handed Bridget another roll, and she fed this to the fish as well, pointing as one catfish came completely out of the water and wriggled across the heads of his peers to get a piece of bread.

Mike remembered the first time they'd come here, when he'd shown Bridget this free bit of tableside entertainment. She had dropped the bread in, laughed with surprise as the fish tore the surface of the water, and then turned and asked him, "What kind of sound are they making?"

Mike had listened for a moment before replying, "Like applause."

Satisfied, Bridget had nodded and smiled, lifting both hands over her head and shaking them like quaking leaves, applauding, as the deaf applaud, back to the fish.

The waitress returned and took their order. When she'd left, Bridget turned to Mike, eyebrows raised. "We need to talk," she told him.

He raised his eyebrows back and handed her another roll, which she turned and dropped whole onto the water.

"I'm worried, Mike," she said, sitting back down.

He offered her another roll. She ignored it.

"I'm worried," she repeated.

"Why?"

She sighed, looked at him for a moment, and then nodded once, a small nod.

"You know why," she said finally.

"Bridge," Mike said, speaking slowly so she could read his lips in the dim light. "Nobody in the world is more ready for the deep dive than I am. Nobody has more experience. Now that Pete's gone, I'm the best there is at this."

"And Pete's gone," Bridget pointed out.

"Things happen. People die every day, driving to work. But we still drive cars. Remember," he said, pointing to himself, "I came back from that dive."

"You almost didn't," Bridget returned. "You told me what happened."

"There was an issue with the lights, Bridge. We fixed that. We'll use Lamar's lights this time. We won't have that problem again."

"You fixed the *lights*," Bridget said.

"What is that supposed to mean?" Mike asked, raising his voice and then feeling foolish for that—raising his voice to someone who could not hear.

"You know what that means," Bridget said.

He sat silent, waiting.

Bridget pursed her lips.

You have lights, she told him, switching to sign. *You have better lights and better gear and even better sponsors this time. But what about you? Last time, you did this because you wanted to. This time, you're acting like you have to. And you don't.*

"I want to do this, Bridge," Mike said.

I don't believe you.

What's the deal? Mike signed back angrily. *Is this where you get possessive? Try to change me? I'm a cave diver. I've been a cave diver since before we met. I'm doing this dive.*

Bridget's eyes moistened in the candlelight.

You're not ready, she signed.

Mike snorted.

How would you know if I'm ready? He signed back to her. *I think you're trying to smother me. Who I am. What I am. And . . .*

"Don't do that, Bridge," he continued aloud. "This is what I do."

It is not! Bridget returned, brow furrowed. *This is not what you do. Being stupid is not what you do!*

Deliberately, he turned his head, looking away, cutting her off. He regretted it as soon as he did it, but he did it nonetheless. He turned back just in time to see Bridget—leaving.

"Oh, Bridge," he said, rising, but this time it was *her* head that was turned.

Mike stepped out of the booth, nearly colliding with the waitress.

"Sir?" She shifted the platter of food on her shoulder. "Is everything all right?"

Mike dug in his pockets, looking for cash, coming up with a five and a ten. Not nearly enough for the meal. He pulled out his wallet, found his Visa card, started to hand it to the waitress, and then thought about it. What was he going to do? Run after Bridget? Her car was right next to the door; she'd be there by now. Was he planning on chasing her BMW down the Parkway in his beat up old van? And even if he caught up with her, then what?

"Sir?" The waitress stood there with the platter, looking at him, the table, him again.

The fish splashed in the darkness below, clamoring for bread that did not fall.

11
DOS OJOS—
AKAMAL, QUINTANA ROO

Bearded, portly, smiling, and polite, Phillip Faranino didn't look like a snake. But he was a snake. One hundred percent, and dangerous as a cobra. Viktor Bellum knew that, and never forgot it for a single moment while he was with the man.

Faranino was technical diving's own Internet wonder, founder of the *Aquasplorer.com* webzine and diving's most accomplished practitioner of the ancient game known as "let's you and him fight." While others had tried launching on-line diving magazines devoted solely to practical information and objective reviews of gear and destination, Faranino had found fortune by observing that, in any group one cared to name, there was always going to be a significant percentage of people who delighted in seeing the dirt on the others.

So Faranino provided the dirt. And he did it so well that there were charter operators the whole world wide who no longer spoke to one another because of quotes that the editor had printed out of context. Along the way he'd discovered a number of people in the industry whom he could depend on to help him keep things stirred up. And without question, one of those people was Viktor Bellum. So the pair formed a symbiotic bond—Bellum had the abrasiveness that could keep people clicking onto the website, and Faranino had the circulation to provide Bellum with a platform from which to lambaste his competition.

That was why, when Faranino had e-mailed to let Bellum know that he was coming down to do a story on the diving around Cozumel, Bellum had been all too happy to invite him down for some cave-diving as well. And that was why, even though he knew that Faranino would torpedo him in a New York minute if he thought it would be good for circulation, Bellum treated the shabby, shady editor as if he were visiting royalty.

Bellum had planned the visit meticulously, right down to asking Faranino to meet him near Akamal rather than bringing the editor all the way down to Tulum. The ancient city of Tulum, with its majestic Mayan pyramids sitting on very shore of the Caribbean, tended to overshadow its local cave diving. And besides, the local Mexican cab drivers liked to drive out and rinse the dust off their taxis at the basin of the one *cenote* where he did most of his Tulum training, so its name, "Carwash Cenote," did not look nearly as intriguing in print as that of Akamal's mainstay cave dive, "Dos Ojos"—Spanish for "two eyes."

Bellum had been careful to give Faranino the full treatment, making several jumps from one guideline to another during the course of their one-hour dive in Dos Ojos to show the journalist as much flowstone and dripstone, as many soda-straw stalactites and other "decoration" as he possibly could.

Now, as their dive gear dripped on the tailgate of Bellum's old International Scout, Faranino relaxed at a rough wooden picnic table, a camera bag at his feet. Not fifty feet away, a worn log dock ran under the broad arch of the stalactite-covered cavern dome and into the jade-and-turquoise waters of Dos Ojos *cenote*. Even in the shadow thrown by the limestone dome, one could see that the water was crystal clear; the divers decompressing twenty feet below could have been floating in air. Only their bubbles spoiled the illusion.

Bellum came back from the truck with two Mexican beers fresh from the cooler, moisture condensing in rolling beads on the sides of the brown long-necked bottles.

"Nothing like a Dos Equis after Dos Ojos, huh?" Bellum chuckled, trying to make the line, which he'd thought up during the decompression stop, sound natural, off the cuff.

"Hey, thanks, Viktor," Faranino smiled. He opened the beer but did not sip it.

"So," Bellum asked, "do you think you got what you need for your story?"

He tried to sound interested and engaged, even though he was certain that Faranino did not intend to print a single word about their dive in Dos Ojos—that, if he mentioned it at all, it would simply be as background for the muckraking that had actually brought him south of the border this time around. But there was a certain choreography that was expected in these things. Bellum knew this, and he was happy to do his part of the dance.

"I think so," Faranino mused. "This cave—it's typical of the dives here in the Yucatan?"

"Typical of some," Bellum mused, setting his beer down, unopened. He'd seen it too often in the Navy—men who drank when the people with them didn't were men who were made fools of in very short order. "I mean, you go to some caves, like Yaxchen, down south of Tulum, and the visibility might be pure junk—only ten or fifteen feet, particularly after a rain. The water has to be filtered by a lot of limestone to get as clear as it is here. Then again, Yaxchen isn't dived much; just a few locals—'explorers' hard up for something to explore. But as far as decorations—the rock formations formed back when the cave was dry—yeah, Dos Ojos is probably typical of most."

"I see." Faranino slipped a microcassette recorder out of his gadget bag and set it on the picnic table next to his beer. He didn't say anything about it, but the tape spindles were turning, and there was enough shadow that Bellum could see the light of the little red "record" diode.

"This cave is one of the bigger ones, though, isn't it?" Faranino asked.

Bellum shrugged.

"This and Nahoch Nah Chich—name's modern Mayan, means 'giant birdcage'—are generally thought to be the most extensive cave systems, wet or dry, in the world," Bellum said. "As to which is bigger, well, that's a matter of debate. Nahoch is just down the road. Teams have been pushing line in both caves for years, and both keep getting bigger. Eventually, they'll probably connect, and when they do, whichever team has the most mapped passage will be able to claim the other cave as part of their own system. Sort of 'big cave eats little cave.'"

"I see," Faranino said again. He had a notebook out as well, now, and he'd uncapped a Mont Blanc pen, but he'd yet to make a single note.

Leading up to it, Bellum thought to himself. The Dos Ojos and Nahoch stuff was all ancient history. *Aquasplorer.com* had done its own cover story on the rivalry years before, and Faranino knew all about it, even if he pretended otherwise.

"How about depth?" Faranino asked. "Are these caves also the deepest?

"No," Bellum shook his head. "In fact, in some passages in Nahoch, you can put your dive computer up against the ceiling and watch the numerals flicker back and forth between one foot and zero—that's how close the passage is to the top of the water table."

"So what's the deepest?" Faranino asked. He had the pen in his hand now, ready to write.

"That'd be inland," Bellum said, knowing that the evasiveness would help what was coming to sound more genuine.

"Cenote X?" Faranino asked.

"Yeah," Bellum nodded. "That's what they're calling it. Cenote X."

"I see."

The paunchy little writer hadn't been much of a diver. He had stirred up some silt; not much, but a good cave diver wouldn't stir up any at all. Had he not had something Bellum wanted—the media exposure—Bellum wouldn't have geared up to go diving with him.

Bellum was one of the few cave instructors in the world who routinely washed students out for not meeting his personal near-military standards of fitness. Those standards had dropped somewhat in recent years, as Bellum himself could no longer do the prodigious number of pushups, chinups, and sit-ups that he had once claimed constituted a "minimum acceptable level." But all that went by the board if you had something Viktor Bellum wanted. So rather than sending Faranino down the road with his usual cursory "You're fat; come back when you're not . . . ," Bellum had taken him diving and rolled out the red carpet for him. But he still couldn't stand the guy, and this continual "I see" stuff was adding to the irritation.

"Cenote X," Faranino repeated, glancing at his notebook. "You're the pioneer, the explorer in these parts. How is it that you've never tried to dive it?"

"Right of access," Bellum shrugged. "Pete Wiley and Mike Bryant locked it up in an agreement with the landowners eight years ago, giving them exclusive diving rights. And prior to that, nobody even suspected that it existed."

That wasn't exactly true. One other person had known that it *existed*, but he hadn't known precisely where it *was*.

Cenote X. Viktor Bellum had grown so resigned to the idea that he would never again see the crash site that it hadn't even occurred to him that it and the *cenote* discovered by Pete Wiley and Mike Bryant might be one and the same. Yet it was, and the perspective as he'd stepped off the Expedition Network's flight had been almost exactly the same as the one he'd had seven years earlier, when he'd stumbled out of the jungle and realized that the reason he'd seen no flames and heard no explosion was because he, Viktor Bellum, a trained and experienced diver, had lost his million-dollar bonanza in a pit full of water.

"You were there when Wiley and Bryant made their dive, weren't you?" Faranino was asking.

Bellum tried not to start as he returned to the present.

"Yeah," he said, attempting to sound grave. "I'm sorry to say I was. Not as part of the team, of course, but as an observer. I did the color for the television crew."

"You'd been critical of the dive beforehand."

"I had." It had been standard operating procedure for Bellum back then—you dived in his region without his involvement, you got "The Treatment." He'd thought of it the way cold-war nations thought of nuclear weapons, as defense through the promise of offense—a deterrent.

"And yet you apologized to Wiley and Bryant, and offered them your support."

Bellum fell silent for a moment. He remembered his mind racing at a hundred miles per hour as he'd stepped to the edge of Cenote X. What he'd lost was in there. But it had yet to be found. And wasn't it just the way his life had been going that, of all the places for a helicopter to crash in the Yucatan, his had gone down into the deepest water-filled cave in the world—one that was now in a media spotlight?

All the months he'd searched, he'd never even suspected it could be like that. Some Yucatan caves were deep—300 feet or better—but he'd never dreamed one could be as deep as Cenote X. He'd always thought that, if he found the crash site, it would be a two-day deal—one day to locate the helicopter and another to get inside, put lift bags on the cargo, and float it up.

And what he was after had gone all the way to the bottom of the *cenote*. He'd been certain of that. Wiley and Bryant had already been to better than 800 feet on their training dives in Cenote X; nobody had said anything about finding a helicopter, and a Huey in full military markings was a pretty hard thing to miss.

So Bellum's first priority on arrival at the *cenote* had been to keep his lost chopper lost. That had required him to think on his feet. But then, he'd always been good at that.

———

Bellum looked up at Faranino, his face composed, somber. Faranino reflected, not for the first time, that the man was a competent actor.

"I did that," Bellum said. "And I regret it. It was—I don't know—spirit of the moment?"

Faranino nodded and kept silent.

"I mean," Bellum continued, "I knew in my heart of hearts that these guys weren't ready for this dive, that their methods were all wrong, that their whole approach was essentially flawed. But we had a film crew there. . . . No need for sour grapes. So I offered an olive branch."

Mixed vegetable metaphors, Faranino mused to himself, but he nodded again.

"I should have put a stop to it before somebody got hurt," Bellum said.

As if you could have, Faranino thought. Aloud, he asked, "You said that 'their methods were all wrong.' Can you elaborate on that?"

"I don't know—I'm speaking from the outside here," Bellum began, knowing that the halting, the fudging, would make him sound all that much more genuine. "And I want to make it clear that this is just my opinion. I'm not accusing anybody of anything. But it just seemed to me that they were sensationalizing the dive, making it seem like more than it actually was."

"But Viktor, it's the deepest known cave dive in the world."

"Sure. But except for depth, Cenote X is not really all that technical a dive. You look at Bushmansgatt in South Africa; that's a cave with an entrance at the bottom of a lake. You're diving passage to get to depth there. Zacaton, up north, has some angle to its drop. But Cenote X is basically a straight up-and-down bounce dive . . ."

Faranino nodded, even though he knew that, in shape, Cenote X was more like an inverted funnel; it wasn't as if it had open water over everything.

". . . When you look at how Wiley and Bryant made an expedition out of the attempt," Bellum continued, "all the so-called 'training dives' and 'practice dives' they made—"

Faranino looked up. Even for *Aquasplorer.com*, this was straining credulity a bit. "Cenote X is something on the order of twelve or thirteen hundred feet," Faranino pointed out. "Are you saying they wouldn't have to work up to that?"

"Sure, but you can do that sort of thing in a chamber."

Silently, Faranino wondered how many hyperbaric chambers there were in the world that could take a diver down to the equivalent of 1,300 feet. Personally, he couldn't think of one. But this was getting too good to interrupt with anything as trivial as the truth. He nodded.

"So, what are you saying, Vik?" He knew that Bellum hated to be called "Vik."

"Hey, I'm not saying anything," Bellum replied, ignoring the prod. "Far be it from me to speak ill of the dead . . ."

Oh, give it a break, Faranino thought, but he kept his face straight, nodding.

". . . But it seems to me a person could say that these guys were milking a pretty simple, if deep, dive for all it was worth, making it more complicated than they needed to, and they got bit by their own monster. Wiley died. By his own account, Bryant nearly bought it as well, and what was his big, pressing, overwhelming problem? Light failure. *Light* failure. I mean, cave divers *train* for light failures. And I'm not just talking explorers. I'm talking your basic, run-of-the-mill tourist diver in Florida. You assume, going in, that you will have no lights coming out. It's a basic safety principle, and it should have been no big deal for any full cave diver at all. So you tell me; were these guys ready for this?"

"What do you say?"

"I say Pete Wiley is dead."

Faranino looked down at his notebook.

"You think they made the dive riskier than it needed to be?"

"Again—I'll let the evidence speak for itself. Pete Wiley is dead."

"So why," Faranino drew a question mark in his notebook, "would they add risk?"

"Well," Bellum began, "although you might not suspect it from the way they did their dives, both Pete Wiley and Mike Bryant were professionals . . ."

Interesting, Faranino thought. *He's talking about Bryant as if he died too.*

"They made their living at this," Bellum said, "and when you're not teaching and guiding, well, sponsorship is what takes up the slack, right?"

"So you're saying that they were grandstanding for the sake of their sponsors?"

"I didn't say that," Bellum said, just a hint of a smile creeping through. "But it's a pretty easy conclusion to draw, isn't it?"

Faranino shrugged and looked back down at his notebook, his pen tracing the page.

"You know," he said, keeping his eyes on the notebook. "Mike Bryant has formed a new expedition to come back and dive Cenote X."

"Well," Bellum said, "I hear he's got sponsors for another try."

"That's not the same thing?"

"That's the problem," Bellum said, trying to put the right hint of exasperation into his voice. "It *is* 'the same thing.' It's the same thing as before. Sponsorship money. Publicity. Three-ring circus. And I can't even say that I blame Bryant for it; he's just taking what's offered. But I do blame his sponsors. They're paying a guy to try again at something, using methods that have already killed somebody."

"So what about you, Vik?" Faranino asked the question without looking up.

"What about me?"

"I understand that you have been seeking permission to dive Cenote X yourself." He lifted his eyes and met Bellum's as he said this.

"I have." Bellum didn't blink.

"You've retained an attorney to do this?"

"Yeah. It's come down to that."

Faranino broke off the eye-contact and blinked, pretending to watch a group of divers getting out of Dos Ojos. He turned back to Bellum.

"Why?"

Bellum shrugged.

"To get it done with," he said.

Faranino had been doing interviews long enough to know that there was nothing that would get a subject to elaborate, maybe even say things he didn't really want to say, like ten or fifteen seconds of empty, open silence, especially when they knew that there was a tape recorder running. And knowing that, he said nothing—just waited with pen poised.

Bellum nodded.

"Cave diving is my life," he finally told Faranino, keeping his face absolutely straight. "It's what I do; it's what I love. It's important to me. Its reputation is important to me. Every week, all over the world, legitimate pioneers are pursuing legitimate exploration in caves all over the world—maybe not as deep as Cenote X, but every bit as important . . ."

Hip boots, Faranino was thinking. *I need hip boots.*

". . . and these people are willing to do it for the love of it, for the reward of simply going where nobody's ever been before," Bellum continued.

And now he's doing what? Faranino thought. *Quoting the voice-over to Star Trek?* But he didn't say a thing; he just nodded.

"I just hate to see that reputation tarnished by the kind of circus they're apparently planning at Cenote X," Bellum said, ". . . like the kind of circus they had there five years ago. I just think that, if I can get in there, do the dive, touch down on the bottom, and be done with it, maybe I can de-fuse this whole situation—give cave diving back to the explorers, and give Cenote X back to the jungle. I mean, all this hoopla is all about being the first, right? If I can be first, then it's done with. There's no interest, no sponsor pressure, nothing. No need to dive. It's . . . like I said: done with."

Faranino arched his eyebrows.

"And what about *your* sponsors, Vik?" Faranino asked.

"I don't have any."

Faranino arched his eyebrows again.

"Not one?"

"I don't need any," Bellum explained. "I live here. Cenote X is like sixty clicks away from my shop. I don't need to bring equipment in-country; I've got it here already. I have all the support personnel I need—and I gotta tell you; it won't be much—just a phone call away. And I won't need to take but two days off from my training and guiding schedule to do it."

"So why do it at all, in that case?"

"I thought I made that clear," Bellum said, feigning exasperation. "To save lives."

Faranino started to chuckle, but caught himself.

"Hey," Bellum said, hands open. "I'm a cave instructor. Safety is what I'm all about. It's always been what I'm about. I just like to see people coming out of caves alive. If I can accomplish that by putting an end to this carnival at Cenote X, then that's what I'm gonna try to do."

Bellum shrugged, picked up his beer, and took a drink.

"But I don't want to go on about that," he said, setting his bottle down. "We're here to talk about diving Dos Ojos, right?"

Oh right, Faranino thought. *Now that you've tarred and feathered Bryant and every one of his sponsors, you don't want to talk about that.*

He clicked off his tape recorder, knocked out the record-protect tab on the tape, and put the tape back into an outer pocket of the gadget bag, zipping it shut. He sipped his own beer. Then, reaching into the main body of the bag, he took out a small, rectangular Canon digital camera.

"Right," Faranino said. "How's about I get some shots of you standing next to the spring?"

"Sure," Bellum smiled. "Want me to get some gear, maybe set it up for the shot?"

"Great idea," Faranino smiled back. "Why don't you do that?"

He held the smile until the other man had started walking back to the truck. Then, drinking his beer, he looked down at the notes he'd scribbled during the brief interview.

Amazing, he thought to himself, savoring the taste of the ice-cold drink. *In less than five minutes, Bellum has managed to discredit both Pete Wiley and Mike Bryant, accuse their sponsors of goading them into something for which they were not qualified, imply that Bryant should be stopped for his own safety, and paint himself as a selfless crusader for truth, justice, and . . . whatever.*

Faranino sipped his beer again and looked at the phrases he'd jotted down, noting all the qualifications, the ways Bellum had answered direct questions with questions of his own, the way he'd implied rather than accused, and made clear that what he was expressing was simply his opinion.

Smart. It was a ball of innuendo; Bellum hadn't spoken a single libelous word. Nothing that he could be taken to court for and, more importantly, nothing that Faranino and *Aquasplorer.com* could be taken to court for. Yet Bellum had smeared Mike Bryant like soft butter. There was no doubt about that.

Faranino finished his beer and then pretended to fiddle with the camera as Bellum carried a set of tanks down to the water's edge. The editor had come here hoping to prod Bellum into saying something newsworthy. Instead, Bellum had played the situation like a virtuoso, using the interview to build a platform for his own agenda. It seemed like a lot to go through to just to trip up a competitor, but Faranino had seen worse done, and done often, in his career. And smearing a competitor came as easily to Bellum, Faranino guessed, as breathing.

He had, Faranino realized, been used. And yet he and his web-zine would come away with exactly what he'd come down here looking for—a little controversy, another scrap of bread to toss among the dogs and start a fight for the entertainment of his readers.

He chucked the empty bottle into a trash can, turned on the camera, and went to take his picture. It was a Friday; if he did some writing before dinner, he could have the whole story written, formatted, reviewed by his lawyer, and uploaded to the Web by midnight. Just in time to get the weekend readers and the weekend word-of-mouth. All those wannabes, clicking their mouse buttons, racking up impressions on the ad tabulators. If he closed his eyes, he could almost see the dollars piling up.

12

SAN MIGUEL DE COZUMEL, QUINTANA ROO, MEXICO— LATE JULY, 2003

What significant changes have you made to your approach to the dive this time around?"

Mike Bryant strained to see who had asked the question. No soap. All he could make out was a silhouette, an amorphous backlit shadow in a small sea of amorphous backlit shadows. Indistinctly, he could make out one guy—standing at the rear of the group, not sitting—somebody he didn't know. In the dim light from the nearby thatch-roofed open-air bar, he could make out baggy khaki pants, a red Hawaiian shirt and sandals, shaggy blonde hair, and a moustache and goatee. The guy looked more like a surfer than a diver. Probably one of the resort guests, Mike decided. And he wasn't the one who had asked the question, anyhow.

It was probably the twentieth time Mike Bryant had done his presentation on Cenote X, but it was the first time he had done it outdoors, under palm trees, with tiki lamps. And all things considered, Costa Club had done an admirable job of turning the apron next to their sprawling pool into a starlit conference room.

The sheet-plastic screen of the projection TV, wired into the video port of Mike's laptop, rippled slightly as the land breeze began to kick up, the air from the warm island beginning to move out toward the sea. They had a name for that elsewhere in the Caribbean, Mike remembered—the "Undertaker's Wind." He missed a beat, almost losing his train of thought.

"Uhm," he stalled as he remembered the question. "Of course, we're using the new Yobatu 1000 high-performance regulators . . ."

He smiled to where the chief Yobatu Scuba rep was sitting with some large dive-center operators. Yobatu was, after all, paying for this shindig.

". . . and we're looking at other equipment improvements—Dive Rite HID lights with compact, low-profile battery canisters, and the new Ni-Tek computers that will allow us to compute all of our gas switches in real time. But overall, our approach to the dive is essentially the same as that used on the last attempt. We had considered going to an underwater habitat, similar to what they've used at both Wakulla Springs and Nahoch Nah Chich, which would allow us to decompress dry and use a combination of oxygen and air breaks even for some of the deeper stops. That would also give us the option of going to intravenous fluids for rehydration—on these really deep dives, you can't stay ahead of the dehydration with oral fluids alone. But in the end, we decided that, given the remote location of the site, the habitat added too much complexity and created new areas of vulnerability. You'll recall that, up at Zacaton, Jim Bowden was forced to abandon one attempt because of issues with his habitat."

The silhouette nodded. Mike wondered how much of the answer his questioner had actually followed. A dive such as Cenote X sounded like it was all guts and glory, but most of it was compressed-gas physics and logistics. Then again, this was a fairly knowledgeable crowd: nearly a hundred dive shop owners with operations large enough, and accounts with Yobatu Scuba substantial enough, to justify the price of a free trip to the Mexican Riviera.

"Any other questions?"

A shadow was moving forward; it was the chief Yobatu representative, a capped-toothed, booth-tanned, blown-dry marketing type from Los Angeles.

"Thanks, Mike," he said, taking the microphone from his hand and turning to the crowd. "Let's give our explorer a hand."

He led a smattering of applause, which he cut off after about five seconds.

"So now you see that Yobatu Scuba is ready to go to thirteen hundred feet later on this year," he said, smiling and adding, "but we'd like to ask you to refrain from jumping the gun and trying it on tomorrow morning's wall dive!"

Polite laughter rippled across the group collected on the resort's darkened lawn.

"And now," he said, "four little words that you've all been waiting for: the bar is open!"

More laughter, more applause, and the group rose to their feet and began moving toward the portable bar set up adjacent to the main tower of the hotel, laughter and conversation growing from all quarters, like herd noises.

Mike shut down his laptop computer and began packing it, together with its various cables and adapters, into a travel-worn Kensington soft case. Behind him, the resort manager was unplugging the projection TV, getting ready to move it indoors, out of the night air.

"Bueno presentacion," said the man, a diver himself.

"Gracias," Mike replied.

At least *somebody* thought it was nice, he thought to himself as he zipped the case shut.

This trip had been planned and publicized for months. Like most manufacturers in the dive industry, Yobatu Scuba did most of its face-to-face schmoozing at the annual Diving Equipment Marketing Association's exposition—the "DEMA show," as it was known—held every autumn. But there were many dive-shop owners and charter operators who didn't make it to DEMA: people from south Florida, the Caribbean, Hawaii, and other places where the show date coincided with the crucial last days of their season, a time when travel was out of the question. So Yobatu also had this four-day program—a combination of new-equipment presentations, training, and marketing seminars—for the off-season operators.

In many ways this off-season meet was more lucrative for Yobatu than DEMA. For one, they didn't have to share their audience with any other manufacturers. And to round off the program, they'd asked Mike to come down and make a presentation on Cenote X.

They'd made the request months before, and he'd eagerly accepted. The initial sponsor support had been enough to purchase most of the supplies they'd need for the training and the dives and to get Mike, his team, and their gear down to Cancún. But they still needed a way to ferry everything inland to the dive site; a medium-duty truck, or at least three weeks' rental of a small fleet of four-wheel-drive pickups. And Mike knew from the last dive that sponsors who were already signed up were the most likely source of contingency cash for last-minute items such as this. So he'd readily agreed to come down and speak.

But that had been before the *Aquasplorer.com* article.

"Underwriting Tragedy?" That had been the headline. And then the subhead: "Are big-money/big-name sponsors pushing ill-prepared 'explorers' too deep, too far . . . too fast?"

Mike had read the Internet article with mounting ire. It had been obvious that Bellum had been out to cut his legs out from under him and that

Faranino had been more than happy to build his circulation by printing the lies.

And build it he had; just about everyone Mike knew had read the deliberately sensational story. Those that Mike counted as friends—people such as Lamar Hires and the Mexican dive operators who had worked with him on the previous dive as support personnel—had registered disgust and outrage—but still, they'd read it. They'd clicked onto the webpage, registered on the hit counters, vindicated the advertisers' decisions to tie themselves to Faranino's muckraking. Mike had even logged on and read it himself.

What he'd seen had sent him reaching for the phone to call Skip Williamson, an attorney who specialized in diving-related litigation. Skip, perennial yuppie that he was, had recognized Mike's number from the caller ID on his cellphone, and answered, "Hey, Mike—I know why you're calling and yeah, I've read it too."

"Good. Then what can I do about it?" Mike had asked.

"My advice? Ignore it."

"What?" Mike had nearly shouted back into the phone.

"Mike," Skip had replied calmly, "Phillip Faranino may be a major-league jerk, but he's not a *stupid* major-league jerk. There's nothing in that article that's litigable."

"But he slandered me," Mike had said.

"Libeled."

"What?"

"He libeled you," Skip had repeated. "Or at least that's what you'd like to think he did. If somebody lies about you in print it's libel. Slander is a something spoken in deliberate mistruth and meant to harm. If you were to accuse anyone of slander, it would be Bellum, and it won't work there, either."

"Why?"

"Look at the article again," Skip had consoled him calmly. "Look at the headline, the subhead. They're questions, not statements. And the whole story's done that way: questions, implication, guarded and carefully identified opinions. Smart. If somebody *says* that you're incompetent, you can sue them down to their socks, and you can usually win. But if somebody merely *questions* your competence, they can simply say that they were being prudent. And they'd be right. It's a free country, Mike. You can say what you like—as long as you're careful how you say it. And either

Faranino is very smart about this sort of thing or he had the foresight to pass the article by a lawyer before he posted it on the Internet."

"But it's not right."

"There's a lot done every day that's not right, Mike," Skip had agreed. "But it happens—because it's legal. Listen, buddy, I feel for you. I really do. And if you want my opinion, nobody deserves a trip to the woodshed more than Phillip Faranino and Viktor Bellum. But you can't nail 'em. Not this time and not on this. They were asking questions, thinking out loud. And that's protected speech. First Amendment stuff, Mike. You don't have a leg to stand on."

"Why is it," Mike had fumed, "that I hear that every time I call you?"

"I wish it weren't so," Skip had chuckled. "But that's the way it is. Hey, guy—I'm at my club now and I've got some clients waiting for me, so I'd better go. Here's some free legal advice, and I'd urge you to take it: forget about this. If you raise a stink, the most you'll do is call attention to it and that could wind up lending it some credibility. Faranino's a jerk, Bellum's a jerk, and everybody knows it. So let 'em be jerks. You're not. Leave it alone."

"But—"

"You'll regret it if you don't."

"Okay. Okay. You're right. Thanks, Skip."

In the end, Skip's advice had proven to be correct, although Mike had learned it the hard way. It was not that Mike had said anything; Yobatu Scuba had.

Without consulting with him, Yobatu had issued a statement in the form of a press release, condemning the implications of the *Aquasplorer.com* article and reiterating their support of, and confidence in, Mike and his team.

It was awful. The release had sounded to Mike like one of those presidential statements of support for a wayward cabinet member—the ones that always seem to come out about forty-eight hours before the guy tenders his resignation.

And once the controversy had become the subject of an official Yobatu Scuba news release, legitimizing it, then even the more solid magazines in the diving world began covering it. *Skin Diver*, *Sport Diver*, and *Scuba Diving* all carried pieces both in the news sections at the front of their books and on their online websites. Mike even got a call from *Diver*, in Great Britain.

Back home in north Florida, where almost all of Mike's friendships and acquaintances seemed to revolve around cave diving, everybody knew about the stories, and everybody reacted. Some people avoided him like a leper, apparently concerned that they might be deemed guilty by association. Others, like his former students and like Lamar and the people at Dive-Rite, went out of their way to show their support for him. And while publicly Mike was thankful for this, privately it made him feel even worse, because there was no quarter in which he could feel normal any longer. Even the Yobatu execs were hesitant to take his calls. The questions, the allegations, were always there—largely unspoken, but there—and they intruded on everything he did and made preparation for the expedition all the more difficult.

There had briefly been one bright spot in the whole thing, and that had been Bridget. Once Bellum's innuendoes had reached the popular magazines, just about all of them sent e-mails off to Bridget, and she responded the same way to all of them, pointing out that Mike was the world record holder; that she had full confidence in his ability to make the dive.

Mike, who had not been in contact with Bridget since that evening at the Crab House—she was not returning his TDD calls, and a combination of pride and concern about causing a scene had kept him from trying to visit her at home or at the hospital—had initially been buoyed when he learned of Bridget's responses. But when she finally did reply to one of his e-mails, the substance had been far less than what he'd hoped for.

"Listen," she'd written. "I won't help a rat like Faranino torpedo you, but don't count on my help for the dive either. I'll stand by you for the PR value, but nothing's changed. Privately, I'm not certain that Bellum was all that far off base."

His cellphone rang and he answered it on the second chirp.

"Hi, Mike," Becky's voice sounded amazingly clear over the digital connection. "You're not still making your presentation, are you?"

"No. Just finished."

"Whew. Good. I never can figure the time in Cozumel. You know, they have that screwy Daylight Savings thing that's out of kilter with everybody else. Sometimes they're on Chicago time, sometimes they're on New York."

"Well, it's . . ." Mike looked around. "Dark."

Becky laughed, an odd and haunting female variant of her father's hearty laugh.

"So, what's up?" Mike asked.

Becky hesitated. Then she said, "Bridget called me."

Mike didn't say anything at first. Bridget and Becky were on the phone regularly; Bridget was sort of an unofficial big sister to the young woman. Even before Pete's death, Bridget had given Becky a TDD unit, so the two could converse over phonelines. There wasn't anything unusual about Bridget calling Becky—unless the conversation had concerned him.

"Yeah?" Mike finally managed.

"She told me, uh, about the two of you," Becky said. "How . . . I guess you could say she said you guys had a blow-up."

"A couple of them, if you count e-mail," Mike agreed. "How'd she sound?"

"Okay, I guess," Becky told him. "I don't know. I always feel learning-disabled, trying to keep up with Bridget on the TDD."

"I know what you mean."

"Mike . . . ," Becky started. Then she stopped again.

"Yeah?"

"Bridget asked me . . ." She stopped once more.

"Asked you what?"

"She asked me," Becky finally said, "to try to talk you out of doing the dive."

"I see," Mike fumed silently. "So—is that why you called?"

"No!"

"Well . . . since you brought it up, how do you feel about it? Do you want me to do it?"

"Do you want to do it?"

"I asked you first," Mike reminded her.

There was a long silence, with just the wind, the palms and the murmur from the bar. Mike almost thought the call had been dropped. Then Becky's voice came back over the air.

"Okay," she finally told him. "Yes, Mike. Yes, I do. If you have any doubts, any doubts whatsoever about whether you should make it and whether it could . . ."

She hesitated again.

"Yeah, I know," Mike said.

"Good," Becky sighed, relieved. "If you have doubts, then I want you to stay home. But if you think this is do-able, I want to see *you* do it, not somebody else, and especially not Bellum. It's what my dad wanted for the two of you. It's what he died trying to do. He didn't want to just dive the *cenote* for himself, Mike. He wanted it for the team."

"Me too."

"Well, then there you are," Becky said. "You're what's left of the team. It's what Dad would want. So it's what I want. I want you to go for it."

"And I'm going to," Mike told her. "Did you tell Bridget this?"

"Yeah . . ."

"How'd she take it?"

"Well . . ." Becky's voice sounded perilously near tears. "You can't really slam the phone in somebody's ear on a TDD, but she gave it a darn good try."

"I'm sorry," Mike said sincerely. "I know you two are close; I didn't mean to be the source of friction."

"We'll get over it," Becky assured him. "It'll just take some time. It's a woman thing, Mike; we take longer to heal."

"Amen to that . . ."

"Listen," she told him. "Do you want me to put together some pro-expedition releases for you—progress reports, that sort of stuff? You know, so you can show how you're proceeding, try to make this just a bump in the road?"

"Sure. I'll send you some information," Mike said. Then he thought of Pete's daughter, all alone out there in California, and he added, "This will all come out okay, Becky. Nobody's going to die, and we'll all be friends again."

"I hope so," Becky told him uncertainly.

Mike was putting away his phone when he caught, out of the corner of his eye, someone moving his way. It was the guy in the red Hawaiian shirt that he'd seen standing at the back of the group.

"Awesome presentation," the guy said, moving closer. He looked to Mike to be in his late twenties.

"Thanks," Mike said shaking his hand. He looked at the guy's shirt pocket—the conference attendees all had name badges that they'd been issued on arrival, although some didn't wear them, scuba divers tending to be an independent lot. Then he looked at his visitor's wrist. Most dive-shop owners had big, complicated, pressure-resistant dive watches with rotating bezels. Some of the more successful ones had Rolexes. Others had the newer slim-line dive computers that doubled as watches. But this guy was wearing a Timex. It was the Expedition model—digital, with a nylon strap—but a Timex nonetheless.

"I'm not with the conference," the guy said, reading the look. "Is that cool? I mean, if you need to talk with some of these folks, that's fine by me. I'll just hang until you're done."

"Naw, that's all right," Mike told him, nodding at the crowd of retreating backs. "Nobody seems to be flooding me with questions. I'm not much competition for the free booze."

"Hey—who is?" Mike's visitor grinned. "Name's Elvis, Mr. Bryant. Elvis Hastings."

"It's Mike," Mike replied, shaking his hand again. He looked at the young man to see if he was putting him on. "Your name's really Elvis?"

"Way," Elvis grinned. "My mom's Hawaiian. The story is, when I was born, my dad asked her what she wanted to name me, and she said, 'Kameahameaha.' And my dad says, like, 'No way! The name's bigger than he is!' So my mom goes, 'C'mon, dude. I wanted to name him after the king.' And my dad says, 'Done deal. We'll call him Elvis.' And wouldn't you know it? She called his bluff. End of story."

"And a good one," Mike laughed. "Deserves a beer. Can I get you one?"

"Make it a Coke and you're on," Elvis grinned.

"Coming right up."

A few minutes later, Mike sidled back through the crowd with two of the familiar red-and-white striped cans, beaded with moisture.

"I forgot to ask," he said. "Did you want a glass and ice?"

"No, thanks," Elvis replied, shaking his head. "It's better this way. I mean, a newer resort like this, the water's probably cool. Most of them have their own purification systems. But down here in the skinny latitudes, I usually try not to drink water or use ice unless the water's out of a bottle or I filtered it myself."

"Wise man," Mike said. "You spend a lot of time in the tropics?"

"Lately," Elvis nodded as they walked away from the noise of the crowd, through the access tunnel to the beach. They sat together on the seawall, legs over the edge, small waves breaking against the concrete a few feet below. "I've spent the last half a year or so on the mainland, over in the Yucatan."

"Really?" Mike asked. "You a diver?"

"No," Elvis answered. "I mean, yes, actually. I do dive—the resort floated me some lessons on Fiji a few years back, when I was staying there, doing a surf clinic. But that's not what brought me down here."

"Well, there's not much surf in the *cenotes*," Mike observed, raising his eyebrows.

"Indeed," Elvis agreed. "Actually, I'm here doing missions work."

"Missions?" Mike asked. "You're a missionary?"

"Guilty."

Mike took in the Hawaiian shirt, the beard, and the baggy khaki pants one more time.

"You don't look like a missionary," he observed.

"Yeah. I get a lot of that."

"You don't even *sound* like a missionary."

"That too."

"So what brings you over to Cozumel? You here for R and R?"

"Not really," Elvis shook his head. "I came to see you."

"Me?" Mike scowled for a moment. "You're here to what—convert me?"

"If you want," Elvis shrugged, grinning. "I'm the local distributor. But actually, I'm here because I was reading your website—"

"You were reading my website?"

"Yeah."

"But you're not a cave diver—"

"Me? Nah. Never done it."

"And you don't even dive regularly."

"No. I mean, diving's cool, but I haven't done much of it lately."

"So what led you to my website?"

"Well," Elvis started. He glanced around, then looked at his watch. "Listen, Mike . . . have you had dinner yet?"

Twenty minutes later they were ordering shrimp-stuffed sea bass at Santiago's, a grill open to the street in downtown San Miguel, and just a five-minute ride away from Costa Club in the Mitsubishi Montero that Elvis had ferried from the mainland. On the ride over they'd talked about Elvis's surfing career and Mike's cave-diving back in Florida, as Elvis dodged the little four-wheel-drive vehicle between tourists on motor scooters, street vendors on pedal-carts, and the ubiquitous white taxicabs. They'd passed the big Mexican flag on the waterfront and the solid stream of laughter and Cuban cigar smoke coming out of Carlos and Charlie's. One of the policemen on the main drag had recognized Elvis's vehicle and raised a hand in greeting as they'd passed. Mike was beginning to really like the outlandish missionary, despite the fact that he still hadn't a clue as to why the young man had crossed the strait to see him.

They'd smelled the restaurant almost as soon as they'd seen it—a rich aroma of garlic and grilled beef and seafood that wafted out into the busy street—and Elvis had parked in the next block, easily threading the SUV into a nook between clusters of motor scooters.

"Okay," Mike said, after Santiago himself had shown them a platter of the evening's grilled specialties and carried the menus away. He stirred his lemonade with his straw—unlike his colleagues back at the conference, he was bearing in mind that he'd be diving in the morning—and sat back in the rattan-backed chair. "So you checked my website . . ."

"Right," Elvis said. "I saw you were coming here to talk, and hey, even on the car ferry, San Miguel is only an hour and a half from Playa del Carmen, so I took the chance of coming."

"Why?"

"I think I can help you," Elvis said.

"How so?"

"Well, to start with, I can offer you a base of operations in Quintana Roo," Elvis explained, trying the lemonade that Santiago's barkeeper made with liquid cane sugar and purified water. "I keep an office here, at Puerto Morelos, with a local Bible student to answer phones, do filing, and so forth. If you need it for a mail drop, a place to receive faxes, check e-mail, crunch spreadsheets, that sort of thing, you're welcome to it."

"I appreciate that," Mike said. "But to tell you the truth, Jorge Yanéz, here in San Miguel, usually does the same thing for me when I'm in-country. And Jorge's a local cave diver—an instructor, in fact, so he'd probably be more knowledgeable than a Bible student about what's important to the expedition—what needs to get radioed on to me in the field, that sort of thing."

"True enough," Elvis agreed. "And if you don't need the office, that's cool. It's there, though, if you do. But I do have one other thing that I think you might find useful."

"What's that?" Mike asked, sipping his own Coke.

"A Sikorsky heavy-lift helicopter," Elvis said matter-of-factly. "I can get every bit of your equipment from Cancún to the edge of your *cenote* in a single two-hour trip."

"You have a helicopter?" Mike asked, sitting up as he said it.

"Well, *I* don't, per se" Elvis told him. "But Faith's Frontier—that's the missions organization I'm with. We're putting in a small medical clinic, deep inland, for people on the Yucatan Peninsula who live too far away from the coastal towns to get to existing medical facilities. We're sending in the building materials, the clinic equipment, medicines, everything, by containerized shipment—you know, the big metal containers, about the size of a semi, that they use to transship materials?"

Mike nodded. He'd seen them quite a bit around Miami; shipping containers that could be loaded on a truck or a train car, either one. And he'd seen pictures of the big Sikorsky helicopters that could pick up one of those big steel containers fully loaded, winch it into a bridge-like span under its fuselage, and transport it just about anywhere that there was a level spot the size of the aircraft's footprint.

"We've chartered to send in three containers of supplies," Elvis explained. The first one—building materials—has already gone in. The next one is going in in a couple of months with the clinic equipment, solar power panels and storage batteries, that sort of stuff. But the last one, with the clinic's actual supplies? That's coming up short. We've got space available."

Mike cocked his head.

"How much are you asking?"

"Nothing," Elvis told him. "We're flying anyhow. Might as well fly with a full load. The charter company doesn't charge anything extra for it. In fact, they prefer it—it balances the load out better, makes everything more stable."

"So why not fill it up with other stuff the people there can use?" Mike opened his hands. "You know—canned goods, sneakers, rain ponchos. Seems to me you could find some use other than giving the space away."

Elvis nodded.

"Yeah," he said. "We could probably make a whole bunch of friends by just filling the excess space up with Ray-Bans and Coca-Cola. At least we would among some of the young people. But the elders probably wouldn't think that was very cool. These are remote, tribal people, bro, and they live where they do because they prefer it that way. So our mission isn't to make little Americans out of them. It's to give them something truly necessary that they lack."

"And preach a little hellfire and brimstone along the way?" Mike asked, eyebrows arched.

"And give them the truth," Elvis replied simply. "That's what Jesus called it. It's there in the book of John: 'Then you will know the truth and the truth will set you free.' So yeah, we'll give them the truth. Because it does set them free and freedom is a very cool thing. And because that's something necessary that they lack, as well."

"Okay," Mike said, scowling slightly and making it clear that he wasn't at all sure that it was okay. "So let's say you've got this space, and you don't want to fill it up with trinkets and trash and turn the local kids into Brittany Spears and the Backstreet Boys. I guess I can see that. But why us? Why our expedition?"

Elvis leaned forward, both hands on the table.

"Because you have something we need," he said.

"And what's that?"

Elvis raised an eyebrow—he was one of those people who could, one brow at a time.

"Your doctor," he told Mike, nodding.

13

Our doctor."

Mike said it that way: a statement, not a question.

"That's right."

"But," Mike scrunched his eyebrows, not understanding, "if your outfit is big enough to hire a helicopter and build a clinic, surely you have your own doctors."

"Oh, we do," Elvis nodded, agreeing. "In fact, we'll have a staff—two doctors and three nurses for the first month, and then a permanent staff, one doctor and one nurse practitioner, a married missionary couple, handling the facility once we've got it established."

"Sounds as if you have things covered, then," Mike said. "Why do you want ours?"

"Because she's the one that the Cháakadon will trust," Elvis said.

"The Cháakadon?"

"Right," Elvis told him. "Maybe I'd better back up."

The waiter arrived with Santiago in tow, the restaurant owner standing somberly in the background as the dishes were presented and the lemonades refilled. Only after both Elvis and Mike had sampled their seabass and voiced their approval did the proprietor smile and return to his post near the entrance.

"The Cháakadon are a group of Mayaans who live in the interior of the Yucatan Peninsula, near its base, down by Guatemala," Elvis explained as he spooned salsa onto his fish. "They take their name from Cháak, the Mayan rain-god."

"I've heard of Cháak," Mike said. "He's depicted on some of the Mayan ruins as having a long, curled nose—"

"Like an elephant's trunk," Elvis agreed. "Only the Mayaans never saw elephants in antiquity, so that raises all kinds of cross-culture contact theories."

"But that's the key, right?" Mike asked. "Antiquity, I mean. All the Mayaans I know now are pretty much assimilated. It's not as if any of them are still building temples, planting by the stars, and making human sacrifices, that sort of thing."

"That's true," Elvis agreed. "At least, it is to a point. The classic Mayaans, the ones who built the temple cities like Chichen Itza and Tulum, were all long gone by the time the Spanish made contact here—most of the temple centers were already falling into ruin. But all of the ancient Mayaans were pantheists, like the ancient Greeks. They believed there was one god that caused the sun to shine, another that brought rain, another that made the corn grow, and so forth. They had a hundred and fifty different gods in all, and a lot of their culture was wrapped up in doing things that they thought would keep all these dudes happy, without making any of them jealous. Cháak, for instance—they wanted him to make it rain enough that the corn would grow, but not so much that he'd send a hurricane.

"Now, if you look around the Mayan region today, you'll find beliefs that are a mixture of the old and beliefs from other cultures, other times. It's the same all over the Caribbean basin, really. Voodoo, in Haiti, is probably the most well-known example. It's this mixture of native beliefs and imported African cultures, with spirits worshiped in ceremonies incorporating elements of the early Spanish Catholic mass. In the Bahamas, there's a folk religion called *obiah* that's similar to Voodoo; it has spells and charms and curses.

"And here in Mayan country, many people still believe in at least some of the old ways. These dudes may scope out as modern in every respect; they might wear Foster Grants and Levis, and they might watch *Baywatch* in Spanish on their color TVs and drive Toyota pickups. But they'll avoid certain areas because they're supposed to be haunted by evil spirits or creatures. Or sometimes outside forces drive an interest in some aspect of the old religion. Take Ixtab, the Mayan god of suicide. He was a relatively minor god, sort of a grommet who was tossed in just to cover all the bases, but there are mainstream people, mainly young people, who are into all the dark, underworld sort of thing—"

"Goths," Mike commented.

"Exactly," Elvis agreed. "A suicide-god just has a natural appeal to people who are into the whole vampire-ritual-Gothic thing. And that gets reflected back into the subculture, and maybe, for some folks, Ixtab gets revived as a god and elevated to a position of higher importance."

"So you're saying there's . . . what—suicide cults around the Mayan region?" Mike asked.

"Not at all," Elvis said. "But what I am saying is that, even in a relatively upbeat and modern place like right here, on Cozumel, the old ways are not completely dead. Not by a long shot. Go to some of the more remote beaches on the south end of the island around the time of the full moon, and you'll find conch shells and driftwood arranged in circles in the sand—"

"I've seen them," Mike said.

"They're altars," Elvis told him. "Sacrificial altars. True, they may not be slaying calves and goats and virgins out there, but they'll leave a plug of tobacco or a bit of salt or sugar cane or whiskey poured on a conch shell and hope that somebody in the spirit world will sit up and take notice and make life just a little bit easier for them."

Mike shrugged. "Giving up what little you have? Hoping against hope that if you let it go you'll get more?" He snorted. "That sounds like most religions in the world to me."

Elvis nodded. "Me too," he agreed.

Mike looked up, surprised. He'd expected at least a token argument on that from somebody in the missionary business. "So what are you saying?" Mike asked.

"The Cháakadon are not typical Mayaans," Elvis explained. "They retreated into the interior of the Yucatan back about the time of the Spanish conquest, and they stayed there."

"Sounds like a wise move," Mike commented.

"Tell me about it," Elvis agreed. "The Spanish didn't come here to exchange diplomatic letters with the locals. Their name for themselves said it all—they were Conquistadors—conquerors. If it was worth money and they could fit it in the hold of a galleon, they were here to take it and haul it back to Madrid.

"But that was like, what—five centuries back, dig? Yet the Cháakadon have stayed in the jungle. At first it was to stay away from the Spanish. Later it was because they weren't sure that the ones who followed were any better. And after a while, well, I think they just stayed in the jungle because they'd always been in the jungle. Two or three hundred years on, it became all that they knew, and they were skeptical, even fearful, of anything that came from beyond it."

"How did they live?" Mike asked.

"The way their Mayan ancestors lived for centuries before them," Elvis said. "They planted corn, hunted wild boar and iguana, grew chili peppers and spices. They acquired goats and chickens from the other Mayan groups, and they integrated these into their agriculture. The women wore simple cotton shifts, and the men worked in loincloths and wore ponchos and simple pants for cool weather and formal occasions. And they often wore elaborate tattoos, which was a throwback, really, to Olmec culture. We're talking frozen in time, here."

"And they're still like that?" Mike asked.

"Yes and no," Elvis answered. "They lived pretty much undisturbed for the better part of four centuries, growing and foraging what they needed in the jungle, and trading very rarely with other Mayan groups—the assimilated Mayans—for what they couldn't grow or fabricate themselves. Then, early in the twentieth century, gemstone prospectors working the Yucatan reported contact with people who dressed oddly and spoke a language similar to that of some other Mayan-descended groups, yet different, with none of the Spanish influence that had crept into most Mayan-language dialects. That got the interest of the government, and they verified that there was an isolated, tribal group of Mayan descendents living in the interior of the Yucatan. But you know how turbulent Mexico's history was throughout the first part of the twentieth century, right? I mean, it kind of started with Pancho Villa and devolved from there. So the dudes in Mexico City sort of figured that they had their hands full and the Cháakadon got overlooked."

"Lost in the system?" Mike asked.

"I guess you could say so," Elvis agreed. "But the record of contact was there; they were known now. And, back in the late 1950s, a missionary named Alfred Bellamy made contact with the Cháakadon and did something no one had ever done with them before. I mean, the standard means of ministering to a small, highly localized tribal group of people such as this had always been to learn enough of their language to witness to them and then to get them fluent in a major language—which would be Spanish in Mexico, right? And then you let them read the Bible in that language. But Bellamy didn't do it that way. He went the extra mile and spent the time with the Cháakadon to begin learning their language."

"How many people are we talking about here?" Mike asked.

"When Bellamy contacted them? About six hundred."

"Wow," Mike sat back. "That seems like a lot to go through, learning an entirely different language just to reach six hundred people. I mean, he could go to Mexico City and reach six million of them."

"I know what you mean," Elvis nodded. "But it's biblical, you know? Jesus told the story in the Bible—in Matthew and Luke both—of the dude who has a hundred sheep and walks away from ninety-nine of them so he can seek out the one that is lost. And Bellamy did more than learn their language."

"How's that?"

"He began translating the Bible for them."

Mike stopped a forkful of stuffed seabass halfway to his mouth. "Translating? The whole Bible?"

"That was the plan—Genesis through Revelation. Actually, he started with Matthew and did the New Testament first. But from what we understand, he was all the way through the Pentateuch—"

"The what?"

"The first five books of the Bible. The ones written by Moses—Genesis through Deuteronomy. Bellamy got at least that far in his Old Testament translation, as well."

Mike nodded, wide-eyed.

"And he did all this," he asked, "into a language only spoken by six hundred people?"

"You got it."

Mike popped the grilled fish into his mouth, chewed, and thought.

"That's preposterous," he finally decided.

Elvis smiled.

"Is it?"

Mike just looked at him.

"Let's say that the Space Station springs a leak or something," Elvis said. "There's like three dudes on board. And they only have enough air left for a week. But you've got a Space Shuttle that can be on the pad and ready to go in forty-eight hours. What do you do?"

"Launch the Shuttle," Mike answered.

"Okay. Now let's say that the Shuttle has this vital, multi-billion-dollar telecommunications satellite on board. It'll have to be jettisoned before you can rescue the Station crew. And no," Elvis smiled, "you don't have time to orbit the satellite and rescue the crew both. It's got to be one or the other. What do you do?"

"Rescue the crew," Mike said.

"Really?" Elvis grinned. "You know, those telecommunications satellites do more than carry phone calls. Doctors can use 'em to show other doctors in remote locations how to do special surgeries. They can be used to do currency transfers that can keep national economies from collapsing, and that can prevent famines and keep millions of people from starving."

"But the Station crew would die without the help," Mike said. "And . . ."

He stopped talking, as if something was dawning on him.

"And to a Christian," Elvis finished for him, "a tribal people, living without God's Word, because it's not available in their tongue, is a million times more tragic than someone dying."

Mike set his fork on the edge of his plate.

"Now wait," he said, brow wrinkled. "What can possibly be worse than dying?"

"'What shall it profit a man if he gain the whole world and lose his soul?'" Elvis asked in return. "We're talking eternity here, bro. Die once—bummer. Die twice—that's a disaster."

Mike picked up his fork again. He wasn't certain he'd followed what Elvis had just said.

"Okay," he said. "Back to the subject. So this guy decides to spend his life translating the Bible into this obsolete language—"

"Not obsolete. For six hundred people, it's their primary tongue."

"Whatever. What does this have to do with our expedition?"

"Well, Bellamy died."

"They killed him?"

"No. No. Nothing like that. Natural causes."

"So somebody else took up his work, right?"

"Not."

Mike helped himself to a tortilla from the basket on the table and offered one to Elvis.

"Bellamy's work was lost," Elvis explained, accepting the basket. "The mission organization was fairly new at the time. Nobody had thought to register Bellamy's work and his research materials in the organization's name. So, when he died, under Mexican law, it had to go to his next of kin."

"Which was?"

"Again, we're not sure. Remember, we're talking decades ago. No computer databases. Just paper records. And paper has a way of getting damaged, getting lost."

"Man," Mike shook his head. "Talk about your exercises in futility. So the translation disappeared?"

"From what I could gather, Faith's Frontier—that's the missions organization—didn't really go looking for the translations for several years. They didn't have the staffing or the funding back then to replace Alfred Bellamy. By the time they did, it was a dead end."

"So what happened?" Mike looked down and was surprised to see that every bit of Santiago's extraordinary cooking was gone. He couldn't even remember finishing it.

"Faith's Frontier sent two more missionaries in. Neither one was even able to make contact. Then, somebody got the bright idea of using LANDSAT photography—"

"The same thing we used to find the *cenotes* on our cave-diving project—"

"Yeah. I read that on your site. Anyhow, we used it to find cleared land. The Cháakadon still slash-and-burn to clear acreage for agriculture, same as the ancient Mayans. We found a couple of likely spots, asked for higher-resolution scans, and we pinpointed a couple of sites with thatched roofs. Traditional Mayan construction."

"So you sent another missionary team there to see them?"

"Not really. From all we'd heard about the Cháakadon, if somebody went straight to one of their villages, they might freak and bolt. So we just sent a single missionary into their territory."

"You?"

"Bingo," Elvis smiled.

"And you made contact."

"I did."

"And?"

"It was square one, you know?" The waiter took the dishes away and Elvis folded his hands atop the table. "I mean, Faith's Frontier's linguistics school put me through a two-month deep dive through the Mayan language, but these folks don't really speak Mayan. Or rather they do, but it's a much more antique form of Mayan than what has survived to the present day. It's like, Virginia or Kentucky accents, you know? Linguists believe that those accents actually closely echo the way British English was spoken by residents of certain English districts back when those regions were originally founded. Only in this case, the difference is a lot more extreme—like Middle English compared to Modern English."

"But you've learned it?"

"I'm beginning to. You've been by the Blue Bubble Dive Shop here in San Miguel? On the front of the shop, they have a sign, 'Broken English spoken perfectly.' Well, that's where I am, bro. I've become a perfect speaker of broken Cháakadon Mayan."

"So they're accepting you."

"As much as they are going to accept an outsider at this point."

"But why are they so shy?" Mike asked. "I mean, this missionary guy—"

"Bellamy."

"Right," Mike nodded. "Bellamy made contact. Sounds as if he was getting along with them. So why couldn't you just pick up with them where he left off?"

"Good question," Elvis said. "First of all, Bellamy died nearly twenty years ago, so there's a whole generation of Cháakadon that never had that initial contact."

"But there's an older generation that did," Mike pointed out.

"Absolutely," Elvis agreed. "Then again, something happened about ten years back."

"What?"

"I'm still not sure," Elvis confessed. "Outsiders—somebody, or something—came in and took something."

"Took what?"

"Something called the 'Children of Days.'"

"Which are?"

"Your guess is as good as mine," Elvis confessed. "You see, part of the Faith's Frontier covenant is that, while we don't intentionally put up any roadblocks that would prevent tribal people from learning a second language, like Spanish or English, the onus is on us to learn *their* language. Village headsmen often aren't crazy about language schools for the simple reason that, if we come in and teach the kids national languages—and the kids will learn faster than anybody else—before you know it, you have a crop of young people who are geared to leave the village and make a go of it in the outside world, working in one of the resort towns or maybe even moving out of the country. Something like that—a whole generation packing up and leaving—can eviscerate a village and kill off a culture, and while these guys might be primitive, they aren't stupid. They know the risks of outside contact.

"So what I've been doing with the Cháakadon is learning their language, rather than teaching them mine. I mean, some of the younger men who hang with me are picking up English, but that's all they're doing—picking it up. I'm not formally teaching it to them. And obviously, they don't have any structured means of teaching me Cháakadon Mayan, so the going is, as you'd might expect, kind of slow. Bottom line—I don't have enough of the language yet to understand exactly what the 'Children of Days' are. I know they aren't people; I asked if they meant that some of their children had been kidnapped, and they fell all over themselves assuring me that wasn't the case, even though some of the elders claimed that what had happened had been far worse."

"What could be worse?"

"You've got me. I haven't a clue."

"You said that something or somebody came in?" Mike asked.

"Yeah," Elvis said. "That's a little nebulous, isn't it? Some of the people just say it was a thief. But most say it was . . . well, a spirit."

"A spirit."

"Actually," Elvis said sheepishly, "the literal translation would be 'a god.'"

Mike looked at the young missionary.

"So whatever this is that was stolen, God took it?"

Elvis shook his head.

"Not God," he said. "A god. One of the Mayan deities. The sun-god, Kunich Ahua."

"Kunich . . ."

". . . Ahua," Elvis nodded.

"So you think there's a Mayan god running around causing trouble in the Yucatan?"

Elvis shook his head.

"Of course not," he said. "But these folks are spooked."

"What's he do? Appear in dreams?"

"Darn near," Elvis told him. "Nobody ever sees him, but they hear him."

"Like out loud?"

"Exactly."

Mike shrugged.

"So he's speaking their language," he said.

"Right. Speaks it perfectly."

"But they're the only people in the whole world who speak this language?"

"As far as anybody knows."

"Well then," Mike shrugged. "He's one of them."

"You'd think so wouldn't you?" Elvis said. "But this is a very small village, just over three hundred people altogether. And they swear it's not the voice of anybody there. Besides, there's been a couple of times when the whole village was there, everybody accounted for, and they've heard his voice coming out of the jungle."

"What's he telling them?"

"Different things at different times. At first, he was telling them not to abandon their old ways. Then he called out some of the young men, asked them to leave the village. There's one younger guy in the village—Kukulcán? His grandfather told me—showed me, really—it was more pantomime than conversation . . . Anyhow, he thinks these guys are ending up in forced labor, processing cocoa paste. And lately, this Kunich Ahua has been telling the villagers to steer clear of outsiders—people like me."

"Sounds as if some drug runner wants an untraceable source of labor."

"Maybe. But I think there's more. I just don't know what it is yet."

The waiter brought two slices of yellow key lime pie, poured two coffees, and left a small, steaming pitcher of milk on the table.

Elvis raised both eyebrows this time.

"Dig in, bro," he said. "Won't be the same unless you eat it while the pie's still cool and the coffee's hot."

Mike followed his host's suggestion, and the pie was amazing—tart but sweet, with tiny bits of candied lime peel grated into the meringue on top. The two men ate their dessert without speaking, and then Elvis added a spoon of cane sugar and a healthy dollop of warm milk to both coffees as the dishes were cleared away.

Mike tried a sip.

"It's good," he said.

"Yeah," Elvis agreed. "*Café con leché* is really supposed to be a breakfast thing, but it's so good after dinner that I'm willing to buck tradition."

Mike took another sip and set his cup down.

"Okay," he said. "It sounds as if you're in a fascinating—and mysterious—line of work. But you haven't told me yet."

"Told you?"

"Why you need our doctor."

Elvis rolled his eyes and grinned.

"Sorry, man," he laughed. "Too many years of surf stories, you know? Where somebody asks you how the break is, and you end up telling them why hula dancers wear grass skirts. But to answer your question, we don't really need your doctor. But she'd sure speed things up."

"Because?"

"The Cháakadon will trust her."

"You said that before," Mike said. "What makes you think that?"

"There was a young woman in the village that was scalded when a cooking pot collapsed," Elvis explained. "The injuries were beyond what the shaman could handle, so two of the men took her to K'uxulch'en."

"Where's that?"

"Your *cenote*. The one you call Cenote X. That's its real name: its Mayan name. It means, 'The Well of Sorrows.'"

Mike nodded slowly, pondering this.

"And when they got there, the men said that the girl was ministered to by—man, it took them two hours to get this one across to me—a green-eyed woman who spoke with her hands."

"Forest," Mike muttered.

"How's that?"

"The girl Bridget treated. That's what we called her," Mike told him. "How is she?"

"Her Mayan name is Ixnitke'," Elvis said. "It means 'lady Plumeria flower.' And she's fine. She's married now to the fellow that I mentioned, my friend Kukulcán."

Mike grinned, despite himself.

"The Cháakadon are still in awe of that 'hand-talking doctor woman,' Mike. They realize that Ixnitke' wouldn't have survived without her help. So I did some research and found that your expedition had been at the *cenote* that year, and it could only have been Dr. Marceau who helped the girl. She did what I've been trying to do for months on end, Mike. She bridged the gap. They trust her. Completely."

Mike was silent for a moment.

"If that's so," he finally said. "I'm not sure Bridget would be willing to abuse that trust. I mean, if these people have really lived isolated for centuries, like you said . . ."

Elvis nodded.

". . . then I'm not certain Bridget would want to use her influence to intrude on them. Modernize them."

Elvis nodded again.

"I'm with you," he said earnestly. "And that's why I'm learning Cháakadon Mayaan, rather than teaching these folks English or Spanish. I'm there to witness to them where they are, rather than bringing them to where I am."

Mike was silent for a moment.

"It sounds as if they already have a faith," he finally said. "Why force yours on them?"

"I'm not," Elvis said. "I'm not here to force, and I'm not here to coerce. God doesn't want it that way. The Bible's clear on that. A decision for Christ should be one made of a person's own free will, or it's not really a decision at all."

"But what if they're happy where they are?"

"Then they'll stay where they are, won't they?"

Mike was silent again.

"You know," he finally said. "The cool thing about Forest showing up when she did . . . It was just nice to know that there were people in the world that haven't been corrupted by TV and politics and—and religion. By all of what we've become."

"I'm not down here to put them in bras and briefs, bro," Elvis replied quietly. "I'm here to bring them the Truth."

"As you see it."

"As God gave it to us."

Mike lifted his coffee cup, set it back down again.

"It's meddling," he said.

"Your doctor meddled," Elvis countered. "She saved a life. I'm doing nothing more than that."

Mike glanced up at the missionary. He wasn't quite certain that he understood what the young man had just said. But on some plane, it made sense to him. And he liked Elvis. They may have only met a couple of hours ago, but he could sense that the missionary was real, not a deceptive bone in his body.

"Can I level with you?" Mike asked.

"Absolutely."

"I don't know why, but I think what you're doing is good."

"I know why," Elvis smiled. "But go on."

"And I really want to help you," Mike continued, looking down at the table, puzzled by the missionary's last statement. "But I've got to be honest. Things between Bridget—Dr. Marceau—and me are . . . well, *strained* right now. To be perfectly frank, I think it would take a miracle just to get her to come along when I make my next attempt on the *cenote*."

He looked up and was perplexed. There sat Elvis, grinning over his coffee cup.

"Dude!" the missionary exclaimed, "miracles are my boss's specialty!"

14
TULUM,
QUINTANA ROO, MEXICO—
AUGUST, 2003

Shirt off, feet on his desk, Viktor Bellum set his condensation-beaded Dos Equis bottle on the floor next to his chair and gazed wordlessly at his visitor.

Hector Gabrillo stood, hat in hand, on the other side of the desk. Bellum had offered him neither a seat nor a drink. The *federale* officer looked like a kid in the principal's office.

"I'm sorry, *Picuda,* but that's what was in the report," Gabrillo said, breaking the silence. "This Bryant, he has filed all the papers to bring his team in next month. They will be flying in the equipment by the helicopter from Cancún. The regional office? They notify me because the *cenote,* she is in my district."

Bellum picked up the beer, turned it in his hands, set it down again without drinking.

"Okay, help me to understand this," Bellum told the policeman in a flat voice. "I'm hearing from my contacts in Florida that Mike Bryant has been run ragged. His sponsors are treating him like a leper. His team was falling apart—even what's-her-name, the deaf chick, was pulling out. And now you tell me that he's coming in a month early? How can that be?"

"I don't know. Maybe . . . maybe he's *desperado, Picuda,*" Gabrillo stammered. "You know. Like he's afraid the money's going to stop coming, so he starts early, while he still has some."

Bellum shook his head.

"No," he said evenly. "That doesn't make sense. The last time he and Wiley went in, they took trucks. And this time, you say they've chartered a chopper? That doesn't sound like a guy who's running out of money to me. If anything, he's found some new support."

"Maybe," Gabrillo agreed.

The *federale* jumped as the beer bottle whistled across the room and shattered against the wall behind him.

"So what are you doing about it, *mi amigo*?" Bellum growled. "Need I remind you that I keep you in *cervesas* and *señoritas* to prevent problems like this?"

Gabrillo shrugged.

"I don't know," he said. "I mean, what do you expect me to do, *Picuda*? Maybe, after he does this thing, this dive, I could plant a little *coca* paste in his equipment, and arrest him. But not now. I mean, why would a gringo smuggle the drugs *into* Mexico?"

"Come on, man, think," Bellum ordered. "You're the law around here. How do you keep him out?"

Gabrillo moved his foot to avoid the puddle creeping toward his shoes. The beer bottle had been half-full.

"Why do you care if this *gringo* dives in this *cenote*, *Picuda*? The Yucatan, she is full of *cenotes*."

"Not like this one," Bellum muttered. He looked up. "And why I care is none of your concern. I'm paying you to *do*, Capitan, not to judge."

Gabrillo looked down at his feet and shuffled sideways. The yeasty puddle of Dos Equis was spreading.

"Think, man," Bellum repeated. "This stinking country loves its paperwork. Can't you find some that needs to be done, or done over?"

Gabrillo shrugged again.

"The papers," he said. "They are not so much since the NAFTA, you know? And this Bryant, he has done this before. No. I checked when you first called me. His papers, they are all in order."

"Then lose some of them, you idiot."

Gabrillo didn't even look up at the insult.

"I don't have them, *Picuda*. This Bryant, he is bringing all of his equipment in through Cancún this time, remember? And Cancún, she is out of my district. There is another *capitan* up there, he handles this."

"Then tell *him* to lose some of their papers," Bellum said, exasperated.

Gabrillo shook his head.

"The Cancún *capitan*, he is new to the area. They just promote him, out of Monterrey. I don't know him. If I ask him to do this thing, maybe he is a straight-shooter? And maybe he arrests me. Or maybe he thinks I try to trap him. So he arrests me to make it look like he is on the high and high—"

"The up and up."

"*Sí*. As you say. Either way, no papers get lost, and I get arrested. It's no good."

"So go up there and steal the papers," Bellum said.

"I could," Gabrillo agreed. "But how would they know they were gone? The papers, they are filed now. Nobody looks at them. What, we are going to steal the papers and then call my brother officer in Cancún and say, 'Hey, *amigo*, how about you check this *gringo*'s papers one more time?' No. I don't think so. It would look very strange."

"Well, come on, Gabrillo," Bellum said, palms up. "There's got to be something."

"I don't know what," the Mexican shrugged. "The *ejido*, the landholders, they have given all of the necessary *permisos*. They are on file. Maybe if there were the rare fish or animals living in the *cenote*, we could go tell the Club Sierra or the Greenpeace or something. Or if there were native people who objected to the *buscada*, the diving in the *cenote*, that would be one thing. But nothing and nobody lives there. Or if Bryant or part of his team were undesirables, maybe we keep them out. But we have nothing on any of them."

Bellum grunted.

"Where'd they get the dough to charter a chopper?"

Gabrillo shrugged.

"I don't know, *Picuda*," he said apologetically. "But I know they don't charter the whole thing."

"What do you mean?"

"How do you say?" Gabrillo asked. "Share. They share it."

"With who?"

"The Frontier of Faith," the policeman said, scowling, trying to remember the bulletin. "Some *missionario*, working with the Indians."

"Him," Bellum said flatly. "Yeah. I know about him."

He looked up at the policeman.

"Okay," he said, disgusted. "You're no use to me. Get out of here."

Bobbing his head, Gabrillo left, relieved.

Bellum shook his head in disgust. Why did he even bother going to Gabrillo for assistance? The man was a career flunky—no clout, no connections, and no brains. He almost felt bad for chewing the guy out.

The whole room stunk of beer now. Bellum got up to get a broom, a dustpan, and a mop. And then, as he opened the door to the closet where he kept the cleaning things, he stopped.

What was it Gabrillo had said?

Suddenly, he realized that there *was* a way to keep Bryant out.

He looked at the calendar. There was a moonless night coming in just two weeks.

That was when he'd do it.

15

AEROMEXICO FLIGHT 612, EN ROUTE TO COZUMEL— SEPTEMBER, 2003

Sir? Something to drink?'

Mike woke with a start to the whining drone of muffled jet engines, the clinking of glass bottles on a stainless-steel cart.

Pretty, Hispanic, uniformed, the AeroMexico flight attendant gazed questioningly at him. Her cart was loaded with full-size fifths of liquor—none of those puny little plastic bottles for an airline whose country had invented *machismo*.

Mike eyed the flat-sided bottle of José Cuervo, and then thought better of it. Cozumel or no, this was no holiday. And even though he wouldn't be diving for several days, he needed to keep a clear head.

"Yo quiero un Coca-Cola, por favor."

It came out in Spanish without his even thinking about it, and the flight attendant smiled, poured him his drink, and gave it to him with the rest of the can. Then she moved her cart, making her way back down the aisle.

Wakulla Springs. That's what he'd been dreaming about. The sidemount passage, such as it was. In the end, he'd had to take off all of his gear—even his fins—and Houdini his way around to get himself turned in the tight, low pipe of a passage. It had taken twenty minutes, he'd gotten stuck twice, and he'd wound up making his exit on the reserve gas, the gas you were supposed to save for emergencies.

A close call, but it had been years ago. Mike wondered why it had come to mind now, shrugged it away, and drank his soft drink.

On the tray table next to him, Bridget had piled her reading: the *Journal of the American Medical Association*, *Mortality and Morbidity*, the *New*

England Journal of Medicine. She was reading *The Lancet*—that was the British one, Mike remembered—and she marked a spot with a yellow highlighter pen as she read. She could study anywhere, a benefit of her handicap. To Bridget, background noise simply did not exist.

Mike studied her profile, framed by the airliner window, backlit by the stark white of cumulous clouds and the silver-blue of the Gulf of Mexico, thirty-five thousand feet below. Had he not just awakened from a dream, he would have suspected that he was dreaming right now.

Bridget.

With him.

On their way back to Mexico.

Would wonders never cease?

Mike had taken to Elvis Hastings more quickly than he ever would have imagined, talking with the affable former surfer with a candor he had never achieved even with old and trusted friends. They'd talked long into the evening in San Miguel, Santiago happily refilling their coffee cups and letting them keep their table, the off-season restaurant traffic being light.

And Mike had unloaded the whole truck—Bridget's objections, the blowup at the Crab House, the phone conversation with Becky. Then Elvis had asked Mike pointblank about his confidence level on the upcoming dive, and Mike had reverted to public relations and damage control, talking about preparations; about the fact that he was the only person in the world who had been as deep as he'd been and returned, unscathed; about the improvements Yobatu Scuba and Lamar had made in the equipment they'd been using this time.

It had been an entirely circumspect reply, and Elvis had gazed at Mike for a long time after he'd given it, saying nothing, until finally Mike had looked down at his coffee cup. And that's when the missionary said, "Listen. I've got a few weeks of home leave coming. Why don't I go back with you? Talk to Bridget?"

He had. It had taken all of forty minutes, the two of them vanishing behind closed doors into Bridget's study at the hospital, Mike unable to hear a word of what was being said, because no words *were* being said, Elvis having proven able to sign quite fluently—part of his training, he'd explained.

And when they'd come out, Elvis had had his arm around Bridget's shoulder, and her eyes had been puffy and red from weeping. Bridget had simply signed to Mike, not looking him in the eyes, *How long should I clear my schedule for? When will we be coming back?*

Stunned, Mike had held his hand up, crooked his finger—the cave-diver's sign for a question, prompting Bridget to sign to Elvis, *Show him.*

And Elvis had handed him a Polaroid photograph: a young woman holding a baby.

Bryant's eyebrows had gone up.

"Why, that's . . ."

"Ixnitke'," Elvis had agreed. "The girl you knew as Forest. Yeah, that's her, bro. And this is her son, who was born last month. I was there. And I don't have much medical training, just first aid, you know? But after a couple of weeks, the baby looked pale—blue—and I do have a stethoscope, and I know a heart murmur when I hear one."

Blue baby—a hole in the heart, Bridget signed, drying her eyes. *For heart surgery, it's a fairly straightforward procedure, especially on an infant. I've done them before.*

She'd sighed and looked at Mike.

You win. I'm going.

And now, here she was, looking radiant in a linen blouse and cotton khaki culottes, her hair pulled back into a pony tail, exposing the long, smooth lines of her neck in a way that left Mike's voice all thick and awkward and husky. He put his hand atop Bridget's and squeezed. She left it there for a second, and then slid her hand away, turning the page of her magazine, not looking up.

Mike sipped his Coke and looked at the in-flight magazine.

Half an hour later, the airplane changed altitude and the engine noise dropped, signaling the beginning of their descent into San Miguel. Bridget put her magazines away in her nylon attaché, and both she and Mike got out the immigration forms they'd been handed on the ground in Atlanta. They each filled out the passport control forms and then Mike held up the customs card and looked Bridget's way, a question on his face. She shook her head and began to fill out one of her own.

Ouch. On all of their previous trips abroad, Bridget had let Mike do the customs cards so they could pass through as a "family unit"—fiancés, Mike would tell the agents, if they asked. Not this time. And it was funny; that troubled Mike more than having her pull her hand away from his. Trying to hide the hurt in his eyes, Mike bent over the tray table, pen in hand, and began filling out his own card.

The airplane door opened onto one of those wheeled, portable stairways, Casablanca style—no jetways at the San Miguel airport. Mike followed Bridget down the steps and across the hot airport tarmac under the watchful eyes of a security guard who looked as if he might one day grow into his uniform. It was, Mike reflected, not for the first time, an anticlimactic finish to an airport arrival that begins with the jet sweeping low along the mainland over Playa del Carmen, then continues with an approach, low over the water, and ends with the descent over the hotel and lighthouse-studded beach, past the northern outskirts of San Miguel itself, and into a jungle-fringed airport of a size something less than that used for most American county seats.

Refusing Mike's help, Bridget had carried her own attaché and carry-on down the stairs. They entered the little terminal, and she stood ahead of him in the passport line in a fashion that suggested there was no connection between the two of them beyond the fact that they had flown the same airline. She even handled the short conversation with the passport agent herself, having practiced the few lines sufficiently that they came out like normal speech.

Mike followed her and then walked to the luggage carousel, where Bridget had already retrieved her two bags and was shoving them along with her foot toward the customs checkpoint. Mike got his two gearbags—the ones full of prototype regulators and dive lights, dive computers, and other delicate and one-of-a-kind instruments that he had not wanted to trust to international airfreight—as well as a duffel of clothes, and fell in line behind Bridget.

He watched as she pushed the customs control button, got a green light, and then pushed-pulled her bags ahead of her, out to the lobby.

Mike stepped to the white line painted on the floor, waited until the customs agent pointed at the button, and then stepped forward and pressed it.

Red light.

Mike groaned. The button-and-light system was random. If it gave you a green light, you skipped the bag check. Red, they went through your stuff. And even though it was luck-of-the-draw, no amount of protest could convince the agents to operate contrary to the will of the light bulb. The agent pointed to a table near the wall and looked at Mike as if he were smuggling counterfeit microchips or something. Nodding, he shrugged the two huge gearbags up by their shoulder straps, grabbed his duffel and his overnight bag, and shuffled over to the table.

The young male customs officer did the carry-on and duffel first, looking discreetly and apologetically into the open bags, lifting a stack of folded clothing for a cursory glance underneath, and then nodding and allowing Mike to zip them back up.

Then he got to the first gear bag.

Mike opened the top of the bag and the agent looked in—and stopped. The whole thing was full of padded nylon bags and cases. The agent called something out in rapid-fire Spanish to his colleague, who began waving the other travelers through the checkpoint without asking them to push the control button. Looking back up to Mike, the agent pointed to the bags and said, "Open, please."

The first padded bag contained extra batteries for the HID lights; squat cubes of grayish-white plastic joined together like wires and looking for all the world like something put together by the Unibomber. The agent looked at them for a moment and asked, "Photo?"

"Luminaria," Mike replied, and the agent shrugged and went on to the next padded bag, which held the docking port for Mike's laptop. He didn't ask anything this time, just set it aside and motioned to the rest of the containers, which Mike opened in turn, exposing high-intensity-discharge bulbs, salinity meters, a small portable spectrograph for performing water-sample analysis, complete sets of rebuild kits for the prototype regulators, dive-computer motherboards and piezo resistors sealed in black Bakelite plastic with attached LCD display screens, a tray of jeweler's screwdrivers and pliers, and a dozen other sundry and electronic devices. When Mike got to the last padded container and opened it to expose an Ikelite modeling substrobe, the agent said, victoriously, "Photo!"

"Si," Mike replied, and the agent looked pleased with himself.

They got to the next gear bag and the agent groaned audibly when Mike opened it and showed that it was full of more of the same. But, again, they went through every bag within, the agent sometimes staring at an object for a full minute or more before nodding for Mike to go on to the next. By the time they were done, both Mike and the agent were sweating, the baggage area had been emptied of all other travelers, and the agent's female colleague was staring bullets at Mike, as if this delay was all his fault and not the light bulb's.

Then, since regulations prevented the agent from physically opening or closing a bag, Mike began the laborious processing of packing everything back up.

As Mike walked out to where Bridget and Jorge Yanéz were waiting in the lobby, the agent said something in slang Spanish behind Mike, and Jorge began laughing.

"What'd he say?" Mike asked.

"He thinks that you are James Bond," the Mexican cave diver replied, reaching down to take Mike's duffel and the heaviest of the two gear bags.

They made their way past a local kid huckstering a time-share walk-through to a pair of tourists and went out into the heat where Jorge's red Ford pickup sat waiting, Bridget's bags already in back next to Jorge's tanks and a pair of stainless steel backplates.

They put Mike's bags in back as well, bungeeing the bags containing electronics so they couldn't move around, then all three divers got up front, leaving the windows down because, like most local vehicles on Cozumel, Jorge's old F-350 was not air-conditioned.

"We'll go to my shop before we take you to your hotel, okay?" Jorge asked. "Señor Hastings, the missionary? He called this morning and said he would call back an hour from now."

"Did he say what it was about?" Mike asked.

"No. Just that it was urgent."

Mike signed the exchange for Bridget. She looked concerned, which he found touching, although he couldn't sympathize. If Elvis had something urgent, it was probably something affecting his missions work. Mike, on the other hand, was already focused on his dive. The only thing he could think of that might remotely affect him was the helicopter. But if it was delayed, he had a broad window of time in which to work. If the chopper was cancelled, then that would pose a problem—a significant problem—but he'd improvise if needed, hump the gear overland on foot if that was what it came down to. They'd done it before. He'd come too far, planned too long, and invested too much of himself to have this fall apart now. If Elvis was having problems with his Indians, then that was too bad, but he wouldn't let it interfere with his dive. He was focused. He reminded himself that he had to be focused.

Costa Maya Expeditions, Jorge's shop, was across the street from Hotel Pepita, a little whitewashed building that was a kilometer away from the resort hotels along the waterfront in distance, and four or five decades away in time. The shop itself was simple: a projector screen and a slide projector, five or six folding chairs that could be arranged into a small classroom, a few framed photographs of cave divers and a couple of cave system maps on the walls, a locked side room for equipment, a closet full of files, and a desk with a computer, at which Rosa, Jorge's pretty young wife, sat in a Costa Maya T-shirt and a pair of cut-offs, her hair pulled back in a single raven-black braid. She looked up as they came in, and beamed.

"Bridget! Mike! We've been missing you guys! Welcome back."

Rosa, an English major in college, had an accent that sounded as if she had been born and raised in Ohio, although she had never been north of the border. She hugged each of the visitors in turn, kissed her husband on the cheek, and offered them soft drinks that were, together with the ancient air conditioner laboring in the side wall, a welcome relief from the heat of the day.

The four old friends caught up with one another for about half an hour, and then the phone sounded, the familiar double ring of the Mexican phone system. Jorge answered it in Spanish and spoke a few more words in that language. Then he turned to Mike and said, "It's Señor Hastings. He wants me to put it on the speaker phone, okay?"

Mike nodded and said, "Hey, Elvis," turning so Bridget could read his lips.

"Mike!" Elvis's voice crackled on the other end of the line. "I'm glad we got through. I'm calling from a biologist's research station about fifteen kilometers from the Cháakadon village."

"What's going on?" Mike asked, signing what Elvis had just said and thinking it strange that there were no words of welcome; he'd already come to think of Elvis as a friend.

"I wanted to give you a heads-up," Elvis replied. "There may be trouble with the dive."

"How's that?"

"Some of the Cháakadon are thinking of protesting it."

"The Cháakadon? What—"

"They had a visitor while I was up north on my home leave. Kunich Ahua."

"'Kunich Ahua?'" Jorge asked, puzzled.

"Local rabble-rouser," Mike whispered as he wrote the name down on a scratch pad for Bridget. Then, aloud, he said to the speakerphone, "I don't get it. Why would this guy give a rip about our dive?"

"Well," Elvis said, "remember I told you that the Cháakadon have their own name for the *cenote*?"

"Yeah. Sure," Mike replied. "You said that they called it 'the Well of Sorrows.'"

"K'uxulch'en. Exactly. And they call it that because it figures in their culture. It has religious significance to them."

"What sort of religious significance?"

There was a pause on the other end of the line. For a moment, the only sound in the room was the rattle and hum of the ancient air conditioner.

"Listen," Elvis said. "I can't be one-hundred-percent sure of this. I mean, I still have beaucoup difficulty with the language, plus this is a topic that even some of the Cháakadon aren't sure about, and the ones that are, well, they're acting pretty coy, you know?"

"I've got you," Mike said. "Grain of salt. So what is it?"

There was another pause.

"When people get critically ill or injured, or when a child is born with crippling defects," Elvis finally said, "they've taken them to the *cenote* and thrown them in."

The air conditioner rattled away as Mike continued to sign what Elvis had said, Bridget's wide eyes registering that she was following the conversation.

"In the past, you mean," Mike said.

"That's what they're admitting to," Elvis said. "The village headmen are smart enough to realize that outsiders would view this as murder. But if you put two and two together, it looks as if it might still be the custom."

"What?"

"Forest," Bridget interjected aloud. "Don't you see? It was what those two men were going to do with Forest. When they brought her to the *cenote*."

"I think Bridget's right," Elvis agreed. "My guess is the two guys were Quatul, the village shaman, and one of his apprentices. When they got to the site and found outsiders there, they couldn't follow through, and she was too sick to take back to the village, so they left her."

Mike said nothing, stunned.

"It's not a traditional Mayan custom," Elvis said. "I mean, the ancients pitched people into *cenotes* all the time—the Sacred Well at Chichen Itza is the best-known example. But those were sacrifices, meant to appease the gods. Usually they threw in prisoners or young virgins, people strong and in the prime of life. But throwing in the sick, the injured—I don't know where that came from. It seems to be unique to this village. From what I've been able to gather—nobody wants to talk about it—they think that the *cenote* is a kind of portal to the afterlife, that Cháak will nourish them, just as the rains nourish the earth, and physically rejuvenate them in some sort of paradise."

"That's crazy," Mike muttered.

"Is it?" Elvis asked. "I believe that I will go to heaven after I die. Am I crazy?"

No one said anything.

"It's the same principle," Elvis said. "It's just a terrible distortion of it."

Turning to Jorge, Mike asked, "This protest. Can it stop the dive?"

"Maybe," the Mexican replied. "After the troubles in Chiapas, a few years back, the government began to pay much closer attention to the demands of native groups. There's a lot of pressure from outside too. Organizations in the United States, in Europe, that lobby for the rights of native people. If these Cháakadon raise a fuss, the federal government may well step in and forbid the dive."

Shoulders sagging, Mike looked around the room and then down at the phone.

"So what do we do?" He asked it to no one, and to everyone in general.

"I think," Elvis replied over the speaker phone, "that you and Bridget had best get over here right away. Tomorrow, if possible."

16
THE YUCATAN PENINSULA

The jungle, which had been absolutely still when they'd first entered it nearly an hour before, was alive now with sound, albeit perpetually in the distance. The screech of parrots, the repetitive hoots of howler monkeys, and the calls of a dozen types of songbirds always seemed to emanate from just around the next bend or just over the next rise in the trail. But every time they got to the seeming source, the immediate vicinity was silent—nature holding its collective breath, waiting for the intruders to pass.

Mike and Bridget had left Cozumel before daybreak, catching the first fast ferry of the day to Playa del Carmen, Mike falling asleep in the airliner-like seat after having met most of the night in a Costa Club conference room with the two Yobatu Scuba project engineers.

Unlike the PR people and the marketing staff, the engineers were totally dedicated to the deep dive project and totally indifferent to anything printed on the *Aquasplorer.com* website. They believed in the dive completely, they were vitally interested in seeing Mike succeed, and they had commuted back and forth between Japan and Florida several times over the previous six months, living, sleeping, and breathing the project; throwing themselves into the task of creating the regulators that would function perfectly at ten times the recreational depth limit.

During the evening meeting, Mike had presented the engineers with the modifications that he and Lamar had made to the prototypes they'd been testing in Florida. The engineers, accustomed to team efforts and collaborative design, had welcomed the expert innovations and spent hours measuring, comparing the modified regulators to the prototype specifications, transmitting data back to Japan, where their peers ran computer simulations even as they met, and asking Mike about nuances of the units' performance. And Mike, in return, had willingly participated in the all-night meeting because the data that resulted from it would be transmitted via encrypted e-mail to Yokohama, where it would be used to create the finished, pre-production models that would be used for the actual dive. These would be completed within two weeks and sent via overnight express courier to Mexico, together with complete rebuild kits and the special tools needed to maintain them, so Mike and his support team could test the equipment thoroughly for a month before subjecting it to the rigors of the deep dive.

That is, if there was a deep dive.

Elvis had been waiting for them in his Montero at the ferry landing, a Thermos of hot coffee at the ready, but even the strong Mexican brew had been insufficient to bring Mike fully awake. He'd slept throughout the drive down the coast, past the seaside resorts and beach clubs, to Tulum, where Elvis had turned inland. And even then, Mike had awakened only long enough to register their location. He'd soon fallen asleep again, coming fully awake only after the Montero had made the transition from paved road, to gravel, to dirt, to a bumpy two-track that had to be driven at walking speed and even then tested every facet of the vehicle's four-wheel-drive capabilities and caused the SUV to pitch and roll like a ship in rough seas.

"Dude!" Elvis had called cheerfully, seeing Mike stirring in the rearview mirror. "Welcome. We're not to the end of the earth yet, but hey—you can sure see it from here!"

Mike had recognized some of the terrain. They were on the same primitive road that he and Pete had used to ferry their gear back to the trailhead during the initial attempts on Cenote X. Then Elvis turned south, toward Guatemala, onto an equally marginal route—more of a path of least resistance through the vegetation than an actual road—until finally they had come to a place where the forest growth was too dense for anything but foot traffic.

Backing the Montero into a tight spot between two cypress trees, Elvis had turned it around the way they had come and then left it, keys above the visor and doors unlocked. He'd pulled three rucksacks out of the SUV and then a small bottle of blue-green liquid, which he'd rubbed into his neck, his arms—any exposed skin.

"It's an organic cleaner, called Basic-H," he'd explained. "Cool stuff—strong enough to take chewing gum out of carpeting, but you can thin it down and use it to rinse fruits and vegetables. I use it undiluted for insect repellent."

"Does it work as well as the regular stuff?" Mike had asked.

"I think so," Elvis had told him. "Mostly I use it because it doesn't smell like bug juice. The Cháakadon used to say something to one another when I put DEET on. And later, when I'd picked up enough of the language, I realized they were griping to one another about how badly I stunk! So I use this now, instead. It's all natural, and pH balanced, so it's safe to wear. And one side-benefit is that later on, when you go to wash up, you're already wearing your soap!"

Mike had smelled the bottle; it hadn't really smelled like anything, not even soap. He'd put some in his hand and then handed the bottle to Bridget, signing *mosquito* as she'd taken it.

Now, after fifty-five minutes of brisk hiking—Elvis was in the lead and had earned new respect from Mike for his prowess with a machete—Mike had to admit that he had not, to the best of his knowledge, been bitten by a single fly or mosquito.

Not that he was bug-free by any means. Tiny, nearly invisible gnats buzzed constantly around his head. Every minute or so a mosquito buzzed in for a close inspection of his ear before deciding that he didn't seem palatable. And even though Mike had been running nearly every morning for the previous seven months, he was sweating profusely in the humid jungle, rivulets of perspiration coursing down his back, his chest, and under and around the red bandana that he had folded and tied into a headband.

Bridget seemed to be faring better, which didn't surprise him. Mike knew that women had, proportionately speaking, more body surface than men. It was the reason most women caught chills more easily, and the reason that Bridget usually needed a bit more insulating undergarment than Mike when they dived in dry suits. This time, that tendency was working in her favor. Bridget's skin glowed, and the hair around her face looked a little damp as she glanced back at Mike to see how he was doing. But she didn't look the way he felt: stuffed in the sauna with the heat stuck on "high."

In the side pockets of their packs, Elvis had given Mike and Bridget translucent plastic Nalgene bottles straight from a cooler. Each bottle had been filled with purified water and then frozen solid. In less than an hour, though, most of the ice had melted. Mike pushed up the sip-top and took a swig, the cool water both refreshing him and replacing a bit of what he was losing with each bead of sweat.

He stopped to put the bottle back in its pocket, and that's when he smelled it: the unmistakable scent of wood-smoke. It wasn't strong, but it was there. Somewhere up ahead, somebody had a fire going.

Twenty feet ahead of him, Elvis turned around and grinned.

"Yeah," he called back to Mike, reading his thoughts by the expression on his face. "We're getting close to the village. Won't be long now. Maybe fifteen, twenty minutes."

Elvis, Mike noticed, looked no more done-in than Bridget. Probably, Mike assumed, because he'd grown accustomed to the climate. It was discouraging, though. Here he was, Mike thought, the world-class explorer, and he was the only one of the three who looked like a dishrag. Despite his concern over the protest, he was relieved when they finally reached the Cháakadon village.

It was laid out with as much care as any planned subdivision that Mike had ever visited back in the States. The houses were oblong affairs, roughly rectangular, but with rounded corners; they had high thatched roofs that made them look as if they were wearing cone-like straw hats. The buildings stood in pairs, Mike saw; one house would have solid wattle-and-daub walls, and its mate would be made of open, spaced branches that let the wind pass through. It was from these ventilated houses that the wood smoke was coming, and when Mike saw a woman emerge from one of them carrying an iron kettle, it dawned on him—each family had two buildings, one for sleeping and one for cooking,

Next to each kitchen structure was a small garden, growing peppers and herbs, and Elvis, Bridget, and Mike approached the village by walking a narrow path through fields that surrounded the village entirely, like a broad, green moat. Some of these were waist-high in corn. Bare-chested men wearing straw hats were trimming others with scythes.

"Fallow fields," Elvis explained. "The Cháakadon plant corn in a field for two years, and then let it rest for one, keeping it trimmed so it won't be hard to re-plow. Same principle taught at all the agricultural schools, only they figured it out for themselves. Pretty cool, huh?"

Outside one of the nearest houses, an elderly man stood shirtless, his black hair streaked with gray, singing as he wove a fishnet-fine hammock on a broad, rudimentary loom, guiding the boat-like shuttle through threads that were all the colors of the rainbow. At the sound of Elvis's voice, the old man looked up, grinned, waved, and called something back to the houses. A few raven-haired heads peeked around doors and through windows. Then shrill laughter erupted from around the village, and children began streaming out of the houses.

There were thirty or forty of them, and they ranged in age from toddlers to early teens, the older ones in embroidered cotton dresses or the short, rough-fabric pants and simple white cotton shirts favored by the adults, the younger ones in long shirts alone, the littlest ones entirely naked. Like a happy swarm of bees, they converged and ran as a group, and in a moment it was plain that they all had a common target—Elvis.

The young missionary laughed and spread his arms wide, eyes closed, as kids of all sizes plowed into him, climbed up on him, and danced around him as if he were some hula-shirted human May-pole.

Elvis hugged the littlest ones and gently peeled them from his body, then he took off his pack and, like some surfer-attired Santa, began handing things out—pads of paper, small pocket knives for the older boys. There was candy too, but Mike noticed that only the littlest ones got it. Anybody old enough to wear clothes received something practical.

When the last gift had been given, Elvis put his pack back on, then picked up the smallest brown child and set him, bare bottom and all, on his shoulders. Surrounded by happy children, Elvis turned to Bridget and Mike, grinned, and said, "C'mon, you guys. Let's go meet the family."

Other people, adults, were coming out of the houses now. A few of the men started walking back from the field, scythes over their shoulders, waving as they came.

"Bix a belex?" they called as they walked, and Elvis responded with a single word, *"Maloob."*

"They're asking how we're doing, and I said, 'Fine,'" he explained to Bridget and Mike. Mike tried the word himself, doubling the children over with laughter. Bridget simply smiled.

A young man, taller than his peers, rounded the corner of the nearest house, grinning broadly. He was wearing faded khaki cargo shorts, a Boardroom Surf Shop T-shirt, and a pair of Ray-Ban Wayfarer sunglasses. A Mayan Elvis, Mike decided.

"Dude!" the young man called out.

Mike broke up. Definitely a Mayan Elvis.

Elvis ran forward and hugged the young man, still balancing the little brown child on his shoulders.

Turning, Elvis said, "Guys, this is my Mayan bro, Kukulcán."

The missionary grinned and added, "He's been picking up a little English from me."

"Looks like he's picked up more than that," Mike said, chuckling at the outfit.

"I haven't taught him to surf yet," Elvis replied. "But give him time."

Kukulcán asked a question in his own tongue and Elvis replied in what was obviously an affirmative.

"He wanted to know if you're the man who wants to dive in K'uxulch'en—in the Well of Sorrows," Elvis told Mike. "I said that you are."

Mike nodded.

"Not cool," Kukulcán said, his face suddenly somber. "Boss guys? Bumming—big time."

"Okay," Mike said to the Mayan directly. "Let's go talk to the boss guys."

Nodding once, Kukulcán turned on his heels and began walking. The three Americans fell in behind him, trailed by a mob of children. A few of the younger ones danced at Mike's knees, tugging on his pant legs. When he looked down, they eagerly held up their hands, fingers pointing toward the sky; understanding, he slapped his hand against theirs, "giving them five," eliciting giggles of excitement.

The procession came to a halt outside a wattle-and-daub house identical to several they'd already passed.

"The headman's house?" Mike asked.

"No," Elvis replied. "Kukulcán has something he wants to show you."

The Mayan went to the doorless entry of the dwelling and beckoned softly. Moments later a young woman, not yet in her twenties, stepped into the opening, the sunlight catching the highlights of her long, jet-black hair and painting shadows on the folds and gathers of the tunic-like, turquoise-blue dress that she wore. When the woman saw Bridget, her eyes brightened and she ran the ten steps between the two of them, throwing her arms around the trauma surgeon and hugging her like a long-lost relative.

"Forest!" Bridget exclaimed, and she hugged her back.

They held their embrace for nearly a minute, and then Forest, her eyes moist with tears, stepped back, held one hand up, and hurried back into her home.

A moment later she was back, carrying a bundled blanket in her arms. Shyly, she stepped up to Bridget and lifted a flap of the blanket back, revealing a tiny brown face with tightly shut eyes, two little balled fists, and a wispy shock of silky black hair. The baby was gray–blue at the tiny moons of his nails and his lips, his skin paler than that of the children milling at the visitor's feet.

"Oh, Forest," Bridget cooed aloud. "He's beautiful."

The Mayan woman beamed proudly, Bridget's meaning obvious to her despite the lack of a common language. Turning to Elvis, Bridget signed, *What's his name?*

No name yet, he signed back. *They don't name their children until the spring after they are born. Right now, he's just "baby."*

"Oh, 'baby,'" Bridget said, carefully accepting the infant from the young Indian woman. "We are going to make sure you grow up big and healthy and strong."

And that was how they walked to the center of the jungle village, Elvis and Kukulcán side-by-side like a pair of unusual twins, Bridget walking with Ixnitke' and carrying the young Mayan woman's baby, and Mike looking like a pale Goliath, surrounded by a sea of brown-skinned children. As they walked, the clusters of women and crop-tenders fell in with them, until finally it was a crowd of nearly two hundred that entered an open, plaza-like area near the center of the village, where somber-faced older women were placing kettles and bowls of food on a set of sturdy wooden tables.

"We talk here?" Mike asked.

"No," Elvis replied. "We eat here. The Cháakadon know that you were up early and that you had a journey to get here. They won't talk until they know that you're fed and refreshed."

"Pretty civilized of them," Mike observed.

"This is probably the way they greeted the Conquistadors," Elvis told him frankly. "They gave the Spanish food and shelter and comfort, and the Spanish robbed them and raped them and ruined them—all under color of authority from the crown. When you look at it that way, I think you'd have to say that they've been 'civilized' a darn sight longer than we have."

"Guess you're right," Mike muttered, impressed at how gently he'd been chastised.

They were in a large common area near the center of the village. On one side, halved logs had been arranged in six rows to form a rough semicircle. Facing the rudimentary benches was a firepit full of dead ashes, with a low wooden platform behind it.

"Town hall?" Mike asked.

"Sort of," Elvis replied. "When I first got here, I taught the gospel house-to-house, visiting and sharing meals. Then Kukulcán saw a letter I was carrying, with a picture of the inside of my home church. He and his brother decided that their village needed something like that as well. So they appropriated one part of the square and built it for us."

"Pretty high compliment to you," Mike observed.

"It is," Elvis agreed, adding, "but it's caused a lot of discord in the village. Some people saw it as institutionalizing an intrusion. There were lots of folks in favor of asking me to leave, until they heard that I was bringing Bridget back."

"Lots of folks?" Mike asked.

Elvis nodded at a small cluster of people, no more than ten brown-skinned men, most of them not much older than Kukulcán. The group was walking toward the makeshift amphitheater purposefully, led by an elderly man who appeared to still be strong and wiry, but walked with the assistance of a staff.

Bridget, startled, looked at the leader of the group and then at Forest, who responded with the tiniest nod possible.

"The opposition party," Elvis observed.

"Who's the leader?" Mike asked. "That shaman you told us about?"

"He's the one," Elvis said. "Although he's more storyteller than shaman. Mayans have mythology, the same as most polytheistic people do. Quatul tells stories about the various gods, teaching the children who they are and what they rule. It's a prestigious position, and it comes with perquisites—like never having to cook a meal, because someone's always hosting you. I guess he sees me as competition."

"How's it going?" Mike asked. "Do you know enough of the language?"

"Well," Elvis mused. "It's this way. Do you speak Spanish?"

"Sure. We've been coming here for years."

"So," Elvis returned. "Are you comfortable enough with your Spanish to, say, explain the nuances of Spanish poetry to native speakers?"

"No way. I might get by teaching a cave course but not something like that."

"There you are." Elvis told him. "Only I'm worse off than you. I can barely speak enough Cháakadon Mayan to invite somebody for a bite to eat. These folks like hearing stories about Jesus. They even readily accept that he's God, which is more than you can say for many Anglos. But when it comes down to what sin is and what Jesus did about that, we're still bridging a gulf. And they don't think that he was all that powerful a God if he allowed himself to be killed. I don't have enough words yet to explain that he wanted that, that he preordained that. To explain why it was necessary, you know?"

Mike didn't know, but a crowd was coming into the square now, women bringing more food, men setting aside their hoes and scythes and washing at wooden troughs that were apparently set up for that purpose. Kukulcán turned to the three Americans and said, "Eat, dudes. Okay?"

Lunch was a spicy meat—wild boar, Elvis told Mike—cooked in a stew and served with rice and beans in a peppery sauce. The square, which had been largely hushed when the three Americans arrived, gradually gave way to fifty or sixty separate conversations, all frequently punctuated by exclamations and laughter, all except for Quatul and his group, who ate by themselves and remained stoically silent, as if banking their resolve. Although plates and platters were used to pass and serve the food, it was eaten off leaves and corn husks, which were simply dropped into the firepit as the gathering finished their meal. Afterward, people passed gourds of water from communal pots, drinking casually from the same implement.

Mike accepted a gourd, drank, and then looked at Elvis, surprised.

"It's cold!"

"Sure," Elvis said. "Or at least it's cooler than you'd expect. It's water from a *cenote*, not a big, geothermal one like yours, but a small sink, about six feet across, leading into a cave that's about twenty feet down. You know how the Yucatan is—just a few rivers—so these folks have to depend on *cenotes* for water. Either that or use rainwater. But from what I understand, they've sited their villages near *cenotes* for centuries."

Accepting a drink of water, Bridget rose and carried the gourd to Quatul, offering it to him. As she drank, she looked at his face, swollen in welts. She turned to Elvis.

"What happened?"

Elvis turned and asked Kukulcán a question, listened to the answer, and then turned back to Bridget, signing, *He's got a sweet tooth. Likes honey. I guess he didn't get enough smoke into the hive before he took some.*

Bridget nodded and then signed, *Ask him if he will allow me to help him.*

Elvis asked Quatul, who said a few words, and Elvis signed, *He wants to know if it will hurt.*

"Yes," Bridget nodded. "But only a little."

When Quatul nodded his assent, Bridget rummaged in her backpack and brought out a small disposable syringe, a vial of antihistamine, and an alcohol swab. Moving Quatul's loincloth aside, she swabbed the edge of his buttocks and gave him an injection, which he stoically ignored. Only after she was finished did he turn to his group, point to the welts on his face, and then point to his buttocks and say something. The whole village roared.

Bridget smiled, shook her head, and told Elvis, "No translation necessary."

As if on cue, Quatul and his group moved over to the edge of the platform, where Mike, Bridget, and Elvis were sitting. Mike stood and then, unsure as to whether these people shook hands, nodded his head in an informal bow.

Quatul nodded back.

Mike motioned to an open bench, and Quatul nodded again. He and his group sat. As if returning to a theater after intermission, the entire village began taking seats on the halved logs. Soon there were no seats left, and the overflow stood in the background, arms crossed, silent. The square became so silent that you could hear birds calling and the wind sighing in the trees beyond the fields. Finally, Quatul spoke.

"He asks why you want to enter the Well of Sorrows," Elvis explained.

"Tell him I want to find the bottom," Mike said.

Elvis translated, and Quatul replied, one word.

"Why?" Elvis translated.

"Ask him if he has ever had the urge to climb the tallest tree in the jungle," Mike said.

Elvis said something in Mayan and listened to Quatul's reply.

"He says no," Elvis said. "He says that monkeys climb all of the trees in the jungle and that he is a man, not a monkey."

"Do the men of this village ever kill jaguars?" Mike asked.

There was another exchange.

"Yes," Elvis said. "When the jaguars lose their fear of men and come too close, then the men kill them, although this has not happened in quite a long time."

"When they did," Mike asked, "was there honor in killing the largest jaguar?"

Elvis spoke and Quatul replied.

"Yes," Elvis said.

"It is the same with the Well of Sorrows."

Quatul harrumphed and said something.

"The Well of Sorrows is a pit of water," Elvis translated. "It is not a jaguar."

Mike scowled, perplexed.

"He knows what you mean," Elvis offered. "He's just messing with you."

"Then tell him," Mike said, "that the Well of Sorrows is as special as the biggest jaguar."

Another exchange.

"Quatul says that the Well is special to the Cháakadon because it is the house of Cháak. He wants to know why it is special to you."

"Because there is none deeper. Not anywhere in the world."

Quatul listened to the translated reply and asked another question.

"How do you know this?" Elvis translated.

"We have instruments and plumb lines—ways of telling."

Elvis translated this with difficulty, substituting the Mayan word for "tools" for "instruments," and "ropes" for "plumb lines."

Quatul harrumphed and barked back a reply, slapping his knee.

"If you know how deep it is, then what is the point in going down into it?" Elvis repeated.

Mike took a breath.

"It is the difference between seeing the biggest jaguar," he said. "And killing the jaguar that troubles the village."

Quatul listened to the reply as it was repeated in Mayan and then shook his head.

"The Well of Sorrows troubles no one," Elvis translated.

"That's not what I hear," Mike said.

"How do you mean?" Elvis asked.

"I hear that it consumes the sick and the infirm of the village."

"Dude," Elvis warned. "Do we really want to go there?"

"Yes," Mike replied instantly. "Tell him."

Quatul sat up as Mike's reply was translated. Looking down, he muttered something.

"Quatul says that you have been listening to foolish stories," Elvis said.

Mike said nothing in reply, and Quatul, uncomfortable with the silence, looked up and spoke again.

"He says," Elvis translated, "that the Well of Sorrows is a portal to the realm of Cháak. That those who go there at Cháak's bidding are—'renewed,' I think is the word he's using—but those who trespass risk Cháak's wrath. He says that Cháak lives at the bottom of the Well of Sorrows, where your ropes and tools have touched. He says that Cháak devours all who come there unbidden. He says that this is what happened to your friend."

"Ask him if this is something that he hears from his friend Kunich Ahua," Mike said.

"Dude—" Elvis warned.

"Elvis," Mike said. "We've got an elephant in the room here. Let's talk about it."

"Okay," Elvis decided. He told Quatul what Mike had asked.

Quatul's dark face reddened. He spat back a reply.

Wary, Elvis told Mike, "He wants to know if you belittle their Mayan gods."

"Tell him that, from what I hear, this Mayan god is a man who whispers in the dark."

Quatul listened to Elvis and spoke back, shaking his head.

"Quatul says that no men beyond this village can speak their tongue as Kunich Ahua can," Elvis said. Then the elder Mayan added something, and Elvis, nodding his head, noted with just the slightest of shrugs, "He says that I'm a prime example."

Bridget, who'd followed the entire exchange wordlessly, smiled as Elvis said this.

Quatul spoke again and Elvis translated, "As for Kunich Ahua being a man, Quatul says that sometimes the spirit of a god can enter a man, and then it is the spirit one hears talking and not the man."

There was a pause, and then another elderly man, the one who'd been weaving a hammock as they arrived, stood up from his seat in the crowd and, moving slowly but steadily, began to walk forward.

"Who's he?" Mike whispered. He remembered seeing him as they'd come in.

"Naum Kaan," Elvis whispered back. "He's Kukulcán's great grandfather."

Speaking in a soft voice that everyone had to strain to hear, Naum Kaan said something and waited, eyebrows raised; obviously, he'd asked a question.

"He's asking me if I believe that the spirit of a god can enter a person and be made manifest through him, just as Quatul has said," Elvis explained. He replied in Mayan, stopping several times to search for the words. Then told Mike and Bridget, "I told him that I believe that there is one God only and that his Spirit not only can enter into people and be made manifest through them, but that it does so all the time. I also told him that I believe that the person who calls himself Kunich Ahua may be inhabited by a spirit but not the spirit of God."

Looking directly into Elvis's eyes, Naum Kaan asked another question, to which Elvis gave a lengthy, stumbling reply. Then the Mayan elder asked another question.

"Can you teach me to cave dive, Mike?" Elvis asked, still looking at the old man.

"What?" Mike asked.

"Naum Kaan just asked me what I believed to be in the Well of Sorrows," Elvis explained. "Whether I believe it to be inhabited by the spirit of Cháak. I told him that I do not believe Cháak is there or anywhere else. I told him that I believe that there is only one God and that he is a god of love and that he is everywhere, so he is in the cave as well. Then he said that, since my God is a god of love and I believe him to be there in the cave and not Cháak, I must not be afraid of the cave. And he asks if I will go into the Well of Sorrows with you, bro. I won't lie to him, dude. If I say I'm going, I'll go. And I'm willing. So will you teach me?"

"Elvis," Mike half whispered. "I can't teach you to do a thousand-foot deep dive. That can't be taught."

"He's not expecting that, Mike," Elvis said, still looking at the Mayan. "He's just wondering if I have faith enough to go into the *cenote*. Fifty feet. A hundred. Whatever. Enough to see you through the door. I've done scuba, but not this stuff. So will you teach me?"

"Sure," Mike said.

"Cool." Elvis nodded to the Mayan and gave him a short answer.

Naum Kaan nodded and turned to Quatul.

"He's telling him that it is his understanding that, to stop you from diving in the Well of Sorrows, the Cháakadon would have to go to the

Mexican federal government, whom they do not trust. He's asking Quatul how wise he thinks that this would be."

Quatul glared back at Naum Kaan and then looked down, saying nothing.

Turning to Mike, Naum Kaan spoke again in his soft, strong voice.

"He's asking you whether you would cancel your plans to dive in the Well of Sorrows if the Cháakadon people asked you to," Elvis explained to Mike. "He's asking if you will accept their authority over this matter."

Mike turned to Bridget, who opened her hands.

Turning back to Naum Kaan, Mike took a breath, nodded, and said, "Yes. I'm the stranger here. I accept their authority."

Nodding his understanding, Naum Kaan turned to Quatul and asked another question.

"Naum Kaan is reminding Quatul that he carried him as a baby when Naum Kaan was a boy," Elvis explained, "and Naum Kaan is asking Quatul if he will bow to his wisdom, seeing as he is the oldest man in the village."

Quatul looked profoundly uncomfortable for a moment. It was obvious that there was only one graceful reply. He made it, somberly nodding his head.

Naum Kaan looked at Quatul and nodded, looked at Mike and did the same. Then, turning to face the village, he began to speak.

"'I am an old man and I remember things that happened long before any of you were born,'" Elvis said, translating Naum Kaan's phrases as he spoke. "'For many years, the Cháakadon have been one village, but I remember a time when we were two. My wife came from the other village, and now she is gone, just as that village is gone, because sickness took them both at different times. But long before there was the time of sickness, there was a man who came, a man who spoke our tongue just as we speak it. He was an Anglo, and maybe it is as this god-man says, that he was filled with the Spirit of God. Certainly I know that he spoke as this god-man speaks, of one God, and of a Son of God, and he had great faith in his god, just as this man does. Quatul does not trust this god-man, and there were those in my wife's village who did not trust that old one either. Yet he never did them harm, and when they sickened, he died with them in their sickness rather than leave them, because he loved them.

"'Any man who loves so much that he will die for that love is a man who must be heard,'" Elvis said, eyes glistening, continuing to translate what Naum Kaan was saying. "'Yet the old gods are the old gods and must be given their respect. So I say this: Let this stranger swim into the Well of Sorrows if he wishes to. He bows to our authority; let us grant it. If Quatul is right, and the Well is the portal to Cháak, then the stranger will see nothing, or perhaps Cháak will take him, if he took his friend. And as for this god-man, let him show his faith and, if Quatul is right and Cháak lives there, perhaps he will take him, as well. But if Cháak is not there, then I believe that this stranger will show us that. And as I have been allowed to speak for our people, then I say that we will allow this test. And I am pleased, because my wife, who died when our second child was born, believed in the Son of God that this god-man teaches, and if he is the One who will take me where my wife has gone, then I want to know this, and I want my family to know it as well. And I thank my old friend Quatul for allowing me to make this decision for all of us. Either way, his permission carves us a sure path to wisdom and truth.'"

And with that, Naum Kaan shuffled back in the direction of his loom, and Quatul, looking as dignified as a man can look after having been given his comeuppance, glanced around at his henchmen and returned the way he had come, and the entire village got up from their rough log benches and began to clear away the food and return to their fields. But before they left, one of Quatul's followers said something to him, and he touched his face, where the welts were already subsiding. He looked at Bridget for a long moment, said nothing, and walked away.

Walking out into the crowd, Bridget picked up Ixnitke's baby again, and then, as her hands were occupied, called aloud, "Elvis! The first parts of the clinic. Where are they?"

"Up top," Elvis said, walking closer to her so she could clearly see his face and signing as he spoke. "We have the basic clinic building set up, although the X-ray equipment and most of the furnishings for staff housing won't be here until two weeks from now, when we chopper it in with your dive equipment. But most of the basic stuff is here, even though a lot of it is in cases. We sited it on a hill about half a kilometer away, so it wouldn't dominate the village when we built it. Want me to take you there?"

"Please," Bridget said.

Elvis and Ixnitke' fell in with her and Mike joined them, taking the baby from Bridget's arms and carrying the infant easily. They walked through the village the opposite way from how they'd come in, passed down another narrow path through half-grown corn fields, and followed a neatly cut path that had boardwalk sections through wet spots and stone steps to cover one small rise. The clinic buildings, customized versions of the PortaKabins used on European construction sites, were neatly arranged around a poured concrete common area in a cleared space just out of sight of the village.

"Naum Kaan seems like a pretty smart guy," Mike commented as he followed Elvis into the clearing.

"He is," Elvis agreed. "Although I'm just now getting enough grasp of the language to realize that. The part about his wife's testimony was news to me, but it explains a lot, especially why Kukulcán was so receptive from day one."

"It was smart of you to say that you believe that human beings can be inhabited by spirits," Mike said. "What made you decide to say that?"

Elvis stopped and turned to face Mike.

"Because I believe it, bro," he said.

"Why would you believe that?"

"Because the Bible is Truth, and it says that such things are facts."

"Oh, come on," Mike said, moving to walk around the missionary.

"Wait," Elvis said. "When I tried to chill you out back there, you went full tilt. Why?"

"I don't know," Mike said. "It felt right."

"So you felt led to say it?"

"Sure."

"So," Elvis grinned. "Who do you think was leading you?"

Mike scowled. "You're trying to say God made me say those things?" He shook his head. "I doubt that he'd do that, Elvis. I'm not sure I even believe in him. Why would he use me?"

"The Bible tells how God used a donkey to talk to a man named Balam," Elvis said. "It recounts how heathen people, who didn't even know God, were used by him to bless the Israelites. God knows what's at stake here. Why wouldn't he use you?"

"Why would he?"

"To enlarge the kingdom, bro."

Mike shifted the baby to a more comfortable position and shook his head.

"This is crazy," he said.

"Nope," Elvis replied, turning and continuing up a set of poured-concrete steps to the nearest clinic building. "On the other hand, I just agreed to follow you into a water-filled pit a quarter-mile deep. Now *that's* crazy."

17

THE CHÁAKADON VILLAGE

Naum Kaan passed the boat-shaped wooden shuttle through the web of string-like colored threads with hands gnarled and knotted by years of this meticulous, fine work. Back and forth, the weave built steadily, the shuttle never slowing. He liked to say that it was his hands that knew the work, not him, and he could talk, sing, even listen and give advice as he worked. His hands would continue to dance the shuttle steadily, never missing a single thread.

The hammock was going to be a fine one, iridescent blue, like a rare bird. He was making it for—he frowned and thought as his hands did their steady work. He could not remember.

That was the way with him these days. The stories of his youth were crisp and fresh in his mind, but little details like the purpose of a trip across the village or what he had eaten at his last meal often slipped his mind. Just the other day, he had gotten up early to finish a hammock for the grand-daughter of a friend, and when he had gone outside to his loom, it was empty. This had puzzled him greatly, as theft was a great rarity among the people of his village. And why would anyone steal a half-finished hammock in the first place?

But it had not been there, so he had gone back into his hut to gather the materials to start anew, and there the hammock had been, lying atop the chest where he kept his materials, tied up in the distinctive fashion that he tied all the thread goods after he had finished them, to keep the open netting from catching on a splinter and being spoiled. Obviously, he had finished it the evening before. But he could not for the life of him recall doing so.

A puzzle.

Two years before, Naum Kaan had begun to show Kukulcán how to make hammocks. Not that the boy would do it for his livelihood anytime soon; making hammocks was an old man's job, something for those too advanced in their years to hunt or travel in search of trade. But Naum Kaan had started teaching him, anyhow, because Naum Kaan was getting on in years, his eyesight poor in low light now, his step less steady than at any time in his life, and one had to pass the craft on while one was still dexterous at it or risk the chance that such talents would be lost to his people forever.

His fingers danced the shuttle through the fishnet-like web of fabric, building the hammock row by row. He tried once again to remember who had ordered it. Nothing.

No matter. Either he would remember it later, or whoever it was that had ordered it would show up tomorrow to claim it and leave him the bundles of dried fish and smoked iguana and other foodstuffs that were his standard barter for such work. And when they picked it up, the mystery of whom it was for would be solved.

Naum Kaan had developed a method of keeping track of his orders—a hank of thread the color of the desired hammock, left hanging on a peg in his hut. One knot in the thread meant it was a regular hammock, two knots was a double, three the *familia* that three children could share. Two such hanks of thread were hanging on his peg now, so he had employment for a week, a way to occupy his time and bring in enough food to share with his considerable extended family. Beyond that, Naum Kaan did not worry.

"You still do wonderful work, my friend."

Naum Kaan almost started at the sudden Mayan voice, but he tugged at a thread to cover the reflex. Quatul was a sneaky old codger, proud of the way that he could walk in even on a seasoned old hunter such as Naum Kaan without being heard, and Naum Kaan refused to give him the satisfaction.

"I'd better," he grunted in their common, ancient language, dancing the shuttle through the weft. "It's the only thing I'm good for any more. Shall I make us some coffee?"

"Kukulcán's wife saw me coming back here," Quatul replied in Cháakadon Mayan. "She said she was putting on a pot for us. She'll bring it when it's ready."

"She's a good woman."

"That she is."

"It would have been terrible if we'd lost her."

This last comment was meant as a jab, and it worked. Quatul said nothing, but he looked away as Naum Kaan gazed straight at him, doing his work by feel.

"So, are the strangers still here in the village?"

"No," Quatul told him. "The woman tended to some sick ones and examined the baby, and then they left."

"She is clever with her hands."

"She is," Quatul agreed reluctantly.

"Is she married to the stranger?"

"I do not think so," Quatul said. "They are familiar, as a husband and wife would be familiar, but she does not follow him as a wife follows her man. And she is coming back soon to work in their place for the sick, to tend to more of the people. Coming back alone. A wife would not do that."

"Not among our people," Naum Kaan agreed. "But they are not our people."

"Precisely."

Now it was Quatul who had made the jab, and Naum Kaan who ignored it.

"Well," the older man said. "It is a pity if they are not married. A woman such as that would make a good wife."

Quatul chuckled and poked Naum Kaan, almost making him drop the shuttle. "Are you thinking for yourself, you old coot?"

Naum Kaan laughed. He had a good, deep, well-practiced laugh. "Don't even think that, Quatul," he chuckled. "Am I such a nuisance to you that you would want to send me to my grave early?"

Quatul said nothing. There was an awkward silence.

"I am sorry if I embarrassed you today, my friend," Naum Kaan finally said.

"No apology is necessary," Quatul said, gazing off across the cornfields at the jungle. "I am sure you said what you said because you think it is best. I just wish we had spoken privately, you and I, before the meeting this morning."

"So do I," Naum Kaan replied, passing the shuttle through the weft. "But you did not come to me before raising your objections in front of the people."

Silence settled in again.

"You're right," Quatul finally agreed. "It was rash of me not to talk with you first."

"No harm was done, my friend."

They paused as Ixnitke' came back behind the hut, carrying two clay cups and a steaming gourd of hot coffee. She expertly knocked the cups against the side of the gourd to settle the grounds, put a chunk of sugar cane in each cup, and then poured the coffee over the cane, letting it steep for a moment before flicking the green-white cane out with her fingers. Quatul was a guest, but Ixnitke' served Naum Kaan first, keeping her eyes downcast as she offered him the cup. He was oldest, and that was the custom among their people. He tried the coffee, smiled, and said, "Excellent, daughter." Then the young woman served Quatul and left.

"I just don't trust strangers," Quatul mused, sipping his coffee.

"You don't?" Naum Kaan asked. "Then why follow one? You and the young men?"

"Kunich Ahua is not a stranger," Quatul objected. "He is an ancient. They created us."

"Is that so?"

"Come now, Naum Kaan," Quatul scolded. "You know the stories as well as I."

"The stories ...," Naum Kaan grunted.

"What of them?"

"They are your vanity, my old friend. You are the keeper of the lore, so you defend the lore. And that makes you jealous of anything that threatens it, anything that suggests that it might be nothing more than woodsmoke and fantasy, the stories of old men dreaming."

Quatul straightened up, offended.

"Naum Kaan," he scolded, "you never showed such irreverence when we were younger. What has come over you?"

"Maybe the truth," Naum Kaan shrugged.

"The truth?"

"'... The truth will—set you free ...,'" Naum Kaan quoted haltingly, remembering the words as he'd learned them in his native Cháakadon Mayan.

"What is that?" asked his friend.

"A thing my wife taught me," Naum Kaan said softly, gazing over the top of his loom at the distant clouds that hung over the jungle canopy.

"Something she learned in her village. It was important to her that I should know that, a very long time ago."

"Naum Kaan," Quatul chided softly in his most patient voice. "Your wife is dead; dead now these twenty summers."

"Perhaps," Naum Kaan mused, remembering the girl of twenty that he had married when his hands had already begun to gnarl. Then he smiled and added, "Perhaps not."

"I mourned with you. I buried her with my own hands."

"I remember."

Quatul scowled at this seeming non sequitur. "Kunich Ahua is not one of us, yet he knows the things we know," he pointed out. "He speaks as we speak. What does that make him, if not a god?"

"A man," Naum Kaan shrugged.

"And what if it pleases a god to cloud our minds and make us hear him as a man?" Quatul asked, scowling unto his cup. Nothing was left of the sweet coffee now but the coarse grounds. "Can a god not do that?"

"He can," Naum Kaan agreed. "But if this man is nothing but a vision, why would he stop and relieve himself against a banyan tree? One night, when he spoke to the village as we gathered around the fire, I walked into the jungle to look. I saw no man, but I found the wet trunk of a banyan, and the smell was that of a man."

"Naum Kaan!" Quatul shrank back in horror. "You spied on him! You defied a god!"

"Did I?" The old man asked it quietly as he passed the shuttle through the weft. "Some of our young men left at his command. We never saw them again. And you know the stories we have heard: The *coca* paste . . . the Anglos."

"You said it yourself," Quatul scoffed. "Stories. Stories and rumor. Did Kunich Ahua not predict our great loss? 'You will lose that which you hold most precious.' He predicted that."

"He did," Naum Kaan agreed. "And I predict that this hammock will be ready by morning. Am I a god? Or do I say that which I know to be true because it is my intention to do it?"

Quatul thought about this for a moment. Then he shook his head.

"Kunich Ahua would not rob us," he said. "He thinks too much of our people. He believes in us, cherishes us as his own."

"Believe what you want, old friend," said Naum Kaan, working the boat up higher in the nearly finished hammock. "But know this as you do. As certain as you and I are standing here, one of us is very, very wrong."

18
K'UXULCH'EN

Coming back to the *cenote* had been eerie for Mike, as if he had never left the dark pit and its sparse jungle clearing at all. For the first day or two, at every turn, as he and Jorge's group of volunteers had put up the tents and begun to prepare for the arrival of the rest of their equipment, cutting a landing space for the helicopter and clearing the old path down to the edge of the *cenote*, it had seemed plausible to look up and expect to see Pete standing there, all shaggy hair and moustache and deep tropical tan, grinning the way Pete always grinned. Then the realization would return—that Pete was dead, and that, in delving back into the mysteries of Cenote X, Mike was doing no less than plumbing the very depths of his best friend's grave.

It cast a further pall on an undertaking already burdened by the stress of mounting the expedition virtually on his own, and by the pot-shots being taken at him by Faranino and his fellow alarmists in the media. Standing on the rim of the *cenote*, looking down into the perpetual twilight of the shadowed waters, ringed by the weathered limestone walls, it was very easy to feel overwhelmed by the prospect of diving there. With Pete long gone and the weight of the expedition falling squarely on his own two shoulders, Mike felt painfully alone. His solitude could not have been deeper had he been the lone sailor on the open ocean in a one-man boat, headed directly into the teeth of a killer storm.

For a while, Mike retreated into the distraction of the work at hand, work that was constant and considerable. Saplings already covered the breadth of the helipad and staging area that he and Pete and their support crew had cleared painstakingly by hand just a few years before. So Mike and Jorge's crew set to work, first with machetes to clear away the entangling underbrush, then with chainsaws. It was lonely work; while Jorge spoke English fluently and Mike had a working knowledge of Spanish, the presence of all the Mexican volunteers kept Jorge speaking almost constantly in his native tongue, using the idiomatic Spanish of the Mexican Riviera that Mike had difficulty following.

Elvis had gone off to the Cháakadon village and Bridget, having found enough urgent medical need among the Cháakadon people to concern her, had gone with him—but only after receiving Mike's assurances that he and the crew would do their best not to drop trees on one another or maim themselves with axes while their doctor was gone.

That was what first jumped to Mike's mind as Jorge came running to him.

"Trouble, amigo," he said.

"What?" Mike looked around. "Who's hurt?"

"The chainsaw," Jorge said. "She is hurt. She stops and we tried to get her going, but *no mas*."

Mike walked with his diving superintendent over to where three of the Mexican work crew were gathered around the saw. Mike picked it up and tried giving the cord a pull. It didn't budge.

"When they fueled the saw," Mike asked, "did they mix in the two-cycle oil?"

Jorge repeated the question in Spanish. The crestfallen look on one worker's face told Mike everything he needed to know.

"That's my fault," Mike said. "I should have reminded everyone that these are two-cycle saws. Go ahead and work with the other. Make sure it's oiled, though. I'll see if this one is terminal."

But when Mike carried the saw back to where the men had pitched their tents, the problem became worse. There was a toolbox full of extra batteries, pliers, twine and the like. The parts and the other extras for the saws, such as the chain sharpener, were supposed to be in there. They were not.

Mike set the saw down and sighed. Somewhere, back in Playa del Carmen, all the stuff he needed to fix the saw was sitting on a bench somewhere.

That left one saw to clear an area the size of a football field and, predictably enough, it played up as well, long before the day was out. First it wore out its chain, dulling it to the point that the saw was burning, rather than cutting, its way through the dense tropical hardwood. So Mike put the crew to work with axes while he tore down both saws, replacing the worn chain on the working saw with the virtually new chain from the saw that had seized.

This gave them a workable saw for several hours. Then, near the end of the day, one of the volunteers cut so deeply into a tree trunk that the weight of the tree settled on the saw blade and, rather than getting help to relieve the pressure, the man tried to horse the saw back out of the cut. Mike heard the sound of its chain snapping halfway across the clearing.

"What now?" Jorge asked.

Mike looked around.

"The nearest chain is in Tulum, maybe Playa," Mike said. "That means a hike out, then a drive, and then the return drive and the hike back in. Two days, minimum, and possibly as many as three or four. I don't know. Maybe we're better off just finishing with hand tools?"

"I agree," Jorge nodded.

They used axes and handsaws the rest of the day, wearing gloves but still raising blisters on more than one city-softened hand. The next day, near noon, Mike was swinging an axe at a tree root when a pair of brown feet suddenly materialized in his peripheral vision. He looked up. The small space they'd cleared was dotted with short, brown-skinned people. Most carried axes and machetes, and two had a large black cooking-pot slung between them on a pole. At first, Mike was concerned—the arrival of the visitors had been eerily noiseless. Then the crowd of visitors had parted and Elvis Hastings and Kukulcán walked up, both dressed in identical aloha shirts and khaki shorts, and both grinning broadly.

"Dude!" Elvis greeted Mike, hugging him enthusiastically despite Mike's grime and sweat. "The Holy Spirit said that you might be in need of a little help."

And that was all the explanation that Mike was able to get out of the missionary. The Mayan crew went to work first near the campsite, taking a total of perhaps two hours to fell, strip, and cut to length the trees needed to erect the frameworks of two traditional Mayan houses. Then three of their number stayed at the camp to weave saplings through the framework to form walls, and to cut and place the thatch for the roofs. The remaining nine, plus Elvis, joined Mike and Jorge and their crew at the work site, where the Yucatan natives, skilled for centuries at clearing land for farming, bent to their task with a speed that had put Mike and his westernized crew to shame.

The Mayan men sang while they worked, filling the growing clearing with the strange consonants of their language, an oddly reassuring sound. It was an amazing and ancient contrast to the frantic shriek of the chainsaws that had pushed back the jungle just a day before. Mike felt it and everyone felt it—a timeless peace and a feeling of being at home that he would not have thought possible in the heart of the Yucatan.

Mike and his crew had been leveling the saplings, digging a shallow pit next to each tree so a chainsaw or an axe could be used to attack the bole and remove the vegetation without leaving a stump. But the Mayans, accustomed to clearing land for agriculture, lopped off the saplings five feet above the ground and then rigged a rope harness to the standing trunk. While three of their number attacked the roots with axes and machetes, the rest of them pulled as a team, literally ripping what was left of the small tree from the earth. The Mayan method worked both better and faster than the way Mike and his crew had been doing it. By midafternoon, Mike's crew had fallen in with Kukulcán's, pulling together despite the lack of a common language, the men sharing water bottles and food— granola bars from the cave divers and dried fruit from the Mayans—as they stopped for breaks.

By day's end, the group had nearly the entire area cleared, a task that Mike had thought would take the rest of the week. Dinner was canned ham and canned vegetables, which the Mayans ate politely, albeit with sidelong glances at one another.

"Prepared foods are unknown in a Cháakadon diet," Elvis explained to Mike as they ate. "This might taste normal to us, but it's extremely salty to them. They'll probably outlive us by a decade or so, bro. They've never taken a multivitamin and they'll never need one. Everything they've ever eaten has been totally natural, with zip preservatives."

After dinner, the Mayan men brought out net-like hammocks and struck them from the rafters and postbeams of the thatched huts they'd thrown up on arrival. As the visitors climbed into their hammocks to sleep in them crossways in the Mayan style, Mike took a glance in and realized with a start that his visitors' "primitive" accommodations, constructed with nothing but that which was readily available from the jungle around them, were considerably more comfortable than the tent, sleeping bag and groundcloth that he'd brought for himself.

As if reading his thoughts, Kukulcán said something to Elvis, who translated, "They normally would have just put the hammocks between trees for a short trip like this. But they threw the huts up so you and Bridget would have a good place to stay for the rest of your visit here, after they're gone. Kukulcán says it's not natural for a man to sleep in a sack."

At this, Mike laughed and nodded his agreement and his thanks. Then Kukulcán said something more and Elvis grinned.

"Kukulcán says that Bridget told his wife that you have two houses back in Florida as well, and he says that this is a good thing, a Christian thing, to live apart until you are married."

The Mayan smiled.

"You. . . Christian?"

He asked the question in English.

"Uhm—me?" Mike stammered. "Well, uh—I went to church when I was a kid."

Kukulcán had raised a single eyebrow adroitly—something Mike hadn't realized was cross-cultural—and said something in Mayan to Elvis before excusing himself and walking off into the night. Elvis smiled again, nodding to himself.

"What'd he say?" Mike asked.

"He asked me," Elvis smiled, "to witness to you. So when you and Bridget married your babies will grow up to be believers."

"Believers?"

"Christians."

"I see," Mike said uncertainly, lowering his eyes. He stayed silent for a moment, then looked up and observed, "Looks like you were doing fine with your mission work among those folks, even before Bridget came on board at your clinic."

"With Kukulcán," Elvis agreed. "And with Ixnitke'—his wife. They were ready almost from the time I got there. And Kukulcán's grandfather, old Naum Kaan . . . He says he follows the old ways, but I don't know. He acts like he's on the fence and, if you ask me, I'd say he's already a closet believer. But the rest of the village? No, the jury is still definitely out."

He paused. Mike nodded.

"So . . . back to what Kukulcán asked," Elvis said. "What do you think Mike? About God?"

"God . . . ," Mike repeated uncomfortably. He'd looked around for a moment and then said, hesitantly, "I'm not really into the God thing."

"I see," Elvis replied. "So. . . are you into the sin thing?"

"Pardon?"

"Sin. It's an either-or proposition, Mike. Either you're following God or you're living with sin. There is no third alternative."

"Well," Mike replied, looking away, toward the darkening jungle. "Sin is all a matter of opinion, isn't it?"

"Sure is," Elvis agreed, "It's a matter of a headstrong human being clinging to the opinion that he knows better than the Creator of the universe."

"Elvis," Mike said wearily, "I appreciate what you're trying to do here. But you don't have to, okay? I'm not one of your Mayans."

"God doesn't make distinctions, Mike," Elvis told him. "He just sees people. And the twenty-eighth chapter of Matthew commands me to take the truth to 'all nations,' not just the folks on my missions agenda."

The distant sound of crickets and tree frogs filled in an uneasy pause in the conversation.

"Listen, Mike," Elvis said, reaching into his pocket. "I can see that this is embarrassing you, so I'll back off. That's cool. But will you do one thing for me? Will you take a look in this?"

He handed Mike a book.

"A Bible?" Mike asked.

"Well, not the whole Bible, but the New Testament and Psalms. It's yours. Read it when you like. It's all good, but the Gospel of John probably says the essential stuff the most clearly."

"Uh, thanks," Mike muttered, looking down at the ground before his feet. "Well, I guess I'd better turn in."

He carried the Bible back to his tent, and set it atop his backpack and got into his sleeping bag for the night. But he wasn't able to fall asleep, seeing the little black book, no larger than a deck of playing cards, lying there in the blue moonlight that fell through the mosquito-net door. So finally he got up and tucked the book away into a pocket of the pack. After that, he was able to sleep, but fitfully, and he awoke before dawn, apprehensive, yet unable to say why.

The next day's work went quickly. With twenty men bent to the task—a dozen of whom actually knew what they were doing—they quickly felled, stripped and cut to length all the trees they'd need to build a dive platform. Sometime around mid-morning, three of the Mayans walked off into the jungle with bows and arrows, coming back half an hour later with five large iguana. This time, it was the cave divers, in their cargo pants and hiking boots, who looked askance at one another. But by the time lunchtime came around, the wonderful aroma coming from the campsite was enough to overcome the qualms of most of the divers, all but one, who accepted a hand-made tortilla on a broad green leaf, looked at the thick, stew-like concoction ladled atop it, and asked, hesitantly, *"Pollo?"*

"The great one-size-fits-all description of new foods," Elvis told Mike, grinning. "'It tastes like chicken . . .'"

Mike tried a bite and saw what Elvis had been laughing about.

"I've never had chicken that tasted this good," he declared to the missionary, adding, "tell you what—we'll be happy to gather firewood and wash dishes, but from now on, your guys are in charge of the cooking. Deal?"

"Deal," Elvis told him, still laughing.

By midafternoon, they were down to marking out helipads. The unusable leaves and smaller branches had been taken to the downwind perimeter of the landing area to be dried before burning, the stouter branches and the trunks trimmed to workable lengths and stockpiled for future use. As Mike mounted a windsock atop a taller pole, guying it in place with cave guideline, he stepped back to realize that the task of clearing the area, which had seen so daunting just a couple of days earlier, had been finished better than three days ahead of schedule.

It was almost something of a shock; the first time in—well he couldn't remember how long—that he found himself with no urgent errand, no crucial task that had to be accomplished for the whole, detail-strewn, complicated expedition to continue.

He missed Bridget, and he wondered if the feeling was reciprocated. It was no idle question; she had made it quite clear that she was in the Yucatan under duress, so to speak, and not as she'd been the last time, because she desired it. Mike knew how she felt about the expedition, and the worst part was that he shared many of her feelings—with very little feeling of adventure and a growing sense of dread.

Having, for the moment at least, nothing to do; dwelling on Bridget; wondering what, if any, future the two of them might have—it was not the state of mind he wanted to have, especially a day's journey deep into the Yucatan. He needed distraction, so he sought Elvis out.

"You said you wanted me to teach you to cave dive," Mike said. "Want to start?"

"Now?" Elvis asked. "I suppose. Can you float me some trunks?"

"We won't need those yet," Mike laughed. "The first day's all on dry land."

They began on camp stools next to the Mayan hut, Mike showing Elvis the differences between cave-diving gear and regular scuba equipment, using as examples the two sets of gear that the team had backpacked in on the chance that some preliminary underwater work might be necessary.

Then he taught him about the gas rules, stressing especially the "rule of thirds"—that, once a cave diver has hit one-third of the gas level noted on entry, he should turn around and leave.

"And that's true even if you are with a buddy and he gets lost," Mike pointed out.

"Now wait a minute," Elvis interrupted. "My buddy gets lost, and I hit my third, so I turn around and leave, and my buddy is still lost in the cave, and I'm outside with one-third of my air still left? That's crazy!"

"Is it?" Mike asked. "Then let's say you stay in. And let's say you breathe your tank down to half, and then you find your buddy but he's out of air. What do you do?"

"Share air," Elvis told him.

"Fine," Mike agreed. "You share air. It took you a third of a tank to get in and it will take you a third of a tank to get out. You've got half a tank left, but you're sharing it between two people. What's going to happen?"

"We ...," Elvis hesitated, the realization suddenly hitting him. "We have a quarter-tank apiece, but we each need a third. We ... both drown."

"Exactly," Mike nodded. "That's why we have this principle. It is never right that two people should die, just because one could not live."

"Wait," Elvis said. "That last part. Can you say it again?"

Mike repeated it: "It is never right that two people should die, just because one could not live."

He noticed that Elvis wrote it down, word for word.

Next they went to line-reel work, with Mike showing the missionary how to unspool line without entangling it and how to reel line back in by feeding it back and forth, the way line is taken up on a baitcasting reel, to keep from jamming the reel.

Then they moved on to dry-land line-reel exercises, a procedure that required some thinking on Mike's part, because he'd always done this portion of the class either on his property back home in Florida or, if he was traveling, in a park of some kind, where he could find trees with open ground in between.

All around the *cenote*, Mike had had trees aplenty, but with little open ground in between; enough light penetrated the canopy for the undergrowth to be thick and plentiful. So he took Elvis to the trail, the same trail that both the cave divers and the Mayans had followed to get to the dive site, and, instructing the missionary to look the other way, Mike strung the eighth-inch braided nylon line from tree to tree, using a small "jump reel" to create a junction at one point, adding directional line arrows, and locking the reel off and securing it after running out about fifty meters of line.

Mike used a third reel to show Elvis the basics—how to encircle his thumb and forefinger around the line like the universal "okay" signal, how to sense, from line pressure against his fingers, whether he was running too high, too low, or too far to one side or the other. Then he blindfolded Elvis with a bandanna and had him walk the trail, following the guideline, checking for guidelines at the junctions. In one area, where Mike had put in a junction with no line arrows, Elvis had to feel to see which line slipped against the other, as the secondary line would always be the one that moved.

Finally, Mike took Elvis' blindfold off and had the missionary take in all the line and then run it back out again, getting accustomed to the peculiarities of the reel. It had been a good exercise, about ninety minutes of line-work all, told, and it had been getting close to dinner time as they packed the reels up for the short walk back to camp. They were just about to step back out into the clearing when Elvis stopped Mike.

"Look," he said, pointing.

"At what?" Mike asked. He hadn't seen anything out of the ordinary, Then, in a small, trampled area in the underbrush, right next to the trail, he spotted what the missionary had been pointing at—there was a platter-size flat rock with a gray powder around its perimeter and, in the center of this gray circle, sat two small rough-carved wooden bowls. One contained something red. The other held a clear liquid.

"What is it?" Mike asked.

"An altar," Elvis told him. "To Cháak. The gray stuff is wood ash—smoke is supposed to be a medium for communication with the spirit world. The clear liquid is water, and it'll be rainwater—that's how you can tell the sacrifice is to Cháak—it's kind of like the address label. And the red stuff will be blood; it's symbolic of appeasement."

"Your people?" Mike asked.

"I don't know," Elvis told him frankly. "Kukulcán is the real deal. Christian, I mean. You heard him the other night; he's become a regular evangelist. The rest of these guys, the ones that are with me, are what I'd call seekers—they're still feeling this stuff out. And even among the ones that are close—well, picture it for yourself. You've been following a certain faith all of your life and then someone comes along with a persuasive case for showing that you've been wrong. That's a really hard jump to make. And even after you've made it, bro, things can get a bit gray, you know? In Japan, for instance, it's common for people to profess to be Christians, and yet visit and worship at Shinto shrines. Now, anybody even remotely acquainted with the Bible knows that's dead wrong; it goes against the very first of the Ten Commandments, the one about strange gods. But it's a comfort thing; people are going to naturally tend to gravitate back to their old culture and their old nature."

Elvis thought about this for a moment and then shook his head.

"No," he said. "It doesn't add up. I mean, even if some of these bros were clinging to the old ways, the *cenote* is considered sacred to Cháak, right? And they pitched sacrifices *into* it; they didn't build altars alongside. So if this is worship, then that's what they would have done. They would have just thrown the blood, or whatever it came from, right into the pit."

"So what's this?" Mike asked.

"It's a warning," Elvis told him, shaking his head. "Or a curse. Take your choice."

"From somebody back in the village?"

"No," Elvis shook his head again. "I mean, don't get me wrong. The village has no lack of elders who are plenty steamed over the idea of ditching Cháak and picking up on Jesus. But they're open about it. This, though—this is sneaking around. After all, it's what, like over eighty degrees out here this afternoon? But look at that bowl of water; it's almost full. And the blood; no flies, no insects of any kind. Naw, that hasn't been here for more than an hour, tops, and I sure haven't seen anybody sneaking out here, have you?"

"I haven't," Mike agreed. "So who's leaving it, then?"

"I've got an idea," Elvis told him. "But you aren't going to like it."

"Try me," Mike grunted.

"Our old pal, Kunich Ahua."

Mike chuckled.

"The sun god is making sacrifices to the rain god?"

"Whoever's masquerading as the sun god is," Elvis asserted.

"Why?"

"For the same reason anybody would masquerade as a Mayan god in the first place," Elvis said. "For power."

Mike had kicked the makeshift altar off into the underbrush, the red blood spattering across the foliage and flashing crimson in the dappled midafternoon light. It made it even more apparent than it had been before, but there was no undoing it.

Line reels in hand, the two men walked back toward the camp, moving slowly across the newly cleared staging area.

"The Cháakadon," Mike asked. "They live here in the Yucatan full-time. So are they . . ."

"Sensitive to their environment?" Elvis finished for him. "Aware if there's someone strange in the neighborhood? I hear you, bro. And the answer is yes. When I first got in this neck of the woods, they were watching my every move for days before they let on that they were onto me."

"And yet you don't think it was one of them."

Elvis shook his head.

"It just wouldn't make sense," he said.

By the time they got back to the camp, it was obvious that theirs was not the only altar that had been found. Kukulcán met them at the camp's border, uttering the single English word he knew for trouble.

"Bummer," he said.

The Mayan men didn't sing together as they gathered wood for the evening fire and prepared the evening meal. Late that night, as orange sparks from the campfire fluttered up into the star-strewn Yucatan sky, every set of eyes glanced nervously time and again to the darkness surrounding the camp, searching for a visitor who made no noise; who did not even interrupt the constant concert of insects and the shrill chorus of a thousand tree-frogs.

The next morning, the entire camp rose to perform the last major task before the helicopter came in with the supplies: setting the primary guideline for the *cenote* dive.

It was a seven-man job, requiring all of the cave divers who had accompanied Mike into the jungle for this preliminary work. They began by rappelling two men down the limestone walls to the water's surface, where they inflated a fourteen-and-a-half-foot inflatable boat, installing a rigid wooden floor to provide a working surface—not an easy task while suspended from kernmantle mountaineering rope. Then the primary guideline was lowered to the boat on its 55-gallon-drum-size nylon spool, which was set into an aluminum cradle that had been fabricated for the task. After that, hundred-meter ropes were attached to the bow, the stern and either side of the stout gray inflatable. These were passed to men who had rappelled down to water level and anchored themselves into the limestone at the four compass-points of the *cenote*.

GPS unit in hand, Mike stood in the bow of the inflatable and motioned to the four rope handlers, telling them when to take in rope or pay it out.

Jorge looked around.

"The line," he said. "You are putting it in where Pete made his dive. Is that right?"

"It is," Mike nodded. "His insurance still hasn't paid. If I can find his body while I'm on the bottom, so much the better. It will settle things."

Jorge nodded, but looked unsure.

Mike held his hand up so all four handlers would take tension in their lines.

"This looks like it," he said. "Get ready to toss the anchor."

With the Mayan men watching from up top, their brown faces just barely visible over the *cenote*'s rim, Jorge's brother stripped about twenty feet of half-inch line off of the big spool and then man-handled a fifty-pound mushroom anchor, with six feet of steel chain attached, out of the stern of the boat. Mike held the rope as Jorge prepared a shackle to attach the line to the anchor. Then the breeze had kicked up for just a moment, jarring the boat ever so slightly, and Jorge's brother, his bare feet wet, slipped on the smooth wooden deck.

Mike would remember what had happened next as if it had been shot in slow motion. The anchor chain, kinked into a coil, had lain in a loop under the Mexican's other foot. His balance lost, Jorge's brother toppled, releasing the anchor with a noisy splash. Mike, still holding the rope with one hand, grabbed the young man's shirt with his other. Then the weight of the anchor yanked them both down into the water, and all sound vanished as Mike and the young Mexican were towed down into the green depths.

Gripping the young man's shirt with all of his might, wishing that he'd had time to take a breath before being dragged underwater, Mike passed the rope up to his mouth, and gripped it in his teeth, hoping that Jorge would have the presence of mind to allow it to spool down out. He had—the rope kept coming with them. Mike could feel his hair being swept back by his passage through the water of the *cenote*, the weight of the anchor tugging them downward.

As his ears began to ache from the growing pressure, Mike climbed down the young man's struggling body, finding the chain, but unable to release it. The water had gotten dark, and his ears ached agonizingly. Just a few feet more, he knew, would be sufficient to implode his eardrums, and that would create vertigo, maybe disorient him and rob him all sense of his orientation to the surface. Passing the rope through the loop spliced into its end, he lassoed the anchor, pulled the rope tight against the chain, and then, still gripping the rope, began swimming for the surface for all he was worth, tugging frantically at the rope, signaling to the surface.

Up top, Jorge must have seen the line jerking, because, scant seconds later, the rope was being drawn upwards in great, strong spurts. Mike kept hold of the line, grabbed Jorge's now-limp brother by the shirt collar, and kept on swimming, the green surface shimmering above and getting closer as he swam.

They wasted no time trying to free the anchor when they got to the surface. Mike simply handed up the chain and Jorge pulled it—anchor and all—into the boat, drawing the young man up with it. With Mike pushing from behind, the Mexican fell heavily onto the plywood decking, the impact shocking life back into his lungs, because he immediately coughed up a white froth and began breathing again. Then Mike clambered back into the boat, exhausted.

A ragged cheer erupted from the four line-handlers stationed around the *cenote* and from Elvis and Kukulcán up top. But the rest of the Mayans remained silent, somberly registering the tragedy that had almost taken place.

19

TULUM

The two Navy footlockers were in the way again.

Viktor Bellum put down the double set of steel 104-cubic-foot scuba tanks that he'd just carried in and shook his head. Lifting the first squat, rectangular box, he grunted and moved it to a far corner of the stockroom, under a block of circuit breakers. He came back, hefted the other one, and then stood with it and shuffled over to put it atop the first.

He finished the job and stood there, sweating, despite the big 10,000-BTU air-conditioner laboring in its framed hole in the wall. He thought of why he kept the footlockers.

With most people it would be sentiment, he supposed, because the contents of the two containers were literally all that he had from his parents.

The stuff had actually shown up in cardboard shipping containers—six of them—near the end of his first hitch in the Navy, eight months after the base chaplain had come calling to let him know that his parents had finally given their lives to his father's screwy business. They had died in some place that the chaplain couldn't pronounce of a disease that, amazingly enough, he could: *Muchapo* virus, the Latin American cousin of Africa's Ebola.

After the containers had arrived, lugged up to Bellum's second-floor apartment by a postman who obviously hadn't cared for the job, Bellum's first inclination had been to carry them back out to the curb. Looking at the shipping labels, recognizing the handwriting of his father's elderly Mexican assistant, Bellum had known that they could be nothing other than his parents' personal effects, and he had been hard-pressed to think of a single thing of theirs that he would ever care to see again.

Then he'd thought better of it. His father had never shown much talent for either making or saving money, but there was always the chance that there was some cash squirreled away somewhere in their things. That or a savings bond, maybe the gold pocket watch of his grandfather's that he'd remembered seeing as a kid. So the shipping containers had sat there for weeks, taking up room in Bellum's tiny off-base studio apartment, until Bellum had finally come up with a holiday weekend with nothing better to do than sort through them.

The first two boxes had been about what he'd expected: his mother's thin cotton dresses, washed too many times; his father's shiny-seated suits, hopelessly out of style. All went straight to the dumpster. And when Bellum had gotten to the third box, he'd thought he'd found more of the same: dozens of manila file folders, crammed with notes hand-pecked onto thin paper by his father's ancient Olivetti typewriter, fat envelopes of black-and-white pictures taken by the old man as he'd traveled.

Then Bellum had started actually reading some of the notes, and what he had seen there had just about stopped his heart. He'd read for the rest of the weekend, and by the time he got done, he'd realized that his father's old assistant had sent Bellum more than just six boxes of junk.

The old man might not have known it, but he'd shipped him the keys to a treasure.

And that's why Bellum kept this stuff—his father's files. He'd needed them to find what had brought him back down here, and eventually he would need them to help sell it off. But until then, they were necessary clutter.

The shrill ringing of a telephone interrupted his reverie. It was the landline, not the satellite phone. Someone calling for the shop. Bellum stepped into the small office and picked up the old-fashion Bakelite receiver.

"Tek Tulum," he said. It was the dive shop's name, and the easiest way to answer a phone when the calls stood a roughly fifty-fifty chance of being in Spanish or English.

"*Hola,*" the male caller said haltingly. "*Señor Bellum . . . por favor.*"

Bellum rolled his eyes—an American trying to remember high-school Spanish.

"This is Viktor Bellum," Bellum replied in English. "What can I do for you?"

"Oh, hi, Mr. Bellum," the caller said, his relief evident. "This is Arthur Kensuth from the Expedition Channel. Do you remember me?"

"Red hair, skinny, assistant producer ... ralphed all over the floor of the chopper on the way in to Cenote X a few years ago," Bellum said.

"Uhm, yes," Kensuth said sheepishly. "Yes, sir. That would be me. I was calling to let you know that we're going to be doing a feature on Mike Bryant's next attempt to dive the *cenote*, and we were wondering if you might be available to do the expert commentary for us again."

"Are you sure there's even going to be a dive?" Bellum asked. "Last I heard, Bryant was having Indian trouble."

"No, sir," Kensuth replied hesitantly. "Not that I'd know of. We got both a fax and an e-mail from the Yucatan Deep Project this morning, confirming that they will be making the dive exactly one month from next Wednesday."

"You're sure of that?" Bellum asked. "I mean, there was nothing in the announcement suggesting that the dive might be delayed?"

"No, sir," Kensuth repeated. "But don't worry. I mean, if anything happens, if there's a postponement or anything like that, we'll still pay a kill fee."

"Kill fee ... ," Bellum repeated dully.

"Yes, sir. You know. We still pay you even if there's no broadcast; nothing for you to do."

"Oh," Bellum said. "I see. No. I wasn't worried about that."

"Great," Kensuth said, a bit of confusion creeping through in his voice. "So we can count on you for the taping?"

"Huh? Oh, sure. Absolutely. When do I report?"

"I'll send you full details in a fax, but basically, we'll send a driver to pick you up the day before the broadcast, and then we'll all chopper down there the morning of the dive."

"I've got a better idea," Bellum said, thinking on his feet. "Why don't we meet up a day earlier and then all get down there the evening before? That way we can get a little background, catch up on the technicalities of the dive, that sort of thing."

"I don't know," Kensuth said slowly. "That would add a day's 'copter rental. And we'd have to arrange for tents, cots, catering—"

"I think I can scare up the tents and cots, no extra charge," Bellum said dismissively. "As for catering, it won't kill you to live on MREs for a day; I did it weeks at a time in the Teams."

Bellum doubted that the civilian would recognize the military reference to "meals, ready to eat," but then again, it never hurt to throw in a subtle reminder of his supposed SEAL background.

"And I think it will be worth whatever it costs to keep the bird on site an extra day," he added. "I mean, you want a quality program, don't you?"

"Yes . . . but I'll have to talk to our producer."

"Have him call me," Bellum told the young man.

"I'll try," Kensuth muttered. "Mr. Lorenzo is a very busy man."

"So am I," Bellum said. "But I'll be free one hour from now. Tell him I'll be waiting for his call then."

"Gee. I don't kn—"

"One hour," Bellum repeated. "I'll talk to him then."

Without waiting for a response, Bellum hung up the phone and looked at it, thinking.

Viktor Bellum had never been a SEAL. That was true. But he had had the full-boat EOD training, in many ways every bit as rigorous as what they dished out at the fabled Coronado school. And one thing the Navy had taught Bellum was that, no matter how simple the assignment seemed, you always had a Plan B.

Always.

Every time.

And sometimes, it didn't hurt to have more than one.

20
CANCÚN

Dual rotors thrashing the air at either end of its fuselage like a pair of gargantuan eggbeaters, the Sikorsky heavy-lift helicopter thundered slowly over the airport tarmac. It maintained a constant fifty feet of altitude, the noise of its passage drowning out even the scream of a Boeing 747 jumbo jet hurtling down an adjacent runway, taking another load of tourists home. Pivoting at its nose, the helicopter approached the big steel shipping container from the downwind side. Then, like a mother hen settling protectively onto her brood, the huge aircraft descended until it was hovering steadily just ten feet over the top of the reinforced metal box.

Standing two hundred feet to its side, his hair whipping in the outwash from the rotor blast, Mike Bryant nodded his approval as he watched the big helicopter keep its place in the steady breeze blowing in from the Caribbean. Despite the wind, the helicopter was perfectly steady, as if it had been tack-welded into its place in the sky.

Mike had a healthy respect for helicopter pilots. Several years before, while scouting for additional apertures into a big cave system in Brazil, a pilot had taken a much smaller helicopter than this up to 2,000 feet, put it into a hover, and invited Mike to take the controls.

Mike could still remember how, the instant the pilot had relinquished his grip on the pitch and altitude controls, the helicopter had seemed to develop a mind of its own, the horizon walking by outside the bubble canopy as it began a slow rotation, the treetops seeming to rise and fall like ocean waves as the rotors pitched and yawed. He had only had the controls for fifteen seconds, possibly fewer, but he could still remember vividly how, even with him devoting a hundred percent of his attention to the skittish aircraft, he had been unable to maintain anything more refined than a drunken wobble. When finally the grinning pilot had resumed control, Mike had been surprised to find himself drenched in sweat, despite the torrent of air jetting at him from the cockpit air conditioner.

And that had been a little helicopter—a two-place job. Mike could only imagine what it must be like to try to rein in one that was nearly the length of two city buses.

The helicopter lowered two hooks on thick, well-greased steel cables, and the men atop the shipping container stepped back, allowing the hooks to touch the roof of the box, grounding out any built-up static electricity before they approached them.

The two men grabbed the hooks and clipped them onto a pair of reinforced steel lifting trusses; two devices that looked like gigantic industrial-strength coat hangers. From either end of these, thick Kevlar lifting straps, like extra-wide loops of fire hose, descended through eyes welded onto the roof of the container to lugs that projected from its base. Both men scrambled to the ground and their coworkers signaled to the pilot.

The steel cables straightened and then went rigid as the helicopter rose. The thunder increased in volume as the pilot added throttle and flattened the pitch of the blades. The shipping container, essentially a boxcar without the undercarriage, quivered slightly as the trusses assumed its weight. A moment later, Mike could see daylight under the big box's base.

He felt a hand on his shoulder.

"Time to go," Elvis Hastings shouted in the cave diver's ear.

Mike nodded, and with one last glance at the shipping container, now being winched up into the cavity between the helicopter's cab and its rear engine nacelle, he walked to a fenced area where a pair of small Bell Jet Ranger helicopters were spooling up on their own pads.

The helicopters, the noisy tarmac, the jetloads of tourists arriving and departing, the distant sprawl of luxury hotels along Cancún's beachfront—Mike found it difficult to believe that he was fewer than 200 kilometers away from the isolation of the small camp at Cenote X.

Cenote X. Mike still thought of it that way, even though the project had already adopted the Mayan name, "K'uxulch'en," in its press releases and project reports.

It had always irked Mike that places got renamed by latecomers. Mount McKinley was a case in point. Named for a politician by a sea captain who had seen it in the distance and never so much as set foot on it, the tallest point in North America had already borne a much more beautiful native name—Denali. And even though the government had made some concession for the mountain by calling the land surrounding it Denali National Park, the fact remained that it was still Mount McKinley as far as the U.S. Geological Survey was concerned, despite the best efforts of wilderness advocates and Native American groups to set the record straight. So Mike was determined that he would not insult the Mayan people of Quintana Roo by repeating the error with the world's deepest known *cenote*.

Still, old habits died hard. K'uxulch'en, that deep, dark abyss in the middle of the jungle had been Cenote X when his best friend had died there. In some part of his mind, it would be Cenote X forever. He thought about the near accident at the *cenote* and marveled again that it was just a short flight away.

That near accident had taken place better than a week earlier. The intervening days had been spent in a press conference down at Tulum (chosen by the media-savvy Becky because the spectacular waterfront ruins, the only ruins so situated in all of Mexico, made a great backdrop for a photo-op). While in Tulum, Mike had taken Elvis out for a check-out dive on scuba, and he'd found the wave-savvy former surfer to be a natural in the water. After that, they'd made Elvis's first cavern and cave dives, and the missionary had proven to be an extraordinarily adept student.

The days had been busy, but there had still been time for Mike to feel Bridget's absence. True, there had been good reasons for her to return to the Cháakadon village and stay there until the Faith's Frontier medical staff had time to arrive and get established in the jungle clinic. But Mike couldn't help but think that the heavy friction between the two of them had helped fuel her decision to remain distant until just before he began the two weeks of practice dives that would precede the actual attempt. He'd missed her; he'd been concerned about her. And yet he'd remained apprehensive about seeing her again. It had not been like the old days, and he'd wondered whether it would ever be like that again.

Their blades were already whirring furiously when the two Americans got to their helicopter. A crewman held open the cockpit door and then handed them each a set of pale green David Clark headsets after they had climbed into the back seat and strapped in. In no time at all, the crewman jumped in the vacant front seat, latched the door, and they were off, the helicopter tilting giddily as they accelerated forward and began to climb. Behind it, the second helicopter, containing the rest of the ground crew, followed.

All three helicopters vectored around the flight paths leading in and out of the airport, and then beat steadily out to sea, gaining altitude as they went. They would, Mike knew from his previous experiences with helicopters, climb to a minimum of a thousand feet. The big Sikorsky carrying the shipping container was a twin-engine aircraft and could, thanks to fuselage-length driveshafts, continue flying even after failure of one engine. But the Jet Rangers were single-engine craft and needed the altitude to give them ample room to switch over to "autogyro," the helicopter's glide mode, should problems develop.

The crewman handed back two pairs of rubberized marine binoculars.

"For the watching," he explained, his voice seeming to come from somewhere in Mike's head. The headsets were the newer, noise-canceling type that reduced the rotor noise and turbine whine to a level less than that of an air conditioner and seemed to heighten the disembodied-voice effect of the cockpit communications.

"What's our ETA at the village?" Mike asked, lifting the headset's boom mike into place.

"One hour ten," the pilot replied. Since English was the international language of aviation, his was better than average. "It'd be shorter as the crow goes, but we're going to have to jog around a few places. So we don't overfly any houses and peoples up here on the coast, *sí*?"

Elvis nodded at the answer and grinned Mike's way. Mike grinned back. It was business but it was also fun.

The three aircraft turned farther out to sea to avoid and pass behind the path of a cruise ship coming into port. Mike used the binoculars to look at early-morning joggers taking turns around the white ship's main deck. Many of the vacationers stopped at the rails to watch the three helicopters. The Sikorsky was on his side, so Mike trained the glasses on it as well.

The binoculars delivered an amazingly crisp image; he could even make out the Dallas Cowboys logo on the pilot's cap as he turned and glanced Mike's way. Mike looked at the helicopter's huge fuselage, the blur of the rotors, the suspended load, the taunt Kevlar straps. He lowered the binoculars.

Then he snatched them back up again.

"Tell them to set down!" He tapped the crewman's shoulder as he said it.

"Eh?"

"*No mas!*" Mike replied hurriedly, using the only Spanish phrase that he could muster under the circumstances. "The cargo strap! It's breaking!"

Instantly, the crewman lifted his own binoculars to his eyes.

Mike raised his for another look as well. It confirmed what he'd already seen; the rear strap on his side—the one that would be out of sight for the Sikorsky's crew—showed a twisting fuzzy patch, like a dandelion seed, where it passed around the lifting lug of the load.

A torrent of Spanish erupted over the headset. Mike could make out a one-word reply from the larger helicopter: "*Por que?*" The crewman on the Americans' helicopter repeated his warning and added something this time. Then the Sikorsky tilted out of view as the Jet Ranger's pilot pushed the stick forward and made a bee-line for the beach. When Mike next saw the Sikorsky, it had turned so it was facing out to sea and it was backing slowly toward the shore.

"He backs to reduce the load on the strap," the crewman explained to his clients.

Off to his right, Mike could see the other Jet Ranger skimming full-bore over the water toward the white sand of a cluster of oceanfront resorts. They passed swiftly over jet skiers and a couple of wind surfers leaning into the breeze on their brilliantly colored boards.

The pilot switched his mike to the loudspeaker mounted on the helicopter's skid and began issuing curt, rapid-fire instructions in Spanish. Listening over the intercom, Mike could make out just one word, "*playa*"—beach. Then the pilot repeated the instructions in English, "Please clear the beach—do not run. Please clear the beach now."

Switching back to radio, the pilot called air traffic control, declaring an emergency. Down on the beach, two lifeguards began ushering bikini- and swim-trunk-clad tourists back to their hotels as a third guard rushed out on a Jet Ski to clear the water in front of the beach. Elvis, Mike noticed, was silent throughout the whole thing. Then Mike glanced his way and saw that his friend's lips were moving wordlessly; the young missionary was praying.

The huge helicopter and its load reached the white surfline and began turning, its rotorwash flattening out the brilliant turquoise Caribbean water. Then, once its pilot had a safe, clear view of the beach, he began inching the monstrous aircraft forward, its load dangling just a few feet above the frothing waves. In less then a minute the big gray helicopter was over the sand, its rotorwash blasting beach towels, chaise lounges, sand buckets, and discarded cover-ups into the surrounding foliage and out to sea. He sank lower and a sandstorm erupted under the blades, sending the crowd of sunburned onlookers up even farther from the impromptu landing site.

"Man," the Jet Ranger's pilot sighed over the intercom. "Are we gonna have the paperwork to fill out on *this* one. . . ."

Finally the storage container kissed the sand and both Jet Rangers set down on the firmer ground just above the waterline. The crewman from the Americans' helicopter popped the hatch and went sprinting out to meet the other three members of the ground crew, who hurriedly tied bandannas over their mouths and noses to shield themselves from the flying sand and then swarmed up the ladder on the side of the container, where they quickly undid the big cargo hooks, freeing the load from the helicopter. One of the crewmen leapt from the top of the box and dashed out onto the sand in front of the hovering aircraft, where the pilot could see him. He signaled an "okay" and then a thumb's-up, and the big helicopter went up a few feet, banked slightly, and then swiftly went back out to sea, rising as it set a course back to the airport, leaving the white-sand beach suddenly calm and virtually deserted.

The Jet Ranger's pilot shut down his engines, grabbed something from the map pocket behind the copilot's seat, and everyone got out. Almost as soon as the rotor noise diminished, Mike could hear animated shouting in Spanish—the resort's manager, wanting to know why a boxcar had suddenly materialized on his beach. The pilot from the other helicopter jogged up to deal with him while Mike, Elvis, and their pilot joined the others at the container. Everyone immediately clustered around the frayed lifting strap.

"Close call, *sí*?" The uniformed Mexican lifted the thing he had brought from the Jet Ranger—a small, silver digital camera—and took several photographs of the damaged strap from various angles. Then he released and held up the business end of the heavy strap. Of its original six inches of width, only two remained intact. The rest was split and fuzzy. The pilot turned the strap over and everyone leaned forward for a closer look. The back side of the strap was blackened and looked partially melted, and when the pilot flexed it, tiny silver-gray particles fell from it.

"What's that?" Elvis asked. "Sand?"

"Aluminum oxide would be my guess," Mike replied, and when Elvis returned him a shocked look, he nodded. "Industrial-grade sandpaper. Like what you probably used to shape surfboards back in California. My guess is that somebody took a belt-sander to this sucker before it got put on the load."

"They knew what they were doing," the pilot grunted as he took two more photos. "They did the back of this strap, where we wouldn't see it when we hooked up—we strap the loads on this way, stitching-side out. And they did the back strap, the one we can't see from the heavy-lift. The rear straps, they are cut about fifteen centimeters longer, yes? To allow for the chopper's attitude in flight."

Elvis looked at Mike.

"What are you thinking, bro?"

"How soon do we have to report this?" Mike asked the pilot.

"None of us here are the experts," the pilot shrugged. "I mean, it *looks* like this strap was tampered with, *si*? But we won't know that for sure until I turn it in for the—how you say—analysis. I have to alert the aviation and transportation departments and make the report, of course. That's standard procedure; we declared the emergency. But this is not America, *si*? I have a day or two to do it. Why? You would like to get going, yes?"

"I would," Mike said. "If somebody's trying to monkey-wrench this shipment, I don't see any reason to lay around here and give them a second shot at it."

He turned to Elvis. "Do you?"

"It's ethical to wait on the report?" Elvis asked the pilot.

"Of course," the Mexican nodded. "I will get this strap to the proper authorities and make out all of the paperwork. It will be done properly. Nothing will be overlooked."

"Then let's get the other strap and boogie," Elvis decided.

The pilot nodded and walked back along the beach to his helicopter to make the radio call. He waved over the other pilot, who had somehow calmed the resort manager, and the second man jogged back to his helicopter, got the rotors turning, and took off low, across the water, heading back to the airport.

By now, all manner of emergency vehicles were arriving. A little white Ford Transit van with POLICIA on the side came weaving back along a hotel sidewalk, using its siren to part the swimsuited onlookers. The policeman stopped prudently short of the sand and began to walk their way, but the pilot intercepted him. Mike listened to their conversation in Spanish. The gist of it was that they had experienced a problem with a lifting strap and had set down here while the helicopter and a tender craft returned to the airport to reinspect the lifting gear and get another strap. And in the meantime, the pilot smiled, would the policeman be so kind as to keep the crowds at bay, as the rotor blades could be dangerous?

Glad for something to do, the policeman began moving the gawkers back. A fire truck arrived and the pilot talked to their captain as well. The firemen all pulled their coats and helmets off and lit cigarettes—it was obvious that the pilot had asked them to wait until all of the choppers were once again airborne. Last to arrive was the news van from the local TV station. The policeman looked their way and the pilot shook his head, so the policeman kept the protesting, gesturing camera crew back behind his line.

Finally, after what seemed to Mike like a lifetime, but was actually only fifteen minutes by his scarred and nicked Citizen Aqualand watch, they all heard the rapid thrumming of the second Jet Ranger skimming in low across the brilliant blue sea. In a matter of seconds, the immaculate red-and-blue helicopter had set down on the sand 100 meters down the beach, and the ground crew was loping toward it. They opened the hatch and began tugging out the coiled strap that had been stuffed into the back seat. Then they all came back to the shipping container, along with the second pilot, who opened a plastic bag and began to hand out white paper-fiber face masks, the kind one would use for spraying paint or plastering, to the crewmen, the other pilot, and Mike and Elvis. They all put them on and, two minutes later, the heavier drumming of the approaching Sikorsky came hollowly across the open water.

The crewmen swiftly stripped the damaged lifting strap off the container and then looked at the strap and up at the senior pilot. The pilot put the mask up on his forehead and scowled; he hadn't thought about what they would do with the extra strap. And they couldn't put it back in either of the two smaller helicopters; they needed the seats for the crew.

"Put it in the shipping container," Elvis suggested, his voice muffled by the paper mask, and the pilot grinned at this obvious solution, barked an order in Spanish, and it was done.

The Sikorsky's drumming grew to a steady, chest-drumming thunder that echoed back loudly from the resort buildings. The crewmen scrambled back into place on the container, and both pilots went back to their machines, snapping canvas covers in place over the intakes, while Mike and Elvis retreated up the beach a safe distance.

The big helicopter came back in and video cameras materialized in the hands of half the tourists queued up behind the policeman's yellow-taped line. The miniature sandstorm repeated itself, and the crewmen squinted and shielded their faces as they hooked up the two lifting-arms. That done, they climbed down and each watched a lug carefully as the second pilot took position out in front of the heavy-lift chopper and directed it to take up tension. All four crewmen then retreated 25 meters. The pilot directing the operation whirled a finger in the air, and the Sikorsky rose with its load once again tucked in place, turned heavily, and headed back out to sea.

Mike and Elvis's pilot had taken the intake shields back off of his machine and was spooling the engine up as they climbed in. They put on their headsets and the crewman climbed in and secured the door. The pilot turned and grinned back at Mike and Elvis.

"Okay," he smiled. "We go now. But no more surprises, *sí?*"

21
THE CHÁAKADON VILLAGE

You have not gone up the hill to wait for the machines that fly." Naum Kaan turned from his loom to see who had addressed him in his native Cháakadon tongue, even though he knew full well that it was Quatul. Sure enough, there the old codger was, his gray-streaked hair damp and his forehead beaded with perspiration.

"But you, my friend, have been up and returned," Naum Kaan observed. "Why is that? I have not heard their machine."

"The whole village went up there this morning, to their place for the sick," Quatul said. "But they did not come when expected. The woman looks at that thing on her wrist, the one they all wear to tell them where the sun is in the sky. . . ."

He paused here to consider giving his opinion on such a thing; that wearing a machine to tell one where the sun or the stars were was like wearing a machine to tell you if you were standing out in the rain. But he decided it would be best to stick to the subject.

"And you can tell that she is worried," Quatul continued. "As well she should be, for I believe that their machine has come to trouble, that the things they wish to bring here have fallen from the sky. I told your daughter-in-law to tell the woman this thing, for I have seen that she knows some of the woman's hand-talk. But Ixnitke' refused to do as I said."

"And why would you believe that the strangers' things have fallen from the sky?" Naum Kaan asked it with his eyebrows raised, making it obvious that he was not going to rise to any bait about a disrespectful daughter-in-law.

"Some of the young men told me."

"And why would *they* believe that?"

"Kunich Ahua," Quatul said. "He spoke to them and told them."

"Kunich Ahua appeared to them?"

"Of course not. He never appears. He is a spirit. But his voice was heard in the young men's hut last night. He told them that he would not let this flying machine come."

"But the machines have already come twice," Naum Kaan pointed out. "To bring the place for the sick. To bring the things that go inside."

"That was when the one who calls himself Elvis was here," Quatul said, almost spitting the name out. "He is a witch."

"A witch," Naum Kaan mused. "So a witch is stronger than a god these days?"

Quatul said nothing.

"You said Kunich Ahua appeared to the young men," Naum Kaan said. "And yet you are the shaman. How is it that he did not come to you?"

"I do not know," Quatul replied, the sorrow of the thought obvious in his face. "I believe he thinks that I have lost my power among our people."

"Quatul," Naum Kaan said softly. "You have done nothing wrong in respecting my wishes. I am the elder. It is our way."

"A god disagrees," the other old man replied curtly.

"I strongly doubt it."

Naum Kaan worked his loom in silence for a moment and then asked, "If you heard of this visitation from Kunich Ahua, how is it that you did not tell me?"

"I thought you would dismiss it as fancy."

"Did you?" Naum Kaan asked. "Or did you believe that I would ask Kukulcán to travel to their camp and ask the men there to use the thing that talks through the air to call and warn them that such a thing was possible? To smother this man's prophecy?"

"Kunich Ahua is not a man," Quatul said, grabbing at the diversion. "He is a god."

"So you say."

"And we have the proof; the flying machine is not coming," Quatul added smugly.

"Do we?" Naum Kaan asked. "Quatul, my friend, have your old ears gotten that feeble?"

Naum Kaan smiled, and in a moment Quatul heard it as well, the distant throbbing of helicopter rotor blades, echoing off the jungle canopy.

"Well," Naum Kaan smiled, locking his loom open and tucking the boat for safekeeping into the open web of the half-finished hammock. "Now, I think, it is time for me to go up the hill. Would you like to join me, my old friend? Or would you rather wait down here and see if Kunich Ahua shows up to prophesy what he thinks about *this?*"

22

Flying over the jungle was like flying over the sea. The scrub vegetation of coastal jungle had given way to the hardwoods of the Yucatan interior, and after that the helicopters moved over a vast and softly undulating, unchanging expanse of green. What they were seeing, Mike knew, was just the top of the canopy. The ground below rarely showed through.

Monkeys lived in the trees below. So did jaguars, snakes, rodents, and any variety of reptiles. But even though Mike knew all of that, he couldn't see any of it from the Bell Jet Ranger helicopter cruising comfortably over the ocean of green foliage. He couldn't even see any birds from his moving seat, high above the terrain. Wisps of fog rising steam-like from the trees were the only sign that what Mike was seeing was real, and not some cleverly painted tableau.

The smaller helicopters had accompanied the Sikorsky with its suspended load until the last *campesino*'s farmhouse was far behind them. Then the pilots had twisted more throttle into the smaller craft, taking them ahead of the larger one, transforming from escort to vanguard.

They couldn't all come in at once. While the Faith's Frontier clinic up on the hill had a helipad, it was only large enough for one of the smaller helicopters at a time, and could not accommodate the Sikorsky at all, so the Jet Rangers would have to land one after the other and discharge their passengers. Then the Sikorsky would lower the shipping container from a hover, after which all three choppers would go on to the camp at the *cenote* and sit on the ground for four hours, the amount of time that Faith's Frontier estimated would be needed to move their equipment and supplies out of the container. There had been some talk about using radios in case the timetable changed, but the distance from the Cháakadon Village to the *cenote* was nearly 30 kilometers, just beyond the range of their handheld avionics. So the timetable assumed tremendous importance; if the operation was not completed in time, the helicopters would not be able to stay on—they had already been chartered by a Meridien construction contractor for the following day. And the emergency setdown on the beach back in Cancún, the time used waiting for the replacement strap to arrive, had not helped at all.

"Village coming up. GPS says ten clicks."

The pilot pointed and Mike squinted through the scratched and crazed acrylic of the helicopter's broad, curved windshield. In the distance, near the horizon, he could just make out several thin threads of woodsmoke rising into the clear Yucatan air from a clearing on the ground and, on a low hill above the village, the orange speck of a windsock hanging at rest.

They banked and vectored straight in toward the sock, the jungle rushing by in a green blur as the helicopter skimmed barely a hundred yards above the treetops. As they flashed over the hilltop clinic, Mike saw a sea of brown faces framed by black hair; a hundred pale palms raised in greeting as the crowd waved at the passing aircraft.

The helicopter kept going, arcing upward in a shallow climb and banking slightly to the left as the pilot put his craft into a wide orbit around the hilltop clinic and the village below.

"We let the other chopper set down first, *sí?*" The pilot nodded straight ahead, where Mike could see the minute red and black shape of the incoming helicopter. "That way, the crew can start making ready for the box, *sí?*"

"Good idea," Elvis said. Mike saw the missionary close the small, worn brown-bound Bible he'd been reading and snap the cover shut. The Californian smiled and winked.

"Looking forward to seeing your girl?" Elvis asked.

"Yeah," Mike replied. It was true. Bridget had rarely been out of his thoughts over the past two weeks, even though he'd assured her that the *cenote* camp would be fine without its doctor as they got things ready for the airlift—both he and Jorge were also trained emergency medical technicians. To make matters worse, the separation would not end today; it would only be interrupted. Bridget would be staying at the Cháakadon village for another week while Mike and his support divers got things ready for the preliminary dives and she transferred her clinic caseload into the hands of the permanent staff.

Mike could see her in his mind's eye, bent over the medical charts as he'd seen her so many times in the ER at Ocala, wearing the small reading glasses that she needed only at the end of a very long shift, sitting in the pool of light cast by the desk lamp, writing in the compact, clear hand that she used on charts and scripts alike. Bridget had no patience with doctors who scrawled their notes or their prescriptions. She refused to allow even the slightest risk that a patient's safety might be compromised because her written observations or instructions were not clear.

Mike loved the orderliness of Bridget's life, so different from the clutter and improvisation—and chaos, he had to admit—of his own. And he was awestruck by the fact that this woman had, for eleven years now, devoted virtually every spare moment of her life to being with him, paying attention to him, edifying him.

Until recently.

Mike hated the absences of the past few months; hated the fact that they were mostly—all—his fault. The result of his stubbornness.

And why? What, he wondered, did it really matter if Viktor Bellum, bullying jerk that he was, dived some pit in the jungle before he did? Forty years from now, when he sat on the porch in High Springs, what would be more important to him; what would have made his life worth living? That he had been first to touch bottom in Cenote X, or that he had gone through his life with Bridget at his side?

He said that he was doing it to preserve Pete's memory. Becky supported him on this, but then again, Becky was very, very young. In the final equation, he really had to wonder if it ultimately added up to nothing more than a matter of protecting his own pride.

And that all contributed to the other thing that he felt: apprehension.

He remembered a time a couple of years before, when, strapped after having paid Becky's college and refunding a deposit from a Swiss group that had cancelled their lessons, he had been waiting for the weekend, for fresh funds to replenish his bank account, when he realized that he had an insurance payment due. He'd written the check, but he'd not been sure that he would have sufficient funds in his account to cover it. It had been evening, but his bank had had one of those 24-hour dial-up services, so his balance was available by phone. But he'd been unable to call because, even though the situation would remain the same regardless of whether he called—there were either sufficient funds to cover the check or there were not—*knowing* that he was out of money would have seemed somehow more dreadful than not knowing. He preferred having the hope to having the truth.

And that was the way it was as the little helicopter circled and he watched the other Jet Ranger touch down and disgorge its four passengers. Bridget had every right to want nothing to do with him. Either they still had a relationship or they did not. But Mike preferred the hope that something might be there over the possibility of discovering that it was all over.

This time he had no choice. The pilot was landing the helicopter, sinking toward the big white "H" outlined with limestone paving-stones in the center of the circle alongside the clinic.

They touched down, and as soon as Mike removed the noise-canceling headphones, noise—the whine of the turbine, the whoosh-whoosh-whoosh of the rotor blades, the background static of the avionics—rushed in all at once. Elvis was smiling and buttoning his Bible away in the cargo pocket of his shorts. The pilot turned and shouted, "Okay, amigos, see you in three plus travel, *sí*?"

Stooping under the whirling rotors, the other crewman and the two Americans walked briskly to the throngs of Cháakadon crowded in around the clinic buildings. Mike looked for Bridget and then saw her, her long hair pulled back in a French braid. She was dressed in a Mayan linen dress with embroidery—birds, flowers, leaves—all up the front, and she was holding a baby in her arms.

For a moment, Mike just stopped. The dress, the child, her waiting for him to arrive—for a moment, the picture that it painted, the possibility, was so moving that it nearly took his breath away. Then he kept moving toward her, and she smiled.

Bridget handed the infant to Ixnitke' and stepped forward, her tanned arms open for an embrace, and Mike gladly put his arms around her and held her. Her hair smelled exotic, woodsmoke and flowers, and he buried his face in it, squeezing her as she squeezed back. But when he stepped back to kiss her, she turned her head ever so slightly, so it landed on her cheek. He'd been missed. He was welcome. What he was not was forgiven.

"We were worried," Bridget shouted over the noise of the helicopter.

We had a problem with one of the straps that holds the container, he signed back. *Had to set down and replace it.*

She nodded. The answer satisfied her, and there was too much confusion to deliver the full-fledged explanation on the spot.

The baby, Mike signed. *Forest's?*

Bridget nodded.

Healed already?

Almost, Bridget signed back—the only communication possible with the chopper noise. *You or I would take months, but babies heal in weeks. Growth hormone.*

The helicopter's rotor noise crescendoed, and they turned to watch the Jet Ranger rise from the ground and hover, bee-like, as it turned. Then it dipped, moved forward, and vanished beyond the treeline. A few seconds later they could see it rising back into the sky, already some distance away, on course for the *cenote* camp.

New look for you, Mike signed.

Yeah, Bridget agreed. *They aren't used to women in shorts around here. So Ixnitke'*—she spelled the name—*made me two dresses. They're both beautiful, but this is the prettiest of the two. Do you like it?*

"Very much," Mike replied aloud.

She smiled, and Mike could have sworn that he saw the hint of a blush in that smile.

The crowd murmured, and a distant whup-whup-whup, accompanied by a low, continuous thunder, rolled in from the east and then seemed to fill the air around them. Mike turned and saw the Sikorsky, farther away than the sound would have suggested, flying toward them with the shipping container winched closely under its fuselage, like an eagle with a fish clutched in its talons.

Bridget followed Mike's pointing finger, and she nodded.

The four ground crewmen went into action. One popped a smoke grenade and set it on the ground on the side of the helipad away from the clinic, where the orange smoke rose vertically into the air, indicating the relative lack of wind. The crowd murmured again, and Mike realized that even such low technology must have seemed like magic to them.

A second crewman took up a position on the clinic steps, where the pilot would be certain to see him, and took out a pair of florescent red ground-crewman's batons. A third man had a handheld radio out and was in contact with the pilot. The fourth watched the crowd and held his palms out, urging them to stay back.

The last part proved unnecessary. As the big Sikorsky loomed closer and closer, its rotor-wash flattening the treetops, the thunder of its two huge turbine engines palpable to the very bone in every man, woman, and child, the crowd shrank back. Mothers covered their children's ears, and small children hid behind the legs of the adults. Bridget's eyes widened, and Mike realized that even she could hear the helicopter.

The big machine went into a hover, and ever so slowly the shipping container descended, steel cables paying out glacially as the pilot riveted his attention on the crewman with the batons. When the box was just inches off the close-cut grass, the crewman crossed the batons and lowered them to waist level; the pilot lowered the entire helicopter a good five feet, the cables went slack, and the crewmen scrambled atop the load to unhook it. They signaled an all-clear to the man with the batons, he whirled both batons at shoulder level, and the cables were withdrawn. Then the helicopter rose, the thunder of its engines increasing, and turned to follow its smaller fellows to the *cenote* camp. Its noise was still echoing off the clinic buildings when the four crewmen began opening the access doors on the shipping container.

We have to work quickly, Mike signed to Bridget. *We're running behind; we won't have the helicopters tomorrow.*

She nodded that she understood and then signed, *Can we talk before you leave here?*

Sure, he returned, adding, *I've missed you.*

She smiled and held up two fingers.

There was no shortage of manpower with which to unload the shipping container, but still, the next three hours were very busy. While not careless, the Cháakadon were a people who did not understand fragility. Clay being a scarce commodity in the jungle, most of their containers were either native gourds or iron pots obtained through third-party trades with other groups. It simply wasn't understood in their culture that some things could be damaged by handling. So Elvis allowed the Cháakadon men to unload bundles of towels and bed dressings, cases of gauze, paper toweling—that sort of thing. But the breakable bottles and cases of medical instruments were all unloaded by Elvis, Mike, and their crew.

That worked until they got to the X-ray machine and its table, which were in a single wooden crate too heavy for even six men to move more than a foot at a time.

"Man," Elvis said after they had shrugged it another foot. "How are we going to get this puppy up the steps?"

"We'll need four more men," Mike agreed. "It's either that or open the crate and carry the individual pieces in. But that would take more time than we have."

"These dudes are eager to help," Elvis agreed. "Still, if anybody drops anything . . ."

Bridget scowled for a moment, then stepped up.

Tell them, she signed to Elvis. *To carry it as if it were a baby. That it can get hurt, like a baby, if they drop or bump it.*

Elvis grinned.

"Why didn't I think of that?"

Because you're a man, Bridget signed smugly. Then she laughed.

Elvis called Kukulkán and three of the other young men forward and said something in their language. They all nodded their understanding. The four Mayans took their places along with the unloading crew and moved the big wooden crate into the clinic building as if it were a piece of cut crystal. That was all of Faith's Frontier's cargo; Mike went into the shipping container with the charter company's crew and helped secure the dive project's equipment for the remaining leg of the voyage.

When he got out he was hot and tired, and Bridget handed him a small cut gourd of sweet, cool water.

"Thanks," he smiled.

Time to talk? Bridget asked.

He nodded, and the two of them went back into the clinic building.

I'm concerned about you . . . , she began, and Mike put his hands on her shoulder.

"Sweetheart, I know that," he said. "But believe me, I'm using every safeguard I can on the dive. Jorge is helping, and you know how thorough he is—"

Now it was Bridget who cut Mike off.

It's not that, she signed.

"Then what is it?"

Signing slowly, picking her words carefully, Bridget signed, *I've had a change in my life.*

The sinking must have been visible in Mike's face, because she immediately added, *No. It's not a bad change. It's a good change. Good for me. Good for you. Good for . . . us.*

"What sort of change?'

I've found—

The door came open and Elvis stuck his head in.

"Hey, guys," he grinned. "Sorry to bother you. But the choppers are coming."

"I'll be right there," Mike told him. Turning back to Bridget, he said, "I'm sorry. You were saying you've found something. What is it?"

Bridget lifted her hands to sign and then sighed.

"You've got to go," she said aloud. "I'll tell you when I get to the camp."

"You're sure?" Mike asked.

She nodded.

You'd better go, she signed.

"Okay," he said, reaching for the door.

"Mike . . . ," Bridget said aloud.

He turned.

She pointed to herself, crossed her hands over her heart, pointed to him.

He took her in his arms, held her, kissed her—the lips this time, not the cheek. Then the doors opened again, the thunder of helicopter rotors filling the small clinic space.

"Dude," Elvis called. "You coming?"

"I am," Mike said. "I'll be right there."

23
NAHOCH PAN, QUINTANA ROO, MEXICO— OCTOBER, 2003

The two divers ascended with glacial slowness from the bottom of the *cenote* basin, exhaust bubbles roiling above them like living creatures of liquid and light, billowing and quivering to the surface. As soon as their heads met the thin film between water and air, both men squeezed the inlet valves for their buoyancy compensators. Inrushing air hissed hollowly as the BCs filled, floating them shoulder-deep at the surface. The men removed their regulators and savored the first deep breath of real, sweet, jungle-scented air.

The sun was shining full on the water, and for a moment Mike Bryant just laid back against his buoyancy compensator and basked in it. What he was enjoying, this reprise, would, he knew, be rarer and rarer over the next few weeks. He felt in between everything. Having choppered back out with Elvis after supplying the camp, Mike had stayed in Cancún waiting for the final set of retooled regulators to come in from Yobatu Scuba, and then there had been one more set of press conferences, during which he had been forced to field more questions about Viktor Bellum and his pretenses toward the dive in Cenote X.

This dive in a small system near the coastal highway had not only helped fulfill an obligation—completing Elvis's cave training—it had contributed the illusion of normalcy, something he'd needed desperately. In just two days' time, Mike, with Bridget, would be back at Cenote X, starting the training dives in preparation for—he could only think of it with initial capitals—The Big Day. But for right now, even if just for a moment, he could relax. Mike floated silently, wanting to give Elvis the chance to speak first. He didn't have to wait long.

"That," the young missionary gasped, "was amazing! I mean—I've never seen anything like it. And what was the deal with all those turtle shells?"

"Casualties," Mike replied. "You'll see 'em in a few caves. Turtles are great breath-hold divers; some species'll even sleep underwater, holding their breath. But eventually, just like you and me, they've got to breathe. When they wander into systems like this and can't find a breathing hole, that's it—they're history."

Mike paused, collecting a memory, and then he continued.

"One time, when we were diving the Peacock system, back home," he said, "Bill Hennigan and I found a turtle swimming along the cave ceiling, poking its head up against the limestone, trying to find a place to breathe. Bill swam up, found a shallow depression in the ceiling, blew a whole bunch of nitrox into it with his regulator, then grabbed the turtle and stuck his head up into it, holding him there so he could breathe. We aimed the little guy toward the exit, and he swam with us, all the way out. Last time I saw him, he was going out the cavern entrance and down the run, heading for the Suwannee."

"Very cool story," Elvis said.

"Yeah," Mike agreed. "Hennigan's a very cool sort of guy."

The two men left the water, staggering out of the *cenote* under the weight of all the dive gear. When they got to Mike's truck, they shed their equipment, changed into T-shirts and cut-offs, and sat on the tailgate to warm themselves in the brilliant Mexican sun.

Mike took two bottles of water from the cooler and handed one to Elvis.

"You did great today," he told Elvis. "Really outstanding. I don't think I've ever had a student push that deep into this system."

"Hey, thanks," the young missionary said, obviously pleased at the compliment. "But it's not like I was the Lone Ranger down there."

"Having me with you helped, huh?"

"Well ...," Elvis said, "to tell you the truth, you aren't the One I was thinking about."

"Uh-oh," Mike faked a grimace. "You gonna get religious on me now?"

"Religious? Hey. Never. Don't have a religious bone in my body. But spiritual? That I am. It's just my nature—just the Spirit's nature. I'm never alone, Mike—not ever."

Mike drank his water, thinking about that.

"That must be comforting," he finally said.

"You've got it, bro," Elvis agreed. "In fact, that's precisely what Jesus called the Holy Spirit—'the Comforter.'"

Mike nodded, thinking about that.

"I envy you, Elvis," he finally said. "I envy your certainty."

Elvis arched his eyebrows.

"Envy me? Whoa. Wrong answer, dude. You don't have to *envy* me. I mean, Mike—there's no reason you can't have the same thing I've got—you can have it right now."

The older diver shook his head.

"Nope," he said. "I don't think so. I think I've got a few decades of atonement before God—if there is a God—decides I'm worth keeping."

He looked up: Elvis was laughing at him.

"What's funny?" Mike asked. It had been a rare introspective moment for him, an almost solemn admission. Laughter seemed an irritating way to respond.

"'Atonement,'" Elvis repeated, chuckling. "I mean, what are you going to do, start sacrificing goats? You can't earn God's mercy through atonement, Mike. It's given through grace—something we get even though we never earned it. It's like—what was the name of your friend, the dude that helped the turtle?"

"Bill. Bill Hennigan."

"Yeah. Bill. Did the turtle do anything to earn Bill's help?"

"No," Mile scowled. "You could just see that he needed it."

"Outstanding," Elvis smiled. "How about once Bill helped him? Did the turtle pay him back? Slip him a few dead presidents? Offer to worship him, be his turtle-slave forever?"

Mike didn't say anything. The answer was obvious.

"That's mercy, bro," Elvis said. "Bill saw the turtle's need and was graceful enough to show mercy. That's what's so cool about the whole thing. The turtle didn't do zip—except decide to breathe when a breath was offered to him."

Mike remained silent.

"Let me guess what you're thinking," Elvis said. "You're thinking that I'm an ordained minister, and I must have spent thousands of midnight hours studying Scripture, and you haven't, so I probably have a whole skid-load of detailed knowledge in this area, and you don't, which puts you at a disadvantage. Am I right?"

Mike nodded.

"Well, you've got a point," Elvis said. "After the Lord called me to the field, I spent two pretty intensive years in Bible college, doing translation and mission studies, and I'm fluent in Old Testament Hebrew and *Koine* Greek. Heck, I'm still doing some graduate study; couple more years, and I'll be *Doctor* Elvis. But all of that study—*all* of it—boils down to one basic, essential truth, Mike, and here it is:

"God is holy, and man is sinful. God loves you. He loves you more than anyone—your mother, Bridget, your best friend—has ever loved you. But God can't embrace you while you are sinful, because a holy God just can't dwell where sin is. So, for you to be one with God, your sin has to be gone. But you can't rid *yourself* of sin, bro. You just don't have the power. That's where the sacrifice of Jesus Christ comes in. You've heard the phrase, 'Christ died for your sins,' right?"

Mike nodded.

Elvis nodded back as he continued, "That *doesn't* mean that mankind is such a decrepit bunch of nasty, sinful, sorry losers that, even when we had the Son of God right here among us, we killed him—although, of course, that's exactly what we did. What it *does* mean is that sin, once committed, has a consequence. It has to be paid for, and that's what Jesus did by giving himself to be sacrificed on the cross. He paid the price for sin, Mike—yours, mine, ours. And if you desire and decide to try for a Christ-led life, as opposed to a sin-led life, and you believe and accept the fact that his sacrifice was made for you—the same way Bill's turtle accepted the opportunity to take a breath—then, hey, your sin'll be gone. Long gone. There'll be nothing left to stand between you and God.

"Dude!" Elvis nudged the silent Mike. "You'll *have* what I have!"

There was a pause. Insects buzzed and treefrogs peeped in the surrounding underbrush.

"Assuming there's a God—," Mike started.

"Outstanding assumption," Elvis said, nodding.

"—and there is such a thing as sin," Mike continued, "I don't know that I could be so good as to avoid all sin, lead that kind of life. I think I'd still screw up."

"Without a doubt," Elvis agreed. "At least I'm certain *I* still do. But there's every difference possible between being sinning—straying off-course and hurting the One who loves you; and remaining sinful—not accepting God's offer to wipe the slate clean."

The insect sounds returned.

"Says all this in the Bible, huh?" Mike asked.

Elvis nodded.

"So how do I know that the Bible's right, or that there's even a God?"

Elvis nodded slowly and tapped his chest, twice, over his heart.

"Faith," he said.

Mike sighed, shook his head.

"There it is," he said. "Faith. . . . Whenever one of you guys gets to going on about this stuff, that's what it always comes down to, isn't it? Faith. Well, I'm sorry, Elvis. I'm afraid I just don't have that kind of faith."

You guys. Even as he said it, Mike was unpleasantly startled by the sound of his own voice. It sounded bitter—old and hardened and bitter.

The two men sat in awkward silence, drinking their water and looking down at the still surface of the small, blue *cenote*. Elvis turned and looked under the pickup's red bed cap, peering at the racks and bins of diving equipment.

"Are those the regulators you're using for the deep gig?" he asked, nodding toward a padded equipment bag.

"Yeah," Mike nodded. "Those are the bottom-mix regs."

"Special stuff, huh?"

"Super-special," Mike told him, reaching to pull out the bag and open it. He was glad for the change of subject; for reasons he couldn't quite fathom, all the talk about God and payment for sin had left him upset, unsettled.

"See?" Mike asked. " It's a side-discharge regulator, same as what we used today, only the body—here, tap on that—is solid, milled titanium, rather than polymer. Super-strong stuff. You can drop a tank on it and it won't crack, and the metal warms the breathing gas better than a plastic. Then the hoses, here, are a larger ID—larger inside diameter—for handling thicker gases at depth. In fact, every aperture on this is slightly larger, just for that reason, and the intermediate pressure is also higher. Makes it a lot harder to overbreathe the regulator."

"Sweet," Elvis murmured. "Lots of testing goes into something like this, huh?"

"You bet," Mike agreed. "We bench-tested it on a breathing machine with some extremely dense gas mixtures, and we also did chamber testing down to target depth. That, plus we dived it at Eagle's Nest—only down to 300 feet, but that was deep enough for us to extrapolate the data, project how it'll perform on the big dive."

"So you're confident it'll do the job?" Elvis asked.

"Absolutely," Mike nodded.

"But you've never actually used it in the Well, at the depth you're aiming for?"

"'Course not," Mike chuckled. "If we had, the project'd be history."

"Hmm," Elvis mused. "Has *anybody* ever used a regulator like this for that kind of dive?"

"No," Mike shook his head, wondering about the nagging line of questioning.

"Yet you're totally confident it'll work?"

"Uh-huh."

"So let me get this straight," Elvis scowled. "You're willing to trust something that you've never actually seen work, under deep, stony conditions that you've never actually experienced—and you're willing to trust it totally, I mean, commit yourself to it? Trust it with your life?"

"Yes," Mike said, his irritation finally showing. "I am. I'm confident it'll all work fine. And this conversation is getting just a tad too weird, Elvis. Why do you keep harping on it?"

The young missionary grinned. "I'm just trying to show you."

"Show me what?"

"That—*dude,*" Elvis replied, exaggerating the surfer-speak, taking his time, screwing the cap back on his bottle and flipping the empty into a trash bag at the far end of the pickup bed. "You *do* have 'that kind of faith.'"

24
CENOTE X—
OCTOBER, 2003

His face immersed in the floating ice-water basin, Mike breathed through the snorkel and tried to ignore the headache.

It was like punching in at the time-clock. As if he had never left this warm, dark water at all. He breathed until the headache left, but the cold water did not become pleasurable this time. It simply felt cold, and then it felt like nothing at all.

A hand on his shoulder. He looked up and saw Bridget. The leap in the heart wasn't there. He was rested; the training regimen called for him to get ten hours of sleep, with the assistance of a sedative if necessary, every night. But he was tired, nonetheless. This was the tenth dive in eight days—there'd been two a day the first three days, while the dives were shallow and on air or nitrox. But as soon as they'd added trimix to the gas planning, they'd cut back to one dive a day, and there had been two full rest days interspersed in there—rests from diving, that is—because the gas physiologists all agreed that three days was about as long as a person could dive without having gases in the tissues carry over from one day to the next.

But Yobatu Scuba had asked the team to tape updates for a Japanese adventure and exploration cable channel, and Becky had wanted to keep the sponsors happy. So there hadn't been a day in which he'd really been able to catch his breath, let alone have the talk he'd promised to Bridget.

He was tired. When he looked at Bridget now, he saw a team member, his doctor, and not much more. They were committed to a schedule now. A dive date had been announced, just three days away, and he had pretty much left emotions behind. He was down to purely intellectual decisions now, intellect and experience, because that was what was going to take him forward. He had another practice dive to get through—this practice dive—and then three days of final prep, and then the dive, the one to the bottom, or not, whichever it was going to be. And that was what his life was right now.

Okay? Bridget signed.

The concern was there, evident in Bridget's eyes. Mike faked a smile and nodded, let her take the snorkel away, put his mask on for him, put the mouthpiece to the small Spare-Air cylinder of oxygen between his lips. He vented his BC and slipped under the water.

He moved over to the 12-foot station and put the travel tanks into their place. It was rote movement now, the way he imagined workers must feel in Detroit when they bolt the seats into SUVs. He handed off the small cylinder to Bridget and put regulator one between his teeth. No "I love you," no "too," he just turned and went. It was just a straight up-and-down rope this time, no jump lines and no complications; with just one diver, a single rope was all that was needed. Mike turned face-down, went negative, and fell through the water.

And it happened the way it always did. Somewhere in the first hundred feet, he went from zoned out to in the zone. There. A creature designed for deep diving.

One gas switch and he was coming up on 300 feet. There was a light, a figure in a rebreather. Jorge. The plucky Mexican had insisted on being the deep safety diver for every dive, and Mike was deeply grateful for the confidence that consistency inspired. He switched the rope from his right hand to his left, balled his right fist and clipped it against Jorge's as he went by. He'd done that three days ago on impulse, and then it had become instant tradition, something they did every dive. As Jorge's knuckles kissed solidly against his, Mike smiled behind his regulator, and this time, there was nothing fake about the smile.

He switched cylinders again 100 feet further down. The blinking digits of the Dive Rite multi-gas dive computer, modified to show seconds as well as minutes, showed him to be within ten seconds of his target time, well within acceptable limits. It felt good, comfortable. It was almost as if he were watching a very realistic movie of somebody else making this dive.

At 750 feet he made his last travel-gas switch, to the fourth of the scuba cylinders that he carried under his arms. He did it without stopping his descent, but he began adding gas to his suit as he passed 775, and at the

800-foot marker, right on the money, Mike came to a complete stop. The dive plan called for a full 30 seconds at this depth to see if the HPNS would appear at the same place he'd experienced it last time.

Mike looked at his dive computer and then aimed the HID light straight down, following the rope. The light was focused to a single bright, blue-white spear, but he could not penetrate the darkness to the floor of the cave, more than 500 feet below. Even the top of the breakdown cone was out of range of his light.

Thirty seconds. No symptoms. The tanks on Mike's back would not be used this dive, but they were full, their mix appropriate for these extreme depths. If he wanted, Mike realized, he could keep on going, touch bottom, get it over with and out of the way right now.

But that wasn't the way it was done. You planned the dive, then you dived the plan. That's what got you back to daylight. Mike considered this for a moment. Then, reluctantly, he added gas to his BC and steadily began swimming up to his first decompression cylinder, hanging fifty feet above him on the line.

25

Hands down, without question, Mike's least favorite part of the entire deep-diving process was the intravenous drip.

Bridget gave him one after every decompression dive that they did here in the jungle. She used Ringer's lactate and sterile saline, the two clear liquids used by hospitals and EMTs around the world as media for diluting and carrying injectable drugs. Only in Mike's case, there were rarely any injectable drugs added. The IV was done simply to replenish lost fluids.

Scuba diving—any scuba diving—tends to dehydrate the diver. To begin with, the simple act of being suspended in water is foreign to the human body and confusing to the central nervous system, causing the body to eliminate liquids. That was why most experienced divers hit the head before jumping in—it was that or spend the whole dive with your teeth gritted. Then there is the tendency for moisture to precipitate out of a gas as the gas is compressed. In scuba, this means that, unless the moisture is removed as the air—or in Mike's case, the nitrox, trimix, and heliox—gets compressed, there will literally be liquid, and often a considerable amount of liquid, sloshing around in the scuba tank. In the wrong attitude, this could result in the regulator delivering water to the diver, rather than air. So all scuba compressors have water separators built into them, extracting the precipitating moisture as the gas gets compressed, and scuba gases are drier than desert air.

This means that, with each breath, the diver breathes away thousands of times more moisture than he takes in. And on the dives that Mike was doing now—even an 800-foot "training dive" had him breathing gases that were more than twenty-four times as dense as the same gases breathed at the surface—the molecules of the dry, incoming gas were packed so closely together that they tended to carry moisture out of his body that much more quickly. He prepared for each dive by drinking a liter or more of a sports drink, and he sipped almost constantly on foil-bagged fruit juices during his decompression hangs, but the tests that Bridget had run on him and Pete during the last dives had shown that it was impossible to replenish by mouth, in a day, the fluids lost by the body during a single deep dive.

Thus the IVs. During the first two days of training dives, he hadn't required any fluid replenishment at all, but on the dives that followed, he'd needed about forty-five minutes of drip to get him back to normal. Four days ago, he had done a "bounce" dive down to 650 feet and back. Bridget had been busy that day, because one of the support divers had managed to gouge his leg while breaking tree limbs for the campfire, so she had divided her time between cleaning and stitching the clumsy support diver and supervising the five-hour IV required after a nearly 20-atmosphere dive.

Today, though, there had not been an accident or calamity of any kind within the camp, and the fluid replenishment would take seven hours, so Bridget had brought in a camp stool and set it up next to Mike's cot.

She was running the IV into the femoral artery, inside of his right thigh. It was an uncomfortable place to have a plastic, needle-like catheter and a tube, and she had taped the whole arrangement in place with surgical tape, which Mike knew would take its share of hair with it when it came off. But he didn't complain. As it was, his chances of getting decompression illness—the bends—during one of these deeper dives was considerably greater than his chances during the routine cave diving he did back in Florida. In fact, Pete, a careful man, had been bent three times during his deep-diving career. And fluid replenishment was crucial in avoiding the bends—without it, his chances of coming off a dive unharmed amounted to a coin-toss. So, while he detested the whole arrangement, he tolerated it nonetheless.

Bridget compressed the skin on the back of his arm with a pair of plastic calipers, held it that way for exactly thirty seconds, and then used a stopwatch to measure how long it took to return to normal after she released it. She was, Mike knew, measuring skin turgor, one of the standard indicators of dehydration.

She clicked the stopwatch, squinted at its face, and made a note on a clipboard full of charts and note papers. Mike tapped her on the knee to get her attention.

"How am I doing, Doc?"

She looked at him for nearly a full minute, looked away blinking, and looked back.

I'm concerned, she signed to him.

"Why? Isn't the IV working?"

"Oh no," she said aloud. "The IV is fine."

"Then what?"

She worked her lips, looked upward for a second. When she looked back his way, Mike was surprised to see her eyes welling up with tears.

"Oh, Bridge," he said, and he sat up to hold her.

"No, don't," she told him. "You'll pull the IV."

Then, switching to sign, she said, *And I have to get this out.*

Mike nodded.

You remember at the village? Bridget signed. *I said that we needed to talk?*

Mike nodded again.

I'm worried, she signed. *About what might happen.*

"Bridge," Mike said. "We've been through this. I've got to do this dive."

I accept that, she nodded. *I accept that you think that you have to do that. I don't understand, but I accept it.*

Mike waited, saying nothing.

But I worry about what comes next.

"You mean after I come back from the dive?"

She shook her head, swaying her bell of auburn hair. Tears began to roll down her cheeks.

No, she signed. *I worry about what comes next if you don't come back.*

"Huh?"

Where you'll be. . . .

"Bridge," Mike whispered, because volume didn't matter with Bridget, and he didn't want anyone outside the hut to hear this. "If I don't come back, I'll be at the bottom of the *cenote.* . . ."

Will you?

"Well, where else could I be?"

Heaven, she signed deliberately. *Heaven . . . or somewhere else.*

"Oh, for Pete's sake," Mike said. Meaning to sit up, he swung his legs off the cot, hit the end of the IV line, yelped, and put his legs back on the cot.

"Hastings!" Mike yelled full force now, not caring who heard. "Hastings! Get in here!"

Thirty seconds later, Elvis knocked at the doorway to the hut, sticking his head into the darkened interior. He gave his eyes a moment to adjust to the dark, took in Bridget, weeping, and Mike, red-faced with anger.

"Dude?" Elvis asked. "You bellowed?"

"What's with you, man?" Mike asked him. "Can't you just stick to your Indians?"

"Huh?"

"What are you doing, trying to brainwash Bridget?"

"Brainwa—," Elvis looked at the two of them. "You mean—"

He beamed.

"Bridget!" Elvis said, looking at her. "Babe! You made a move!"

She nodded and Elvis embraced her.

"This," he said, "is so very cool."

"Wait," Mike interjected. "You mean, you didn't know about this?"

Elvis shook his head.

"Then how—"

"Ix-nit-ke'," Bridget said, pushing the syllables out slowly.

Elvis released her. He and Mike looked at her, astounded.

I-X-N-I-T-K-E—she spelled the name—*told me.*

"Ixnitke'," Mike said, "doesn't even speak English."

You're right, Bridget agreed. *But she's very expressive in sign. Maybe not ASL*—spelling again—*but she can make herself understood. She told me how God came from the sky and let himself be hung on a tree for . . .*

Tears again.

. . . For all the bad things we've done. She told me how we are paupers to God, not able to pay for our sins, so he paid for them himself. That trusting him, wanting to follow him, is what puts us back in his company. She made me remember things that I had almost learned before, and then forgotten, a long time ago. When I was a little girl.

"Ixnitke' told you this. . . ," Elvis murmured. He hugged her again. She hugged back.

"Guys," Mike said. "Guys!"

They stopped hugging and looked his way.

"Look," he said. "I know you mean well. I know you . . . both . . . mean well. But I've got this dive coming up in three days. I've got Viktor scum-of-the-earth Bellum running around trying to smear me and get me to let him do the dive, instead. I've got the Yucatan press corps showing up within the week to put us under a microscope here. I . . . just . . . don't . . . need . . . anything else right now. Okay? Can you get that? Can you give this a rest?"

They looked at him. The concern in their faces was as deep as the Well of Sorrows.

"Bridge . . . Elv . . . just let me rest. Okay? For a while? We'll talk later."
They nodded and left the hut.

Mike laid there, scowling up at the timbers and the thatched ceiling for close to half an hour. Then he looked at his backpack. It was within reach, and he pulled it closer to the cot.

He opened the pocket, took out the little New Testament and Psalms. He looked at the black leatherette cover for a minute or more, leafed through the thin, onionskin pages for a few moments, found the Book of John, and began to read.

26
CANCÚN

Dominic Lorenzo, producer for the Expedition Channel, sat in a small office in a hangar at the Cancún airport and went through the satchel-like black bag that contained all of his pills.

There were the vitamins and supplements, of course. A multivitamin with zinc, B-complex, vitamin E, vitamin C with rosehip extract, a triangular little iron supplement that looked like a hard little lump of tar, ginkgo biloba, vitamin D from organically raised eggshell, two compounds to improve memory and nervous-system function, three to improve cardiac health, and a dozen more little tablets and capsules, each resting treasure-like with its peers in a compartmented case that was about the size of a laptop computer, only thicker. Lorenzo barely glanced at all of these, because he took them every day, washing them down with a strawberry-flavored mineral drink that was supposed to make his synapses fire faster or something.

He wasn't really sure what all the pills did, but his dietician, a Los Angeles nutritionist who worked with everybody that was anybody, swore by all the stuff, and the man didn't look a day over forty-five even though he was actually fifty-two. Everybody said so.

No, Lorenzo was more interested in the Zip-Loc bag that contained the pills and other medications that he'd either gotten prescriptions for back in the States or obtained here at the pharmacies in Mexico, where the definition of a controlled substance was a little more lax.

There was Lomotil for traveler's diarrhea and an aspirin-codeine compound for pain. He had six different kinds of ointments for insect bites, insect stings, poisonous plants, scrapes, sunburn, and fungal infections.

He had five kinds of antibiotics, an ointment for an insect-borne virus that caused irritation of the tear ducts (he'd read about this on the Internet), topical anesthetics for scrapes, stings, and tooth pain, and a powdered mouthwash that, when mixed with water, was supposed to wipe out certain types of throat-thriving yeast infections that were found only in the tropics.

He put the bag away and sighed. It was a formidable arsenal, but it wasn't enough. He knew that. Some bug, somewhere out there in the jungle right now, was carrying bacteria for some pestilence or fever that had Dominic Lorenzo's name on it, and with his luck, that bug would find him, and then it would be curtains on his short, unhappy life.

Lorenzo hated jungles, detested toilets that did not flush, and was not terribly excited about the prospect of yet another helicopter ride. He was even less excited about a helicopter ride in an aircraft that had been manufactured by Soviet workers and would be piloted by a person who spoke English only as a second language.

He wished he were back in Los Angeles, making TV commercials.

But L.A. had not been kind to him, which was why he, a man who paled at the thought of life outside a city, found himself working as a producer with the Expedition Channel.

Shark dives, rock climbs, big oceans in small boats—they all terrified him and bored him speechless at the same time. He wasn't really even fond of any activity that risked his skin to sun exposure. But he had found his niche here, or, more accurately, the niche had found him, and here he was, getting ready once again to fly rickety aircraft out to some place with pit toilets, when all he really wanted was a nice urban location shoot, something where he could have his own air-conditioned trailer with an espresso machine and a caterer onsite who knew how to make a decent cannelloni.

Raised voices, both Spanish and English, filtered in through the thin walls from the aircraft hangar. Lorenzo tried to ignore it, but the voices only escalated. Sighing, he put his medications back into the largest of the five pieces of luggage that he was carrying out to the shoot, and opened the door to the hangar. Immediately, the sound went up a decibel or two.

"What," Lorenzo asked, "is all the commotion?"

"Your pilot," Viktor Bellum told him. "He doesn't want to carry my equipment."

Lorenzo looked at the pile of duffels and gear bags stacked on the hangar floor.

"You brought the cots and the tents?"

Bellum nodded.

"Is not the cots and the tents," the pilot, a paunchy little Mexican in a Yankees ball cap insisted. "He wants to be taking these too."

He waved at a collection of scuba cylinders—one doubles set on a back-plate, plus eight single cylinders of various sizes.

Lorenzo looked at them, then looked back at the pilot.

"The tanks, they are full," the pilot said. "Is too dangerous."

"Bunk," Bellum said. "We flew with full tanks every day in the Teams."

"I don't like," the pilot insisted.

"Wait," said a voice from the open hangar door. "Who's taking dive gear?"

They all turned. Jake Stiles, the underwater cameraman, was standing there, hands on his hips. Behind him sat a rental van with its rear hatch open.

"I'm taking it," Bellum told Stiles.

"Why?"

"Just in case."

"In case," Stiles asked, "of what?"

Bellum shrugged.

"Who knows," he told the Floridian. "Bryant might invite me to dive with him."

Stiles rolled his eyes.

"I thought you were going along for color commentary," he said.

"I am," Bellum said. "But it's stupid not to be ready if the opportunity presents itself."

"Señor Jake, he flies with the dive gear empty, *sí*?" the pilot butted in. He was gesturing in Stiles' direction.

"But this one," he nodded toward Bellum. "He flies with tanks full. Too dangerous."

"Jake will get his tanks filled from the expedition's gases," Bellum told Lorenzo. "But they might not let me do the same thing."

"I'd bet on it," Stiles grunted. "In fact, I'd bet that the expedition won't even let you get a foot wet in the *cenote*. So why haul the junk along?"

"We've got the room," Bellum observed.

"What do you think?" Stiles asked Lorenzo.

The producer looked at the pile of gear, at the pilot, at Stiles. When his eyes met Bellum's, the ex-Navy diver nodded toward the office door, picked up an olive-drab canvas briefcase, and said simply, "Let's have a word."

As soon as the door closed behind him, Dominic Lorenzo sighed, shrugged, and said, "Listen, Viktor, I appreciate your initiative, but if the pilot says it's too dangerous to fly your gear—"

"You want me to bring it," Bellum said curtly, interrupting the pale, thin man. "And you want me to bring it full. In fact, if I were you, I would arrange to either spend a few extra days on site or be prepared to do a hot-turn here, resupply, and fly back after you finish the Yucatan Deep project shoot."

"I think not," Lorenzo said, just as curtly. "We are already straining our budget, mister. I'm not ready to—"

"Sure you are," Bellum interrupted again. He opened his briefcase and pulled out a legal-size manila envelope, closed with a string clasp and bearing the indicia of the Mexican federal court in Meridien. "And here's why."

The producer opened the envelope, scanned the document within, and then read the translator's transcript that was attached. He looked at Bellum, who nodded, and then he went back and read it again.

"This is just between you and me for right now," Bellum said. "Understand?"

"Sure," Lorenzo stammered, staring at the document. "Do you really think you can—"

"I can and I will," Bellum told him. "Will that get you a few extra viewers—or what?"

Lorenzo raised his eyebrows, sighed again, and handed the envelope back to Bellum. Opening the door to the hangar, he called out, "Load the equipment . . . load all of it."

27
CENOTE X

"Wait a minute," Mike Bryant asked Jorge. "We had how many oxygen whips to start with?"

"Three," Jorge said.

"And now we have none that are working?"

"That's right."

Mike went ahead and let the astonishment show on his face. Together with an occasional voice, the sounds of the jungle afternoon—the birds and the background drone of insects—crept in from all around. The oxygen "whip" was actually a one-meter length of high-pressure hose with a DIN valve ferrule—one that would connect to Mike's scuba tank valves on one end, and an adapter that would allow the whip to be connected to a high-pressure tank of oxygen on the other. It was the only piece of equipment that could be used to "cascade" oxygen from the storage tanks into Mike's bottom-mix tanks. Without it, the team couldn't prepare his doubles-set cylinders for the next morning's attempt to reach the bottom of the *cenote*.

"I've used the same oxygen whip for something like eight years back in Florida," Mike said. "I've never had anything go wrong with it. And now we've trashed three of them in a month? How did we do that?"

"One was just a bad hose," Jorge said. "It ballooned up the first time we tried using it. Another one got damaged when a doubles-set fell over while we were filling it—it pulled the hose at the crimp. And we just found out that the third one got eaten."

"Eaten?"

"Tooth marks all over it," Jorge explained. "Probably some small animal smelled salt from our sweat on it and started chewing. Some of the guys say iguana, but my guess is a mouse or rodent of some kind."

Mike couldn't help but laugh. Here he was on the eve of the most important dive of his life, and the whole show was coming to a screeching halt because of a mouse.

"And we can't just cobble one together from regular hose," he asked, knowing the answer even as he asked it, "because the regular hose isn't O-two cleaned, right?"

"Bingo," Jorge said. "We didn't want to run the risk that they might be contaminated by grease or other combustibles and start a flash-fire."

Mike nodded. That had been smart. Oxygen rises dramatically in temperature as it is compressed. If anything combustible were in the line while that was happening, it could ignite and, in the presence of pure oxygen, the fire that resulted could be the same as an explosion.

"Don't worry about this," Jorge urged Mike. "I made a call on the shortwave to my wife this afternoon and had her take two of the O-two whips out of my shop and run them on the ferry over to Playa del Carmen, and then drive them up to the airport in Cancún. She's gonna give them to the guys from *Sports Illustrated,* and they'll bring them along when they chopper in tomorrow morning. They're coming in just after sunrise tomorrow to get the set-up shots. I'll have plenty of time to make up the bottom mix. And this way, we won't even have to flip the tanks before you gear up."

Mike nodded. When helium is pumped into a tank of oxygen to make heliox, the two gases mix pretty thoroughly from the velocity of the incoming gas. But after a tank of heliox has set for several hours, the helium, being lighter, begins to separate out and lie in a broad layer on top of the oxygen. Heliox divers liked to agitate their tanks before diving.

"No problem with the *Sports Illustrated* guys bringing the whips for us?" Mike asked.

"Are you kidding?" Jorge asked. "I can see the story now: 'SI Saves the Day for Yucatan Dive Team.' Don't worry. They'll bring them. They'll fall all over themselves to bring them. I think we could probably . . ."

The Mexican stopped talking so he could listen. Mike turned toward the door of the hut and listened as well. Faintly, he could hear it: singing. Not English and not Spanish.

Mayan—he recognized the liquid Ls and hard consonants of the Cháakadon language that Elvis and the local people had spoken in the village—and it was a lot of voices.

Mike and Jorge walked outside into the bright, late afternoon sunlight gilding the staging area. A considerable group of people—it looked to him to be almost all of the men that had attended the meeting in the village, and now, as they got closer, he could see that it was *only* men—was crossing the broad, cleared area that had been prepared to handle the morning's incoming helicopters. At the group's head were two people who could only be Elvis and Kukulcán, and they were flanking a third, an elderly man who walked with the aid of a wooden staff but stood straight and tall. Mike squinted in the tropical sunlight.

Naum Kaan. That's who it was. The elder of the Cháakadon village: the one who had been open to the dive in the *cenote* and the testing of his community's ancient beliefs.

Mike clapped Jorge on the shoulder and walked toward the approaching crowd; Elvis trotted forward as well. Behind Mike, the support divers and other crew members had stopped what they were doing and were standing around the perimeter of the camp, watching. It was as if he and Elvis were the generals of two small armies, coming out to parlay before the battle. Only the expression on the missionary's face spoiled the illusion. He was grinning broadly, hands outstretched as if to hug, even though he was still nearly a hundred feet away.

For one fleeting moment Mike had an image of the dog he'd had when he was a boy: a small dog; a beagle. His father had gotten it as a dog to hunt rabbits with, but the friendly little puppy had proven far too energetic and excitable for anything so methodical as fieldwork. So it had become Mike's dog instead, and while Mike had felt that he could either take or leave having a dog to come along on walks and forays into the woods near his home, the little beagle had bonded to him instantly. Every time Mike had left the house, the dog would be there, waiting to see if it was being invited along, beside itself with happiness if it was. And when summer ended and Mike had resumed school, the dog would be waiting every day when Mike walked up the lane. It would go positively wild with excitement when it caught sight of him—a coil spring wrapped in brown, tan, and white fur, the pink undersides of its ears flapping up and down as it bounded in joyous circles about the lawn.

Elvis was a lot like that. Not that he was slavishly servile or simple or anything like that. But he was easily given to joy; he didn't feel obliged to act guardedly or to keep his emotions in check. If you were a friend—and despite Mike's irritation over all the religion of late, they *were* friends— then Elvis was glad to see you. And he showed it.

Elvis jogged the last few yards and threw his sinewy, suntanned arms around Mike.

Mike patted him on the back and stepped back. Twenty-first century or not, Mike was still uncomfortable about men hugging men. Where he'd grown up, that got you some funny looks.

"Welcome back," Mike told the missionary. "Looks as if you've brought a few friends."

"To see you dive," Elvis nodded. "Actually, to see *me* dive and then to see you dive."

Walking steadily, leaning on his staff, Naum Kaan had now caught up with Elvis, Kukulcán respectfully at his side. Mike turned and offered his hand to the old man, who looked puzzled for just the barest hint of a moment. Then his face brightened as he remembered the European custom. He seized Mike's hand in his and pumped it up and down vigorously.

"Well, the rest of the group sounds happy enough after their long walk," Mike said as his arm was being flopped up and down.

Elvis translated for the Mayans. Naum Kaan laughed and said something in return.

"Naum Kaan says it's not cheerfulness," Elvis translated. "It's fear. Quatul started the men with him singing a good two miles back. The songs are supposed to alert the gods that we are coming, so they don't freak."

"Freak?'" Mike asked, eyebrows raised. "He said that?"

"Loose translation," Elvis grinned. "This is their equivalent of whistling past a graveyard."

"But I noticed that Naum Kaan and his grandson aren't singing," Mike said.

Elvis translated. Naum Kaan shrugged—Mike was amused that the gesture apparently crossed cultures—and said a few words. Mike recognized a phrase that sounded almost like "*cenote,*" and then he remembered that the term was Mayan in origin.

"Naum Kaan says that the *cenote* is a hole full of water," Elvis told Mike. "He has no fear of it as long as he's not actually in it."

"He thinks the spirits can get him if he goes in?" Mike asked. Elvis translated and grinned as Naum Kaan replied.

"No," Elvis told Mike. "He says he can't swim."

Mike laughed.

"Please ask Naum Kaan and his grandson to hang their hammocks in my hut," Mike said, and the two Mayans made a little head bow as Elvis translated.

"And ask if Quatul would be good enough to do likewise," Mike requested as the singing group of men drew closer.

After Elvis had translated this, Naum Kaan looked at Mike, nodded, and said something.

"He says that it is no wonder that you are chief of this camp," Elvis told Mike. "He says that you are wise."

Suddenly all of the Mayan men were raising their hands in greeting. Elvis did so as well, and Mike didn't even have to turn to know that Bridget was walking out from the camp to join them. But he turned anyhow, and his heart melted a degree or two at the sight of her in her khaki shorts and a light denim shirt. Her auburn hair looked like dark flame in the light breeze.

"Have you eaten?" Bridget asked Elvis.

"Some of the dudes aced a few iguana on the way here," Elvis told her. "And they've brought corn and some greens. They were planning on cooking after setting up camp."

Let them, Mike signed to Bridget. *They're much better cooks than Jorge's people.*

Bridget smiled and nodded her head. Still singing, some of the Mayan men fanned into the surrounding trees to forage for firewood while others began attacking the undergrowth with machetes, clearing spaces between tree trunks on which to hang their hammocks. By the time Bridget, Mike, Elvis, Naum Kaan, and Kukulcán had walked the short distance to Mike's hut, the Cháakadon men already had a small fire going.

Three hours later, the fire had been banked against the coming dusk and Mike sat outside his hut, satisfied—he wondered if there was such a thing as an authentic Mayan restaurant—as he waxed the zippers on his DUI dry suit and trickle-charged his dive lights from a bank of ten 12-volt batteries hooked in series. It was an oddly relaxing moment, and he relished it. Then, just as the pit of the *cenote* was plunged into shadow by the setting sun, he heard it—the unmistakable *thump-thump-thump* of an approaching helicopter. A big one.

Mike sighed and put the maintenance items away. All of the project personnel were in place except for Becky, who'd been handling the public-relations work from Cozumel and would be arriving in the morning with the *Outside* magazine writer and photographer on their chartered helicopter. And *Sports Illustrated*, *Men's Journal*, the Spanish-language periodicals, and the newspaper people were choppering in in the morning as well. So this could only be the Expedition Channel film crew.

The good news, Mike thought, was that Jake Stiles would be on this helicopter. Mike liked Jake, trusted him, and saw the seasoned underwater cinematographer as an asset on any dive. As for the rest of them, he had little use. And that went double for Viktor Bellum. Becky had confirmed a month earlier that the Expedition Channel people had again signed Bellum on as their expert commentator, even though Becky and Mike had offered Lamar Hires and several others as suggested alternatives. But the producer had stuck to his guns.

Mike's gut instinct had been to close the site to them. But the Expedition Channel was well-watched by the recreational divers who kept Yobatu Scuba thriving, and the Japanese company had made it clear that they thought coverage by the popular cable-TV and satellite channel was quite a PR coup—one that had entered heavily into their decision to bankroll the expedition. So Mike was stuck with them.

He could see the helicopter now, a big, bulbous-nosed beast of a flying machine with anticollision lights strobing in the golden half-light of the setting jungle sun. Mike was half-tempted to just let it land and keep his distance. But he reminded himself that Jake Stiles was on this flight as well. So he got up, dusted his hands against his khaki camp trousers, and joined the growing throng of support personnel and Cháakadon collecting on the fringe of the staging area, watching the big Russian-made helicopter come in.

The ungainly aircraft hovered slightly nose-high over the staging area, flattening the scrub grass with its rotorwash, sending dust billowing out in a great, tan doughnut that made Mike and the others shield their eyes. Then the helicopter settled to earth, the engine noise stopped, and the dust subsided to a minor storm.

In seconds the side door slid open and a muscular, curly headed bear of a man jumped out and ran, hunched over, to where Mike stood. The two greeted one another like the old friends that they were, and then Stiles said, speaking loudly over the noise of the still-spinning blades, "I wanted to give you a head's-up. Lorenzo wants to do an interview with you tonight."

"Tonight?" Mike's face sank. "Jake, I dive tomorrow. I've got a hundred things to do."

"I know," the other diver said. "I tried telling these guys. But Lorenzo's set on it. And he's making noise about griping to your sponsors if you don't cooperate."

"'Cooperate . . . ,'" Mike repeated. "Man, Jake. You remember when diving was just something we did on the weekend, out of a van? Without vultures like these?"

Stiles shrugged.

"That was bush league, Mikey," he said. Jake Stiles was one of the few people in the world that could get away with calling Mike Bryant "Mikey."

"This is the bigs," Jake continued. "A different set of rules, you know?"

"I know," Mike said. Over at the helicopter, other people were piling out now. He recognized the lanky frame of the series producer and the burnished crewcut of Viktor Bellum: Mr. Hollywood in a skin-tight U.S. Navy T-shirt and wraparound sunglasses. Mike didn't feel like talking to them just at the moment.

"Okay," he told Stiles. "Tell them to set up over by the fire pit; they'll probably like the campfire for ambience. I'll be over in an hour."

The sun had set and the fire was playing its dancing orange light over the expedition's tents when Mike walked over to where the TV crew had set up its fill-lights and camera.

Mike was alone. Bridget was busy running checks on her medical tent, the portable recompression chamber, her instruments—all the things that she would need, or might need, for the morning's dive. Elvis was speaking to his Cháakadon contingent, assuring them that he too was going to dive in the *cenote* in the morning, and that truth was going to have its way. And Jorge was out on the surface of the *cenote* in an inflatable boat, winching up the down-lines in preparation for sun-up, when he would clip each tank of ascent gas into its place on the line, along with a Cymalume stick, as he relowered the line in preparation for the dive.

Mike got closer to where the film crew was set up and scowled. The cameraman was a stranger, some guy with a snowboarder's goatee and a bleached blond ponytail, as was the soundman—a scrawny kid with thick glasses. The other two were familiar: Arthur Kensuth, the gofer for the crew, and Dominic Lorenzo, the producer. But Kensuth was a nobody, and as for Lorenzo—well, Mike didn't trust *him* as far as he could throw him. The guy was just . . . *oily* was the word that came to Mike's mind. He didn't doubt for a second that most of the draw that the Yucatan Deep Project had for the producer was in the tantalizing prospect that Mike might follow Pete's example and die during the dive.

"Mike!" The way Lorenzo said it, you'd have thought they'd been friends for years. "You're right on time. Ready to start?"

"Uh, sure," Mike said as he took his place on a camp stool and the sound guy began clipping a lavaliere microphone onto the placket of his khaki camp shirt. "Where's Jake?"

"Stiles?" Lorenzo asked, as if there was more than one "Jake" in camp. "I've got him getting his gear ready for tomorrow. He's the *under*water photographer. We don't need him for this. That is, unless you'd rather that he be here."

Mike *did* rather. He rathered very much. But he didn't want to come off as a dilettante, and he certainly didn't want to appear weak or uncertain in front of the likes of Lorenzo. So he simply shook his head and said, "No. That's fine. Let's get started."

"Let's," Lorenzo agreed. He nodded his head; the lights came up a notch. The soundman counted down with his fingers, and then Lorenzo began talking.

"Mike, you have quite a contingent of native people here in camp this evening," Lorenzo read from his clipboard. He didn't look up at the camera, and he didn't bother to disguise the fact that he was reading, as his part of the exchange would all be edited out when the final program was put together. "Can you tell us what that is all about?"

"Sure," Mike nodded. "The Cháakadon—that's what the native people are called—assign certain mystic properties to the *cenote*. They believe that it is a portal to the afterlife. They've decided to come here and witness the dive themselves, to see whether it is the spiritual center that myth holds it to be or whether it is simply an extremely deep pit full of water."

"So you've taken it upon yourself to dispute their religious beliefs?"

Mike shook his head.

"I'm not making the dive on any agenda other than trying to reach the bottom of the *cenote*," he explained. "What I see there will be what I see. The Cháakadon have simply come to answer their own questions."

"But you did partner with a missionary on this dive," Lorenzo pointed out.

"We're not partners," Mike objected. "Faith's Frontier gave us local air transportation in exchange for some medical assistance from our project."

"Oh," Lorenzo feigned surprise. "I must be mistaken, then. I thought that a Faith's Frontier missionary was diving with you tomorrow."

"Not diving with me, per se," Mike said. "Elvis Hastings, who is working with the Cháakadon, will make a short dive in the *cenote* to demonstrate his confidence that it's simply a geological feature and nothing more. It was a condition we agreed to in order to get the Cháakadon's approval of our attempt."

"Approval?" Lorenzo blinked. "Do the Cháakadon own the *cenote*?"

"No," Mike said. "It belongs in common to a Mexican landholding group. But as the Cháakadon are the traditional inhabitants of this part of the Yucatan, and the *cenote* figures into their culture, we felt it appropriate to ask their blessing on the attempt."

"But you don't feel that you are meddling with their culture?"

"The Cháakadon are not doing anything the Cháakadon do not want to do," Mike replied, surprising himself with the force of his answer. "Now, do you mind if we get back to the dive?"

"Of course," Lorenzo said. "Are you suicidal?"

Mike just stared at him for a moment.

"No," he finally said.

"Could you put that into a sentence, Mike?" Lorenzo asked. "We need it in context, so it will make sense after editing."

Mike shrugged.

"I am not suicidal," he said. "I'm an explorer."

"Yet there are many people who claim that attempting a dive such as this by yourself is tantamount to suicide," Lorenzo said.

"Who says that?" Mike asked. "Solo diving is widely accepted as the least risky way of making an attempt such as this. Nobody is going to be rescuing anybody a thousand feet underwater. Diving in numbers just increases the probability of failure."

"Not everyone agrees," Lorenzo said. Then, before Mike could reply, he added, "Mike, we'd like you to listen to an idea and give it your careful consideration."

There was the sound of another campstool being set down. Mike turned and saw Viktor Bellum, already wired up with his own lavaliere microphone, taking a place at his elbow. Bellum was still wearing glasses—orange-tinted Bausch & Lomb shooting glasses this time—and his hair was brushed back perfectly into the military cut that he favored. It even looked as if there might be a touch of powder on his face, as if they had made him up for the event.

"Mike," Bellum began, "we've been friends now for quite a while . . ."

"What are you talking about?" Mike asked.

Bellum paused—giving the tape editors some room to work with, Mike realized—and then he started talking again.

"I'm concerned, Mike," Bellum said, his voice even, almost convincing. "I think that you've bitten off maybe more than you can chew here, and I want to help."

"You want to help . . ." Mike said back to him, incredulous.

"That's right."

"You . . . want to help . . . me," Mike said slowly again.

"That's right, Mike. I do."

"And how would you propose that you do that?" Mike asked.

Bellum did a prolonged stage-sigh and turned to look directly into the camera's lens.

"Let me do this dive with you, Mike."

"What?" Mike didn't even bother trying to cover his astonishment.

"I brought all my own gear, all my own gases, my own lights, everything," Bellum said. "All you have to do is agree. Let's do this thing together Mike—okay?"

Mike just stared at him for a moment.

"First of all," Mike said. "If anything would be suicidal, *that* would."

He turned to Lorenzo.

"This guy," Mike said, pointing to Bellum, "has never been below 500 feet in his life. This *cenote* is better that twice that depth. To dive this without training for it—that's nuts!"

He looked up, and the camera's red "record" light blinked back on. It had not, Mike realized, recorded anything that he had just said.

"Are you saying that you won't allow me to dive with you, Mike?" Bellum asked.

"I wouldn't dive with you if you were the last diver on earth," Mike spat back. "You are a snake in the grass, and an imposter, and a conniver, and if my sponsors hadn't specifically asked me to accommodate this film crew, I would be brooming all of you off this campsite. Do you understand me?"

Bellum held his hand up, his face the mask of empathy and concern.

"I know that you're under a lot of stress, Mike, but won't you at least consider my offer?"

Mike pulled off the little lavaliere microphone and threw it in the dirt.

"This 'interview' is over," he said. He walked purposefully away from the campfire and the camera followed him. And this time the red "record" indicator was lit.

Jorge Yanéz walked quietly in the moonlight, trying not to wake the sleeping camp. He had his sleeping bag over his shoulder and his folded cot and a light jacket in his hands, and that didn't leave any way to conveniently hold a flashlight, so he walked slowly, careful not to bump into anything as he made his way toward the large tent where they kept the scuba cylinders.

He'd gone to bed an hour earlier, but he hadn't been able to sleep, thinking about the last oxygen whip and how some animal had chewed it. That bothered him, and even though he had double-checked every last bit of gear after finding the damaged whip, he had been worried that whatever had found the neoprene-coated hose delectable might do the same with some other vital piece of gear. So Jorge had decided that the only logical thing to do had been to move into the gas-storage tent for the night and hope that the presence of a sleeping human might somehow scare away whatever was literally eating into the project's chances of success.

He was fifty feet away from the tent when he heard it, a short but clear "psshhht" of gas being released under pressure. Jorge filled tanks for the project every day; when he did, he had a small knurled knob that he turned on the hose to release the internal pressure and allow him to disconnect the hose fitting from the tank valve. This had sounded just like the sound that the valve made when you equalized the hose pressure.

There was a brief circle of light as a flashlight played briefly over the thin nylon wall of the tent. Jorge put down the cot and jacket and fished his own small penlight out of his trousers pocket. Still wearing his sleeping bag over his shoulder like a quilted nylon bandoleer, Jorge pulled the flap of the tent open and snapped the flashlight on.

At the far end of the tent, in the midst of the neat rows of stored scuba tanks, Viktor Bellum quickly straightened up. From the look on his face, he'd clearly been surprised.

"What are you doing?" Jorge demanded.

"Oh," Bellum's face instantly reverted to a semblance of composure. "It's Yanéz, right? The guy from Cozumel?"

"That's right," Jorge said. "What are you doing here?"

"Just checking out your gear, *amigo*," Bellum said amicably.

Jorge looked at his watch.

"At one in the morning?"

Bellum shrugged.

"You know these TV guys," he said. "They ask me for details on how you guys are equipped, they're gonna want answers right now. They don't wanna hear, 'I don't know.' And I was getting ready to turn in when I remembered that I hadn't looked at your gear yet. I didn't want to get in the way in the morning; I figured you'd have your hands full as it was."

"I heard a hose being purged," Jorge said.

"No," Bellum said evenly. "I bumped one of the tank valves open. Sorry. I closed it down as soon as I heard it."

"Well you need to be out of here," Jorge told him. "We don't open this area to the media."

"Yanéz, c'mon," Bellum said. "I'm not media. I'm a diver. Like you."

"You need to go," Jorge repeated.

Bellum looked at him for a moment, long enough to give Jorge the distinct impression that he was being sized up. Then Bellum broke into a smile.

"Well," he said. "I've seen what I need to see. It looks like you guys are set to go."

Jorge didn't say anything.

"You are, right?" Bellum asked. "Set to go, I mean?"

Jorge shrugged.

"Sure," he said. "We're set to go. We need to top some cylinders off, that's all."

"Well, g'night then," Bellum said as he crossed the tent and shouldered past Jorge in the entrance. "I'll see ya in the morning."

"Sure," Jorge told him. He waited until he was sure that the American was gone, then he walked over and played his light over the tanks and other equipment. It all seemed in order, and nothing seemed to be missing. Yawning, he set up his cot and sleeping bag near a long wire rack full of regulators, hoses, and gas whips. In a matter of minutes, he was sound asleep.

28

Jorge Yanéz awoke at five-thirty to the insistent beeping of his wrist-watch. He sat up in his bunk, the sleeping bag still draped around his shoulders, and blinked at his surroundings—scuba tanks and hoses, the smell of cured rubber thick and inescapable in the closed canvas tent. Then he remembered moving into the gas storage area the evening before, shrugged the sleeping bag down to his waist, and looked once again at his watch. Had the alarm feature not gone off, he knew that he would easily have slept at least three hours more. But there was work to do, and rest could come later.

He got out of his sleeping bag altogether, pulling on his trousers, rolling up the tropical-weight sleeping bag, and folding up his cot to get it out of the way. Then he walked over, barefooted, to where a group of twelve scuba cylinders were isolated—all the tanks that still needed oxygen decanted into them. He found the two single cylinders and the doubles set marked "MB"—Mike's tanks. He decided to set them aside so he could fill them first, just as soon as the oxygen whips arrived.

As he lifted the doubles set, he grimaced—the set weighed several pounds more than he'd thought that they would. They'd feel heavier if they still held a considerable amount of gas, but all the tanks in this row were supposed to be nearly empty. Scowling, Jorge took a pressure gauge off the workbench, screwed it into the double set's manifold valve, and cracked the valve. The needle shot up to nearly 2,000 pounds per square inch.

Jorge scowled again. Helium was expensive—a single tank of the ultra-light gas could cost more than ninety dollars—so most cave divers didn't empty a scuba tank of its mixed gas before refilling it, particularly with a simple, two-gas mix such as heliox. They just read the percentage of oxygen present in the partially full tank with an oxygen analyzer, noted the pressure, and calculated how much oxygen and helium were required to add to bring it up to the desired mix and pressure. But Jorge hadn't been doing that with Mike's tanks. He'd been draining them down to almost zero pressure after every dive, purging them with air, and then redraining them down to just 300 psi—storage pressure—before filling them again with the mixed gases. And he could have sworn that he had drained Mike's doubles set after the last training dive. But they still held just under two-fifths of their working pressure.

Jorge shook his head. A certain amount of stress was inevitable when a team was doing something serious such as this—something in which lives could be at stake if anything went wrong. Still, he hadn't thought he'd been affected by it, yet here were these tanks, still holding pressure, even though they were set in the place where he normally placed drained and purged cylinders. And it wasn't as if he could blame anybody else; Jorge made certain that he, as team crew chief, was the only one who handled Mike's cylinders.

Shaking his head at the thought that he could be so forgetful, Jorge cracked both valves and allowed the gas to start hissing out of the two scuba cylinders in Mike's deep-gas set. It would take at least an hour for the set to drain down to the few hundred pounds he wanted in them before purging them with air, and the hiss of the escaping gas was annoying, like a snake sounding a sustained warning. So he pulled on his sandals and left the storage area, heading over in the dim pre-dawn light to the cook tent, to see if any coffee had been started.

Hugging a fresh towel and a clean change of clothes to her chest, Bridget crossed the camp in her bathrobe, headed for a small, eye-level-high wooden cubicle standing under a large tree at the north side of the staging area.

The cubicle was part of a minor technical marvel that Pete and Mike had designed for Bridget and Becky in the weeks prior to the first attempt on the *cenote*. The cabinet on the ground was simply a modesty shield; the business end was a water-filled, black plastic 55-gallon drum suspended fully thirty feet up in the tree, between two carefully trimmed branches, where the intense tropical sunlight would strike it all day long.

Connected to a pulsing showerhead by fifty feet of heavy-duty garden hose, the apparatus created water pressure worthy of a luxury hotel, and the black plastic absorbed heat every moment that sunlight hit it.

The shower did have one quirk, in that, once the barrel was refilled, it took more than a day for the water to truly get warm. But after two full days, with no evening to cool down, the water was so hot that it felt nearly scalding. So the women had learned to take their showers in the morning, two days apart, in order to bathe at a warm, but not uncomfortable temperature.

The two women were the only ones who used the shower. The men all made do with basins of camp-stove-heated water, the equivalent of GIs bathing in their steel-pot helmets.

Indeed, most of Bridget's baths over the past month had been precisely like that. The Mayan women bathed from basins, so, when in Rome. . . . And even though Ixnitke' had helped her to wash her hair, pouring pitcher after pitcher of wood-fire-heated water over it after she'd shampooed, Bridget had not had a real, honest-to-goodness shower since leaving Cozumel, so she was looking forward to really cleaning up before the media arrived.

Bridget opened the door to the shower and cautiously checked the interior. The Yucatan was, after all, a jungle, and as such, it was home to all manner of snakes, reptiles, spiders, and sundry insects, many of them venomous. But the little wooden cabinet was empty, nothing more threatening than a bar of Neutrogena soap and a bottle of Becky's Herbal Essence shampoo sitting in the small wire basket on the wall.

Bridget closed the shower door, put her clean clothes and towel in a bin hung high in one corner for just that purpose, and took her own shampoo and conditioner out of her bathrobe pockets, setting them in the wire basket. Then she slipped off the robe and draped it over the side of the shower.

There were no knobs to the shower, just a simple on/off valve screwed into the hose immediately above the shower head; the shower temperature was whatever the temperature of the water was in the barrel, high above in the tree. So Bridget flipped the valve open, gasped for a moment at the first few seconds of water, which were always cold, and then stepped more fully into the stream as the hot water from the barrel began to pulse from the showerhead.

Bridget turned and enjoyed the sensation of warm water streaming down over her shoulders, her torso, her legs. She stretched and felt knotted muscles loosen under the warm, rhythmic pulse of the water; then she soaked her hair and felt the water coursing from it down onto her back. She lathered herself with Becky's bar of Neutrogena, rinsed, lathered, and rinsed again. Then she re-wet her hair and shampooed it twice, rinsing thoroughly each time. That done, she squeezed the excess moisture out of her hair and then worked in a generous helping of thick, creamy conditioner.

The conditioner needed to sit on her hair for at least three minutes, and while the 55-gallon drum provided a generous amount of water for showering, Bridget always worried that it would run out, leaving her with conditioner gooed all over her hair. So she shut the shower off and waited, the predawn breeze wafting around the little shower cabinet and raising goosebumps all over her body. Then, after she'd counted slowly to 180, Bridget turned the shower back on and began to rinse the conditioner out of her hair.

She was almost done when she realized that, showers having been at a premium over the last month, it had been several weeks since she'd done her regular self-exam.

Bridget silently chided herself for the oversight, reminding herself that she could just as easily have done the procedure while lying in her cot. If anyone should be conscientious about such a thing, certainly it would be a doctor. But the shower had become her habit, and with no shower at hand, she had simply forgotten to check for a while. So she soaped her hands under the shower's stream, put her right arm up over her head, and dragged the fingertips of her left hand along the curve of her right breast, feeling up to the nipple, and finding nothing more than the usual smooth, resilient feel of the tissue beneath the skin.

She did that twice, then she switched sides, absentmindedly wondering what time all the media would be arriving as she checked her left breast. She ran the fingers of her right hand from the armpit toward the nipple, and wasn't even halfway there when she stopped.

Concerned, Bridget resoaped her hand and repeated the same section of her left breast. There. She had not been mistaken. She could feel it again, a small lump, about the size of a very tiny pea, and so deep in the tissue that she'd had to feel twice to be sure. She ran her fingers from another direction; it was there and it did not move.

Instantly the surgeon within Bridget took over. The mass did not move; that was not a good sign. But neither was it conclusive. Was it smooth or rough-edged? Spherical or flattened? Smooth and round was better than rough and flat, even though they were still nothing more than indicators, not anything on which a diagnosis might be based. Certainly she had not felt anything at all in the area during her last breast self-exam, which had been when? Six weeks before? Seven? But did that mean that it was fast-growing and had appeared in the interim, or did it simply mean that it had been too small to detect previously?

She had no answer to this question, nor could she even feel the shape of the mass; it was just too far under the skin. So then, once the surgeon had exhausted all of her immediate questions, the person within Bridget took over, and she thought about the fact that she was hundreds and hundreds of miles from home, that all of the doctor-friends and institutional connections she had to whom she would gladly trust her diagnosis and care were back home: back there, in Miami, and in Fort Lauderdale, and in Daytona and Jacksonville and Atlanta, and none of them were in Mexico, or anywhere near Mexico, let alone in a distant piece of seemingly endless jungle in the middle of the Yucatan Peninsula. She felt alone, and she felt small, and she felt suddenly very vulnerable, and she thought about that and the fact that the man with whom she'd hoped to spend her future was going, in just a few hours, to dive to the bottom of a very deep, very dark pit that had already killed his best friend. As she thought about all of these things, suddenly it all just broke through like a dam caving in on her. She sank to the bottom of the makeshift shower stall, and she cowered on the slats there where the water ran through, and the warm water rained down on her, and she wept.

———

The tool tent was just what it sounded like; an old-fashioned canvas wall tent where the team stored their shovels, axes, the still-broken chain saws, a spare generator, and various other bits and pieces of hardware that a group of people, living in the jungle for weeks on end, might require. And in the midst of it, between a Honda generator and a barrel-size coil of polypropylene rope, Elvis Hastings knelt in prayer.

The tool tent hadn't been his first choice or even his second. He would have preferred to communicate with God on the rim of the *cenote*, where the dive would be taking place. But he had worried that some of the Cháakadon might see him there and interpret his prayer as being *to* the *cenote* and its supposed divine inhabitant, rather than *near* it. So then he had considered simply walking off into the jungle to pray, but the same hesitance had overcome him; of the 150 or so Mayan deities, several were associated with the jungle, and it was very important to Elvis that he avoid all possibility of ambiguity. He was "the god man" to the Cháakadon. When they looked at him, he wanted them to see someone who worshipped the one, true God of heaven and no other. So ultimately he had decided to come and kneel alone in the tool tent. It was isolated and quiet, God was as much in there as he was anywhere else, and as far as Elvis knew, the Cháakadon had not yet assigned gods to Honda generators or screwdrivers.

The Yucatan Deep Project had been a welcome break for Elvis, not only because of the mystery and adventure of the task at hand but because speaking with Mike, Bridget, and their American team had put him back in touch with people who spoke English. Since his work rarely took him to the tourist areas where Anglos congregated, Elvis spent most of his time speaking Quintana-Roo-accented Spanish and various of the more than thirty dialects of Mayan. Add to this the fact that he also read considerably each day in both Hebrew and Greek, and it was little wonder that he had long become accustomed to thinking in several languages.

But in prayer, he rarely used any of them. Like most prayerful people, Elvis had begun his prayer life by thinking of prayer as a little speech that one made to God: generally a want-list with a few worship elements thrown in for good measure. Then he had begun to understand that prayer was a dialogue, in which listening was as important as speaking one's mind. Still later, once he had arrived at that point, he had come to understand that, as God knew what was on his mind anyhow, it was the listening that was most important. And these days, unless he was voicing a special supplication or a request someone else had made, Elvis rarely used words at all when he prayed. Rather, he just opened his heart and asked God to fill it. And generally he came away calm and comforted and soothed, like a child who has just spent an hour or so in the security of his loving father's arms.

But this time, Elvis had no sooner knelt than he was filled with a sense of trouble and unease. His first thought was of Mike and the dive, but as soon as he considered his new American friend, the troubled sense disappeared and a calm returned. So he reviewed the people in his life one by one: his mother; his father, his surfer friends back in California and his seminary friends in missions around the world, the office staff and volunteers with Faith's Frontiers, his flock at the Cháakadon village, Jorge Mendoza and the Mexican dive crew. The impression of peace continued.

But when Elvis thought of Bridget, the sense of disturbance returned to him immediately.

Elvis didn't try to shake it away. He knew when the Holy Spirit was talking to him. So he quickly thanked God for his watchfulness over the expedition; asked him for his blessing on the day's dive, and asked God's protection on everyone in the camp.

Then Elvis got back to his feet, dusted off his knees, and went looking for Bridget. He decided to try the cook tent first.

Mike Bryant woke up angry. Boiling angry. Naum Kaan, Quatul, and Kukulcán were still sleeping in the traditional Mayan style, snoring crossways in their respective hammocks. And Elvis's hammock was already vacant, which, Mike thought, was good. If the missionary was still here, Mike thought to himself as he got out of his sleeping bag and rummaged beneath his cot for his boots, he would no doubt be sharing that bit of Scripture about not letting the sun go down upon your wrath.

Mike vaguely wondered if the Bible had anything to say about inviting the enemy into your camp. Because that was what he had done, as surely as he breathed, as certainly as if he had opened the doors to his home and said, "Come on in; beat me senseless and rob me blind."

He stood up, buttoned his shirt, realized he'd missed a button at the bottom, cursed, unbuttoned it, and rebuttoned it. Then he walked out of the hut, wanting to stomp in his consternation but making no noise out of consideration to the three men who were still sleeping in the hammocks above.

Coffee, Mike decided. Maybe coffee would help, even though he couldn't have more than a cup, and he couldn't have any at all once he got within four hours of starting the dive. Coffee was a stimulant, which would accelerate both his respiration and his heartbeat; and it was a diuretic, meaning it would cause his body to dehydrate more rapidly. Neither of these effects was conducive to good health on a deep dive.

Mike stepped out into the cool pre-dawn air. The sounds of the awakening jungle—the calling of birds and the sporadic hoots of howler monkeys—calmed him, as they always did. There were millions of people, he knew, who would never set foot outside a city throughout the entirety of their lives. They would never awaken to anything other than the droning hum of traffic, the Doppler shriek of sirens and jet planes, or the rattle and rumble of construction. That he got to spend weeks at a time in the midst of an unspoiled, trackless wilderness was, Mike knew, an unbelievably rare privilege, one that he should savor.

So he did. For a full two minutes, maybe more, he stood and drank in the peace, and the solitude, and the dim and shadowed green. He let the soft blue light of the sky and the distant radiance of the last two visible stars wash down over him, and felt a peace begin to take hold.

Then he turned and saw the Expedition Channel's ancient Soviet helicopter tied down in the staging area, its broad windscreens covered with the protective tarp that made it look like a blindfolded grasshopper. And the helicopter reminded Mike of the film crew, and the film crew reminded him of Lorenzo, and Lorenzo reminded him of Bellum, and as soon as Mike thought again of Bellum, whatever tranquility he'd gained vanished in an instant, like the white mists rising from the geothermally warmed waters of the Well of Sorrows.

He'd been ambushed the night before. Set up and ambushed; Mike was certain of that. Lorenzo's line of questioning; Bellum's sudden arrival on the set; Bellum's obsequious manner, even as he made his outrageous request—all seemed orchestrated to produce exactly what they had produced: outrage on Mike's part. And that business with turning the camera on and off, deliberately recording only those portions that might lend credibility to Bellum's request, deliberately taking out anything that might make Mike appear reasonable and even-tempered, arranging the soundbites so he would appear to be a raging jerk, instead . . . They had tried to rile him, they had succeeded, and the realization that they had done so riled him even more. Worse still, he was certain that there had been a purpose behind all the stage-acting, but Mike couldn't for the life of him decide what it might be. And the uncertainty only served to make him angrier still. He couldn't make the deep dive while he was seething like this; that would be suicidal. He had to calm down. He kicked at a hunk of wood on the ground next to the smoldering fire-ring and walked heavily on toward the cook tent.

Half the camp was already gathered in the big central commissary tent by the time Mike got there. At a table at the far end of the twenty-by-thirty-foot tent, Elvis, Jorge, and Becky all leaned forward in conversation with one another, their faces thrown into shadow by the yellow light of a suspended Coleman lantern. Support divers and workers—mostly Mexican cave divers who had given up vacation time to come assist Mike in his effort—sat at three of the other five tables. Four Cháakadon men, dressed in woven ponchos and the calf-length trousers that they favored in cooler weather, carefully carried Styrofoam serving trays of scrambled eggs and sausage over to one of the vacant spots and stood there for a moment, confused, before sitting down with their feet and legs outside the picnic-style table. Then, after numerous sidelong glances at the other breakfasters, one of the four figured out how the table was supposed to work and put his legs inside. He said something to his companions, who put their legs inside as well, and then they all shared a good laugh at something that the first man said.

Swallowing, taking a deep breath, Mike put on the best game-face he had in his admittedly meager supply and walked over to the table where Jorge and the two Americans were sitting. As he got closer, he couldn't help but actually smile; Elvis and Jorge were both looking pretty rumpled—much as one might expect of a couple of men camped in the jungles of the Yucatan Peninsula. But Becky was neat as a pin in a crisply pressed light blue chambray shirt and smartly creased khaki hiking shorts that perfectly set off her long California-suntanned legs. Her size-five feet were sheathed in ragg socks and hiking boots that looked fresh out of the box, and her sunstreaked hair, cropped helmet-short, was neatly parted and trimmed to perfection. She'd even found some way in the pre-dawn wilderness gloom to put on the lightest touch of mascara, blush, eye shadow, and lipstick. She was ready to meet the news crews, and to Mike, who'd known Becky since she was ten, the effect was startling.

It reminded him that there was a fellow in Becky's life now, a twenty-something account executive at the agency where she was interning. This bit of news, something that Mike would have thought he'd find pleasing, had triggered an entirely different response. Mike had instead come up with his own version of Twenty Questions: Who was this guy? Was he married, divorced, single? What were his intentions? How far had the relationship gone? Was he talking marriage? And if so, how was he prepared to support a family? And so on.

All this had amused Becky, who had the right answers to all of Mike's questions, and it had pleased Bridget, who had told Mike that his concern was simply evidence that "God was working" in his life—an observation that he had found grating, patronizing, and somehow typical of a new Bridget with whom he felt less and less comfortable. But Mike did suppose that, with Pete gone, his relationship with Becky had become more and more paternal. He thought of her as a father would think of his daughter. And that triggered a fresh worry, because if things went badly on the dive today, then who would Becky have to depend on?

The logical answer was that she would have Bridget, who was better prepared financially and—Mike hated to admit this, but it was true—emotionally to care for Pete Wiley's orphaned daughter. But Mike's concerns were from a sphere that existed outside of logic; that stemmed from something that slumbered in the heart's deep core. He did not want to leave Becky stranded and alone again.

And from that thought, it was but a short jump to fresh consideration of Lorenzo and Bellum and the Expedition Channel team's interview/ambush of the evening before, and how angry it had left him and how he felt this threatened both the dive and his safety and—by association—Becky's security. And this angered him all over again, and he actually had to stop, right there and take a deep breath and calm himself back down.

This wasn't good. At the depths Mike would be going to, just getting out of breath would be fatal. Deep dives required an icy calm, and he was nowhere near that. He pushed the thought aside, put the game face back on, and walked up to the table.

"Well," he said with forced joviality. "Here's the usual suspects. Where's Bridget?"

"Hey," Elvis smiled. "I was looking for her myself."

"It's her morning for the shower," Becky said. "Probably milking it for all it's worth. I know I would. I bathed out of a bucket this morning. Yucky."

"Well, you'd never know," Mike said, giving her a peck on the cheek. He turned to Jorge. "Are we ready to roll?"

"We will be," the Mexican cave diver told him. "You have your lights charged?"

Mike nodded.

"I've had the rest of the team's lights charging off of the battery bank all night," Jorge told him. "I'll close them up when I get back to the gear tent. And I'm bleeding down your double set right now, so we can fill just as soon as the O-two whips get here."

"Bleeding them now?" Mike asked. "I thought you already did that after the last dive."

"So did I," Jorge told him, shaking his head in disappointment. "But the tanks were holding like 135 bars when I checked them this morning. I can't believe I overlooked something like that. But apparently I did."

"Don't be too hard on yourself," Mike told him kindly. "We're all under a lot of pressure right now. And you've filled and emptied those tanks so often over the last three weeks that it's understandable that you might think you already did something. Just use your checklists when you get the gear ready. And I'll do the same. That's why we have a system like that."

Jorge nodded and smiled weakly.

Elvis looked Mike straight in the eyes, saying nothing. Mike looked away, glanced around the tent, kept the smile on his face.

"Tell me, bro," Elvis said kindly. "What kind of pressure are *you* under this morning?"

Mike waved to one of the support workers across the tent and pretended not to hear.

"Did you get a good night's sleep?" Elvis asked.

Mike looked up, prepared to lie, ready to tell them all that he was A-okay, all systems green, the usual aphorisms. But then his eyes met Elvis's, and he had this sudden urge to unburden himself, to tell the truth. "Not really," Mike finally compromised. "No."

"That's understandable," Jorge said. "A big dive like this, I don't think I'd sleep a wink."

"It's not that," Mike said. He looked back up at Elvis, and the missionary's eyes were warm, compassionate.

"Tell us," Elvis urged him.

So he did. Mike told them all about the previous evening's taping with the Expedition Channel, about Bellum's staged "drop-in," about his proposal.

"Those *scum*bags!" Becky erupted. The whole tent fell silent as she shot to her feet. "That's it. I'm telling them to pack their junk and clear out of here."

"No," Mike told her, rising to his feet as well. "Those guys might be jerks, but they're jerks we need. The sponsors want the coverage."

"The sponsors," Becky told him, "also want you alive. C'mon Mike. Nobody expects you to dive under these circumstances."

Mike heard her out. Then he shook his head.

"I don't know what game these guys are playing here," he said. "But I do know that they are messing with me for a purpose, whatever it might be, and I absolutely refuse to play into that hand. No, Becky. This is the way it has to be. They stay. And I dive."

"Dude," Elvis said, his voice almost a whisper. "You'll at least let Bridget check you out before you do this, right?"

"I always do," Mike said.

"Okay. That's cool."

A faint, flat, repetitive pounding sounded in the distance.

"Choppers," Jorge said, finishing his coffee and getting to his feet. "Those'll be our oxygen whips."

"And that'll be my cue to get to work," Becky said. She turned to Mike and added, "You'd better be safe. You hear me?"

"Yes, ma'am," Mike smiled. He hugged her quickly, then she and Jorge left the tent.

Elvis gazed at Mike, not speaking.

"What's on your mind?" Mike asked.

Elvis shrugged.

"I think you know," he said.

"Oh," Mike replied. *"That."*

He sighed. "Please, Elv, no God-talk right now, okay? It's just not the time."

"I'd beg to differ," Elvis said. "But okay. If that's what you want, I'll shut up. But it's important, Mike. It truly is. Just think about that, all right?"

"Sure," Mike told him. "I'll think about it."

With a towel wrapped turban-like around her hair, Bridget held her robe closed at the throat and walked back to camp along the faint path that led from the shower. Her extraordinary peripheral vision had noted the helicopters' approach while they were still better than two miles out, coming in along a glide path that would take them from 3,000 feet in altitude to touchdown at the staging area, where several members of the support crew already stood next to the makeshift wind sock.

She entertained no illusions about going out to meet the helicopters. Even if she did not take the time to dry her hair—and she would not; as she would be diving later on in the day, it was simpler to just leave it wet and braid it—the helicopters would still be on the ground and emptied by the time she could run back to her hut and change. And she wasn't in the mood to be meeting the news crews, just now, anyhow. She wasn't in the mood to be meeting anyone.

A lump in her breast—a lump that had not been there just seven short weeks before. Bridget knew exactly what she would have told one of her patients with the same signs. She would have recommended immediate examination via either a needle or a core biopsy: the same day, if possible. She was all too aware of the math; cancer cells often multiplied at an exponential rate, many times more rapidly than normal, healthy cells. Every day, every hour of delay between discovery and diagnosis, could be critical. At some point, many cancers—ductal carcinoma included—metastasized. They spread to other sites in the body and took hold there, as well. And once cancer had spread to multiple locations in the lymph system, or once it had taken hold in bone, as well as the primary sites, it would be difficult, if not impossible, to eradicate. Bridget was not an oncologist, but she was familiar enough with the literature. At some point, you didn't even bother with trying to cure. You just made the patient comfortable and braced them and their loved ones for the inevitable.

That prospect terrified her—but not as much as it once would have. Intellectually, at least, she no longer viewed death as the terminus, as some black and empty pit at the nether end of vitality. She now knew it would be a transition to the eternal, to perpetual life in the presence of Christ, the Creator of the universe. But while that prospect dampened her terror, it did not shield her from the raw, animal fear of death, from the sadness of knowing that her life could be threatened in a very immediate fashion. She had so much she wanted to do, so much she wanted to see. She had never been a bride, never been a mother. She wanted to see Becky grow in happiness with her young man, wanted to see Mike fulfilled as a husband—*her* husband—as well as an explorer. She wanted to teach, to learn new things. She wanted to grow in her new love for Christ and expose others to that same great happiness.

Certainly, becoming a Christian had gained Bridget access to heaven, but she didn't want Christianity just for that. She hadn't believed simply as a means of eternal fire insurance. She wanted to know, in the here and now, more of the joy that she had known ever since Ixnitke' had reminded her, in halting sign, what she had read but never truly learned as a child: that Christ's grace-driven sacrifice, and that sacrifice alone, was sufficient to pay for her—for anyone's—sins. She wanted to tell others about this same true joy and knew that she, as an articulate deaf person who could communicate with other deaf people, was in a unique position to spread that wonderful message. She wanted, in short, to be used by God in this life, as well as to be alive with him in the next, and she was heartbroken at the thought that she might be denied this opportunity. She wasn't even sure how to—what was the word that Elvis used? Witness. She wasn't even sure how to witness. It was just all so new to her. She wanted to live long enough for it not to be new.

There was a chance that the lump was nothing. She knew that. It was possible and it was even probable. But until such time as it had been proven benign, it was imprudent to treat it as anything but a potentially lethal disease. She had given the lecture herself, dozens of times; she knew it by heart. She knew it entirely too well.

Bridget sighed, dried her eyes, pulled herself together. The expedition didn't have its own helicopter, and the ones Faith's Frontier had chartered, the ones used to supply the Cháakadon clinic, were up north on a charter in Meridien right now and no longer available. Even if she were to leave right now, and strand the expedition without its doctor, it would take her most of a day to hike out to where the trucks were parked at the trailhead, and most of another to drive out to Cancún, the nearest city with an international airport. Depending on when she arrived there, it might take another day to arrange a flight to Miami and maybe a day after that to get on one of her oncologist friends' schedules. So, left to her own devices, she was at least four days away from competent American medical assistance. And that was assuming that she was willing to walk off and allow Mike to do the dive without her there to support him medically, which she would never do, not even if her life depended on it.

If, on the other hand, she saw the dive through, then it wouldn't be any problem at all to hitch a ride out with one of the news crews in their helicopters—none would be leaving until they'd gotten their post-dive interviews with Mike, and she wouldn't allow media access to Mike until he'd been rehydrated and thoroughly checked out, anyhow. Flying out with the newsies would shrink two days of travel down to less than an hour. And if her timing was right, it was even possible that she would catch a flight out of Cancún right away. She could be in the hands of one of the top oncologists in the field inside of two days. So that cinched it. It was time to—how was it that Mike and his guy friends put it?—suck it up. It was time to suck it up, grab some courage, keep her news to herself, and get through the thing at hand, so she could deal with her own problem in its own time. It made her feel good to know that she wasn't abandoning Mike when he needed her. It made sense.

So why was it that she felt so isolated?

And why was it that she felt so scared?

"Hey, Jorge—how're you doing?"

Jorge looked up from the tank he was filling and broke into a broad smile.

"Jake!" He jumped up and shook the big man's hand. "I saw you g
the chopper last night, but I haven't seen you since."

Jake Stiles nodded.

"You know how it is," he said. "I've got two cine cameras and three
cameras in housings, and six strobes and four cine lights, and every sin
one is gonna want to flood in a heartbeat unless I've got the O-rings s
coned and seated just right. So I was up taking care of those and gettii
things charged, until late last night."

Jorge nodded.

"I know how it is," he said. "Is there anything I can do to help you
out?"

Stiles nodded back.

"There is," he said, holding up a small scuba cylinder about the size of
a Thermos bottle. "I know you're doing my mix after you get Mike's tanks
filled, but can I trouble you for some argon, as well? I decided at the last
minute to dive dry this time."

"Sure," Jorge said, accepting the small aluminum tank. He carried it
over to a large orange industrial-gas cylinder and began to hook it up.
Then he looked at the gauge on the argon cylinder and shook his head.

"What's up?" Stiles asked.

"This cylinder. I thought it was nearly full, but it's down to less than
2,000 psi."

"Leaky valve?" Stiles asked.

"Must be," Jorge shrugged.

"Well, fill Mike's first," Stiles said. "As long as I have enough to put a
couple of toots into my suit when I get to depth: I'm not planning on getting any deeper than 300 feet. So four, five hundred psi will be fine."

"Oh, it's not a problem," Jorge assured him. "We have a Haskell pump
to boost the helium pressure when I fill Mike's tanks, anyhow. I can always
run the argon through that if I need to."

"Just don't go getting the argon and the helium confused," Stiles joked.

"No kidding," Jorge agreed. "Argon's so narcotic, it will set you on your
ear at twenty feet. Anybody ever tried breathing it at a thousand feet, that'd
be all she wrote, for sure."

He filled the little tank for Stiles, who thanked him and left. Then Jorge
pondered for a moment what they'd just talked about. He shook the
thought away and went on filling the team's tanks.

"Hey, sailor."

In the semidarkness of his little hut, Mike Bryant looked up to the doorway from the decompression schedule that he was reviewing and smiled. Damp hair and all, Bridget was a sight for sore eyes.

"Hey," he replied, motioning for her to come inside. Then he added in sign, *Lots of folks have been looking for you.*

"Well," she replied aloud. "Here I am."

Bridget dangled the blood-pressure cuff in front of him and he sighed, offering his left arm. As she wrapped the cuff around his upper arm and slid a thermometer under his tongue, Mike studied her face, noticing the way she avoided eye contact. It wasn't like her. Because she couldn't hear sighs or inflection, Bridget was extraordinarily visual. Uncomfortable with it at first, Mike had long grown used to having her eyes fixed on his when they were together.

He was literally speechless. The thermometer was under his tongue. So he went to sign: *Is everything all right?*

"Don't move," she told him, not looking up. "I can't get a reading if you move."

He felt the cuff constrict around his lower bicep, then felt the pressure gradually decrease, followed by the soft hiss as Bridget released the remaining pressure from the cuff. She took the thermometer out of his mouth and scrutinized it. Still no eye contact. Finally she set the cuff and the thermometer down on his cot and looked at him.

Your temperature is fine, she signed to him. *But your blood pressure and pulse are both high. Well within normal range, but high for you.*

"Well," he attempted a grin. "It is a big day for me, you know?"

It's not that, Bridget signed back. *Your pulse and BP*—she signed this as letters—*are usually up just a little for a big dive. Maybe ten percent. This is almost twenty-five. What's going on?*

Mike studied her face.

He touched the two fingers of his right hand to the palm of his left: *Again.* He lifted his left arm, offering it for the cuff.

"Don't snow me," Bridget said, adding in sign, *I know that you can make them go down temporarily.*

"So what's up?" she asked again.

He lifted his eyes to hers and nodded. Then he told her. It took him a while, because he did it in sign; no need to spill it publicly, just in case one of the reporters was listening outside the hut. And when he was done, he shrugged and looked at Bridget, questioning.

If I asked you to scrub this dive, Bridget signed, *would you do it?*

Mike took a deep breath and thought of the preparation, of the people from *Sports Illustrated* and *Outside* and the rest of the media that were waiting out in the staging area. He shook his head, the movement nearly, but not quite, imperceptible.

Bridget looked at him and blinked, the pain evident in her green eyes. *Well, you're going to have to set this aside if this is going to work*, she signed. *You dive while you're upset, like this, and you'll overbreathe your gas supply. You won't have enough.*

"I know," Mike said. "I know."

Bridget studied him again, and then she did something very undoctorly. She took him in her arms and she held him. Sitting next to him on his cot in the dark little wattle-and-daub hut, she held him and put his head in the crook of her neck and stroked his hair and pressed her hand against his back, and she held him and rocked him gently back and forth. She did that for several minutes, until she felt him relax. Then she released him and stood up.

"Thank you," Mike said softly. Then he looked at her and signed, *How are you doing?*

"I'll be fine," she said, hugging him again, whispering, her voice almost not even there. "You just do this dive and come back to me—and I'll be fine."

––––––––

Around the rim of K'uxulch'en, a new feature had been added: bright orange nylon tape had been strung on stakes to mark a no-go zone and help keep the media people from stumbling over the edge.

Standing on a crate near the tape, Becky welcomed the various media people, easily switching back and forth between English and Spanish. She gave a brief backgrounder on the *cenote* and the previous attempts, courageously soldiering on past the part where she spoke of her own father's death. Then she got on to the day's agenda and opened for questions.

Viktor Bellum raised his hand.

"You said that you'll be starting in two hours," he said. "Given the amount of decompression that will be required, I would have thought that you'd want to start as soon as possible. Is there a delay?"

"What's the matter, Viktor?" Becky asked, her eyes twinkling. Her composure betrayed none of the animosity that she felt toward Bellum and his producer. "Got a hot date waiting for you back in Cancún?"

The rest of the reporters chuckled and Bellum glowered.

"Actually," Becky said, "We had an issue with our oxygen whips."

She turned to the reporters from the general-interest magazines and explained, "Those are the special hoses we use to get oxygen out of the big tanks that we store it in and into the scuba tanks that Mike will be using during the dive. And I want to add, again, our thanks to the guys from *Sports Illustrated* for being so kind as to fly a couple of our spare whips in with them when they choppered in this morning."

"Well, it was either that or try to organize a footrace, so we'd have something to cover," the *SI* reporter joked good-naturedly.

"Still," Bellum objected. "How long does it take to pump a couple of tanks full of heliox?"

"Well, I know that it's important to get a cold fill, so the gas doesn't contract," Becky told him. "And as we are filling Mike's bottom set to better than 340 atmospheres, or 5,000 psi, the tendency is for the tank to heat up even more than normal, so Jorge, our divemaster, is immersing the tanks in ice water while he fills them, and filling them very, very slowly. And I understand that we had to blow Mike's tanks down this morning—let the old gas out of them—and you want to do that slowly too, so you don't frost the valve."

"You *blew them down*?" Bellum asked.

Becky looked up; the man actually sounded shocked. She nodded.

"But heliox is *expensive*," Bellum muttered. Then, more to himself than anyone else, he wondered aloud, "Why would you blow it down?"

"Well, don't worry Viktor," Becky said. "We aren't charging *you* for it."

More chuckles from the assembled journos, and this time Bellum's face definitely reddened, so Becky covered and added, "Actually, Viktor's right. We generally do just top off mix, because it's so pricey. In fact, I'm diving tri-mix in my support work, and that's exactly what we do with my tanks. But because it's so important to us that we have exactly the right mix in Mike's tanks, Jorge is blowing his down every time before we fill them."

She looked up. Bellum actually looked pale for a moment. Then she looked back, and he was back to his usual arrogant self.

"Okay then," she said. "If there aren't any other questions. Let me remind you that we are only going to allow working divers, which would be our crew and then Jake Stiles, here on the platform. I've got to go get geared up, and we will see you back here at the *cenote* in two hours."

As they watched Viktor Bellum walk off with two of the Expedition Channel crew members, one of the *Sports Illustrated* reporters nodded in his direction and asked Becky, "What's wrong with him today?"

Becky shrugged.

"What's wrong with him *every* day?" she asked.

The worry evident, etched on his face, Kukulcán watched as Elvis pulled on a three-millimeter-thick neoprene wetsuit, tugging up the back-opening zipper. The wetsuit was the one piece of dive gear with which the missionary was truly familiar. Except for the fact that it was black and gray rather than the fluorescent colors that his sponsors had favored, the suit was virtually identical to the ones that he had worn in his days as a competitive surfer.

"Dude," Elvis smiled to his Mayan friend. "Chill out. Really. I'll be fine."

The young Cháakadon man nodded, concern fixed on his classic Mayan features.

Elvis cuffed up the legs of his wetsuit, getting ready to pull his dive boots on. He stopped.

"Okay," he told Kukulcán. "Let's have it. What's bothering you?"

Kukulcán looked out the doorway of the Mayan-style hut and then back at his good friend.

"Kunich Ahua," he whispered.

Elvis rolled his eyes.

"Quatul said that he was *here*," Kukulcán insisted.

Elvis just looked at him, his expression blank.

"Last night," Kukulcán said. "Quatul told me Kunich Ahua *spoke* to him."

"Quatul was dreaming," Elvis told him.

"No!" Kukulcán insisted. "He was not asleep! He was outside to . . . to go to the trees."

"Okay," Elvis said. "Nature called. Then what?"

Kukulcán nodded.

"While he was . . . while he was there, Kunich Ahua came up behind him and spoke."

"Okay," Elvis said. "So we've got what? The Mayan sun god trotting around in the middle of the night? Anything wrong with this picture? Go on."

Kukulcán looked out of the doorway again.

"Quatul said Kunich Ahua told him . . ."

"Go on," Elvis told him.

"He told him a man dies in K'uxulch'en today," Kukulcán said. Elvis could actually see the whites all around his eyes.

"Kukulcán," Elvis said calmly. "Do you believe in Jesus?"

The Mayan nodded.

"Do you believe that Jesus is God?"

Another nod.

"And what about God the Father and the Holy Spirit? Are they God?"

"Yes."

"And how many gods are they? Three?"

Kukulcán shook his head.

"One," he said.

"And how many gods are there?" Elvis asked him quietly.

Kukulcán took a breath.

"One," he said. "Only one."

Elvis nodded.

"Then if there is only one God, is Kunich Ahua a god?"

Kukulcán shook his head.

"Then who spoke to Quatul?"

Kukulcán nodded in understanding.

"A man," he said.

"That's right," Elvis said. "A man. A man who has been messing with your people's heads for far too long. Kukulcán, the Holy Spirit spoke to me this morning."

"How?" Kukulcán asked. "He walked up behind you?"

"No," Elvis told him. "I have never heard him speak in a voice like a man."

"Then how do you hear him?"

"Here," Elvis said, placing his hand over his heart. Kukulcán nodded.

"And the Holy Spirit said nothing about a man dying in the *cenote* today, bro."

Kukulcán nodded again.

"He warned you of nothing?" he asked the missionary.

"I didn't say that," Elvis said. He told his friend about his concerns for Bridget.

Kukulcán's eyes narrowed. He knew that his wife would have died five years before, had it not been for Bridget.

"The doctor," he said. "She will not die here, will she?"

"I don't believe so; no," Elvis told him.

"And the Holy Spirit told you this as well?"

"He did not," Elvis said. "But it is what I believe."

"Then," Kukulcán decided, "I will pray for Bridget."

"That's the right thing to do," Elvis assured him. "That's exactly the right thing to do."

There was no easy way down into the *cenote*. A small, stubby, hand-cranked pipe-and-timber swiveling crane had been set up next to the most overhanging section of the limestone pit. This was used to lower scuba tanks and other gear off to the one end of the floating work platform that was anchored in two places to the limestone walls. People had to get down to the water's edge by half-rappelling, half-downclimbing a steep lime-stone incline to the other end of the platform. Mike had designed the system using safety methods he'd employed to enter deep systems in Brazil: each person going down the rope had a mechanical brake, called a *prussick*, to catch them and keep them on the rope if they slipped. There was also a top rope to belay each person as he or she made the descent. It was a good system, but it created a bottleneck every time the team had to send people into or out of the *cenote*.

A cluster of people—Mike, Jorge, Bridget, Becky, and four or five other wetsuited people who would not be diving but were there to help handle equipment—were already gathered at the top of the rappel when Elvis got there. They greeted him warmly. As Elvis hugged Bridget, he stepped back, looked her full in the face so she could read his lips, and mouthed, "I need to talk with you later, okay?" She looked surprised for a moment, then she nodded in agreement.

To Elvis's surprise, Mike asked him to lead the group in prayer. So the missionary did, his hands on Mike's shoulders, with most of the group, including a few of the reporters, joining in. Then they began shuttling people to the bottom.

Elvis debated telling Mike about the nocturnal visit of the supposed Kunich Ahua. He decided against it. The guy had already been sufficiently ruffled by the way the Expedition Channel had set him up the evening before. But it wouldn't have been right to just sit on the information, so Elvis got Jorge aside and told him as the first support people made their way down the rope to the water.

Stern, somber, the Mexican shook his head slightly and asked, "Who is this guy?"

Elvis shrugged.

"We've brought more than sixty men from the village," he told Jorge in Spanish. "And with the reporters, the crew here, that's another forty or so. It could be anybody."

The Expedition Channel crew set up a camera on a tripod and began shooting tape of the team descending to the platform. As they did, Viktor Bellum, still in his Navy SEAL T-shirt, but wearing metallic-gold-lensed Oakleys this time, shouldered his way through the group, stopping at the edge of the people clustered around Mike.

"Buddy," Bellum said from about six feet away. "Have you thought about what I said?"

All conversation stopped. It was a weird way to conduct a dialogue, with the two men standing several feet apart from one another. Then Elvis noticed that the camera crew had stopped shooting the people going down the rope and was focused on the group at the rim of the pit. This was being done, Elvis realized, for the benefit of the camera. He made his way over to Becky, tapped her on the shoulder, and nodded toward the lens pointed their way.

"I want to help you, buddy," Bellum repeated, a seemingly warm smile on his tanned face. "Won't you let me do this with you?"

Mike looked ready to say something, then Becky stepped in front of Bellum.

"You'll need to move to the side, Viktor," she told him. "This area is for dive crew only."

The smile vanished from Bellum's face, and he stared at Becky, the metallic lenses of the sunglasses hiding his eyes. The two of them were almost exactly the same height, but he was nearly two of her in terms of weight. He shrugged and walked over to join his camera crew.

But when Elvis glanced over at Mike, he saw that the cave diver's face was flushed, nearly crimson. Bridget was talking to him, her hand on his shoulder, and he was nodding, calming down. But it was obvious that he had been riled.

The rest of the preparation was so set, so rote, that even as he participated in it, it seemed to Elvis that he was an observer, someone on the outside looking in. Once they got to the platform, none of the divers tarried there; the wetsuits and, in the case of Mike and Jake, the even heavier dry suits, dictated a transition into the water as quickly as possible. Even though it was geothermally warmed, the *cenote* water was already cooler than the jungle air.

They geared up floating in the water next to the platform, the support people handing them each piece of gear—fins, BCDs, lights, reels, masks—as they needed them. Elvis saw Bridget handing Jorge two plain white Styrofoam cups, which he stuffed into the pocket of his rebreather vest. It was something new that they'd added to the routine: when Jorge got to his stop, he'd release the first cup and let it float to the surface, letting the rest of the crew know that it was okay to start the dive. Then, when he saw Mike coming back up to the safety stop, he'd take the other cup out of his pocket and release it as well. It was a very reliable, if low-tech, means of letting those on the surface know that Mike had come back and was okay.

Like dominoes falling, one against the other, the pre-dive regimen clicked into place. Elvis got Mike's travel tanks. That would be his job today—to hand Mike the tanks once he'd gotten submerged. They swam as a group to the marker buoy, a scant forty feet from the platform, where Jorge immediately descended to his stop. Five minutes later, the cup popped to the surface. Up on the rim, the Mayan men and the reporters were gathered, right up against the caution tape, watching everything.

Elvis saw Mike and Bridget hold hands. She kissed him, and it took the explorer a moment to respond, as if he was lost in his thoughts. Then they brought out the ice-water basin, and Mike began snorkel-breathing.

Buddied with Becky, Elvis put his regulator into his mouth, vented his BC, and slipped beneath the surface, the two extra tanks clumsy at first, then easier to handle once he was completely underwater. The transition was sudden, from a sunny, breezeless day, to a world of green mottled light, the depths of the *cenote* black beneath their fins, the yellow polypropylene rope dropping laser-straight down into the depths, vanishing after less than a hundred feet.

They could see Mike, Bridget, and two support people at the surface, their legs dangling down like decorations hanging from a ceiling. Then the support people moved off, and Bridget and Mike began to descend, feet-first. Once they were completely underwater, Bridget took Mike by the elbow and guided him over to Elvis, who handed him one tank and then the other.

They'd done this on the training dives, and always, Mike had winked and smiled as Elvis handed him the tanks, the crinkles at the edges of his eyes, behind the mask, showing warmth, recognition. But it wasn't there today. Mike's eyes seemed unfocussed, almost as if he were looking, but not seeing. Yet he handled the tanks with practiced ease, gave a thumb-down "diving" signal to no one in particular, and began to descend. In moments, he had transitioned to a sky-diver-like orientation in the water, his fingers brushing the descent rope, his cave-light snapping on. They watched him slip down into the blackness, and then the blackness simply swallowed him up.

Elvis, Bridget, and Becky slowly surfaced, Becky immediately kicking over to the work platform, where she would get on a handheld radio and send a progress report to the journalists up on the rim. Elvis turned in the water until he saw Kukulcán standing with his grandfather and the rest of the Mayan men at the top of the limestone cliffs. Elvis gave them a *shaka*, the traditional surfer's "howdy," thumb and little finger outstretched. Sixty Mayan hands returned the signal, and even from the distance, Elvis could see the relief etched on Kukulcán's face, the satisfaction on Naum Kaan's, the consternation on Quatul's.

Elvis turned to Bridget. He took off his dive mask, and she did the same.

"So," he said, "tell me."

"Tell you what?" she asked aloud.

Elvis pointed to himself, touched his open hand to his forehead: *I know.*

For a moment, all color drained out of Bridget's face. She bobbed as a stray breeze stirred the surface of the *cenote*, and then she touched her open hand to her forehead and traced a quick question-mark in the air: *Know what?*

Elvis looked at her for a moment, sighed, and took her hand, squeezing it in reassurance.

"Why," he asked, "don't you tell me?"

———————

Mike took a full, deep breath, and as the 200-hundred-foot marker slipped by on the rope, finally relaxed a degree or so. He hated it that he'd let Viktor Bellum get his goat. He knew that Bellum was playing to the cameras just to get him riled, and it upset him to know that he'd allowed himself to get upset, which made no sense at all, but there it was.

But all that was topside, and it was slipping away now, and Mike was in an element that he understood. He relaxed another degree and noted light below on the line. That would be Jorge, waiting at 300 feet.

Jorge was looking up, the twin, fat hoses of the rebreather apparatus curling away behind his head, his dark hair looking thinner here, underwater, than it did topside. The two men exchanged "okay" signals and then Jorge clenched his fist and held it out: Mike tapped his own fist against the other man's as he passed him on the way down, their knuckles clicking together in the familiar salute.

Mike switched regulators to his midpoint travel mix and tried to pace his breathing. He was more relaxed now, but he still wasn't into the zone, still wasn't into the running-on-autopilot calm that he wanted for a big dive such as this. He thought of Bellum and wondered why the man seemed to feel he had to monkey-wrench the dive like this, but that just elevated his respiration, and he pushed the thought away. Peaceful thoughts. Calm thoughts. He reached for them, but few came.

The 500-foot marker came up, and Mike looked at the submersible pressure gauge, sticking up on its stubby little stand-off hose out of the travel-bottle's first stage. He read the gauge, then read it again, and then he stopped his descent. Hovering next to the line, Mike reached into a zippered pocket and pulled out the plastic slate on which he had marked, in permanent felt-tip marker, the go/no-go pressures for every checkpoint in the dive. And sure enough, there on the slate, it said that the minimum pressure on his travel-tank at 500 feet had to be 2,650 psi.

He was just under 2,500.

No good; his respiration rate had been too high. This wasn't going to work.

It was close. Tantalizingly close. And for just a split second he debated with himself, wondered whether he could slow his breathing enough to compensate, still pull this off. But to do that would violate every standard he taught by. It would definitely flatten his chances of making it back to the surface.

Viktor Bellum. For a moment, Mike enjoyed the fantasy of squeezing the jerk's fireplug neck until his head popped off. Then he added a touch of gas to his dry suit and began to swim his way back up the line. He felt relief at having turned the dive, and he felt guilty for feeling relieved. But he was alive, and alive felt pretty darn good.

Bridget told Elvis. She told him everything: what she had found in the shower, how she felt, what her fears were. She did it all in sign, making sure her back was to Becky, and she slumped, head back on her buoyancy compensator, after she had finished.

Elvis swam closer and, to the extent that the equipment would allow it, he hugged her.

You're going to tell Mike, he signed. He didn't add the question-mark. It wasn't a question.

Bridget nodded.

After the dive, she signed. Then her eyes went wide, and she pointed past Elvis.

"He's coming up," she said.

On the water, next to the buoy, a second Styrofoam cup bobbed at the surface, jostled by the bubbles coming up from below.

"He's early," Bridget added. She didn't need to add the rest; they both knew that Mike must have aborted the dive.

Elvis turned Bridget in the water so she was looking at him.

"Listen," he said aloud, mouthing the words carefully so she couldn't mistake what he was saying. "You still have to tell him. You have to tell him today."

She didn't reply.

Have you been reading the Bible I gave you? Elvis asked her.

Bridget nodded.

In Exodus 20:16—Elvis spelled out the name of the Biblical book—*also Matthew 15:19 and several other places, it talks about "false witness." Seen that anywhere?*

Bridget nodded again.

It means telling the whole truth, Elvis signed. *If you keep this thing from Mike, let him make his decisions based on just part of the information? It's not right. It's the same thing as lying to him.*

She still didn't say anything, and Elvis added aloud, "Bridget—God's will is very clear on this. Are you going to listen to him or not?"

Finally she nodded a third time.

"I'll tell Becky right now," she told him. "She can get another doctor in here, maybe by tomorrow. You're right. I'll tell him."

Turning the dive at 500 feet had shortened Mike's decompression time, but it had not eliminated it, not by a long shot. And while Bridget would have been capable of signing the news to him underwater, she had not. She and Becky and Elvis had gone down to meet Mike at 200 feet, then Becky had surfaced to make a progress report, and Bridget and Elvis had kept Mike company through two hours of decompression. When they surfaced, they swam him over to the platform, where he got out of the water, pulled off his dry suit and insulating undergarment, and lay there on the wooden deck in swim trunks and a T-shirt, breathing pure oxygen from a long, green, skinny tank.

Bridget, Becky, and Elvis gathered around him, and he looked at them questioningly, and then Bridget had simply said, "Tell him." So Elvis had, with no editorializing, other than to add, "And Bridget wants you to know that this is not like a diagnosis or anything. But it is a cause for concern. It's something that has to get checked out right away."

"I've been on the horn to Cancún," Becky added. "There's a doctor there who's trained in hyperbaric medicine. No cave cert, but he's dived caverns. We can get him in here day after tomorrow. He's clearing his schedule right now—"

"No," Mike told her, cutting her off. He pulled off the oxygen mask and said, "Call him back and tell him we won't need him. And get the reporters together and tell them that our next attempt will be in two . . . better make it three . . . weeks' time. Set a date with them. Three weeks. I'm going back to Florida with Bridget."

"No," Bridget protested, tears flowing down her cheeks.

"Yes," Mike told her, squeezing both of her hands. Then he released them so he could sign, *Life has priorities.*

29

THE UNIVERSITY OF MIAMI
MEDICAL CENTER

Mike woke up and looked at the clock on the waiting-room wall. He'd been asleep for forty-five minutes. High in the corner of the sea-foam-green room, a TV set was playing with the sound turned all the way down. One of those fake-courtroom shows; two roommates suing one another over a dead boa constrictor.

He needed a shower. He'd changed to fresh clothes before they'd left the *cenote*, but that had been nearly eighteen hours earlier. The media had all seemed sympathetic, which was encouraging. The producer's assistant from the Expedition Channel had even asked if it was all right for them to leave their tents and most of their gear on site, so they wouldn't have to set it all back up again in three weeks, and when Mike had told him that would be fine, the young man had wished him and Bridget the best of luck.

Still, it had come as a relief when he had seen the Expedition Channel's helicopter lift off a good hour before any of the rest of the media. He wouldn't have wanted to have left with any of that crew still in his camp.

Just as soon as Bridget had pushed a half-liter of saline into him, he, Bridget, Becky, and Elvis had all hitched rides out to Cancún with the rest of the media. He and Bridget had gotten into the chopper with the guys from *Sports Illustrated*, Becky had accepted a lift with the team from *Outside*, and Elvis had ridden with a newspaper photographer and his pilot in a small helicopter that had only two seats but a generous baggage area, where the plucky missionary had sat atop his backpack for the entire flight.

Their exit had been a hurried affair, and they had traveled light, each person taking just one pack of clothes and personal effects, Becky bringing her laptop along so she could hammer out press releases on the flight back to Miami.

And it had all gone swiftly—astoundingly so. After the *SI* pilot had radioed ahead and described the situation, an AeroMexico agent had gotten on the radio, taken Bridget's American Express Card number—she would not hear of the rest of them paying their own way—and written tickets that were sent with the flight crew out to the next Miami flight. A baggage handler had been waiting when the helicopters landed, and in a move that would have been impossible in the United States, they had piled with their bags into the handler's tractor-drawn cart, and he had driven them over to the waiting airliner, where a gate agent had given them the most cursory of inspections with a scanner wand and then trundled them onto the airplane.

Working from the list Bridget had given her, Becky had made phone calls while they were still rumbling across the tarmac in the cart. Bridget's oncologist of choice had cleared her schedule for the next morning, the hospital had arranged hotel rooms near the airport, and just two hours after leaving the camp, the four of them had been in the air en route to Miami, where Bridget had a firm appointment with one of the best cancer docs in the Southeast. Mike had been impressed; it usually took him two weeks just to get in to see his dentist.

Two seats away, Elvis had his Bible open on his lap. Mike watched him for a moment, saying nothing. It seemed like Elvis always had a Bible open, and one would have thought he would have memorized it by this point—in fact, the way he dropped Bible verses into conversation, Mike figured that he already had.

Mike hadn't seen much of Elvis the previous night. The girls had stayed in a room adjoining theirs, and Elvis had spent much of the evening over there, talking with them, praying with them. It was the first time Mike realized that Bridget had apparently talked to Becky about this Christianity thing, and Becky had apparently welcomed the talk. It made him feel lonely, and he was surprised by that. He remembered something he'd heard in a philosophy course during college, some guy who said that, if you woke up one day and everyone around you had turned into a rhinoceros, then, by the end of the day, you'd want to be a rhinoceros as well.

Mike stretched, and Elvis looked his way, smiling.

"Good nap, bro?"

"It was a nap," Mike said. "How much longer do you think they'll be?"

"Not long," Elvis assured him. "The doc said that this is a very simple procedure. They don't even put her out for it. You want some coffee or anything?"

Mike shook his head.

"Want to pray together?" Elvis offered.

Mike considered this.

"Think it could change anything?" he asked.

"Absolutely."

"But what's there—what's inside Bridget—it already is whatever it is, right? How could prayer possibly change that?"

Elvis grinned.

"Are you familiar with the concept of divine prescience?" he asked.

"What's that?"

"A fifty-cent way of saying that God knows about everything, even things that haven't happened yet."

"Oh." Mike sat up. "Sure. That makes sense."

"Well," Elvis explained. "If you understand that, then it's just a very short step to understanding that, to God, it's *all* past tense. So no matter what you pray for, even if it's for the health of your grandchildren when you've yet to even have children, to God you're praying about something that may just as well have already happened, and he is able to have shaped and influenced that outcome, if that is his will. Same with the lump. If his will is for it to be nothing, it's nothing."

"Okay," Mike said, even though Elvis had lost him somewhere around the grandchildren. "Pray away."

So Elvis had come next to him, and the missionary had prayed. And it wasn't a flowery, thee-and-thou speech, nothing like Mike had expected. Rather, the young missionary just talked to Jesus as if Jesus was sitting there, huddled with the two of them. Elvis mentioned to Jesus some of the things that Mike had read about, like the raising of Lazarus and curing a leper, and some things Mike hadn't heard about, like healing a blind man's eyes with mud or God opening an elderly woman's womb. And by the time Elvis had finished reminding Jesus, reminding God, of all the wonders he had worked, then keeping Bridget safe suddenly seemed to Mike like a very easy thing for God to do.

Elvis finished and Mike told him, sincerely, "Thank you. That made me feel better."

The missionary smiled and squeezed his shoulder.

"You talk to Jesus like he's here," Mike observed.

Elvis smiled.

"Mike," he said, "Jesus is here. I have his word on that. It says in the Bible that whenever two or three are gathered together in his name, he will be there also."

Mike shrugged.

"I don't know," he said. "I'm not sure I count as one of the two or three."

"Why wouldn't you?"

"I . . . I don't believe the way you and Bridget believe. I don't see why Jesus would listen to someone who isn't already . . . you know. Inside."

"Mike," Elvis smiled kindly. "In my life, Bridget's life, every believer's life, there was a time when we prayed to Jesus and told him that we knew that we were sinners and that we had only one hope and that he was that hope, and we asked him to save us from our sin and to help guide us in a life that would steer us away from sin and toward his will."

"Yeah?"

"Yeah, and when we spoke to Jesus like that, we weren't 'inside' either. We were outside, coming in. So don't go thinking that God is deaf to your pleas. He hears you."

Mike nodded.

"But you've been thinking about it, haven't you?" Elvis asked.

"Thinking?"

"That New Testament I gave you," Elvis said. "I notice that it's getting a little wear. In fact, I noticed that it wasn't left next to your cot after you packed to come here."

"Yeah," Mike admitted sheepishly. "I brought it along."

"Well?"

"Well?"

"Is there anything you want to tell me?" Elvis asked. "Or God?"

Mike cleared his throat.

"I guess that I . . ."

"Guys!" Becky rounded the turn from the hall into the waiting-room doorway. "Come on with me, okay? You can come in and see her now."

Bridget was sitting up atop the covers on one of those tilting and reclining hospital beds. The room, labeled "Procedure Room 7" on its door, had the usual hospital-room accoutrements—a small attached bath, a night-stand, and a small closet, through the open door of which Mike could see

Bridget's jeans and shirt hanging on plastic hangers. But the room also had a sink, medicinal cabinets, and a wall-mounted lightbox for viewing X-rays.

Bridget was wearing some sort of hospital gown that flapped over itself in the front. She looked like she was getting ready to cut somebody's hair.

"Hey," Mike said.

"Hey yourself," she told him, and he kissed her gingerly.

"I don't want to bump anything," he said.

"Everything's numb," Bridget told him. "They gave me a local. You could bump it with a Mack truck and I wouldn't care. When that wears off, though, I might be a little sore."

She smiled.

"Becky's a real trooper," she said. "She stayed right here through the whole thing."

"I almost provided them with another patient," Becky added wanly. "I mean, the incision was very tiny—maybe half an inch. But there was *blood*."

She shivered at the memory, and Mike hugged her.

There was a knock at the door, and Elvis let in a woman in white.

"Hi," she said, signing as she spoke. "I'm Shelly. I'm an oncological RN"—she spelled out the letters—"and I'm also an interpreter for the hearing-impaired. I know that Dr. Marceau . . ."

"Bridget," Bridget piped up.

"Okay, doctor! Bridget! I know that Bridget can read lips as well as most of us can hear, but hospital policy is that if someone doesn't hear, we sign."

"That's fine," Mike said. "In fact, up to a minute ago, I didn't even know that there was a sign for 'oncological.'"

"Doctor Perkins will be here in ten minutes or so to give you the results of the biopsy."

"That fast?" Mike asked.

The nurse nodded.

"We do sentinel-node biopsies in a lot of our breast surgeries here," she said. "That's where, rather than taking out a bunch of lymph nodes, you just take out the one that's closest to the tumor, and you examine it while the patient is still on the table. If it's clear, you can close, and if it's not, you go ahead and do the regular procedure, where you take out all the Level One and Level Two nodes. We didn't do any nodes on Dr. Mar . . . on Bridget, but we did excise the entire mass in question, as it was so small that it might have moved if we tried to examine it with a needle, and we wanted to make sure that we got a good sample of the questionable tissue. And since our lab is set up for quick turnarounds, we had them quick-freeze and section it. They're examining it under a microscope and writing a report right now. We don't normally do that for breast lumps, but this lady has quite a few friends on staff here."

Bridget smiled.

There was another knock at the door. A tall woman with gray hair and glasses came in.

"Hey, Fran," Bridget said.

"Hey, adventure woman," the doctor said. "You want full report or bottom line?"

"Bottom line," Bridget, Becky, Mike, and Elvis all said at the same time.

"Okay," the doctor said, looking down at her chart. "Bottom line. Get dressed and get out of here, girl. You're fine."

The bed bounced as all three friends converged on Bridget at once. Bridget's head emerged from the jumble and she said, "Good thing I'm still numb. Not precancerous?"

"No," the doctor told her as the nurse signed. "I'll tell you the truth; it looked suspicious when I took it out. I didn't like the shape or the color. But the lab sliced and diced it six ways to Sunday, and there isn't an abnormal cell in it. My guess is you must have bumped a door on the way to the bathroom in the dark. This was just a little fibroid tissue, like what you get sometimes after a bruise goes away."

"Wait," Mike asked the doctor, straightening up. "You said it looked suspicious?"

"It did, when I took it out," she agreed. "In fact, I was certain that I'd be coming in here with bad news. I've never had one that looked like that come back as anything but cancer."

"W-well," Mike stammered. "Are we being premature here? Is there a chance some samples got mixed or something?"

"Not a chance," the doctor insisted. "The specimen went from my hand to the pathologist's. Besides, they're having a slow day down there— Bridget's was the only fresh specimen in the lab. And I'm confident of the results . . ."

She blushed slightly as she said this. " . . . I mean, I know it's not good to second-guess your pathologist, but—this being Bridget and all—I got on the 'scope and checked everything again myself. This lady is clear as a bell."

"Sounds pretty definitive to me," Becky said.

Mike looked at Elvis.

Elvis just grinned.

"Thanks, Fran," Bridget smiled as Mike, Becky, and Elvis got off her bed.

"Don't mention it," the doctor said. "I'd better get out of here; I've got rounds. You get dressed and Shelly will bring you the discharge papers, okay?"

The two medical personnel left, and the four friends were left in the room alone, grinning at one another.

Bridget nodded at the phone on Mike's belt.

"You've got a message, buddy," she said.

"Huh?" Mike looked down. The screen was blinking. "Oh. I had the ringer turned off."

He took the phone off his belt and pushed a button.

"It's a text-page from Lamar," he said. He pushed another button, read the screen, and the grin dropped from his face. He paged up and read it again.

"Mike?" Becky asked. "What is it?"

He handed her the phone.

"CALL STILES ASAP," it said, giving the underwater photographer's satellite phone number. "BELLUM HAS DIVED CENOTE X. REACHED BOTTOM. 1,283 FEET. SORRY TO BE THE BEARER. LAMAR."

30

COURTYARD BY MARRIOTT, MIAMI INTERNATIONAL AIRPORT

"Mike, I am so, so sorry. I never had the slightest idea that this might happen."

The satellite phone clarity was amazing. It was as if Jake was standing right there in the hotel room with them.

"Don't apologize," Mike told the speakerphone. "I'm sure you didn't have anything to do with it. What happened?"

"Well, we deedee'd right out of there, like you saw," Jake said. "But when we landed at Cancún, and I went to pull my gear off the chopper, Lorenzo tells me to leave it. He says I can hit the head if I want, but that I shouldn't go far from the chopper. And then, about half an hour later, this carload of *federales* shows up, and two of them climb in the chopper with us. Next thing I know, we're flying back to the *cenote*. We land, and of course Jorge is out there, asking what gives, and one of the cops shows him this paper. It's a court order. It directs Bellum to seek a cooperative dive with you, and it says that if you don't, or you die or abandon the site, he has the right to dive it, and the *ejido* has to grant him permission. And get this: the cop says that you were served with a copy of the order."

"Either he got bought off or he served it on someone he thought was you," Elvis told Mike. "We're not talking the world's most sophisticated legal system. Not in Quintana Roo."

"Okay," Mike said. "Go on."

"Well, naturally, Jorge's madder than a wet hen, but what can he do?" Stiles said. "He tried calling you, but your phone was out of range."

"I was probably on the flight to Miami," Mike said.

Becky, easily the fastest signer in the group, next to Bridget, had been translating the conversation for her, and now Bridget began to tear up.

It's my fault, Bridget signed to Mike. *If I hadn't taken you away . . .*

"Don't go there," Mike said. "My guess is that Bellum had some other idea for trying to either incapacitate me or get me off site. Your situation just turned out to be a good break for him, that's all."

He turned back to the phone.

"Did you film the dive, Jake?"

"I'm sorry to say that I did," Stiles voice came back. "I didn't want to, but Lorenzo was muttering lawsuit if I didn't."

"Did Bellum actually do it?" Mike asked.

Stiles was silent for a second.

"Well, he went in with his dive computer zeroed," the photographer said. "And when he came back up, it read a max of 1,283 feet."

"That'd be about right for the side of the debris cone," Mike mused. "What kind of computer?"

"Cochran," Jake said. "A Commander, I think."

"Hmm," Mike mused. "No way to program in a fake depth on that, that I'm aware of."

"I think he actually did it, Mike," Jake said.

"Who safety dived for him?" Becky asked.

"Nobody," Jake said. "He went solo, top to bottom, and carried all his gas."

"That's crazy," Bridget said as Becky signed Jake's reply.

"Well," Stiles said, "sanity never has been Bellum's long suit."

"And you're sure about the computer readings?" Mike asked.

"Positive," Stiles said. "In fact, I shot digital stills of him, just as he started the dive, and later on when I met him at the 200-foot safety stop."

"Where are you now?" Mike asked.

"My hotel in Cancún," Stiles said.

"Oh, man," Mike apologized. "And here I am burning up your satellite phone time."

"Don't mention it," Stiles said. "I'm still on assignment until I get back in-country, so I'm charging Lorenzo for every second of this. What do you need?"

"Can you send us copies of your digital photos?"

"Sure," Stiles said. "I can e-mail you the whole batch. There aren't that many because I cull the images right in the camera and just keep what I can use."

"Use this address," Becky said, giving him her AOL screen name.

"You got it," Stiles said. "Anything else?"

"Where will you be over the next few hours?" Mike asked.

"Just chillin' in the room," Stiles said. "My flight out isn't until tomorrow."

He gave Mike the number, and Mike thanked him and hung up.

"No safety diver?" Bridget asked. "That sounds pretty strange to me."

"Well," Mike shrugged, "he might have been acclimatizing by doing deep ocean dives on the sly. And as for no safety man—Jake said it: Bellum's bizarre."

Becky came back from her and Bridget's room about fifteen minutes later, the open laptop in her hands.

"Got the pix," she announced. "And it doesn't look good. It's just like Jake said."

She set the computer down and clicked through the images as the other three gathered around. The very first shot showed Bellum's computer reading 10 feet—probably shot just after he submerged. There were a few establishment shots of Bellum hovering in the water, and one eerie one of him descending, backlit by his own cave light.

The next set showed Bellum hovering next to the line, the 200-foot marker visible on it. The photos progressively moved in on his dive computer. The last shot clearly showed him to be at 198 feet with a maximum depth of 1,283 feet logged on the dive.

"I just have a real hard time believing this," Mike sighed.

"Wait!" Bridget said. She turned to Becky and signed, *Can you keep this one on the screen and make it smaller?*

Becky nodded and reduced the photo to half the screen size.

Now, Bridget signed, *put the first picture of the dive computer next to it.* Becky did it.

"It's the same computer," Mike said. "It's even scratched in the same places."

"But look," Bridget said, pointing at the strap of the computer.

They all looked.

Do you see? Bridget signed. *The strap is sticking out . . . different. Like he rebuckled it, but only got the strap though half the buckle.*

Becky jumped ahead to some shots of Bellum getting out of the water.

"It looks okay here," she said.

"He rebuckled it," Bridget explained.

"That doesn't mean anything," Mike said, signing as he talked. "The suit squeezes—gets tighter from the water pressure—when you dive. The computer tends to get loose. It isn't uncommon to rebuckle it a couple of times when you're dealing with big changes in depth. Otherwise, as the suit squeezes, the computer wants to fall off."

Okay, Bridget signed to Becky. *Now—the beginning and the safety stop, side by side.*

She did.

"I'm looking," Mike said. "What am I seeing?"

"This," Bridget said. She pointed to Bellum's line reels—a big "exploration" reel and a smaller "gap" reel, both visible just above the tanks on his left side.

"Yeah . . . ," Mike said. "He's got two reels. Nothing unusual in that. Most cave divers carry two reels. You might not need them on a simple bounce like this *cenote*, but you get used to diving what you train with."

That big? Bridget signed.

"It is a pretty big reel," Mike agreed. "But again, maybe it's what Bellum usually carries. Like I said, you get used to certain equipment, you carry it."

"Okay," Bridget said aloud. She pointed to the second picture. "So where is it?"

All four heads bent closer to the screen. Only one reel showed in the second photo.

"Maybe it's hidden by the tank," Mike said. "Let's look at some others."

Becky slowly paged through the other photos, including the ones shot after Bellum had emerged from the water, grinning for the camera, the perennial sunglasses back on his face. The big reel wasn't there; not in any of the pictures.

"Dude," Elvis said. "It's gone."

Mike dialed Jake's hotel room down in Mexico.

"Jake," Mike said as Becky signed for Bridget. "Do me a favor. Think carefully. Anything strange about Bellum's dive?"

"Well, no safety diver," Stiles said. "That was pretty odd."

"Granted," Mike agreed. "Anything else?"

The line went silent for a moment as Stiles thought.

"Yes," he finally said. "Two things. For one," he explained, "as you saw from the shots, I didn't go down to 200 and wait for him. My rebreather isn't re-engineered like yours are; mine's only rated to 140 feet, so I was on scuba. That being the case, I just shot Bellum at the beginning of the dive, surfaced, and then waited there until he was just about due at 200. Then I went down to shoot the grand finale."

"Okay, understood," Mike said.

"And when I was on my way down?" Stiles said. "A whole bunch of bubbles came up. Two bunches, in fact. Not normal exhaust bubbles; it was like diving above humpback whales. I figured maybe Bellum blew an O-ring, except neither bunch lasted more than a minute. And when I got to Bellum, he seemed fine—not freaked out or anything."

"Was he coming up to the stop when you got to him, or was he already there?" Mike asked.

"Already there, and that surprised me a little," Stiles said. "I left early, hoping to get him coming up, and when I got there, he was already hanging. I remember thinking that he was too quick, that he was gonna get bent. But he didn't."

"Okay," Mike said. "Anything else?"

"Yes," Stiles told him. "I could have sworn that I saw Bellum drop something."

Mike looked around at the group.

"What'd he drop?"

"I can't say," Stiles said. "I just saw movement. Then it was gone."

"Any color?"

"Red maybe. I don't know. Maybe white. It was just when my light hit him and then it was gone, and he was still some distance away."

"Think about this, Jake," Mike asked him. "Could it have been his line reel? The big one?"

"Yeah! Yes, indeed—it sure could have. And—let me look at my laptop—yeah, the big reel's not there in the later pictures."

The line fell dead for a second. Then Stiles came back on.

"You don't think he did a dive, do you?"

"I think he did," Mike said. "I think he did a dive to 200 feet, lowered his computer on the line reel, purged his travel tanks so they wouldn't have too much pressure when you met him—that was the bubbles you saw— but then he jammed his reel when he was bringing the computer back up. And you surprised him. You got there a minute before he expected you. So he just wound the line around the reel, maybe brought it up hand over hand, got the computer off of it, and then chucked the reel so you wouldn't see that it was all messed up."

The four friends looked at one another in the Miami hotel room.

"That makes sense," Stiles said. "What're you going to do?"

"We're practically at the airport now," Mike told him. "We're catching the next flight out of here. If you still want to shoot me doing this dive, be at the *cenote*, day after tomorrow."

"Should I tell Lorenzo?"

"Absolutely. The more witnesses, the better."

31
CENOTE X

The trail from the last vestige of the dirt road, the place where they had parked the trucks, was like a green tunnel though the jungle. Birds and frogs called from all around. An occasional monkey added its low, hooting howl to the chorus. Then, as the four friends neared a brighter area in the green, a different call, birdlike in tone, reached them from a distance.

Elvis smiled. The recognition signal had been one of the first Cháakadon customs that Kukulcán had taught him. Elvis returned it, a whistle ending on a high note. Three minutes later, the familiar Hawaiian shirt emerged from the jungle at the far end of the trail.

There was no "dude," no *shaka* this time. The two friends simply embraced one another.

"I'm glad you're here," Elvis told his Mayan friend. "Is your grandpa still at the camp?"

"He is," Kukulcán said. "Quatul too."

"Very cool," Elvis smiled. "Sounds as if we're ready."

They were ready. He was fairly certain of that. Mike had been on the hotel phone for better than two hours before they left Miami, calling Skip Williamson, his American attorney, and then Juan Carlos, the *ejido* president. Then Skip had called back, conferenced in both Juan Carlos and a Mexican attorney in Playa del Carmen, and they had talked for another hour. After that, Mike had spent half an hour talking with Jorge's wife on the cell phone, giving her instructions to radio on to Jorge.

The five of them—Elvis, Kukulcán, Becky, Bridget, and Mike—were just emerging from the jungle when they saw two men, one in uniform, and the other with a crewcut and sunglasses, walking their way across the broad, clear-cut staging area.

It didn't surprise Mike to see Bellum. They'd heard a helicopter passing over them in the pre-dawn gloom as they hiked in. He'd assumed it would be the bunch from the Expedition Channel. And the guy with Bellum was a policeman. That didn't surprise him either.

"Mike," Bellum said when they were still fifty feet away.

"Vik." Mike knew he hated the nickname.

"What're you up to, buddy?"

"Going for a dive. And I'm not your buddy."

"I don't think so."

Bellum turned and said something in Spanish to the young police officer, who shuffled forward, obviously uncomfortable with the situation.

"*Señor*, there can be none of the diving here," he told Mike in hesitant English. "There has been a court order to those who control the *cenote*."

"And who might that be?" Mike asked pleasantly.

"Why . . ." The policeman took a folded sheet of paper out of his pocket and consulted it. "*Ejido Mono*. Why?"

"Because they no longer control either the *cenote* or the land around it."

He handed the policeman a folder. Inside were several legal documents.

"What's this?" Bellum growled.

"A lease," Mike told him. "The *ejido* has leased me the *cenote* for five years."

"Give me that . . ."

Bellum snatched the papers out of the *federale*'s hand and read them.

"This is ridiculous. It says here you leased the property for a hundred pesos. That's ten dollars."

"Actually, eleven dollars, twenty-two cents, at yesterday's exchange rate."

"This is a ploy," Bellum said. "It won't stand up in court."

"Oh," Mike nodded, "it will stand long enough."

People began to emerge from the camp: the Yucatan Deep Project support divers, Quatul and Naum Kaan, various members of the Expedition Channel film crew. They had, Mike noticed, a camera set up at the edge of the clearing. But nobody was filming right now.

"What's going on?" Lorenzo called as he walked out to meet the group.

"You're the one who choppered in from Cancún," Mike replied. "Why don't you tell me?"

"Well, I understand you're disputing Viktor's claim to have dived the *cenote*."

Mike glanced out of the corner of his eye. The crew had the camera running again.

"Disputing? No. I wouldn't put it that strongly. Let's just say that I would like to see for myself whether he's been there."

"And how," Bellum asked, "would you propose to do that?"

"Easily. What's on the bottom of the *cenote*, Viktor?"

Bellum looked around, as if gathering support.

"I've already said what's on the bottom of the *cenote*. There's nothing on the bottom of the *cenote*. Nothing but broken limestone and silt. It's like the surface of the moon."

"Fine," Mike said. "Then I'll look myself. If there nothing's there, that's the end of it."

"Well . . . what are you expecting to find?"

"Maybe nothing," Mike shrugged. "Or maybe a line reel, Viktor. Maybe a line reel that somebody used to lower a depth computer to the bottom of the *cenote*."

"That's slander!" Bellum shouted to the camera.

"I said, 'Maybe.'" Mike pointed out.

"You can't dive here," Lorenzo asserted smugly. "Isn't that right, lieutenant?"

"It *was* right," the police officer agreed. "It isn't right, now."

He snatched the papers back out of Bellum's hands and showed them to Lorenzo.

"That lease says that the *cenote* is mine, to do with as if I owned it," Mike explained. "And the first thing I'm going to do is clear you and your people off my property."

Lorenzo just stared at him.

"Mike!" An accented voice rang out. "Your gear is set. We're ready to go."

Jorge came trotting out, shaking Mike's hand, Elvis's hand, hugging Bridget and Becky.

"You can't do this," Lorenzo warned. "You can't order us off. Your sponsors will hang you out to dry. We're the only media that's here, Bryant. The magazines and newspapers all left two days ago. The dive's a done deal. You're old news. Non-news."

"You're right," Mike said over his shoulder as he walked back to the camp. "Jake can stay, if he wants."

"I want," Stiles replied.

"That's great. The rest of you—clear out."

Lorenzo crossed his arms.

"I won't do it."

Mike stopped, turned, and walked back to the *federale*.

"You've heard me ask these people to leave. Is that a lawful request, sir?"

The little policeman nodded and smiled just a little. It was clear that he'd had more than his fill of Bellum and Lorenzo.

"*Señor*." He turned to Lorenzo as he carefully handed the lease back to Mike. "These papers are in order. We must go."

Twenty minutes later, Mike was in his hut, pulling on his dry suit, when he heard the sound of the Expedition Channel's big Russian helicopter spooling up. Earlier in the week, the sound had been an awful intrusion on the project's peace. Now, it was music to his ears.

The sun was just coming up as he trotted out to the edge of the *cenote*, where the rest of the team was gathering. Jake Stiles caught up with him as he walked.

"I cobbled something together for you. Here."

It was a digital still camera in an underwater housing, hooked to a submersible underwater strobe. Atop the clear housing was a dry-suit inlet valve. On the bottom was an exhaust valve.

"Just hook that up to your BC's low-pressure inflator and give it enough air to make it bubble every 300 feet or so," Stiles said. "The housing is only designed for 100 meters, but if you air it up as you go down, the air pressure should offset the water pressure and keep it from imploding. Any luck, it'll stand up long enough for you to get some pictures of the bottom."

Mike smiled.

"Jake—that's a great idea."

"Hey. If it'll help put the truth out on Bellum, I'm all for it."

Elvis was already in harness and rappelling down to the waterline. Becky was ready to go next. Bridget wasn't in her wetsuit—her doctor had simply told her, "Warm tropical freshwater and a fresh incision? You tell me what *you* think, Doctor."

Mike looked around.

"Where's Jorge?"

Down on the edge of the platform, in deep shadow not yet struck by the rising sun, a figure in a black dry suit and a rebreather pack waved up at him. Mike waved back and the figure backrolled into the water.

"Well," he said. "Jorge's raring to go."

Mike skipped the ice bath and the snorkel. He'd never liked it anyhow, he felt more calm than he'd felt in years, and, while he thought it highly unlikely that Bellum and Lorenzo would find a Mexican magistrate to listen to their complaints at seven in the morning, he wanted to be underwater and on his way in case they did, so even a radio call would not be able to stop him. He simply blew up his BC and lay at the surface for five minutes instead, his eyes closed, his lips barely moving. Becky and Bridget, over on the platform, assumed that he was meditating, slowing his heartbeat. Only Elvis, floating next to him, knew the truth—that he was praying.

"You go with God, buddy," the missionary whispered to him.

They descended and did the tank handoff. Without looking back, Mike flipped on his primary light and began his descent into the dark water below. There was no hypertension, no anxiety this time around. He was good to go.

Two hundred feet and he could see the glow of the safety diver's station. Fifty feet more, and Mike could make out details—the rebreather hoses, the seams on the man's hood, the panes of the mask. The light below whirled in a circle, and Mike returned the signal: *okay*. He added a puff of air to the camera case and it burped obligingly. Then, as he dove steadily past the safety station, he held his clinched fist out, ready for the salute.

He went right past. There was no answering kiss of knuckles against knuckles.

It was early, Mike thought. Maybe Jorge was still half asleep.

32
THE EXPEDITION CHANNEL HELICOPTER, EN ROUTE TO CANCUN

Dominic Lorenzo was beyond irritated. This made the third time he'd found himself choppering back from the location shoot in an insect-infested jungle in the last two weeks. And what did he have to show for it? One failure by the Yucatan Deep Project team and, if what Bryant was saying was true, one fraud by his own color commentator.

The helicopter vibrated with its passage, reminding Lorenzo that he was flying in a product of Soviet technology, many years after "Soviet" had ceased to be a viable term.

He hoped Bryant was wrong; hoped it was all bruised ego and wounded pride talking. If Viktor Bellum had indeed dived to the bottom of Cenote X, as he'd claimed he had, then Lorenzo had a story—a great story with a startling twist. Possibly the best story of his career.

But that had been before Mike Bryant's allegations. Those threatened all of it. Right now, it boiled down to a case of one diver's word and opinion against the other diver's claim, and while Bellum's dive computer had once seemed irrefutable proof that he'd made the dive, it was now highly suspect evidence. The whole thing was just one big mess. Lorenzo stuffed two wads of cotton more deeply into his ears in a vain attempt to protect himself from the aircraft's incredible noise level. As he did, he thought once again about how much it had cost him for this helicopter charter, the crew, the supplies. He rummaged in his medical bag for antacids.

Lorenzo popped two of the chalk-like tablets into his mouth and looked for the tenth time since takeoff at the door to the helicopter's lavatory. It wasn't a real lavatory, just a metal compartment with a chemical toilet and a box of moist towelettes instead of a sink. But he had refused to use the primitive slit-trench latrine back at the *cenote* camp. He'd used these facilities instead, despite the pilot's insistence that the toilet was for in-flight use only.

Well, Lorenzo had to use it right now—had needed to use it ever since they'd taken off, half an hour before. But he'd seen Viktor Bellum heading for it as the rest of the crew had walked back and forth with bundled tents, camera cases, and lights, hastily loading up.

"Gotta hit the head," was how Bellum had put it in his usual brusque, macho pseudo-military way of speaking. "Head." Not "lavatory," not "restroom." As if, even with something so simple as a call of nature, Bellum felt compelled to remind everyone that he'd spent time in the Navy.

Except Lorenzo was pretty sure that it wasn't a call of nature that had sent Mr. Macho, Mr. Supposedly World-Record-Holder-Cave-Diver into the little compartment at the back of the helicopter's cargo bay. When Lorenzo had finally helped toss the last duffel of cables into the cargo space, the door had still been shut and had remained that way as they'd lifted off in a cloud of dust and climbed to altitude.

He was pretty sure that Bellum was just hiding in there, avoiding contact, avoiding conversation, avoiding confrontation with the fact that his actions over the past two weeks now stood to severely dent Dominic Lorenzo's already depressed career.

His stomach cramping, Lorenzo walked to the lavatory door.

"Bellum!" He shouted it, aware that the old Russian helicopter's rotor noise made intelligible conversation all but impossible. "You about done in there?"

No answer.

Lorenzo pounded on the door. Waited. Pounded on the door again. Nothing.

He tried the latch. It turned, but the door wouldn't budge.

"Oh, for Pete's sake . . . ," Lorenzo grumbled.

He tried the latch and pounded again.

Lorenzo made his way forward through his half-asleep film crew, past the little police officer, who was looking a bit green in the face, obviously not ready to make any effort for the personal comfort of any *gringo*. The producer ducked through the passage into the sun-bleached cockpit, where he tapped the pilot on the shoulder.

The pilot turned; looking at him through dark green Ray-Ban Aviator sunglasses.

"Bellum's been locked in the washroom since we took off," Lorenzo shouted.

The pilot said nothing.

"I pounded on the door," Lorenzo said. "There's no answer."

The pilot sighed, looked out the window at the ground—solid trees to the horizon.

"Tell me, *señor*," he said to the producer. "You know how to fly this thing?"

"Of course not," Lorenzo told him.

"Well, then, we will have to wait until we land before I can do anything about that."

Lorenzo rolled his eyes.

"I am sorry, *Señor* Lorenzo," the pilot said. "But the chopper—somebody has to fly her, *sí*? Don't worry. We land at Cancún in twenty, twenty-five minutes, tops."

Lorenzo sighed and went back to the cargo bay, slumped onto one of the uncomfortable jump seats bolted to the wall, and felt the helicopter thundering against his back.

It was nearly thirty minutes later when the helicopter touched down at the airport. The little policeman was off before the rotors had even stopped, glad to be freed of his flying torture.

Lorenzo didn't really care about the lavatory anymore; there was a flush toilet and a sink in the charter company's offices. But as much as he desperately needed both of those things, he wanted even more to give Viktor Bellum a piece of his mind. The pilot came back into the bay, and as the crew opened the cargo door and began off-loading equipment, Lorenzo motioned, hands-up, toward the still-shut lavatory door.

Nodding, the pilot took out a small, red Swiss army knife, put it near the latch, and then stopped. Bending down, he slid the blade into the seam of the door and tugged it sideways. Two five-peso coins came popping out.

"What's that?" Lorenzo asked.

"The door," the pilot replied, peering at the top seam and popping two more coins out. "She was jammed."

"You mean locked," Lorenzo corrected him.

"No, *señor*. I mean jammed. From the outside. Here. See." He wiggled the latch and then swung the door open.

Except for the squat green plastic chemical toilet bolted to the center of the floor, the little metal compartment was empty.

33
CENOTE X

As Mike closed in on 600 feet, he gave the little camera housing another puff of air. A couple of bubbles worked their way out of the plastic housing's exhaust valve and wobbled, jelly-like, up past his dive mask. He rechecked the pressure on his travel tanks. He was well within his reserves. He even had a couple of hundred pounds to spare.

At 625, his high-intensity dive light began to flicker. The beam was just as strong as ever, but the light was going on and off, like the beam from an old-fashioned movie projector. Scowling, Mike shut the light down, plunging himself into darkness, waited for ten seconds as he felt the guide-rope pulling along through his fingers, and then turned the light back on again.

The beam shot out in a strong and uninterrupted blue-white beam for five seconds, no more. Then it began to flicker again.

That cinched it. He was running out of juice. The battery was either uncharged, which he found very hard to believe—Jorge had become obsessive about his checklists—or something had happened to discharge it. Maybe it had gotten bumped on the way down to the work platform. But if that had happened, the brilliant HID light would have lit up the pre-pawn *cenote* like a Hollywood premiere. Mike supposed it could be flooded, as well, but a flooded light usually didn't flicker. It just quit.

Leaving the primary light burning, Mike took the safety shield off his backup. The safety shield was actually an insulated beer-can holder—it even had the *Tecate* label still printed on it, but Mike had never found anything that worked better at protecting the extremely expensive HID bulb. He let the cover go and turned on his secondary light, and then turned off his primary. Technically, he still had the primary light—it was weak, but it hadn't failed. He knew he should turn around, but his case was still defensible. None of his lights had failed. Not yet.

Twenty feet later, the secondary began to flicker as well.

Mike came to a stop next to the rope. What in blue blazes was going on? He looked at the dive computer on his wrist. He was at 725 feet, and he had been underwater for just under ten minutes. Right on schedule. And the extremely powerful HID dive lights—each one of them—produced thirty-nine minutes of sun-bright light at full charge. His whole trip, from the surface down to the bottom, and back up to 300 feet, was calculated to take no longer than thirty-seven minutes, so he should easily have been able to accomplish the whole dive on a single light.

As if in answer, his secondary light flickered one more time, and went dead.

That cinched it. He was going up.

Mike flipped the primary light back on and made it to 600 feet by the time it went dead, as well. The luminous face of his dive computer was more than bright enough for him to read in the pitch-black of the *cenote*, so he just followed the rope up in the darkness, keeping his ascent rate at seventy feet per minute until he could see the green glow of the Cymalume stick on his stage tank at 500 feet. Then, with a moment of prayer, he pulled a back-up light off his shoulder strap and twisted it. He got light. Nothing like the HID light, but it didn't flicker, and it kept burning.

Mike did a mental calculation and realized that the tanks on his back, which he had not even touched yet, were still breathable. The mix was 1.4 percent oxygen, which at 500 feet would be the same as breathing 20.58 percent oxygen at sea level—almost the same as breathing regular air at sea level. He did another quick calculation and came to the conclusion that he could safely breathe his bottom mix all the way up to 300 feet. After that, it would become dicey. At somewhere around 240 feet, the equivalent percentage of oxygen in his bottom mix would fall below 10 percent: the amount required just to retain consciousness.

Rationalizing that he might as well breathe now what he wouldn't be able to breathe later, Mike went to his bottom mix. The sound of the gurgling regulator shifted, from down under his arm, on the travel tank, to up behind his head, on the double-set manifold. He immediately felt just a little tired, but ignored it. That was the diminished oxygen, he knew.

He lifted his stage tank off the up-line, clicked it into place on his harness, clipped the nearly-empty travel tank off on the rope, and timed off 90 seconds as he did his first deep decompression stop.

At 90 seconds he moved, still breathing off the double set. He hadn't even opened the valve on the stage bottle. Despite the fact that he was diving on his second backup light, Mike had plenty of breathable gas on his back. And the stage bottle that he'd just picked up, mixed to deliver the equivalent of 40 percent oxygen at 500 feet, would still be usable—just barely—at 140. Once he got to 140 feet, he could bolt back to the surface, just swim upwards and exhale, if he really needed to. He'd get bent, but he wouldn't drown.

At 400 feet, he did his next stop. The schedule called for 210 seconds here—that was three-and-a-half minutes.

Mike looked up. The light from Jorge's safety-diver station at 300 feet was shining straight down at him. Mike painted a circle with his backup light, but the cave-light up above didn't move, just remained still. Mike realized that his little backup light might be too puny to be seen 100 feet away. But it seemed to him that Jorge wouldn't be able to miss his bubbles, now running straight up the rope. Mike painted another circle with his light. Still no response.

He was feeling tired. The bottom mix was now delivering him—it took him nearly two minutes to do the calculation—just under the equivalent of 16 percent oxygen at the surface. That was like being in a crowded room with no ventilation. It would make you sleepy.

He switched back to his stage bottle and began to move up again. His head cleared immediately; even at 300 feet, the stage bottle would still deliver more oxygen per breath than a regular lungful of sea-level air.

Mike got to 370 and circled his light again. The light above made no reply.

Now Mike was worried. Was Jorge injured? Ill? If the computer malfunctioned on the safety diver's rebreather, it could give him too little oxygen to remain awake—or so much that he would go into convulsions—but he'd get an alarm if that happened, and a diver as experienced as Jorge would know to go to the ascent gas that was sitting right there with him.

Mike was at 350 feet now. Jorge had to see him. Suddenly, the light above winked away.

Almost too late, Mike realized what was happening. Something had come between him and the dive light above; something that was falling.

Immediately he kicked to the side with more force than he would have thought possible. He was rocked by an impact and the water around him sounded as if he'd been trapped inside of a giant, clanging bell. Dizzy and disoriented, he aimed his light down and caught just a glimpse of what it was that had struck the stage bottle clipped under his right arm. It was another scuba tank—the ascent bottle from the 300-foot stop, he suddenly understood.

Mike batted his light up and down rapidly. He was angry now. The dropped scuba tank could have cracked one of his and burst it. If the dropped tank had hit him in the head, that would have been all she wrote—the water in between might have cushioned the blow, but only slightly. It still would have been enough to knock him cold and send him to the bottom of K'uxulch'en, and the *cenote* would have been worthy of its name.

Mike batted the light up and down again. Still no response from above. Now, his anger faded back to worry. Maybe Jorge had been going for the stage cylinder when he blacked out or something. Maybe, Mike realized, his friend was up there dying. That was it. Mike forgot about the ascent rate and began pulling himself up the rope just as quickly as he possibly could.

He was just thirty feet away when the light above winked out completely. Mike stopped kicking and coasted up the rope, stopping when his hand closed on the empty stainless-steel D-ring where the stage bottle had been. He played the light around: no Jorge, no anything. Just empty, black water. He pirouetted in the water, shining the small backup light in front of him.

He'd made half a turn and was just exhaling when his whole body shook, and he saw stars. He head was jerked back a second time, banging against the crossover valve on his tank manifold, and now it was just piercing, shooting, roll-up-into-the-fetal-position-and-cringe painful. Blinking away the bright crimson spots blossoming in front of his eyes, he tried to take a breath, got a mouthful of water, coughed, forced himself to keep from inhaling again, and reached for his mouth. All that was there was the mouthpiece. The regulator was gone.

Grabbing his other travel-gas regulator, Mike spat the useless mouthpiece out, got the new regulator into his mouth, and had just taken one breath when it too was pulled away. But this regulator was on a rubber shock-cord , so it didn't get yanked that far. It just turned his head, and when it did, he caught a glimpse of feral, yellow-gold eyes.

Bellum.

Unclipping the stage tank from his harness, Mike thrust it behind him with all the force he could muster and felt the *thunk* of rolled steel against bone. He pulled the hose back, crammed the neck of the mouthpiece-less regulator into his mouth, took a breath, and turned.

Bellum was rubbing his chest and shaking his head.

Trying to psyche me out, Mike thought. *Make me think I can't hurt him.* It was working.

Kicking at his attacker was out of the question. The fins slowed him down too much, and Mike didn't harbor any illusions about Bellum giving him time to take them off.

Bellum turned his dive-light back on and aimed it directly into Mike's eyes, blinding him. Mike sensed, rather than saw, the other man moving to his side, and he lashed out with his own dive light, knocking Bellum's dive mask up onto his forehead.

Fresh spots danced in Mike's vision. He saw Bellum calmly pull the mask onto his face, blow it full of air through his nose, and shake his head again.

Mike's mind raced. He had never believed the stories about Bellum being a SEAL. But he was certain that Bellum had received some sort of military training. While Mike had spent a lifetime learning to survive underwater, coming out on the best side of a fistfight wasn't part of it. He had no doubt that, given enough time, Bellum would drown him.

Mike glanced at his depth computer: 270 feet. They were drifting up, but slowly. Then he remembered something—Bellum blowing air back into his divemask. And Bellum was on a rebreather. A little bit of gas, being breathed over and over again.

Mike formed the ghost of a plan.

Glancing down at his compass, hoping that it was reading correctly, Mike started swimming east, toward the center of the *cenote*, away from the rope. He knew he couldn't get away from the other diver; Mike was carrying four tanks, while Bellum just had the single, streamlined rebreather. But he could get Bellum swimming after him, make him work. Mike swam for all he was worth for ten seconds. Then he wheeled and pushed out with his scuba tank again. He connected enough to knock Bellum's mask askew a second time.

Mike glanced at the computer as Bellum resecured his mask: 245 feet. Not shallow enough. He struck out with the heel of his hand, knocked the mask loose enough to get a little water into it, and kicked furiously to work his way upward as Bellum blew air back into his mask yet a third time.

Close. He had to be close. Mike looked at his gauge: 200 feet. Good enough. Bellum came in and tried to pull the regulator out of his mouth. Mike raised the camera Stiles had given him, pressed the shutter and fired the flash directly into Bellum's eyes. The other man blinked, blinded, and Mike pulled on Bellum's mask again, flooding it completely one more time.

Shaking his head as if to show how pathetic he felt Mike's actions to be, Bellum pushed against the top of his mask with the heel of his hand and calmly blew the water out of it: the classic scuba-instructor's demonstration maneuver.

Then his expression changed.

Both hands went to his mouthpiece. He was vigorously pulling, drawing on it.

He was out of air.

It had only been a matter of time. Rebreathers, as Mike well knew, are designed to allow hours of time underwater, but they work by using the same gas over and over again. If gas is lost—as it is when a mask is flooded—it has to be replaced from small tanks, containing only a few cubic feet each of compressed oxygen and diluent—in this case, helium. At the pressure of 200 feet, there was enough gas in the system for a diver to clear a mask—but only a few times. Then the unit would run out of breathing gas. That was what Mike had banked on—sheer, unalterable gas physics.

They were far from the rope now, floating in the deep green of the middle of the *cenote*, no features in sight, nothing but the steely luminescence of the surface 200 feet above them.

Bellum lunged at Mike, but Mike easily kicked away from him; a man dying for lack of a breath cannot move swiftly for very long. Then, when Bellum's struggles began to slow, Mike cautiously approached him, took the long-hosed regulator from his own double set of bottom mix, and offered it to the other man.

Eagerly, working on instinct, Bellum crammed the regulator into his mouth and took three deep breaths. Then, behind his mask, his pupils dilated for a moment. His eyelids drooped.

The first part had been physics. This part was physiology. Still, Mike didn't move until he was certain that the other man was out cold.

He was. The bottom mix contained only the equivalent of 8.25 percent oxygen at this depth—not nearly enough to sustain consciousness, particularly in someone who had nearly suffocated.

Mike reached into his BC pocket and found four black nylon zip strips that he kept there for underwater repairs. Four was enough. He linked two of them together in a figure-eight, raised Bellum's limp arms over his head, slipped the zip-strips over Bellum's wrists, and pulled them snug. He wondered if they were too tight and then pulled them even tighter. Then he looped a third zip-strip over the shoulder-strap to Bellum's rebreather and joined the fourth strip between the ones on Bellum's wrists and the one on the rebreather.

Mike inspected his work. It looked as if it would hold.

Swimming due west by his compass, Mike used Bellum's dive light to search for the rope, towing the other man easily behind him. He found the rope, located his bottle of deco gas, and switched off to it. Then he clipped Bellum's body, plus the stage tank, off on the rope.

He found a spare mouthpiece in his BC pocket, twisted it onto the stage bottle regulator, turned Bellum around, and pulled his backup regulator out of the unconscious man's mouth. Pushing the new regulator into Bellum's mouth, Mike gave the purge button a push.

In moments, Bellum's eyelids began to quiver. His eyes opened. He began to struggle.

Calmly, Mike wrote on a slate and held it up before Bellum's eyes.

I WOULDN'T, IF I WERE YOU, it read. THIS TANK DOESN'T HAVE MUCH GAS.

Everybody—even Bridget, sutures and all—ended up coming down to 200 feet to meet him. They had found Jorge, his hands and feet duct-taped together, and his mouth gagged, in the gas storage tent. Then, shortly after that, the Expedition Channel helicopter had returned, looking for Bellum. Sending the helicopter on to Tulum to fetch the *federales*—it was closer than Cancún—Becky, Bridget, Jorge, Stiles, and even Elvis had come down on double-sets and rebreathers, charging in with lights blazing.

Then, when they saw Bellum trussed up the way that he was, they had all gathered around Mike in relief. Afterward, Stiles shot a few photos of Mike next to Bellum. He showed them around on the digital camera back—they looked like shots of a hunter and his deer. A very upset deer.

But the most sobering moment of all came when they had pulled Bellum from the water and guided him up the steep, roped incline to the *cenote*'s rim. Jorge had stayed down with Mike to tend him through his decompression, but other than the two of them, everyone in the camp, including the Cháakadon men, had gathered to see what was going on. As Bellum was led through the Mayans, he spat out a remark that seemed unintelligible to most of the *anglos* present. Yet the Mayans fell immediately silent, staying that way until Quatul said something to Elvis, speaking in his native tongue.

"Well," Elvis had said, turning to Becky as Jake and Jorge tied the prisoner to a tree at the edge of the sun-lit jungle. "That solves *that* mystery."

"How's that?"

"Bellum," Elvis said. "He just called these people cowards. He did it in perfect, unaccented Cháakadon Mayan. And he did it, Quatul tells me, in the voice of Kunich Ahua."

Lying back on his bunk, the IV drip running into his forearm, a constant-flow oxygen mask held over his mouth and nose, Mike heard the knock at the door of his hut and pulled the mask away long enough to call, "Come in."

An unkempt police officer, his shirt-tail half hanging out, coffee stains on his uniform tie, wearing the insignia of a captain in the *federales*, came into the half-light of the hut.

"Oh, hi," Mike said. "I heard the chopper come in. Please excuse me for not getting up."

"But of course," the policeman said. Then he noticed the oxygen lines and the IV.

"*Madre.* The Bellum. He did this to you?"

"This?" Mike looked at the tubing and laughed. "No. This is me most days. But Bellum did try to kill me."

"You are certain of this? You will testify?"

"He dropped a scuba tank on me. He was aiming for my head. He pulled my regulator out of my mouth at 300 feet. Several times. He tried to drown me."

The *federale* shrugged.

"I do not know much about this sport," he said. "After all, the football, they push and kick, but nobody gets arrested."

"The football, they do not try to drown people." Mike replied evenly. "And he also jumped my divemaster, tied him up and stuck him under a load of regulator hoses. And I'm pretty sure he sabotaged my lights, probably by turning them on down on the dive platform and then covering them up so nobody would see them burning while he ran the batteries down. Oh, and if you talk to the Mayan people in the camp here, I think you'll learn that he has tried to recruit native people for the drug trade. Is that enough for you to arrest him?"

The officer considered what he'd just heard.

"Is enough," he said.

"Okay," Mike told him. "Jake and Jorge have him tied up to a tree out at the edge of the clearing. They've both been watching him; he'll still be there. Take him away—far away from here. All right?"

"*Sí.*"

The policeman got up to leave. Mike sat up.

"*Capitan?*"

The policeman turned.

"My name? For the report? It's Mike Bryant."

The policeman pulled out a thin notebook and wrote.

"Bryant. Miguel. *Gracias.*"

"And may I ask your name, captain?"

The policeman nodded.

"It is Gabrillo, *Señor* Bryant. *Capitan* Hector Gabrillo. Of the Tulum post."

34

No one had ever done it before, which was why they were trying to do it.

To Mike Bryant, floating at the surface of more than fifty billion gallons of geothermally warmed water, a deep aquamarine pool in the middle of trackless green jungle, such reasoning—thinking that had seemed logical, even inspired, back home in Florida—was making more and more sense by the minute.

He'd been hard-pressed to explain that to the rest of the team.

When he'd said that he'd wanted to do the dive again the very next morning, the chorus of nays had been deafening. Jorge had wanted two days to completely check out all of Mike's dive gear and make certain nothing else had been sabotaged. Becky had begged for two days to call *Sports Illustrated* and *Outside* and the rest of the media and see who she could get back in, which turned out to be everybody except for the Expedition Channel crew; they would be represented by Jake Stiles alone. The story of the fight in the *cenote* and Bellum's subsequent arrest had simply been too enticing for any red-blooded American—or Central American—writer, and Bridget had asked for two days just because she was sure Mike wouldn't agree to three. As for Elvis, he had simply tapped on the New Testament with his finger and said, "Tell you what, bro. Why don't you just chill out for a couple of days and read this?"

So Mike had done that. And he had asked Elvis to have Kukulcán go back to his village and bring back as many of the men as he could.

"Bellum put a lot of time and energy into messing with these people's minds," Mike had told Elvis. "And he put in a lot of effort to keep us from seeing what's on the bottom of the *cenote*."

"So what is down there?"

"I don't know," Mike had said truthfully. "There's a lot of area down there, and even if I make this dive, make it all the way down, I won't see but a little bit of it. So the chances are that I won't find anything. But I just feel—moved to have the people here. I can't explain it."

"I can."

Mike had sighed.

"Just send the kid to go get the people, okay?"

"I will," Elvis had told him. "But let's talk this through, okay? I mean, I saw your face when Fran told us Bridget was free and clear; you know a sign when you see one, bro. And it's not as if you deny the existence of God; I've seen you pray. So what is it?"

"I . . . I don't know," Mike said honestly.

They'd both sat there quietly. Then Elvis had offered, "I think maybe I know."

"Try me," Mike had said.

"The reason you came here. The reason you wanted to make another attempt. That was never for you, was it?"

Mike had nodded and Elvis had paused, taking a breath.

"Listen, Mike," Elvis had finally said. "I never met Pete. I've heard he was a great guy, but I never met him. But I'm going to hazard a guess here. He never made a decision like this either, did he?"

Sorrow, heavy and cloying, had fallen over Mike.

"No," he'd told the missionary. "I don't believe he ever did."

"Then maybe, just maybe, is it possible that you are hesitant to take that step because you don't want to leave your friend, that the thought of a heaven without Pete is just freaking you out more than you can imagine?"

Mike had blinked, stunned.

"Maybe," he'd admitted.

"Then I need to share with you something you once shared with me," Elvis had said. And opening up his notebook, he'd read aloud: "'It is never right that two people should die, just because one could not live.'

"That's your rule," Elvis had told him.

Mike had said nothing.

"All right," Elvis had finally said. "I'll send Kukulcán to get the people."

All that had been two days before.

Becky was staying dry today. There were just too many reporters, and the job of dealing with them all was like herding cats. And Jorge—this time, Mike was certain it was Jorge—had already headed down to his safety position at 300 feet.

Jake came out, swimming easily on his back, the camera gear balanced on his broad chest the way a sea otter would balance its lunch. He got to Mike and gave him the same digital camera that had helped save the diver's life just three days earlier.

"And it's working," Stiles had told him. "You got a great shot of Bellum looking all snarly and ticked off. I downloaded that one already, so the flash memory card is clear."

Mike thanked him and hooked the camera to his low-pressure inflator hose.

Bridget was next out. She brought him a cold bottle of water, which he needed. The *cenote* may have been freshwater, but it was warm, sulfurous, and populated in its upper regions with algae. A person would have to be mighty thirsty to want to drink it.

"You are not supposed to be in here," Mike told her. "Doctor's orders, remember?"

I have been bathing, she signed, *in*—she thought about it for a moment and then spelled the word out—B-A-C-T-I-N-E.

"Well *this* isn't Bactine," he said. "Tell you what. You go wait this one out on the beach, and when I get done, I'll take you to the Crab House for dinner, okay?"

Your treat?

Of course.

She kissed him full on the lips and whispered, "You be careful. Come back. You hear?"

I hear, he signed looking straight into her green eyes. *And I promise.*

She nodded and swam back so he couldn't see her crying.

Elvis was the last one out, carrying the two travel tanks.

"Last of the wise men," Mike joked.

"Gold, frankincense, and trimix. That's me."

They floated at the surface of K'uxulch'en, at the very entrance to the Well of Sorrows, and said nothing for a full minute.

"You ready?" Elvis asked.

"You bet."

"You know," he said. "What you decide . . . it's not like you have to tell me to have it 'take.' It's what you tell Jesus, what you tell God. And the Bible says that 'now is the day of salvation.' Today."

"I'll think about that, Elvis. I promise."

The young missionary gazed at him.

"Okay, bro. Ready when you are."

"Diving."

They sank in perfect unison, descending along the bright yellow down-line, as Elvis adroitly vented air and handed off first one tank and then the other to Mike. Finally, at 130 feet, Mike gave a final okay and turned to face down into the blackness. Elvis stopped sinking and watched him go. The dive-light snapped on and a blue-white spear shot down into the empty water. Then it swallowed him.

Elvis closed his eyes for a moment. Then he headed back up.

The suit was squeezing a little. Mike added just enough gas to offset the pressure and gave the camera housing a short shot as well, stopping when bubbles burped out of the exhaust valve.

Lights coming up. Jorge. Fist out this time. Definitely Jorge. Mike clicked his fist against the divemaster's and then switched to his second travel tank. The pressures looked good. The time looked good. It should have, he decided. He'd had enough practice. But inside, he was pleased. This was actually going easily.

Four hundred swept by. Five hundred.

Six.

Seven.

Eight.

Nine hundred feet, and he switched over to the Kahunas. It was *dark* dark now. If he put the lamp head against his suit it was like falling face-first down into a coal chute. The helium tremors came and went, but very quickly this time, not even fifteen seconds, and very mild. He waited for them to come back stronger. They never did.

He passed a grand without even thinking about it. Then came 1,100—the exhaust bubbles were hitting the diaphragm of his regulator like buckshot now, they were so dense, but the pressure on the gauge was still well above his minimums. Eleven ninety-seven, ninety-eight, ninety-nine. He watched the numbers wink by on his dive computer. Twelve hundred.

Aqua incognita; where no man had dived before. He passed 1,250, and his dive-light was picking out patches of gray and tan off to his right. The debris cone. He was lower than the top of the debris cone. He began adding gas to his suit.

Twelve seventy, and the bottom was definitely coming up. He remembered the camera—it was actually dented in on the sides—and he added gas to it until they popped back out again. No leaks; it looked as if he'd caught it in time. Then he added more argon to his dry suit in long, five-second blasts, one after the other, and felt his descent begin to slow. He timed the last blast perfectly and came to a hover just three feet above the silt of the cave floor.

Mike held up the camera and leaned forward, touching the sleeping silt and taking a picture of his finger raising a tiny cloud of sediment. There. He had proof. He'd touched bottom. It was official. He could go back up.

But he didn't. He still had a several hundred pounds of pressure above his turn point. It wasn't much, but he could look around a little. He played his light off to his left and picked out something that looked like spaghetti, with something red lying next to it.

Viktor Bellum's line reel.

Tying his own reel off to the up-line, Mike swam over to where Bellum's reel lay, and he shot a picture of it, the strobe whining like a small insect as it recharged. Then he saw something round, like a softball, lying in the silt just a few feet away. He swam closer.

It was a skull. A human skull.

And it wasn't alone. As Mike played the brilliant blue-white light beam around, he picked out more, dozens of them. Skulls, and rib cages, and the white sticks of arm and leg bones. Most were old. A few had badly tarnished silver amulets or pendants draped among them. But some still had bits of leather and cloth sticking to them. And next to one was a pocket knife.

Mike shot another picture. And another.

It was time to turn. He was past his third. But he could see a shape lying downslope, something that he could almost, but not quite, make out.

Mike checked his depth. He was at 1,320 feet. This was nuts. He needed to get back, or he was a dead man.

He swam closer to the shape.

It was a helicopter, a Vietnam-style Huey, its cargo door open and the rotors broken off. But other than that, it sat on its skids at a twenty-degree list, as if some dead pilot's skill had brought it in to a final landing in this pitch-black, watery LZ.

Mike took a picture and looked at the little display on the back of the camera. It looked snowy; too much sediment in suspension in the water between him and the chopper. He needed to get closer. The little man in his head started chanting: *gotta go, gotta go, gotta go.*

True enough. He needed to get back to the line. He was supposed to be at 1,100 feet and climbing by now. Mike knew that. But he swam closer to the chopper and then he saw it; a pallet strapped down in the cargo area, brick upon white brick of some plastic-wrapped substance. *Gotta GO!* He took a picture—you could tell it was a helicopter now, and you could see the Mexican military markings on the tail. Then he swam right up to the door.

Gottagogottagogottagogotta.... Careful not to touch the fuselage, Mike swam into the aircraft with the same caution that he would have used entering a room with a ceiling full of delicate stalactites. There were two skeletons in ragged blue jeans and what must have once been polo shirts strapped into the cockpit, a rusting M–16 lying on the deck between them. No GPS equipment and no digital gauges. Everything looked analog. Mike guessed that the chopper had been down here at least eight or ten years. He turned and looked at the cargo pallet, touching one of the clear-plastic-wrapped bricks. It gave at his touch—waterlogged.

He touched a few others and they were all that way, soaked through. Mike had never seen coca paste before, but he knew that was what this had to be.

Was this what Bellum had been defending? Some long-lost drug shipment? That was crazy. It just didn't make sense. Mike was no pharmacist, but it seemed to him that the narcotic, undoubtedly worth thousands, maybe hundreds of thousands of dollars when it had gone into this warm water, was now long past the point of potency or salability.

He was 400 pounds below his turn point now. The little man in his head was screaming. Time to boogey. Mike took out a Z-knife, a razor blade embedded in the "V" of a plastic handle, and worked the hidden blade up and down against the cargo netting that strapped the pallet down. In seconds, he had it loose enough to work a brick out.

It was amazingly heavy, so heavy it pulled him to the deck of the chopper. Mike pulled a net bag out of his BC pocket, put the brick in there, and added argon to his suit until he was hovering.

There was a creak.

A loud creak.

Time to go. NOW!

He turned.

But he was too late. The entire palletload of coca paste slumped to the port wall of the aircraft, and the helicopter, already listing, heeled up on its left skid and rolled over ...

. . . Mike was still inside.

Silt jumped up like an explosion. The helicopter came to a rest again, but Mike had lost all of his orientation. He felt for his line reel, and found it, but when he tried to take up slack, he just came to a frayed end. The line had parted, probably cut when the old helicopter had rolled against it.

Mike felt around in the blackness. He reached for his light head, felt it, and felt the broken glass of the bulb. The secondary was still in one piece, and it worked—he could see a brown ball when he pointed it right at his own face—but the silt was still too thick to use it. So he turned it off again and felt his surroundings.

Amazingly enough, the man in his head fell silent.

The chopper had rolled completely over and come to rest on its right side. Not good. The door that he'd swum in through was now flat against the cave floor, bricks of coca paste now piled on that side of the helicopter.

Mike tried to remember pictures he'd seen of Hueys. They had two doors, as he recalled. One on either side. He found the latch for the port side, but no amount of pulling could budge it. It was shut. Jammed shut or rusted.

He found the backs of the pilot's and co-pilot's seats, felt the jagged flutes of vertebrae—the skulls had apparently fallen off when the chopper had rolled—and worked his way by touch to the instrument panel. His tanks were hanging up on everything now, but he didn't dare take them off and set them down. He'd never find them again in the silt-out.

The right side of the windscreen was intact, but the left side was broken, the Plexiglas hanging in jagged teeth that he could feel but not see. Mike did take one of his travel tanks off now, and he used it to knock the broken plastic-like material away, until he had a hole that he could scrape, bump, and claw his way through. His tanks hung up, his net bag hung up, his light-head hung up. But after a full minute of squirming, he was out—still in the silt-out, and still more than 130 stories underwater, but he was out.

For a split second, Mike considered the fact that he had a safety sausage—a nylon signal bag—in his BC pocket. He could blow that up, and tie it to the camera housing, and it would have enough lift to carry the camera up to the surface of the *cenote*, 1,300 feet above, to let his companions know what he'd found, just in case he didn't make it.

Mike didn't do it.

Years before, he'd dived into Peacock Springs and brought out the body of an open-water diver who'd gotten lost back in the system. Knowing that he was going to drown, the diver had gotten out his slate and calmly written a note to his family, to tell them how much he loved them. And when the local sheriff's deputy had begun to go on about how brave the young man had been, Mike had simply lost it.

"He's not brave," he could remember shouting at the startled lawman. "He was stupid! He was an idiot! He gave up! He gave in! You *never* do that. Not ever. You keep fighting. You keep looking—for a way out, for an air pocket, for anything that will give you even one second more of life. And you do that until you can't do it anymore. You never, never, *ever* give up."

So Mike didn't give up. He knew that, even if he found his way back to the up-line, he was now far too deep into his bottom mix to have enough to make it up to the stage bottle at 800 feet—nearly two football fields above him in the stygian blackness. But he thought about how he had found the helicopter and about the fact that it had rolled, but it had not tumbled. He felt his way over the aircraft's skin in the darkness and found the rotor shaft. That was the top of the helicopter. And the shaft would, as the chopper had simply rolled about its axis, be pointing in the general direction of his up-line.

He tried the light again. It was a lighter brown blur now, almost a tan. Not as much sediment suspended in the water, now. So he left the light burning.

Mike felt his way across the deeply silted floor of the cave, touching broken rock, bones, crania, the enameled regularity of teeth, the pits of empty eye sockets. His regulator began to breathe very, very smoothly.

Not a good sign.

Sure enough, the next breath was less than full, and the one after that, even though he drew on it as hard as he could, was smaller still. And finally the apparatus would give him nothing to breathe at all.

He could read his dive computer now if he brought it almost all the way up to his face: 1,301 feet. An absurdly high figure, but he was slowly working upslope. That was good. The place where the up-line started wasn't too much shallower than this.

Mike took the bottom-mix regulator out of his mouth and started breathing travel mix.

Almost immediately, his mind felt super-sharp. That was the oxygen. There was way too much oxygen in the travel mix for this depth. Just where oxygen became toxic was a matter of some debate, but just about everybody agreed that a partial pressure of 1.6—a place where the oxygen in the mix would be equal, if such a thing were possible, to breathing 160 percent pure oxygen. The deep travel mix was 5 percent oxygen, a partial pressure of 1.9 at this depth.

Too high. Sooner or later, he was going to convulse, breathing this mix at this depth. The question was when. Everybody's resistance varied. Mike had seen that in chamber treatments—some people could breathe pure oxygen at a simulated depth of 60 feet for half an hour with no problem. Others would take three or four breaths and go into convulsions. And if he went into convulsions right now, he would lose the regulator from his mouth and he would drown.

Mike wondered how much pressure was left in the travel tank. He didn't bother looking. There wasn't enough. That much was sure. Not enough to get him up to where the next stage tank was, providing he didn't convulse first. He was already searching for the up-line with as much haste as he could muster, without running himself out of breath. There was no speeding the prospect up. This wasn't working. He was as good as dead.

He needed a miracle.

He remembered the prayer that Elvis had said back at the hospital in Miami, reminding God of all the wonders that he had done, and asking for just one more. Still searching, still feeling across the silt with his free hand, Mike closed his eyes and prayed, *Lord Jesus, you healed the blind, made crippled people walk, raised the dead. All the things that Elvis talked about. You can do anything. I believe that. So please give me more to breathe under all this water. And please get me out of here alive.*

Mike opened his eyes and reviewed what he'd just prayed. That about covered it.

Amen.

He was hoping Elvis had been right about God listening even to people who didn't know him when, suddenly, for just a moment, he had a glimpse of clear water. He was getting near the top of the silt cloud. Making sure that he was in a hover, with nothing dragging in the silt, pulling the net bag with the heavy coca brick inside of it up and tucking it under his BC waistband, Mike played the light around. There was another clear patch and he saw, for just a moment, a thin strand of white. He groped where the white strand had been and found it: his guideline. Pulling, praying anew, he got tension on the line, felt resistance. It was still tied off to the ascent line.

Mike tied the loose end of the guideline off on a rock, working by feel, and began following the thin strand of braided nylon. It worked upslope slightly, and brought him to a large block of limestone. The silt-out was thick again here, and he couldn't see the block at all. But he could feel carving in it—eye sockets, a tongue, nostrils. The baroque and stylized convolutions of ancient Mayan sculpture.

He hadn't seen this on the way to the chopper. Mike realized that, when the wreck had rolled, it had swept his line with it, like the second-hand of a clock, arcing it over onto ground he had not covered earlier.

Mike followed the line up, feeling the carved features—for some reason, when he explored them by touch, it made him think *monkey*—and then he got to the top of the block and he felt a very familiar shape: thick rubber ribs, rectangular vents . . . ScubaPro Jet dive fins.

He'd found Pete.

His old friend was lying face-down atop the limestone block. The dry suit was intact, but the body within was mostly gone. The silt was clearing rapidly now, and Mike could see a few details: Pete's reels were still in place, the lamphead was still mounted on the back of a skeletal hand. He checked the pressure gauge for Pete's double set: it showed zero—breathed empty.

Mike reached out and closed both of the double set valves, retaining whatever gas was left inside so it could be analyzed later on. He realized that he had, without even thinking about it, begun the forensic procedures for a body recovery.

This was crazy. He wasn't going to get himself off the floor of this sink, let alone Pete.

Or was he?

Mike checked the stubby submersible pressure gauge standing off of Pete's number-two tank, his deep travel mix. It still held nearly 3,000 psi of pressure. An idea began forming.

Pulling up the inflator hose from the dead man's BC, trying not to look at Pete's face as he did it, Mike blew a few breaths of air into the BC air bladder. The body lifted off the bottom a few inches. Mike took hold of the corpse by the double-set manifold and tugged. It was like lifting something that weighed almost nothing at all. He could see his guideline clearly now, and he had swum only 60 feet in this fashion when his dive light picked out a straight yellow rope rising up in the blackness. The up-line.

His travel-mix regulator had begun to breathe smoothly. Running out. He was amazed that he hadn't convulsed yet.

Mike clipped Pete's body off on the bottom of the up-line, just above the 40-pound mushroom anchor, and, working quickly now because the regulator was getting harder to breathe, he unclipped the travel mix from Pete's body, made sure the valve was open, swished the mud out of the regulator in the water around him, and stuck it in his mouth. Praying again—he was amazed how easily that came to him, now—he touched the purge button.

Cool gas rushed into his throat. Mike was astounded. It worked. Better still, it worked and it did not free-flow. Mike dropped his empty travel tank onto the silt, clipped Pete's in its place, added a puff of gas to his BC, and rose slowly off the bottom.

He looked at the rope. He remembered something he'd heard postulated at a deep-diving seminar—that, under 300 feet, it didn't really matter how fast you ascended. The pressure changes were too small. He'd always wondered if that was really true.

No time like the present.

Mike grabbed the rope and began a pull-and-glide upwards, smoothly building his tempo until he was virtually flying up the yellow polypropylene line. He went as fast as he could without breathing hard. The convulsions had to come soon; he was sure of that. He'd been breathing an over-oxygenated mix for close to ten minutes now.

Depth tags swept by on the rope and still he climbed. He allowed himself a moment of exhilaration. It actually looked as if he might make it.

What was it that Elvis had said to him up top? "Now is the day of salvation"?

In one sense, it was beginning to look as if that were true.

Green glow ahead. It was the 800-foot stage tank. His regulator had smoothed out and was clamping down now, but it didn't matter. He could reach it. His reg' stopped working altogether, and he simply unclipped the travel bottle and dropped it, realizing as he did that this made three tanks and regulator sets that he'd dropped in this *cenote*. Oh, well . . .

He grabbed the stage bottle with both hands and both knees, not wanting to float up past it. He cracked the valve, opened it all the way, and put the regulator in his mouth just as his body began shaking uncontrollably. Oh man—*now* he was getting the convulsions. Pushing the purge button with what little control he had left, Mike forced himself to take three deep breaths.

Just like that, the convulsions went away.

There was no time to celebrate. He unclipped the tank from the rope, clipped it onto his harness, and began to head up again.

"Now is the day of salvation."

Coming home.

He got to 500 feet and switched tanks. He wondered what his deco schedule should look like, decided to go with what he'd planned, and lengthen the stops up top, where gas would be easier to come by. So that made it 90 seconds at this depth. He looked at his computer and started timing the stop.

The seconds clicked away, black digital numerals steadily dissolving into one another.

Mike watched the computer.

It had always been the odd part of deep diving for him. No matter what happened on the dive below, no matter how action-packed things had been on the bottom . . .

That seemed to him like understatement.

. . .It didn't matter. Regardless of how the dive had gone, it was always followed by these deco stops, these long moments of just hanging there, with nothing whatsoever to do.

Nothing, that is, but think.

Mike thought.

He thought about Bridget, the lump. "Highly suspicious," Fran had said. But it was benign.

After prayer.

Climbing out of the wrecked chopper, he'd groped in the dark for the guideline, and then he'd found it.

After prayer.

And then, under 1,300 feet of water he'd found the one thing that he could breathe.

After prayer.

Which meant someone was listening.

And he knew who that someone was.

The computer winked to zero, and Mike moved up.

He got to 400 feet, the water of the cenote was definitely getting lighter, sunlight filtering down into the deep. He had four and a half minutes at this stop. Two hundred and seventy seconds. He looked at the computer, closed his eyes, and thought.

Pete was dead. He'd known that for several years now, and now he had undeniable proof. He'd found him, but he could not give him life again. That just wasn't possible.

And God was real. Mike was certain of that. He wondered if Pete was with him. He didn't think he was. But much as Mike had loved Pete, as much of a mentor and a friend Pete had been to Mike, Mike could no more change where Pete was now than he could bring Pete back to life. And he thought of the cave-diving principle that Elvis had turned and offered back to him.

It is never right that two people should die, just because one could not live.

His rule.

His words.

Elvis had said that no one else had to be there. That it was fine for it to be between him and God.

Well, he supposed. *Elvis should know.*

So Mike Bryant took a breath and bowed his head.

Dear God, he prayed. *I've depended on myself for so long. And where has that gotten me? Into mess after mess. But I believe you're real . . . Jesus, I believe you're real. And I accept what you've been offering, if you'll accept what I have to offer. Wipe out all the bad and the ugly and the . . . sin . . . in my life and fill it with your good. Turn me around. Make me yours.*

He thought.

What else?

Thank you, he added.

And when he opened his eyes, there was Jorge's light, just 100 feet up the rope, circling and circling, asking the question.

Mike answered. He circled his light.

To say that Jorge was ecstatic would have been an understatement. The Mexican diver pounded Mike's back like a tom-tom and kept pointing at his watch. Mike looked at his own dive computer and understood. He was 14 minutes behind schedule. There was no way he should be alive and breathing. He wondered what had kept Jorge at his post for so long. Then he realized that his bubbles had been coming up the line all this time. He motioned for Jorge to give him a slate.

FOUND PETE, he wrote.

Jorge nodded somberly.

TIED ON DOWNLINE, Mike wrote. NEED TO ANALYZE HIS BOTTOM GAS.

Jorge nodded and made a motion, as if he were holding an oxygen analyzer to a tank valve.

Mike erased the slate.

NOT JUST O_2 ANALYSIS, he wrote. SPECTROLYSIS.

Jorge's eyes widened, but he nodded. He pointed at the white brick tucked under Mike's waistbelt and crooked his index finger into a question-mark.

COCAINE, Mike wrote, and Jorge's eyes became platters behind his dive mask.

Mike got the brick out of the net bag. It was very mushy now, and he could feel something hard in the center of it. He made a cutting motion, and Jorge handed him a small, straight-bladed knife.

Mike slit the plastic of the bag and handed the knife back to Jorge. What was once a few hundred dollars-worth of coca paste wafted out through the slit and into the waters of the *cenote*. Mike worked whatever it was inside toward the slit and saw metal—yellow metal and green stone. He worked the object through the slit and waved it back and forth on the water, washing the white narcotic paste off of it.

He held it up and the two men stared at it as they hovered there, 300 feet underwater.

It was a figurine, about four inches high, the features classic Toltec, the eyes and other details inlaid in green malachite.

And the body was solid gold.

Mike thought it would be anticlimactic when he finally came out of the water, seven hours later, but it wasn't. Applause erupted around the rim of the *cenote*, and the dive platform was afire with photostrobes. Finally, Becky managed to shoo all the newsies back up to the rim. She started to move Kukulcán, Naum Kaan, and Quatul up the rope as well, but Mike called out, "No. Leave them."

Elvis helped him from the water and Mike fished the little figurine out of his pocket and showed it to the Mayan men.

They gasped.

Then Naum Kaan began to chuckle as Quatul started speaking in rapid-fire Mayan.

"What's he saying?" Mike asked Kukulcán.

"He says that you have brought back one of the Children of Days."

"Well," Mike said, "tell him that there's a lot more where that came from."

Elvis bustled around Mike, taking his gear off, doing the work so the diver could remain as relaxed as possible.

"Outstanding dive, bro," the Californian told him.

"Yes."

Elvis stopped unbuckling the BC and looked at Mike.

"Dude," he said quietly. "Anything you want to tell me?"

"Yes."

Elvis stared, and then broke into a broad grin.

"You mean . . ."

"Mum's the word," Mike told him. "I want to tell Bridget myself."

"Sure," the missionary agreed. "But man . . . oh, this is so cool. This rocks!"

He threw his arms around Mike and hugged him, and then Mike shushed him.

"Bridget's coming."

The woman doctor fairly flew down the rope from the rim. Behind her, crew members were moving several cylinders of oxygen that she'd asked to have brought to the platform. She ran to Mike, threw her arms around him, and held on for all that he was worth.

The diver laughed.

"Elvis? I can't talk to her like this. She has to see me."

Elvis stepped behind Mike so Bridget could see his face.

Mike has something to tell you, he signed.

Bridget nodded and broke the hug, stepping back so she could see Mike.

Bridget, I . . . Mike started.

Then his face screwed up in pain and his knees began to buckle.

I need to get to a chamber, he signed. *I think I'm bent.*

35

Dude! How're you feeling?"
Elvis's voice sounded tinny over the recompression chamber's "voice-powered" phone.

Mike smiled at him through the thick, bolthead-encircled porthole.

"Good. I feel good. Great, in fact. Hot, but great."

Hot was an understatement. Hyperbaric chambers will heat up to better than 100 degrees as the air within them becomes dense from pressure. The chamber staff had been locking fresh towels in to Mike all night. They'd even given him a fishnet T-shirt to wear, as regular cotton would just become sodden and stick to the skin.

Mike looked at the pressure gauge.

"They've got me up to nine meters now—that's only two atmospheres, and I don't feel any symptoms at all. I'm sure I'm going to be fine."

Elvis nodded, searching for words.

"You were right," he said, "about the gas in Pete's tanks. Jorge sent them out for gas spectrolysis. They were twenty-five percent argon."

"Twenty-five percent," Mike said. He waited a moment, then spoke again, "He would have blacked out at the first breath. Wonder why he didn't do the same with mine?"

"No time," Elvis said. "I figure he was making it up as he went. Is there any way your lights could have been sabotaged?"

"Sure," Mike mused. "If you scored them on the inside of the battery casing—yeah, that would have created a weak point."

"There you go. And Jorge figures Bellum tried the same tank trick with you this time around. Remember how your doubles were half-full after

Jorge thought he'd purged them? And then he couldn't figure out where his argon had gone. Jorge put two and two together—realized that Bellum must have tried to doctor your tanks as well."

"And a regular analysis wouldn't show it," Mike said, "because the analyzer is only calibrated to detect oxygen."

In the porthole, Elvis nodded.

"Well," Mike shrugged. "Hopefully that's enough evidence to convict Bellum."

"Oh. You haven't heard."

"Heard what?"

Elvis pursed his lips.

"Bellum got away, bro. Shot that police captain with his own gun and got out of Dodge."

"No. Shot him dead?"

Elvis nodded.

"There's an upside, though," he said. "They searched Bellum's dive shop and found two footlockers full of notes. Alfred Bellamy's notes on the Cháakadon language and culture. I guess it's obvious now that you think about it. Vincent Bellamy—Viktor Bellum. Same guy. He was Bellamy's son."

"That explains his command of the Cháakadon language."

"Exactly. He grew up speaking it."

"You get the files?"

"Copies now, but the courts are going to release originals in a few weeks. It's all there. Linguistics files, grammars, cultural graphics, everything. And he had almost the entire Bible translated. This is gonna put my work here years ahead of itself."

"That's great. But Bellum didn't seem like anybody's loyal son. I wonder why he kept the notes?"

Elvis nodded.

"The Children of Days," he said. "First it was his game plan, and then it was his certificate of authenticity. Get this. That figurine you brought up? It's one of 365. One for every day in the Mayan calendar. And apparently they became sort of the local equivalent of El Dorado. Old people up and down the coast talked about them. Legend says they had once belonged to Naum Paat, the king of Cozumel, and they got handed down through the ages, but then they disappeared about the time of the Spanish conquest. Growing up here, Bellum would have heard the legends, and he would have dismissed them as nothing but a myth.

"But his father knew something that no other Anglo did—that the Cháakadon people became the custodians of the artifacts in the years after the Spanish conquest. Apparently there were two Cháakadon villages at one time, and the other one had custody of the figurines. They kept them for centuries, worshipped them, in fact, until that village got wiped out by illness; all too common with tribal people. Then my group got custody of the idols, back about the time that Alfred Bellamy was really getting into the thick of his work here, a few years after his son got sent back to the States."

"So," Mike mused. "Alfred Bellamy's notes . . ."

"Established the Children of Days as genuine antiquities and described where they were kept," Elvis said. "Those, together with the rest of Bellamy's notes, gave Bellum a virtual blueprint for stealing them. And he'd made copies of some of the photographs and his father's notes on the artifacts; looks like he sent those out to drum up buyers. Once he had a market lined up, all he had to do was use his EOD training to sneak into the Cháakadon village and use his command of the language to whisper to them in the dark. They knew that nobody spoke their language but them, so they were all too ready to believe he was Kunich Ahua."

"But that figurine was heavy," Mike objected. How would he get more than three hundred of them out of the village, right under the Cháakadon's nose?"

"My guess?" Elvis replied. "He never did. Remember why I said I didn't march straight to the Cháakadon village—because I figured they'd book? Well, Bellamy had noted the same tendency, and Bellum had that highlighted in the notes. And one other consistency about these villages was that they always had to be near water, and the best source for that around here, as you well know, is a *cenote*. Maybe not as big as the one you dived, but a *cenote*."

"I remember," Mike said. "And Bellum's a cave diver . . ."

"Exactly. I figure he sneaks in at night and carries the figurines, three or four at a time, to this cenote, where he dumps them in. If he's barefooted, there's nothing to track, because the Cháakadon go to this 'well' all the time. So Bellum dumps them in, the Cháakadon discover the theft, and they pull up stakes, and then . . ."

"All Bellum has to do is come in when he wants with his cave gear," Mike said. "And get them out at his leisure. That's pretty crafty."

"Nobody ever said he was a fool."

They thought about that for a moment, and then Elvis continued, "Of course that's all theory, but we know for sure how he got the chopper. Becky ran the numbers from your pictures. It was a Mexican army UH-1B, an old Vietnam-era bird. Government records show that an American flight crew had been hired to ferry it down to a military post near the Guatemalan border. Bellum obviously paid them to do a little extra-curricular work en route, and it crashed before they got where they were going."

Mike thought for a moment about everything he'd just heard.

"But why keep up the Kunich Ahua act," he asked, "even after the artifacts were lost? And why would he convince them to revive the old custom of throwing sick people into the *cenote*?"

"A couple of reasons," Elvis said. "At first, he used the sun-god ploy to get young men to come work the drug trade for him, when he thought the figurines were gone forever. Alternate source of income, right? And later—well, remember what the Cháakadon wanted when they first accepted me? Bridget—a doctor. Bellum figured it was just a matter of time before the Cháakadon began to desire the wonders of western medicine, so he was trying to dry up the need by getting them to pitch their really sick people into the *cenote*."

"Killing dozens of people in the process."

"You've got it."

"And now the Cháakadon know where their idols are," Mike observed. "Are you worried about them returning to their old ways?"

"No. Your return from the *cenote,* and your pictures that showed that the bottom of the *cenote* was a graveyard rather than a portal—that all kind of blew away the rain-god mystique. But the Children of Days might still prove useful. The government has offered a deal. If the figurines can be recovered, they'll pay handsomely for the recovery. They can put them on display around the world, charge admissions—this stuff is going to make King Tut's treasures seem like dime-store junk. And the Cháakadon people get to benefit. They can build a school—whatever they want."

"That sounds great."

"So you'll do it?"

"Do what?"

"Accept the recovery contract, bro. You're the only one who knows where this stuff is. And you're still lessee on the *cenote*, remember? There's gonna be big bucks in getting these things out of the water."

"Well," Mike mused. "I'll never dive down there again. But I could do what Bellum must have been planning on doing, guide an ROV—a submersible—to the site, recover them that way. Still, it would take time, and . . ."

Elvis grinned.

"Would the decision be easier to make if you knew that Bridget was going to be over at my clinic while you worked here?"

"It would."

"I think we can make a deal."

"Where is she?"

"She's giving the chamber staff the third degree," Elvis laughed. "Making sure she gets you back in good operating condition."

He squinted at Mike through the porthole and cocked his head.

"Have you told her yet?" he asked.

"Not yet," Mike said. "Bring her to the window."

Bridget was there in no time. For nearly a minute, Mike just looked at her. She was radiant, wonderful. Here he was, hair slicked back with sweat, stinking, and she looked like a picture out of a magazine. She smiled and his heart melted.

Mike drew a question mark in the air. *Will . . .*

He pointed at her. *. . . . you . . .*

Bridget cocked her head, eyebrows raised.

Mike squeezed both of his hands together. *. . . . marry . . .*

Bridget gasped.

Mike pointed to himself. *. . . . me?*

Mike waited for an answer.

Bridget began to tear up. She touched the new cross that hung on a chain around her neck, looked over at Elvis, back at Mike. Mike knew what she was thinking. He'd read the Bible verse about being unequally yoked. He smiled.

Mike pointed to himself, touched his open hand to his forehead, and squeezed both hands together: *I believe.*

Bridget's eyes grew wide. She drew a rapid question mark, pointed at him, touched her forehead, squeezed her hands: *You believe?*

Mike nodded, and Bridget looked, confused, at Elvis, who nodded as well.

Mike repeated his original question.

Bridget was openly weeping now. She drew closer to the porthole, knocked in the air, knocked again and again and again and again with exaggerated emphasis.

Yes.

Yes.

Yes.

Yes.

YES!

EPILOGUE
CAYMAN BRAC,
THE CAYMAN ISLANDS

Viktor Bellum opened the sliding glass doors, and the pine-needle aroma of the iced gin and tonic in his hand was replaced by the fresh, salty scent of the beach air outside.

Except he wasn't Viktor Bellum any longer. Just as he hadn't been Vincent Bellamy for . . .

. . . For how long?

Half his life, he realized. Nearly half his life.

His new name was . . . well, it didn't really matter what his new name was. He hadn't even chosen it, just found it among the death notices in the back issues of a small-town newspaper in Ponce de Leon, Florida. It was the back-up identity that he'd created at the same time that he'd invented Viktor Bellum. Like the man said, always have a Plan B.

And all that mattered was that the identification and the passport and, most importantly, the name on the secure offshore account at the Georgetown branch of the Scotia Bank branch over on Grand Cayman all matched and together assured him of relative peace and privacy and comfort—for the time being.

There was the matter of his fingerprints. He'd been printed when he joined the Navy, just as everyone in the service had gotten printed ever since the military started using fingerprints as a standard means of identifying battlefield remains. He'd gotten out before they'd started DNA swabbing as well, but the fingerprints were enough. Now that they knew who Viktor Bellum had been back before he'd left the United States to return to Mexico, it didn't take a genius to use the prints of Vincent Bellamy, discharged twenty years ago from the United States Navy, as tools in the search for Viktor Bellum, a felon many times over, a double murderer and a fugitive at large.

He felt the sun, warm on his back; he looked out at the sun-washed sea. The he turned and looked at the house. It was beautiful, solid, put together by craftsmen who knew how to build for the hurricane belt.

He was positive that the house would endure for decades but wondered how long he would be able to stay in it.

He wasn't all that worried about being extradited. If American or Mexican law enforcement had traced him to the Caymans, they would have been here by now. He'd gotten out of Mexico on a forged tourist's card, turning it in at the airport on Cozumel, where fewer people knew him, and boarding an AeroMexico flight to Atlanta. From there he'd flown to Charlotte, and from Charlotte he'd caught a direct flight in to the Brac, where a flustered paralegal, called in from his Georgetown barrister's office on just a few hours' notice, had been waiting to deliver him a Suzuki Samurai and the keys to the house.

He sipped at the drink and grimaced. It was too strong; he had poured it much too hastily. He had done far too many things much too hastily.

Paradise came with a price. There were ways around the background checks and the reference requirements for Caymans citizenship, but none around the financial end. To live here in the Cayman Islands permanently, you had to have least $650,000 on deposit in a Cayman Islands bank.

Bellum didn't have this. He would have had it, and many times over, if only the artifacts had not gone down with the helicopter into the *cenote*, and if the Yucatan Deep Project had not come along wanting to dive there before he'd figured out where the *cenote* was and how to get the priceless gold figurines out. But he hadn't done that, so he didn't have the necessary funds, and happily ever after in the Cayman Islands simply wasn't going to happen.

He'd had enough to get a six-month residency permit, but that was it.

So he had six months of moratorium ahead of him. But after that, there was a judgement coming. Two murders, forgery, artifact theft, and all the rest—he had no doubt it was enough to get a man hunted to the ends of the earth. He wondered where he'd be in half a year's time. Africa, Asia, some other place in the tropics? All were possibilities, but wherever it was, he knew he'd still be obsessed with the same thing: where to run next.

He took another sip of the drink, grimaced, and threw the heavy crystal tumbler as hard as he could out over the shore-break and into the blue beyond. It landed with a disappointingly tiny white splash. He was heavy with regret, not the type born of remorse or repentance, but the sort that comes on the heels of disillusionment.

He turned his back on the great, broad, wind-washed blue sea and trudged into the darkness of his regal, silent house.

ACKNOWLEDGEMENTS

For close to a decade, reaching 1,000 feet in depth—the feat ascribed to Mike Bryant in the second chapter of this novel—has been scuba diving's four-minute mile. For the record (no pun intended), this novel was in its final edits when that depth was ultimately achieved by John Bennett in an ocean dive off the Philippines, where John is a technical diving instructor-trainer with Atlantis Dive Resort, in Puerto Galera. John graciously allowed me to interview him for *Skin Diver* magazine just days after his record dive, and the things I learned helped shape the final edition of my manuscript for this novel. I briefly debated having Mike achieve some other record on his early dive, but having gone into this book knowing that the 1,000-foot mark would one day be achieved, I decided to leave things as they were. As John himself told me, "No other depth has the same ring to it as a thousand."

As this book goes to press, though, 1,000 feet of depth *in a cave* has yet to be achieved. The person closest to that mark is explorer Jim Bowden of Austin, Texas, who reached a depth in excess of 925 feet on April 6, 1994, in the hauntingly beautiful *cenote* known as Zacaton, in northeastern Mexico. Jim calls Zacaton his "underwater Everest," and with good reason. It has been sounded to well over 1,080 feet, considerably deeper than the Eiffel Tower is tall, and it is Zacaton, and not K'uxulch'en (Cenote X), that holds the distinction of being the deepest known water-filled cave in the world; K'uxulch'en exists only in the geography of imagination.

Those who closely follow cave diving and technical diving will notice certain general similarities between Mike Bryant's initial attempt to reach the bottom of K'uxulch'en and Jim Bowden's 1994 record dive. In both dives, two divers made simultaneous attempts to reach the bottom, and in both dives, the more experienced of the two perished in the attempt. Those familiar with the Proyecto de Buceo Espeleologico Mexico y America Central (Bowden's team) will also note that Ann Kristovich, a senior team member and the women's record holder for depth in a cave, is, like my character Bridget Marceau, a physician. But I would caution readers against inferring too much from this. K'uxulch'en is not Zacaton, Ann is not Bridget, and Jim most certainly is not Mike. In fact, Zacaton and its principal divers are all referred to by characters in this novel.

I asked Jim to read certain portions of the manuscript to satisfy myself that my fiction was sufficiently distanced from his fact, and he, a wonderful friend, not only did that but read the entire novel in its draft form and became, in effect, one of the project's key sounding boards and *ad hoc* technical advisor. That said, I should point out that this is a work of fiction, and as such, liberties have been taken in numerous areas—history, physics, biology, and geography, to name just a few—so anyone attempting to use it as a textbook is going to wind up sadly disappointed. Many of the diving practices described in this book are departures from fact, and some are sheer invention, created for dramatic effect. In addition, many of the procedures used by deep and technical diving teams are intellectual property, every bit as proprietary as, say, the formula for Coca-Cola. Rather than give such information away, I invented substitutes, so the processes described in this book cannot and should not be used as a blueprint for diving to four- or even three-figure depths—kids, don't try this at home.

This book comes with all the caveats customarily ascribed to fiction, and the characters are my invention and nothing more. There are two exceptions. One is Santiago, owner of a wonderful restaurant in Cozumel, which is faithfully depicted in this book. The other is the cave diver Lamar Hires, president of Dive Rite, who is based on . . . cave diver Lamar Hires, president of Dive Rite. Lamar's wisdom, good nature, and dedication to his craft and his friends are legendary in technical diving; I realized early on that any character patterned on him would be instantly recognizable. So I decided to drop any pretense and simply use him as a character in the book. This was done with his knowledge and consent, and actions and statements attributed herein to Lamar, while fictitious, were nonetheless shown to him before publication. Ever generous, he didn't ask me to change a single word.

I am a deep diver and hold a "full cave" card from the National Speleological Society—Cave Diving Section (NSS-CDS). That said, I neither deep-dive nor cave-dive to anywhere near the depths and extents described in this book. So, for background, I am indebted to countless conversations with Jim Bowden and others who do true, exploration-class diving—Brett Gilliam, Eric Hutcheson, Dustin Clesi ,and Bill Rennecker are just a few of the names that pop immediately to mind.

For helping to get me steeped in local lore, I thank Ty Sawyer, editor of *Sport Diver* magazine, who gave me an assignment that would see me to Quintana Roo and back at a time when this book needed it most. While I was there, German Yañez Mendoza, of Yucatech Expeditions, was kind enough to lend me a doubles set and show me some of the beautiful cave systems of the region. I came away from the experience not only familiarized but a better cave diver to boot. And Costa Club, Mike Bryant's base of operations while he was in San Miguel, served as the same for me, and kept me in great comfort while I was there.

I cannot begin to number the wonderful and generous Mayan people who gladly shared with me information on foods, on clothing, on building technique, on hammock-making and use, and on the wonderfully rich Mayan culture in general. I hope that some hint of that depth came across in these pages.

Writing this book also required the development of Cháakadon, a fictitious dialect of the Mayan language—a task for which I was hopelessly ill-prepared. I am indebted to the University of Calgary's Dr. Marc Zender, who not only coached me through the fundamentals but came up with the wonderful-sounding (and -looking) "K'uxulch'en" as a likely Yucatan-region Mayan translation of "The Well of Sorrows."

New Tribes Bible Institute, the theological teaching arm of New Tribes Missions, patiently endured my questions as I formed "Faith's Frontier," the fictitious mission group described in this book. For that I'd like to thank New Tribes and especially J.P. Marr, the head of their Development and Promotions department. And I would especially like to recommend New Tribes missionaries, with their goal of taking the gospel to the last unreached tribal peoples on earth, as especially deserving of support by Christians and Christian churches everywhere.

Lisa Samson, Alton Gansky, and Bill Myers—all wonderful friends and my betters when it comes to this business of Christian fiction—steadily cheered me on as this project progressed. I'm grateful for their encouragement and covet especially their endless prayers of support.

And of course, I would like to thank the wonderful people at Zondervan. When you enter Zondervan's headquarters in Grand Rapids, Michigan, the first thing you see is a magnificent fountain sculpture of Jesus washing the feet of Peter; that image aptly summarizes the servant's heart of all who work there. From the marketing department to the designers who create covers and pages, I was constantly aware that I was dealing with people who not only were doing their jobs but were earnest about seeing this novel succeed. The staff there also prays for their authors on a daily basis. I'm sure that happens in the secular world, as well, but at Zondervan, it is generally an act of dedication, as opposed to desperation. Hopefully, that was the case here.

My editor, Dave Lambert, was there when this novel emerged as a single-sentence idea, and saw it through to fruition. Dave has that remarkable ability of being able to make you feel good about how well you hold the gun even as he points out that you've just managed to shoot yourself in the foot. Patient to the Jobian extreme, it was he who pointed out to me that "Kalashnikov" has an "a" after the initial "K," that I had best limit the number of species I was fictionally transporting overseas into the jungles of the Yucatan (either that, or seek a name-change to Noah), and that, as I refer to a scuba regulator a few dozen times during the course of this novel, I might eventually want to get around to explaining what one is. Later, Robert Hudson added a second expert set of editor's eyes to the review process. I thank both of them for being this project's readers' advocates and champions of clarity.

And lastly, I'd like to thank my Savior, Author of all goodness. If you found some in this book, He put it there.

Tom Morrisey
Jackson County, Michigan

We want to hear from you. Please send your comments about this book to us in care of the address below. Thank you.

ZONDERVAN™

GRAND RAPIDS, MICHIGAN 49530 USA

WWW.ZONDERVAN.COM